FRACTURED MAGIC

VOLUME I

EMERIC ROWENE

Queer Enigma Books

Cover art: littlestpersimmon
Interior Map: Emeric Rowene
Interior Illustrations: Nipinet Landsem

www.queerenigma.com

Published by Queer Enigma Books.

ISBN: 979-8-9989210-0-1

To my webserial readers,
who've supported me from the start.

A full list of content warnings is available at the back of the book.

THE LAND OF
CALAIDIA
VE
TROAS
CORINIDOS
EJERA
DAMAEL
ALFHEIM
ALFHEIMR

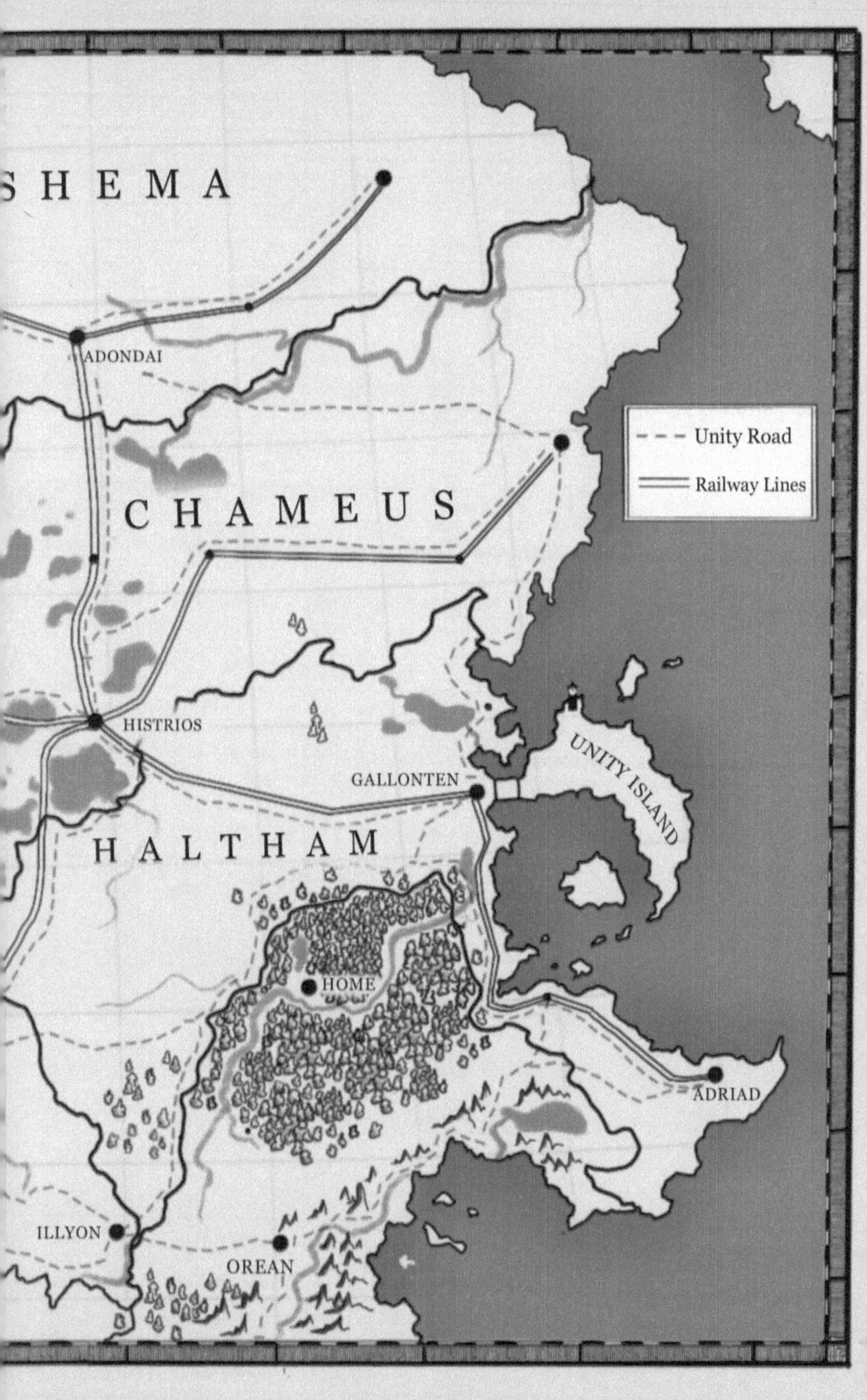

SHEMA
ADONDAI
CHAMEUS
HISTRIOS
GALLONTEN
HALTHAM
HOME
UNITY ISLAND
ADRIAD
ILLYON
OREAN
Unity Road
Railway Lines

CHAPTER ONE

LEANDROS NOCHDVOR HAD A SECRET: he loved ghost stories, especially the trashy, serialized variety that sold on street corners for a penny. Losing himself in a whirlwind romance and dubious haunting was easier than confronting his own ghosts, the failures and losses that clung to him like cobwebs.

As far as guilty pleasures went, this one was relatively harmless. Before today, it had never caused him any problems.

He'd been browsing market stalls with his cousin when he'd spotted it: the latest installment of his favorite serial, taunting him from a newsstand across the street. The author was known for her scandalous content, and her cover illustrations were no exception. This one depicted a scantily-dressed woman wrapped in her lover's arms, a dark house looming behind them, and Leandros couldn't imagine buying it in front of the Crown Princess of Alfheimr. The trouble was that he might not get another chance.

Penny dreadfuls, even popular ones, had limited print runs that sold out fast. While anyone else could borrow copies off friends and neighbors if they missed a week, Leandros was a prince of Alfheimr. More than that, he was the son of a traitor and the man who killed

Egil. His reputation was poor enough; if anyone learned about these little indulgences of his, it would sink even lower.

Back home, he had a strategy. Once a week, he donned a disguise, stole out of the palace, and holed up in a dark café to read. Unfortunately, traveling with family afforded few chances for sneaking out. When they weren't on the road, they were guests in someone else's home. When Leandros did manage to sneak away, his cousin stuck to him like papier-mâché.

Kitty, the naïve heroine of The Carmine Brooch, ended the last installment locked in her evil godfather's attic, the hero a day's ride away. Leandros hadn't been thinking about that then, when he'd agreed to this trip, and he regretted that now.

Leandros looked back at the newsstand, then over at his cousin — only to find she'd wandered off. All he could see of her was her parasol, her back to him as she perused a jeweler's stall. It was now or never. Penny already in hand, Leandros stepped off the sidewalk into the street, but before he made it even a step further, someone crashed into him with all the force of a freight train.

It knocked Leandros into a florist's stall, where he collided face-first with bundles of flowers hung to dry. The florist jumped back in alarm, and tipped over a tub of wilting roses, all that sickly sweet water pouring right toward Leandros, then right down his trousers. It was *freezing*. Muttering an ungentlemanly string of curses, Leandros swiped away the dried bouquets, shook off as much water as he could, and whirled to confront whoever had run into him.

He found her on the ground, pushing herself unsteadily to her hands and knees, and all the fight bled out of him. He didn't even mind the cold anymore. Around them, people were pointing and whispering, but he paid them no mind.

"You're not hurt, are you?" he asked, offering the stranger a hand. Her face was hidden beneath a hood, but she shook her head as

Leandros pulled her up. It was only once she was stable and steadied that she looked up at him and he glimpsed the face beneath the hood.

Goosebumps broke out along his skin.

Leandros loved ghost stories, but ghosts were never supposed to be real. They were only metaphor, feeling. Still, he could think of no better word to describe this woman.

A mask covered the lower half of her face, but by her long ears, Leandros could tell she was one of the orinians that lived across the valley. What skin was visible was bloated and mottled like a corpse, parts of it torn open by gaping wounds. She met his eyes, her own feverish and bright, and then took off running. Leandros did the only thing he could think to do: he gave chase.

"Leandros!" he heard Rhea call, her voice barely audible above the florist's shouts and the onlookers' rippling murmurs. At first, the crowd resisted him, but when they pushed, he pushed harder. He elbowed his way through until he finally shot free of them like a bullet from the barrel of a pistol, and then he sprinted after the woman.

He didn't even know what he wanted from her—to help her, to question her, or simply to stop her—but he was no stranger to trouble. He trusted his instincts, and right now, every instinct told him that losing this woman would be a mistake. He kept the back of her raggedy cloak in his sights until it disappeared around a corner ahead. Putting on a burst of speed, Leandros turned the corner himself only seconds later.

She was gone. The street was empty. There were no alleys, no side roads, not even open storefronts that Leandros could see. There was nowhere to escape to. Leandros slid to a stop.

"Damn," he swore, pushing his sweaty hair out of his face. He kicked a loose cobblestone and sent it flying. "*Damn!*"

He should have expected this. Leandros Nochdvor was made up of good intentions that always met bad ends. Why should this have ended any differently?

When his anger cooled, he looked around and realized he'd followed the woman halfway across the city. Even worse, he'd followed her to the last place in Illyon he wanted to visit: Egil's old neighborhood. Of all the ghosts Leandros wished to avoid, this was the worst of them.

The neighborhood had taken a downward turn since Leandros' last visit, the cobblestone pock-marked and the houses neglected. Illyon had always been a dingy, self-important little city, "progressive" in a way that only meant progress for the lucky, but Egil had made it bright. He had made everything bright. Today, factory smoke filled Illyon's skies, burying the suns and casting the city in shadow. Beneath the smog was a stench so foul it hurt to breathe, the product of a sewage system that hadn't grown to fit its increasing population. If Illyon was good for anything these days, it was this: ill omens, bad feelings, and reminding Leandros of everything he'd lost.

Still hoping to find his mystery orinian, he hurried down the street, but he knew in his heart she'd become just another ghost.

He found himself outside Egil's old house before long. He hadn't meant to come this way, not consciously, but now that he was here, he couldn't seem to leave. It was a small building, better maintained than most in the neighborhood, with cheerful windows and a door that stood unexpectedly open. It had been turned into a museum, he remembered now, the eight-foot-tall statue of Egil that stood on the front lawn jogging his memory. It looked nothing at all like the famous hero. Egil would have loved it.

Leandros wondered what it looked like inside. Was the guest bedroom still there, the one Egil had ready for him whenever he'd wanted it? Were the halls still lined with the blue wood of the ibal trees he and Egil had hauled in from Troas? What had happened to this place, which had once been more of a home to him than his own?

A sigh escaped Leandros. As an alfar, he'd always been warned that humans died young, but he'd never been taught how to live on without them. He couldn't help but think that if Egil had been here, the orinian wouldn't have gotten away. Egil would have known what was wrong with her. Egil would have known how to help.

Across the narrow street, a group of children played jump rope, chanting an old rhyme to the beat:

Taurel, taurel, old stone and coral
Where do you end your reign?
Spread through the valley, down to the trees.
You will be Egil's bane.

As Leandros turned, watching them without seeing, the young girl holding one end of the ropes slowed, almost tripping her friend in the middle. "Ansel, what's taurel?" she called. "It sounds made up."

The boy holding the other end shrugged.

"It's a blue flower that grows far north of here," Leandros answered. When the kids all turned to look at him, he held out his forefinger and thumb, about an inch of space between them. "They're about this big, and they smell like every beautiful thing."

"Have you seen them?" the girl asked.

"Many times, but they only grow on Unity Island. The rhyme is about Unity."

"But it wasn't *Unity* that killed Egil," Ansel argued, regarding Leandros with suspicion. He looked older than the other children, and like Leandros, he was alfar, with pointed ears and sharp features. "Egil went mad and killed a hundred people and even Unity couldn't stop him! That's why Prince Leandros had to do it."

"Ms. Olsen says Egil was a great hero," argued the middle girl. She stopped her jumping to glare at Ansel. "Heroes don't kill people."

"They do if they go mad."

The girls looked conflicted about this. Feeling vaguely ill, Leandros didn't notice the carriage rattling up the street until it stopped behind him and a familiar voice called, "Leandros!"

Leandros was about to swear again when he remembered the children in front of him. He bit his tongue and turned to find his cousin climbing out of a hansom cab.

Rheamaren Nochdvor wasn't like Leandros. Though younger, she was the perfect in alfar in ways Leandros had never pulled off: collected. Composed. Controlled. She never ran; she only walked. She didn't get waylaid by mysterious strangers or inquisitive children. She never cursed, *especially* in front of kids, but Leandros could tell by the set of her mouth that she dearly wanted to, right now.

They were supposed to be discreet, sneaking around the city without an escort, but even if she hadn't just broadcast Leandros' identity, anyone could tell at a glance that Rhea was royalty. She was tall and elegant, dressed in a deep red dress with a full skirt and mutton sleeves. As a symbol of her status, she wore her long, golden hair down, the pointed tips of her ears sticking out from beneath it.

She looked back at the house, then down at the children, and finally at Leandros. "Am I interrupting something?"

"We were just discussing Egil," Leandros said with a wry smile. It softened when he glanced back at the kids, and he gave them a playful bow. The two girls grinned and curtsied back, but Ansel only stared, open-mouthed. "I'm sorry to have kept you from your game. Please, excuse me."

Rhea glanced at the children disinterestedly before returning to the cab, imperiously holding a hand out for Leandros to help her up. Once they were both settled in the shared seat, she asked, "Egil, really? I don't know why you do this to yourself."

"It wasn't intentional, believe it or not."

"You ran off and ended up at Egil's old house on accident? I *don't* believe it. What in the world made you take off like that?"

Leandros scratched his chin, now embarrassed to say. Maybe he'd only imagined that woman. Maybe he'd been reading too many penny dreadfuls. "It doesn't matter anymore. I thought I saw someone strange and was trying to follow her."

"And abandoned *me* in the process," Rhea complained. "What if something happened to me? What would you have done? What would you have told my father?"

"You're more than capable of handling yourself, Rhea."

"*Hmph*," Rhea said. "What was so strange about her?"

"It's hard to describe. She was orinian, but she—"

"Orean is a day's ride away, Leandros," Rhea interrupted. Her voice was flat and measured, flawless as cold stone. "Of course there will be orinians here."

"Let me *finish*, Rhea!" Leandros snapped. Normally, he tried to be patient with his cousin, but the cold wind blowing through the cab made it impossible to forget his wet clothing, and *that* only reminded him of the rest of this miserable day—the Carmine Brooch installment, the lost orinian, the unwelcome memories. There was only one silver lining he could see: his mourning blacks had at least preserved his dignity. If he'd been wearing a trendy white linen suit instead, he would have had a *truly* terrible day, instead of just an irritating one. "Something was wrong with her, Rhea. Really wrong."

"Not with her endurance, given how fast she ran from you," Rhea said. She paused, then, and examined her cousin's expression more closely. His unease must have been obvious, given how quickly her tone changed. "Well, where did she go? Should we keep looking for her?"

Leandros sighed and checked his watch. "There's no time," he said. Besides, he suspected they wouldn't find her even if they did look. "We can make it back for your father's reception if your driver's any good."

"He's not *my* driver. I had to hail a public cab when you ran off," Rhea grumbled. Still, she sat forward and called back to the driver, "To Hampstead Hall, and there's more in it for you if you're quick."

"How did you find me, by the by?" Leandros asked.

"I had to stop and ask a dozen people along the way. You made quite the impression, with your mad dash through the streets."

"Ah," Leandros said, sheepish.

The carriage rattled easily through the streets, the crowds parting for it in a way they hadn't for fellow pedestrians. Leandros kept checking his watch on the way, watching the smooth ride shave minutes off their arrival time. It was an old watch, the front dented and the metal tarnished, but it still ticked steadily in Leandros' hand. When he shut it again, his eyes carefully avoided the initial engraved on the inside lid.

"Only two minutes late," he said smugly.

"You're the one who made us late, so why do you sound so proud?" Rhea asked. "There are flowers in your hair, by the way."

Leandros frowned and ran his hands through his hair. It was the same golden color as Rhea's and was cut fashionably at chin length, though a single, stubborn lock tended to fall rather *un*fashionably into his eyes. Sure enough, a handful of dried petals fell into his lap.

"I had to pay for all those roses you ruined," Rhea added. "I expect you to pay me back."

Leandros scoffed. "Those roses were already as good as dead. Whatever you paid, it was too much."

"And what was I supposed to do? You didn't exactly give me time to barter!"

"I don't believe you even know *how* to barter, but fine. I'll pay you back if your father doesn't kill me for making you late."

"He won't. You know how he always defends you. Besides, he's too glad you finally left the palace to be angry." Rhea watched, unimpressed, as he continued to shake out his hair, then took pity and plucked the last bit out for him. "I'm sorry, by the way."

Leandros paused. That wasn't a common thing to hear from Rhea. "For what?"

"I finally coaxed you out of Alfheim and then all of this happened," she said, gesturing at Leandros. "I feel responsible."

Leandros shook his head. "My rotten luck has nothing to do with you."

A small furrow appeared between Rhea's brows. All alfar expressions were subtle, Rhea's more than most, but Leandros knew where to look. "Are you all right?" she asked softly. This wasn't about the roses or the orinian; this was about Egil.

Leandros' expressions were *not* subtle. He looked out the window to hide his face. "You were right; I can't hide from the world forever. It sounds strange, but I think seeing the house gave me the closure I needed. In a way, that strange orinian was a gift." Turning back to his cousin, he added, lighter, "I just wish they hadn't turned the house into a *museum*."

Rhea smiled, a small, private expression Leandros had seen enough times to count on one hand. "So buy the building. We've arrived, by the way. Would you like to complain more, or shall we go?"

"By all means, let's go. I can complain on the way."

———

If the guards of Hampstead Hall were surprised to see their guests of honor on the wrong side of the gates, they didn't show it, just pointedly informed Rhea and Leandros that His Majesty the King was meeting with the mayor in the east tower. Past the guard post, the two alfar stopped in an empty, echoing courtyard to brush the road dust from their clothes. By now, Leandros' trousers had mostly dried, though they'd dried stiff and crunchy.

Around them, the unique silver brick of Hampstead's walls caught in the sunslight, making the place feel like a glittering mosaic. Now and then, servants scurried along the upper corridors, disappearing and reappearing between ivy-covered columns and glancing over the edge to catch sight of the princess and her infamous cousin. More than used to being a subject of curiosity, Leandros ignored them.

From there, they climbed the spiral stairs to the east tower, stopping before a pair of gilded doors that were opened for them by the guards posted on either side. Rhea swept inside first. She treated her arrival like it was a gift to everyone within, and Leandros had to wipe a smile from his face before he could follow. In Illyon, as in the whole Alfheimr province, expression was a weakness that would be used against him.

The reception hall was a round room circled on all sides by arched windows. The nobles inside made Leandros squint even more than the suns outside; their sparkling gowns and bright jewelry refracted light along the domed ceiling as they circled a man at the room's center, planets circling a bright sun. Nobles and politicians, circling the King of Alfheimr.

Amos Nochdvor turned when Rhea and Leandros swept in, tall and regal and golden. He didn't smile—that would be boorish—but his eyebrows lifted. It was the warmest welcome he could afford to give them, and Leandros felt a rush of fondness. "There you are."

Rhea and Leandros both bowed. As she straightened again, Rhea said, "Apologies, father. I asked Leandros to show me the city."

At the mention of Leandros' name, scorn whispered through the room, more than a few nobles tilting their heads to look down their noses at him. "You couldn't have chosen a better time for your tour?" Amos asked. His sharp blue eyes pinned Leandros in place. Leandros had the same eyes, as had his father before him.

Leandros bowed again. "The fault is mine."

The whispers swelled around them.

"It's a beautiful day and you're both young. I cannot blame you, and neither can anyone else," Amos said pointedly, silencing the whispers in an instant. When the king again met Leandros' gaze, the ice in his eyes had thawed. "But we *will* discuss your leaving without an escort later."

With that, he returned to the conversation they'd interrupted. It was an obvious dismissal, and Rhea tugged Leandros toward the windows, out of the way. Even after his uncle defended him, he could still feel eyes on him, weighing and judging, so he leaned out the open window. Slowly, conversations resumed around them.

Alfheimr treasured stoicism: hide how you feel. Never say what you mean. Be private, be discreet, and give your enemies nothing. Leandros had a history of breaking these rules—he'd traveled too often and too far in his youth. He'd spent too long in the very *human* hero's company. He'd lost what made him alfar. To his people, he was something of an oddity. Without his uncle always accepting and defending him, he didn't know where he'd be.

"Shouldn't you mingle?" he asked his cousin.

"If anyone wishes to speak with me, *they* can come to *me*."

"They won't, as long as I'm beside you."

Rhea nodded. "Yes, exactly."

Alfheimr meetings started notoriously slowly, alfar engaging in business like hesitant new partners at the start of a dance. Leandros had no use for dancing, no use for gossip or small talk, so he continued admiring the view. From here, Illyon sprawled below him like a map, plumes of factory smoke curling at one end and the rooftops of Hampstead Hall sloping beneath him at the other. A valley stretched beyond the city's walls, and the independent city-state of Orean sat even further, little more than a spot on the horizon.

Leandros was trying to make out the shape of the city when the doors opened again and the captain of Hampstead's guard entered to kneel before the king. Everyone in the wide room quieted. "A messenger from Orean has come to speak with you, Your Majesty," he said.

Leandros wouldn't have thought it possible, but the nobles reacted even more disdainfully to the mention of *Orean* than they had to his name. Orean was always the subject of empty grumbling, like bad weather or a favored horse losing at the tracks, but this was different. Leandros had heard whispers of rising tensions and disputes over valley resources, but whispers were normal. He'd *thought* they were normal, but now he wasn't sure.

"Were you expecting anyone?" Amos asked the woman beside him—Illyon's mayor, Leandros remembered from earlier introductions. "No matter. We'll hear them out."

"Yes, Your Majesty," the captain said. He turned to leave, then hesitated. "If you don't mind my saying, there's something off about this woman. Something unnatural."

Rhea and Leandros shared a look. Rhea grabbed for Leandros' sleeve, but Leandros was already stepping forward. "Your Majesty, if I may," he said. "Did she have a black cloak and red hair?"

Eyebrows raised, the captain nodded, and Leandros felt his stomach drop. Every bad feeling he'd had while chasing the woman returned in an instant. "Princess Rheamaren and I ran into her on our way here, I believe."

"Explain," Amos ordered.

Leandros bowed. "Yes, Your Majesty. I only saw her for a moment, but her face was full of cuts from no weapon I've seen. She ran before I could speak with her."

Amos considered this. "Do you suggest I invite her up, or turn her away?" he asked. Behind him, a dozen nobles stared unblinkingly at Leandros.

"Invite her up, but be wary. She may have something important to say, but—" *She gave me a bad feeling*, he'd been about to say. Fortunately, he realized how childish the words sounded before he spoke them. "Just be wary."

"Invite her up, then. I won't turn away a missive from Orean."

———

The captain hadn't been gone long before the doors opened again.

The smell hit first, like rancid meat and spoiled perfume, then the darkness: shadows stretched preternaturally through the doors, reaching along the walls and floor like grasping claws, snuffing out the dancing lights cast by all the glitter and gold. The woman followed them inside. Since their meeting in the marketplace, she'd removed her cloak; etched onto leather armor so old it belonged in a history text, she wore Orean's insignia.

She moved forward with a jerky sway, like a puppet guided by an inexperienced puppeteer. Only then did she lower her mask, and amidst a chorus of gasps, everyone who could backed away.

She looked even worse than Leandros had realized: her skin was gray, almost translucent, and framed by curls as red as blood. Like all orinians, she had long, calf-like ears and a tail that hung behind her, twitching like a cat on the hunt's. The wounds Leandros had glimpsed before stretched across her skin in a mockery of an orinian's birthmarks, and where muscle and bone should have been visible beneath instead swirled a strange magma, orange and sluggish and hypnotic. Her eyes, alight with the same glow, fixed unblinkingly on the king.

"Madam," the king gasped. "You're ill. Let us call a physician."

Leandros felt ill simply from looking at her. Near him, one of Illyon's nobles fainted in a heap of heavy skirts, her friends too entranced by their flyblown visitor to catch her. Faced with everyone's horror, the woman only smiled. At least, Leandros thought it was supposed to be a smile—only half her face cooperated, the other cut through by those awful lacerations. Beneath the cruor, she was tragically beautiful.

Beyond her appearance, beyond her smile, beyond even the smell of death that clung to her like perfume, something about her unsettled Leandros. It was something bigger, a presence behind her eyes, looking out. It made Leandros feel very small, looking at something too large to even see. It hid in the swirl of that glow on her skin, and it had Leandros' hand going to the revolver he wore at his hip. He needed to get Amos away from her, and Amos seemed to have the same realization. "Guards!" the king shouted, his voice breaking on the word. *"Guards!"*

There was no answer from the hallway beyond, only fingers of blood creeping along the floor from without. When the orinian woman took a step toward the king, the mayor bravely moved to block her way.

"Don't!" Leandros warned, but too late. The orinian caught the mayor by the throat, her graying fingers swollen, and lifted her off the ground like she weighed nothing.

"Release her!" the king commanded. "Release her and tell us what you want!"

The orinian tilted her head to one side, considering the command, then let the mayor drop. "Very well," she said in an accent as old as her clothing, as old as the impossible presence that wore her like a shell. "I want *you*. Will you come with me?"

Leandros drew his gun and aimed it at the woman. His hands were steady. "He's not going anywhere."

The woman glanced at Leandros and seemed to dismiss him, but then she looked again. "It's you," she observed. "What is your name?"

Leandros hesitated, then answered, "Leandros Nochdvor."

The woman nodded, as if committing it to memory. "It was kind of you to help me stand, before. I'm sorry, but I will have this king."

When she took another step, Leandros fired.

The crack of the gun echoed through the room. Someone shouted and ducked, but the bullet struck its target, tearing into the woman's shoulder. While she stumbled and lost her stride, she didn't so much as glance down before pressing forward again. Instead of blood, the wound oozed black sludge. Again, Leandros shot. This time, she barely slowed. It was impossible. Inhuman. Leandros shot her again and again and again, shot until his gun ran out of bullets and the orinian reached his king. Standing before Amos, she pressed a single finger to his chest.

Leandros watched his uncle crumple like a broken doll.

Rhea screamed and surged forward, but Leandros caught her by the wrist and dragged her back. Finally, others were moving as well. They rushed toward Amos, but before they could reach him, the orinian swept a hand through the air and something erupted from her palm—something like lightning and something like fire, something that glowed with the same crimson as the magma beneath her skin. It hung in a ring around herself and the fallen king, keeping everyone back. It cracked and sputtered, and as she hoisted Amos off the ground and threw him over her shoulder, it expanded to singe anyone standing close enough.

Despite Rhea's struggling, Leandros dragged her further back, only stopping when the backs of his thighs hit the windowsill. He tore his eyes from his uncle's limp form to watch the flames: every few seconds, they sparked and spread, growing wider and wider. By the time he looked back at the orinian, what he saw made him grip Rhea's wrist so hard she gasped. The orinian's had changed, shadow eclipsing pupil, iris, and sclera and leaving her eyes entirely black. Leandros was frozen in place. He'd seen eyes like those only once before. Egil's had looked the same on the day that he died.

Before he could do anything else, the woman disappeared into thin air, the king disappearing with her. Rhea sobbed and tried to pry free Leandros' grip, but even though the orinian was gone, her flames were not. It sputtered, molten sparks flying. Leandros could feel the heat, now, even from where he stood. He made a decision, then. He turned, caught Rhea by the waist, and launched them both out the open window.

Rhea screamed as they fell, only to be drowned out by a final, deafening pop from behind them. When the women's flames exploded, every window in the eastern tower burst. The alfar fell amidst a shower of glass and flame.

They hit flat rooftop a few fleeting seconds later, searing pain shooting up Leandros' shoulder at his landing. He grunted in pain but immediately pushed himself up, holding himself over his cousin to protect her from the falling glass. It hit his back and arms, cutting and slicing even as the smaller shards dug into his palms. After what felt like ages, it stopped, and only then did he collapse atop the debris.

It gave him a perfect view of the charred tower, its bricks no longer sparkling. Before he could process the sight, Rhea entered his field of vision, her cheeks streaked with tiers. "Leandros!" she cried, voice hoarse. "Leandros, she took my father! What do we do?"

Leandros shook his head. His ears rang, but he could hear the distant sound of fire bells. When he closed his eyes, he saw all-black ones staring back. The answer came to him easily: "We get him back."

Chapter Two

Gareth Ranulf spun on the phone box stool, its receiver held to his ear. "I'll see you soon, my dear," he cooed, listening to the tinny reply before adding, "Yes, ideally with Moira in tow, but you know how she can be. There's some sort of event happening on the island today. Knowing her, she'll need to stay."

Through the glossy windows, he watched strangers hurry past—more than he would've expected from Unity on a Saturday. There were secretaries and politicians, socialites and more than the usual number of reporters. A group of the latter stopped in front of Gareth's phone box, the sleek dragon in their midst sitting her bulk right in front of his door. Gareth frowned, rapped on the glass to get her attention, and nearly missed his wife's reply.

"Come again?" he asked, swiveling back around to face the transmitter. "Yes, I'll tell her. Isobel, I have to let you go; I've been trapped in my phone box. No, it's nothing to worry about. I'll meet up with you and Ofelia on the hour, all right? I love you, Boop."

As he hung up the phone, he clicked his tongue. What sort of person went around blocking phone boxes without checking whether anyone was inside? Gareth knocked on the glass again, deciding to give this stranger a piece of his mind. When that didn't help, he shoved the door open until it hit her blue flank. She finally looked back at that, her eyes widening enough to reveal the full rectangles of her pupils. "Apologies," she rumbled, shuffling aside.

Gareth's bluster left him all at once. "No, it's no bother at all! I should be the one apologizing. I didn't mean to interrupt your conversation. Terribly sorry. Please, pardon me."

Freed from his box, Gareth couldn't help but pause to listen in on their conversation. Maybe he'd learn why the island was so busy.

"Well I'm not surprised by any of this," one of the dragon's reporter friends was saying. "The royal family has another scandal every few decades. We were overdue."

Gareth bent and pretended to tie his boot laces. Eavesdropping had always been a horrible habit of his; at some point, he'd given up resisting it. He wondered which royal family the man meant. There were several options: of the six provinces under Unity's banner, four of them had reigning monarchs. The Sheman royal family in the north won for petty drama, but Ejera in the west had seen the most recent political upheaval.

"Be serious, Arthur," said an alfar girl. She appeared younger than the others, with piercings along her pointed ears and strawberry-blonde hair that she'd braided out of her face. Knowing how alfar biology worked, however, she may well have been the oldest of the group. "Whatever happened must be serious. Both the princess *and* prince came here in person."

"Is that supposed to mean something?" Arther asked.

"The prince hasn't left Alfheimr in sixty years," Gareth's dragon supplied.

"And we were better without him," the alfar girl said. "If you ask me, he's gone as mad as Egil did."

Arthur met Gareth's eyes. "I say, sir, can we help you?"

Gareth stood quickly, his face flushing. "No, not at all. Excuse me." His heart beat fast in his chest as he stepped out onto Unity's cobbled footpaths, but it had less to do with being caught listening and more to do with the thought of *Leandros Nochdvor* being here on the island. The prince was famous, and not just for killing Egil in Histrios—he'd worked closely with the Oracle of Damael, negotiated the first ever trade agreements with the frìth, and even uncovered a coup in Alfheim. He was a hero in his own right, but after Histrios, he'd simply vanished.

The questions Gareth would ask, if he caught a moment alone with the man! Maybe, if he asked nicely, his sister would arrange an introduction. He found himself walking with a quicker step at the thought, his path lined with taurel and other late summer blooms. Above his head, oranges and reds crept along the edges of crisp green leaves. Normally, Gareth hated this time of year, but he was so giddy now that he found he didn't mind it.

This was a season of change, a season for looking back on what you had and forward to what you may yet get. It was normally a season of celebration and relief, but for Gareth, it had always been a season of responsibilities. Unity, the world's inter-provincial governing body, held a week's worth of conferences in Gallonten every fall. All the world's important people flocked to the capital city to attend, and every fall, Gareth was forced to join them.

If it were up to him, he'd be home working on his book, playing in the fallen leaves with his daughter, or walking his estate grounds with his wife. But this year, if he could get an interview with Leandros Nochdvor, his pilgrimage to Gallonten may just have been worth it. Getting a firsthand account from the man who killed Egil was just what his book needed!

His destination was a courthouse that towered against the rocky coast, its pointed arches and stone spires grasping for the gray sky. Unity's famous clock tower stood beside it, adding to the island's famous silhouette. With salty ocean breeze washing over him, Gareth looked up at the clock's face and did some quick math: he had just under an hour to get inside, coax Moira out, and meet up with Isobel across the bridge in Gallonten.

He hurried up the stairs, between bronze statues of the gods Ellaes and Atuos, and into the courthouse only to stop in the doorway at the unexpected crowd. He had never in his life seen the atrium so full. The crowds, clustered together in groups, had stopped whispering when he'd come in, but they started right back up when they realized he was nobody special. Gareth self-consciously adjusted the strap of his writing bag and pushed past, straining to hear the whispers as he went.

"—All the way from Illyon," one man said to his friends.

At the next grouping, a nympherai whispered, "It's the alfar king. I hear he's sick. That's why he didn't come himself."

Passing a third group, Gareth caught only one word: "Orean."

By the time he reached the stairs, his curiosity blazed even brighter than before. He hurried up toward the representatives' offices, his eyes sliding over Unity's decadence—the oil paintings and velvet hangings, the wooden carvings and gilded railings. He was used to it all. At the top of the stairs, the hallway split in three directions, one for each branch of Unity, one branch for each of Calaidia's species. Though dragons didn't grow much taller than draft horses, the ceilings down the center hall were specially vaulted. At twenty-three hands, the draconic magistrate was the exception to the rule, though they said red dragons used to grow even taller. Gareth took the more reasonably sized hallway to the left, following it to the human representatives' wing.

Calaidia's species shared Unity's power equally: each had twelve seats on the Congregation, which created and enforced laws for the provinces to follow, and each appointed one Magistrate to oversee them. The Magistrates were, by far, the most powerful people on the continent—more powerful than the representatives, and more powerful than the leaders of the individual provinces. They were also the *busiest* people on the continent, so Gareth wasn't surprised to find Moira's office empty.

"She's in a meeting," one of Moira's clerks explained. "Would you like me to take a message for you?"

"That's quite all right. I'll just catch up with her later," Gareth said. Before turning to leave, though, he asked, "Is there something happening downstairs? There was a crowd when I passed through."

The clerk smiled amiably. "I don't know anything about that, sir."

"Is that so? I heard it has something to do with the Alfheimr royal family?"

"That's an interesting theory."

"Right," Gareth said, taking the hint. "Well. It's supposed to be your day off, isn't it? Don't let my sister overwork you."

"Yes, Mr. Ranulf. Thank you."

Gareth took the long way out, past the representatives' offices. Almost everyone was in today, and Gareth suspected that if he performed a similar inspection in the other two wings, he'd find more of the same. It was odd: the conference season was for seeing and being seen, not for serious political work. You rarely saw this level of turnout on actual conference days, let alone on the weekend before. Whatever had brought the Nochdvors here must be serious.

Moira wouldn't tell him anything even if he did find her, but Gareth was a stubborn man with an insatiable curiosity; it was why he did so well in academia. As long as he found her, he was sure he could squeeze something interesting out of her. Deciding to check one more place for her, he returned to the atrium. From there, he circled the empty courtroom to the private hallway that led to the Magis-trates' Chambers. Before he could knock at the raised door, though, raised voices stilled his hand.

He couldn't quite make out the words, so he inched closer, stood on the tips of his toes, and peered through the door's narrow window. Inside, he saw four people, two familiar and two new.

"This was your idea, Moira?" asked Malong, one of the Magistrates of the Congregation of Unity. She stood with her back to the far windows, the sunslight catching on her diamond-clear scales and sending rainbows cascading along the walls. Gareth shrunk down, trying to hide as much of himself as possible. Malong was a fearsome sight, and having known her all his life had only made Gareth fear her *more*. Fortunately, her attention was fixed on Moira, who lounged comfortably on a leather sofa.

"Does it matter? Our *esteemed guests* vetoed this one, too," Moira said, sounding bored. Gareth could only see the back of her head, but he'd grown up with that tone. He could imagine the matching expression perfectly.

"It will take too long," said one of the strangers, an alfar woman with hair like spun gold. Her catlike pupils had narrowed to slits in the sunslight. "We don't have time."

The Princess of Alfheimr, Rheamaren Nochdvor. If Gareth hadn't heard the gossip, he might not have recognized her. Aside from her golden hair, she had little in common with her father, her eyes dark and her features soft. Gareth had met Amos only once, as a child, but he could never forget it. The alfar had been a vision, exactly what a young boy imagined a powerful king should be. While Rheamaren was arresting, she didn't have his commanding presence. Not yet.

Then she stepped forward, revealing more of the man beside her. For a moment, Gareth thought it actually *was* Amos Nochdvor, here after all, but this person was too young. The resemblance was uncanny.

Leandros Nochdvor was tall, with a handsome face and the same golden hair as his cousin. Like his cousin, he wore a closely-tailored suit, ornate in a way only Alfheimr could produce. But while hers was green and gold, in line with Alfheimr's love of bright colors and shiny things, his was all black, as if he was in mourning. What presence Rheamaren lacked, Leandros had; Gareth had no trouble fitting him into legends alongside Egil and the Oracle of Damael. Leandros' expression was a sheet of ice over a frozen lake, and every so often, Gareth glimpsed dangerous shadows churning underneath.

His expression was as flat as any alfar's, but the intensity radiating off him made Gareth shift uncomfortably.

"I urge you to reconsider, Your Highness," a thin voice said from a corner of the chambers Gareth couldn't see. He recognized it, though: it belonged to Diomis, the third and final of Unity's Magistrates. Diomis continued, "We understand the need for urgency, but this situation must be handled delicately. Delicacy takes time, and we do not wish to needlessly escalate things."

Gareth held his breath. Situation?

Leandros lifted his chin at Diomis' words, the small gesture somehow dripping contempt, and Gareth noticed an old scar that stretched from his cheekbone to his jaw. Still, he didn't speak.

"With all due respect, Orean escalated the situation when they *kidnapped my father*," the princess hissed, making Gareth gasp in the quiet hallway. "Leandros and I didn't come here to be careful. We came to ask for Unity's assistance—barring that, your permission—to do whatever it takes to rescue our king. I fear your plan, tiptoeing around Orean, *negotiating* with them, won't be enough."

"We understand your concerns, Your Highness," Moira said. "You've expressed them several times over. But Unity won't sanction a war based on one girl's fear."

Gareth winced at his sister's harsh words. That was just like Moira, candid to a fault. In her defense, her position allowed her to be. Rheamaren didn't react, but Leandros' brows drew together. A bold expression, for someone from Alfheimr. "I never said anything about war," the princess corrected. "I only want to—"

"To ride to Orean with an army and demand the king's return?" Moira finished. "Where do you think that will lead? Do you think they'll fall over themselves apologizing and return him to you, as easy as that? After the atrocities they committed to get him?"

Rheamaren's expression was even flatter than her cousin's. It had always unsettled Gareth, on his research trips to Alfheimr, how masterfully its people could mask their emotions. "Don't sanction anything, then," Rheamaren said. "Just don't get in our way."

"Princess, try to understand," Diomis said, still only a disembodied voice. "Regardless of intent, the rest of the world would see our silence as permission. We cannot allow this violence until we know more."

"*Allow?*"

"Yes, allow," Moira said firmly. "Alfheimr will not engage with Orean if we say it cannot."

"We can find a different solution, then," the princess said, glancing at her cousin—for assistance? For support? Gareth couldn't get a read on their relationship, but watching Leandros' face, he caught another shadow shift beneath the ice.

"No," Moira said. "We've done nothing all day but try to compromise, but the discussion is over. Alfheimr is prohibited from engaging with Orean and *Unity* will investigate King Nochdvor's disappearance and facilitate his return. That is that."

Rheamaren frowned, the thick mask of Alfheimr restraint cracking. "Why won't you just—"

"Rhea," Leandros warned. The single word silenced the princess.

Malong smiled, one corner of her lip curling up to reveal sharp fangs. "Best listen to him."

"Leandros?" the princess asked.

"Yes, you've been very quiet all this time, Prince Nochdvor. I'm surprised you even came here today. You used to be quite against Unity in your youth, if I recall. I suppose that rebellious nature of yours changed after Histrios?"

A muscle in Leandros' jaw jumped; his hands curled into fists at his sides.

"We are not here to speak of past affairs," Rheamaren said.

"Forgive Malong. It's clear that you need Unity's help, and we are willing to give it," Diomis soothed, finally stepping into Gareth's field of view. The two alfar were tall for humans, but the nympherai Magistrate stood heads taller than them both. Their legs tilted oddly as they stepped forward, enough to draw attention to their smooth gait and the hooves peeking out from beneath their skirts. Atop their head sat something like a crown made of kelp. "We have people who are trained to handle situations like these. Leave this to us; His Majesty will be safe in our hands."

"What of that woman? Do you have people trained to handle *her*?" Rheamaren asked, making the Magistrates exchange looks.

Diomis laid a bony hand on Rheamaren's shoulder. "Whoever you saw that day was only human. I am sure there is a scientific explanation for the rest. Forget this orinian woman."

"Are you saying we lied?" Rheamaren asked. An accusation like that seemed strange paired with such a blank expression.

"Of course not," Diomis replied. "You are distressed, and you witnessed something terrible. Your mind filled in a fantasy to make sense of it, which is understandable."

"What we do know is Orean is ready and willing to use vio-lence," Moira said. "Whether that violence was alchemical or something else entirely matters little to us. We also know that responding in kind could drive them to further extremes. While they have your father, that's dangerous."

"But—"

"Rhea," Leandros said again, so quietly this time that Gareth almost missed it. Rheamaren turned to look at him, so Gareth couldn't see her expression. What he *did* see was Leandros' subtle nod and the way Rheamaren's shoulders slumped in answer. Finally, Leandros turned to the Magistrates. While his words remained deferential, his voice soothing, Gareth could finally make out the shape of the emotion that thrashed behind the alfar's icy eyes: it was anger. "I hope you'll forgive our hesitation, Magistrates. It's been three days since my uncle's abduction—three days of stress and little sleep. You've not only conceived a plan that will keep the continent peaceful, but considered our king's safety in making it. We should be thanking you."

Gareth could practically see Moira relax into the couch, relieved to be talking to someone with sense again. He saw her perceived victory in the slow curve of her smile, but then Leandros continued.

"However, I'm sure you can understand that Alfheimr needs to be the one to bring him home—for our relationship with Orean, for our people's confidence in their future queen, and for the rest of the world, looking on. If you force us out, it will not go well for us, but it will go just as badly for you," Leandros said.

Moira sat up again. "How do you figure?" she asked.

Leandros smiled, as self-satisfied as a cat in the sun. It was more expression than Gareth had ever seen from an alfar, and he found it even more unsettling than Rheamaren's blank stare. "Everyone knows how Unity feels about Orean, and they know how long you've been waiting for a chance to challenge them. I'm sure you don't want the world to learn how you insisted on taking over this mission, despite our acting queen's refusal. I'm also sure you don't want them to learn the truth of what Rheamaren and I saw in the tower that day. You don't want them thinking you have ulterior motives, do you?"

The threat was clear: if the Magistrates insisted on this route, he would tell everyone what he had seen. But what had he seen?

"The *truth*," Malong spat. "You saw nothing in that tower that day. You were in shock. Going around and spouting nonsense about magic—no one would believe you, even if you tried to tell them."

Diomis shot her a warning look, but Leandros only shrugged. "There's only one way to find out. Suspicion spreads like poison, swift and lethal," he said. Silence fell while the Magistrates considered this. As if he didn't even feel the hostility radiating off them, Leandros continued, "There are other truths I could tell them, as well. Ones I have kept secret on your behalf. Again: shall we see who they believe?"

Moira's brows drew together and Diomis stared, their ichthyic eyes unblinking. Malong seemed to have the strongest reaction, her tail whipping angrily behind her. "What do you want," she ground out.

"I'm glad you asked. I've thought of a compromise that I believe will satisfy us all."

"Go on," Diomis said.

"Unity wants a team to investigate and negotiate Amos' return," Leandros summarized, "And Alfheimr would like to have a hand in rescuing our own king. Having a representative on the team that we trust, one with a personal stake in seeing Amos safely home, would go a long way toward assuaging my cousin's concerns, I'm sure. Surely, that is not an unfair ask?"

"I suppose not," Diomis agreed.

Again, that smug smile. Gareth realized it was more like a chess master's, having just made a winning play. "Then I volunteer for the position."

"*You* want to join the team?" Moira clarified.

"Not quite. I want to *lead* it."

At that, Moira laughed. "You have quite the pair on you, boy!"

"Respectfully, Magistrate, I'm over twice your age," Leandros said, smiling pleasantly, as if they were sharing a joke. "And you'll find that I am *also* trained for this position. I've led similar missions for the Oracle of Damael, have direct personal knowledge of Orean, and hold a dual degree in psychology and law. I also have, as Magistrate Malong kindly pointed out, a reputation that will make Orean more inclined to trust *me* than any of you."

"Absolutely not," Malong hissed. "With your history? Your *father's* history? Your threats? Do you really expect us to believe you're impartial?"

Leandros nodded as if he'd expected this. "I'm from Alfheimr, aren't I? Impartiality is what we do best." More earnestly, he continued: "Magistrates, I'm asking to work *with* you to get him back. As you've made clear, we can't do this alone, but neither can you."

Gareth didn't understand the significance of any of this, of the references to magic and motives and secrets and histories, but he knew how his sister looked when she was close to giving in. And though Rheamaren stared at her cousin with wide eyes, she straightened her shoulders and joined in: "My cousin's compromise sounds reasonable to me. If he leads the team, then you'll hear no more objections from me or Alfheimr. Leandros will report to you, and the team itself will still be yours to assemble."

Moira twitched, crossing and uncrossing her legs. It was Diomis who finally spoke, a rueful smile on their thin lips. "You make reasonable points."

"You're not actually considering this?" Malong hissed at them.

Diomis shrugged. "Having the Hero of Histrios join with Unity once more...it's a compelling narrative."

It was only because Gareth watched Leandros so closely that he noticed Leandros react: he blinked twice, rapidly, his mouth twitching down into a frown. Gareth imagined it was the alfar equivalent of flinching.

"Do you use that law degree of yours, Prince Nochdvor?" Moira asked.

"Not currently."

Moira harrumphed. "You should."

"You've given us much to think about," Diomis said. "Crown Princess Nochdvor, Prince Nochdvor, may we have some time to discuss it? I propose we meet here again in an hour."

Gareth scrambled back from the door before he was caught, but not fast enough. Rheamaren Nochdvor threw it open with such force that it nearly hit him. He landed on his backside, the contents of his bag spilling out over the hallway. The princess barely seemed to notice, storming off in a random direction with a frighteningly controlled expression, and Gareth pushed himself up onto his elbows just in time for Leandros to follow. Unlike his cousin, his own expression was far from controlled: it was fiery and *furious*, though it fell into surprise when he saw Gareth.

Gareth blinked at him. Leandros blinked back. Then Leandros Nochdvor did the unthinkable: he crouched and started to gather Gareth's scattered papers while the doors swung shut behind him.

"Please don't!" Gareth whispered, mortified. "Really, that's not necessary. You can just leave them."

"Nonsense." Leandros tapped a bundle of papers against the ground to straighten them. "That was my cousin that crashed into you just now; if she won't take responsibility, I will. Forgive her, she's had a difficult week." He glanced up at Gareth, his catlike pupils blown wide in the dim hallway. "Were you on your way to see the Magistrates?"

Outside the tension of the Magistrates' Chambers, he seemed a different person. A *gentler* person. It made his resemblance to his uncle even more uncanny, and for a moment, Gareth could only stare. He realized Leandros was waiting for a response. "Ah! Yes. Moira is..." he said, trailing off when the alfar's attention dropped to the small pamphlet he'd found among Gareth's papers. Gareth made a grab for it. "Please, pay that no mind!"

Leandros held the pamphlet out of reach and turned it so Gareth could see the scandalous black-and-white illustration on the cover. The alfar raised a questioning eyebrow at him while Gareth struggled to make an excuse. Then Leandros surprised Gareth again by asking: "Are you finished with this? Would you let me borrow it?"

Gareth's brain stuttered to a stop all at once. "Are you...a fan of the story?"

Leandros ran his thumb over the penny dreadful's cover. "Something like that."

"Then by all means, it's yours. It's my wife's, but she'll be thrilled to have someone make good use of it."

Leandros almost smiled at Gareth, the expression barely there. "You're certain?" he asked. He climbed to his feet, then offered a hand to help Gareth up as well. He was stronger, broader than he'd seemed from a distance, and Gareth felt embarrassed at how easily he was pulled up.

"Quite," Gareth managed.

Leandros made a soft, pleased sound and tucked the pamphlet into an inner coat pocket. "Thank you, sir. For what it's worth, you've made one of the worst days of my life slightly more bearable."

"I'm glad I could help," Gareth said. Then, in the awkward silence that followed, he blurted, "I'm sorry for your loss."

It was an admission of guilt, a confession that he'd been eavesdropping, but Leandros didn't seem bothered by it—or if he was, he didn't show it. Instead, he simply said, "I've heard that again and again, these last few days, but you're the first one who's said it and seemed genuine. Thank you."

Awkwardly, Gareth held out his hand. "Gareth Ranulf," he said. Seeing the recognition in Leandros' eyes when he said his last name, he added, "And please forgive my sister. She cares more than she lets on."

Leandros shook Gareth's hand. "I should go find my cousin, but thank you again for the chapter. I thought I'd missed my chance to read it. And please...don't tell anyone about this."

Gareth couldn't tell whether he meant the kidnapping or the penny dreadful, but he nodded and moved out of Leandros' way. "The princess went that way."

Leandros bowed before following his cousin's stormy path. Gareth watched him go, waited for him to round the corner, then snuck quietly away before anyone else found him there. He had best leave Moira to her work, after all.

Chapter Three

LEANDROS FOLLOWED HIS COUSIN'S TRAIL out of the building, then down the courthouse paths to a bench overlooking the sea. Rhea didn't look at him, even when his boots crunched on gravel and announced his approach, so he sat beside her and breathed in the salty air. It was heavy with the weight of an oncoming storm, a thunderous end to a thunderous day.

He didn't know what had come over him with the Magistrates. He'd acted out of instinct and emotion, but all this time he, he'd thought the part of him that *fought* and *felt* died with Egil. It was a shame it took losing his uncle to find it again.

Out of the corner of his eye, he saw Rhea's expression shift, saw her jaw grind as she chewed on her own anger. Leandros wasn't an experienced hunter like his uncle, but he knew that some animals in the wild often saw eye contact as a sign of aggression. In his experience, his younger cousin was much the same. He kept his eyes on the water, knowing she'd speak when she was ready.

"What were you thinking?" she finally snapped, her voice cracking like a whip. It surprised Leandros so much that he broke his own rule and looked at her. He'd known she was angry—angry at *him*, even—but he'd never expected her to lose control over it. For a moment, her expression was hot fury, but it had cooled again by the time she looked away.

"I'm sorry if I surprised you," Leandros said, choosing his words carefully, "But things weren't going well in there. I had to make the gamble."

"We're Nochdvors. We do not *gamble*." Rhea looked down her nose at him as she said this, lighting the kindling of Leandros' own temper, which he'd fought so hard to hold back with the Magistrates. He was tired of being looked at that way.

"Did you have a better plan? Pray, enlighten me, because it looked like *you* were quickly running out of chances. This solution may not be perfect, but it's better than anything you came up with and it's better than them cutting us out—and I know you know that, otherwise you wouldn't have vouched for me."

"You didn't give me a choice."

"You never had one to begin with. You can't fight them."

"Stop talking to me like I'm a child, Leandros. Until my father is back, I'm your queen."

Leandros sighed. "That's exactly why I'm warning you. *You* can't fight with them, Rhea. *You.* If we can't get Amos back and it falls on you to lead—"

"Don't say that."

"I'm sorry, but I must. The Magistrates remember their grudges. You need to stay on their good side, but you heard Magistrate Malong: they already have their grudges against me. What's one more?"

"This is more than a grudge. Do you really think you can threaten them without consequences?" Rhea asked. She lowered her voice before adding, "Unity is even more dangerous than Orean. You know what happens when someone offends them."

"I'll worry about that *after* your father is safely home."

"Why did you stop me before? When we were talking about that woman?"

That woman. She meant the orinian, of course. They still hadn't found the words to describe her, and it didn't help that everyone—Magistrates, Unity Representatives, even Alfheim officials—kept telling them they were in shock, that they'd misinterpreted what they saw. "The Magistrates will never believe us. If we want their help, we have to play their game: hold the truth until the time is right, and in the meantime, use their resources to get Amos back."

Rhea made a complicated expression and wrapped her arms around herself. He'd never seen her guard crumble so far, but that still didn't make her easy to read. "I need a moment."

Leandros gave it to her. He turned away, watched a seagull drift down and land on the water. He knew how Rhea felt. He felt much the same. Grief, rage, frustration: they coiled inside him like a ring of magical flame, hot anger encircling his heart. It made it hard to think, hard to breathe. The truth was that every ounce of his energy, every second of every day, was spent keeping that anger in check. He had none left over for social niceties, and *that* was why he'd spoken to the Magistrates the way he had. He wished it was courage. Really, it was just exhaustion.

It wasn't until Rhea wiped her eyes that Leandros realized his cousin was crying. He reached a hand toward her, then let it drop again. "Rhea? Can I help?"

Rhea shook her head, Leandros' question only making the tears fall faster. She wiped at them with a frustrated noise. "You've done enough," she said. "You're right, though. I don't know what I would have done if you hadn't stepped in. It makes me so angry. *You* make me so angry."

Leandros stared at his cousin, shocked. "Me?"

"You're supposed to be the one losing control! *I'm* supposed to be better at this than you." She said "supposed" like it was law. She scrubbed at her eyes again before continuing, "It's silly, but I used to be so proud of it. Before everything happened with your father, you were the favorite. Everyone loved you best. The people loved you. Egil loved you. Even *my father* loved you. I hated you for it, I was so sick with envy. But at least I could restrain myself. I could do something you couldn't and fit in somewhere you never would: home." Rhea glanced at Leandros, her eyes and nose rimmed red. "I wish I could've talked to the Magistrates the way you did. But Leandros, I don't envy you what comes next. Are you sure you want to do this?"

Leandros gave the question due consideration. Rhea deserved no less. The aftermath of the explosion had passed in a blur, as had the journey back to Alfheim. There, they'd been greeted with fear and anger disguised as pity, and they hadn't had been given even a moment to grieve before being forced on a train to Gallonten to beg Unity for help. They were both exhausted and numb, which left little room for surety. Still, Leandros was as sure as he could be.

"We grieve in different ways. I can't sit and wait for news; I have to *do* something to get him back. I owe him my life, and I have to be the one to bring him home." Leandros looked back at the courthouse looming behind them. This place, this island, was civil and clean and quiet, unlike Illyon. The paths were surrounded by fields of flowers as blue as shallow waters off a southern shore. As they swayed in the breeze, Leandros thought of the children back in Illyon. "Have you heard the rhyme? *Taurel, taurel, old stone and coral?*"

Rhea glanced dully at the flowers, unimpressed. She narrowed her eyes at Leandros. "Is this going to be about Egil?"

Leandros gave her an apologetic smile. "Yes. Maybe this won't surprise you, but I think of him often, even after all this time. I wonder what he'd do or say, how he'd approach a situation. For him, problems like these were easy. There was only ever one solution: the solution that would save everyone. Whenever I try to take the same route, I end up failing everyone instead. This time, I'd like to just save *one* person. I'd like to do whatever it takes to get Amos back."

After Leandros' father betrayed and abandoned him, Amos had been there. After Egil died and left Leandros behind, Amos had been there. When Leandros had no one else, he'd still had Amos. Rhea peeked at Leandros past her long bangs. For decades after Histrios, Leandros had barely spoken to either of them—to Rhea or to Amos. He regretted it now, regretted the distance it wedged between them. Something wavered in Rhea's expression and for a moment, Leandros worried she'd cry again.

"I should let you go, but I don't like it."

"Thank you for your sacrifice, then," Leandros said, biting back a smile. "I'm sorry I'm leaving you to face Alfheimr alone."

"I don't care about that. It's what I was raised to do," Rhea said. She studied Leandros like she wanted to dissect him, like she could see through him to the storm inside, darker than the sky. "If you repeat what I'm about to say to anyone, as your new queen, I will have you executed." Leandros hid a smile and nodded as Rhea continued: "I lost my father, maybe for good, and next to him you're the person I'm closest to in all the world. I don't want to lose you, too."

"You won't," Leandros said. He knew it may well be a lie. "Trust me, Rhea. Trust that this is something I can do."

"Only if you promise to be more careful with the Magistrates." As if afraid of being heard, Rhea glanced back at the island. There was no one there, just the courthouse blotting out the sky. "Do you really think they have ulterior motives, or was that a bluff?"

"It was only a bluff," Leandros said. A much easier lie.

Rhea nodded, her brow unknitting. "And if you run into that woman...be doubly careful. Even Unity might be in over their heads, with her."

Neither of them had said it out loud, but they knew what the woman was. The word was at the front of their minds, heavy on their tongues: *magic*. Strange, fantastic things happened all the time, but nothing so impossible as what they saw that day in Illyon. That woman was *magic*, and magic wasn't supposed to be real. Not even in Leandros' world of folk heroes and oracles had he seen someone like her. Except...

"Rhea, back in Illyon, did you notice anything strange about the woman's eyes?"

He hadn't been able to get the image out of his mind, the whites of her eyes eclipsed by black. Just like Egil's.

"They were glowing," Rhea said. "Bright orange."

"Not that," Leandros said. "Did you notice anything else? Right at the end?"

"No," Rhea said. When Leandros stayed thoughtfully silent, she asked, "Why? Did you?"

"I thought—no, I must have imagined it," he said. It was another lie, of course. He often doubted himself, but never his memory. At his cousin's pout, he smiled and leaned into her, just enough to knock shoulders. It was the most affection he'd shown her in decades; the most shocking part was that she allowed it, even leaned into it. "Don't worry, Rhea. Magistrates permitting, Unity and I will find that orinian and rescue your father, and we'll be back in Alfheim before you even miss me."

"Fool," Rhea said through a smile, "I'll miss you the moment I leave this place. Be sure to write with updates."

"I will."

Leandros let Rhea lead the way back, back to the courthouse and back into the chambers where the Magistrates waited. And afterward, Leandros escorted Rhea to the train station as the new Captain of Unity's rescue mission. He and Rhea spoke little on the journey, and when they reached their destination there were no tearful farewells. Alfheim guards stood by to escort their Queen home; it wouldn't do to show weakness in front of them, so early into her reign.

All she said was, "Good luck, Captain Nochdvor. Bring my father back. Make Alfheimr proud."

Leandros responded with a low bow. As the train departed, he walked back to Unity Island alone, the anger in his heart settling like silt at the bottom of a river.

Chapter Four

Halfway back to Gallonten, Gareth paused on Unity's bridge to lean as far as he could over its stone walls. Hungry black water churned below, but Gareth wasn't worried about the old brick giving way. It had stood for two thousand years and would stand two thousand more. To Gareth, this bridge marked a passage between worlds. Above, below. Unity, Gallonten. The change started somewhere around the third set of lampposts, where Gallonten fell away behind and the bridge stretched on ahead until all that remained was *Unity,* alone against an endless horizon. Gareth was always relieved to cross back over to Gallonten, to descend from these distant heavens.

He'd heard the two places referred to interchangeably: Gallonten meant Unity and Unity meant Gallonten. That was nothing short of offensive to Gallonten's bursting population. If you'd seen both, if you'd crossed this bridge and stood on Unity's cobbled paths, then you'd know how different they were. Physically, "Unity" referred to the small island off the coast, set apart from the mainland to create an illusion of impartiality. By contrast, Gallonten was just a city.

Gareth ran his hands over the stone, the cold seeping up through his palms, and looked back at the island. From here, it looked peaceful, the clock tower ticking on while two alfar changed the world Gareth knew it. His eyes were drawn habitually toward the clock's glowing face.

"Blast!" he suddenly swore, taking off down the bridge at a run. It was five minutes to the hour. He was going to be late. He hurried through the public square, weaving and murmuring litanies of "Terribly sorry," and "Pardon me," as he jostled bodies. From there, he turned down a side street, then two more. His destination wasn't far from the island, at least, and he reached it just as the clock struck the hour.

While chimes rang out over the city, Gareth stopped beneath a colorful archway to catch his breath, the words "Rinehart Festival Grounds" painted on its fluttering canvas in friendly lettering. A ticket booth sat ahead, a dryad girl with flowers in her hair and skin the texture of birch lounging behind its counter. A line of people spiraled out from it, and Gareth had just started scanning the faces for anyone familiar when small hands grabbed the leg of his trousers and piping voice yelled, "Surprise!"

Gareth whirled to face the newcomer, his hand flying to his heart in a feint of shock. "Ofelia! By the Three, how sneaky you are!"

A round-faced girl in a neat purple dress grinned up at him. She laughed as Gareth scooped her up. "Hah! Momma said you wouldn't be fooled."

"Your mother was wrong. My, you've grown so much since I left that I barely recognized you!" Gareth said, smiling as Isobel joined them. "Hi, Bel."

"It's only been a week, Gareth," Isobel said with a fondly exasperated smile. She leaned up for a kiss, then hesitated and drew back to study her husband. "Why are you out of breath? Darling, what's wrong?"

"It's nothing; I just lost track of time on the island," Gareth said. He wouldn't say any more. He'd made up his mind not to say any more. The Nochdvor's secret wasn't his to share. But sharing secrets with his wife was like sharing secrets with himself, so surely she didn't count? He glanced around, noticed there was no one within earshot, and blurted, "Orean kidnapped Amos Nochdvor. Alfheimr wants to go to war."

Isobel clapped her hands over Ofelia's ears and also looked around. "Are you supposed to be telling me this?" she hissed.

"I wasn't even meant to hear it! It was an accident! Ah, well...*mostly* an accident."

"You were eavesdropping again, weren't you? On who? Moira?"

"All three of them. And the alfar prince and princess," Gareth said weakly.

"Oh dear," Isobel said in a matching tone. "Tell me more."

Quickly, quietly, Gareth recounted everything he'd heard, Isobel fiddling with the ribbons on her sleeve as she listened. "Something seems off about all this. Why are they so sure it was Orean?" she asked when he'd finished.

"Well," Gareth hedged, thinking back, "It sounded like an orinian did it."

"Just one? *One* orinian managed to kidnap a king?"

"Multiple orinians, must've been," Gareth guessed. The mention of *magic* didn't seem worth repeating. Leandros Nochdvor's threats about secrets and poison stuck with him, though. There was definitely more to the story.

"Must have," Isobel said, also sounding unsure. "Leandros Nochdvor. Isn't he the one who—"

"Who killed Egil in Histrios," Gareth finished. "Yes."

Isobel raised an eyebrow. "Did you ask him about it?"

"Believe me, I wanted to. It didn't seem like the right time."

Tired of being ignored, Ofelia tugged on Gareth's sleeves. "Do you think that man will be here?" she asked loudly. "The one from last year? With the fire whip?"

"I'm sure he will be," Gareth said. Sharing these secrets with another had helped settle his nerves, but so had just being with his family. Isobel and Ofelia always had a grounding effect on him. Leaving them for Gallonten was the thing he hated most about fall, which was why this year, Isobel suggested she and Ofelia join him.

Ofelia nodded solemnly. She looked like her mother, with dark hair and round features, but she had Gareth's smile. "Let's go find him."

"We have to get inside first, dear," Isobel said. She and Gareth each took one of Ofelia's hands and they joined the short line curling out from the ticket booth. It was usually busier—the darkening clouds might have frightened away other would-be festival goers, but Gareth was willing to put up with a little rain for a break after the morning he had. He tried not to think about it anymore, focusing on the present instead.

"You look beautiful today," he said to his wife while they waited, leaning over to kiss her on the cheek. She wore an elegant blue day dress, recently altered to accommodate her pregnant belly, and a hat to match. She smiled at the compliment and twined her free hand with Gareth's, and they stayed that way until they reached the ticket booth. While Gareth fished out his pocketbook, the nympherai ticket-girl leaned over the counter and waved at Ofelia. Ofelia waved back, staring with wide eyes at the pinks and purples of the girl's hair.

"You like them?" the girl asked.

Ofelia nodded and the girl laughed, the flowers swaying with the movement. She passed three tickets to Gareth, then plucked one of the flowers from her hair and tucked it behind Ofelia's ear. Isobel thanked the girl as they continued through the archway, and there, the path widened as cobblestone street gave way to a dirt trail packed down by thousands of feet over hundreds of years. A wave of colors, sounds, noises and smells hit the Ranulfs at once. While Gareth and Isobel paused to adjust, Ofelia forged ahead, already pointing out all the things that caught her eye.

Gallonten, an amalgam of all the peoples under Unity's banner, offered plenty of distractions, but none were so famous as the Rinehart Festival. It ran alongside Unity's conferences every fall and attracted performers and artisans from all corners of the continent.

As they walked along, Ofelia tried to stop at every juggler, stilt-walker, and fire-breather that caught her fancy, only dissuaded when Gareth entreated: "Let's see what they've got further along. The gentleman with the fire whip could be just around the corner." Here, a maranet sat on the corner selling tapestries colored with vivid dyes. There, a pair of nympherai dancers whirled in tiered skirts on a platform, lending their hooves to the beat like a percussive force. Up ahead, a half-alfar sold handmade lace and ribbons that fluttered into the path when the wind blew their way. Gareth even saw one orinian, though they were uncommon in Gallonten.

They played games, shopped, watched a puppet show, and bought toys and treats for Ofelia. After a while, when their feet started to drag and Gareth's pocketbook was feeling thin, Gareth bought them all meat pies and hunted for a place for them to sit. They ended up awkwardly perched on the fence separating the lawn from the paths.

"Gather round, gather round! This is a show you won't want to miss!" a voice called. "Hey, you three! We have benches open if you'd like real seats, though far be it from me to critique where such a lovely family eats." The speaker stepped into the Ranulfs' path, silhouetted against stormy gray clouds. He was a young, pretty-faced man, sapien like Gareth and Isobel and dressed in a showy red suit and feather-plumed hat. He knelt in front of Ofelia and flashed a boyish, dimpled smile. "Do you like Egil stories, little one?"

Isobel laughed and covered her mouth with her hand. *"Someone in this family certainly does,"* she murmured, quiet enough so that only Gareth could hear—at least, it *should* have been quiet enough, but the hatted man followed her gaze over to Gareth. He was striking beneath the hat, with light brown skin and large, thick-lashed dark eyes, but there was a weight in his gaze Gareth hadn't expected. He seemed out of place here among the commoners; Gareth would have been less surprised to see him on the stage.

"I take it the lady means you, sir?"

Gareth cleared his throat. "Yes, I study Egil folklore."

"He's writing a book on Egil," Isobel explained on his behalf.

Something in the young man's smile dimmed, but he gestured to an outdoor auditorium off the main path. "Then I can't promise you haven't heard the story before, but I *can* guarantee we'll still make it worth your while." He leaned in as if to share a secret. "The Webhon Players are rising stars in the world of theater. They're performing for Unity itself next week."

"Which story is it?" Gareth asked.

"The Castle of Eide."

It was a lesser known Egil story—still common enough, but the most common version was based off a novel that had taken significant creative liberties. The original story, though...well. Gareth couldn't keep from saying, "How strange."

The young man hadn't expected that answer. "Strange?" he asked.

"Well, the story is originally based on the old coup in Alfheim, you know. Did you do that on purpose?"

"Do what?" the young man asked, still not following.

"Prince Nochdvor is here in Gallonten today—his first time leaving Alfheimr in over sixty years," Gareth said.

The young man looked like he'd been struck. For a moment, he simply stared at Gareth with wide, dark eyes, and then stood. "I didn't realize," he said, his voice too calm for all of the emotions flickering across his face. "It's just a coincidence. We've been performing this show all season."

"O-oh," Gareth said, not sure what he'd said wrong.

Isobel looked between them, eyebrows raised, then cut the tension. "We may as well stay, Gareth; I'd like to have some time off my feet."

The young man flashed a grateful smile, though it was a mere shadow of the one from before. "A smart choice," he said, ushering them toward the benches. "Enjoy the show!"

Gareth, Isobel, and Ofelia had only just settled in their seats when shadows shifted in the wings and fog crept onto the stage in thick tendrils. Paired with the overcast skies above and stone skene behind, it set a dreary mood. The feather-hatted young man jumped onto the stage and waited. Even when the crowd quieted, he continued to wait until every whisper had ceased, every fan had stilled, every eye had turned his way. When he breathed, it was like he cast a spell: the audience leaned in with his inhale, back again with his exhale. The spell crested when he finally spoke, his voice softer, more solemn than it had been before.

"Heroes rise and fall," he simply said. "In the years following the Great War, we saw the cycle again and again. Hope, then defeat. Determination, then corruption. And before his fall, Egil shone the brightest. But where did that fall begin?"

The young man paused while the crowd clapped; Gareth joined in, his excitement rising.

"Egil, as you seem to already know," the man said with a twist of his lips, a little mischief making its way back onto his face, "Became the world's guiding star after the Great War. He saved lives, ended wars, and made trouble as much as he made a name for himself. But like all heroes, he had doubts. Like heroes inevitably do, he grew tired of bearing the people's hope. He retired, settled in a golden city that has since passed into memory. The city was ruled by a king who had seen the rise and fall of the Great War, and Egil enjoyed peace there for a time. But when the King fell ill, the people turned on the ruler who made them what they were. Let us take you back in time and tell you how Egil saved a king and lost his peace."

The young man backed off the stage as he spoke, and from the other wing, two men walked on. The first was dressed in golden fabrics draped over and around him, secured by delicate fastenings. He was elegant and soft, in stark contrast with the man beside him.

"How fares thy father this evening?" the second asked. This one wore an archetypal hero's ensemble, stage armor with a sword at his side, and had a full beard with graying hair around his temples. He had to be Egil. The other was the King's "son," a steady friend who appeared in many Egil stories. Having seen the real thing in person just that morning, the imitation paled in comparison.

"His state remains unchanged," answered the prince, "And the Council grows restless. I fear what will happen should they take matters into their own hands."

"He will improve before they do. I am certain of it," Egil said. Then, both hero and prince stopped abruptly as a woman entered from upstage left. "Ho! Who approaches at this late hour?"

The newcomer to the stage, a young woman, moved toward Egil as if guided on a breeze. She was dressed in an old gown decked in glittering gold. Anyone who knew Egil also knew her, the woman who flitted at the periphery of all the world's stories, heralded strange comings, and foretold calamities: the Oracle of Damael. Her path wound inextricably with Egil's, the Oracle warning of troubles and Egil preventing them.

"My Lady Oracle," Egil said stiffly. "What bringest thou to me?"

"My Lord Egil, a warning I must share with thee."

"Then the sun shines and the wind blows, ev'rything as ever it was. My friend, may I present to thee the Oracle of Damael? Whilst a dear friend she be, I suggest thou leavest ere she speaks her portents. They are never kind to those unfortunate enough to hear."

Before the prince could leave, the oracle stopped him. "I bid thee stay. This concerns thee, young prince. There is one in the castle who would see thy father killed. Stop him before he sees it true."

They really were quite good, Gareth thought as the show continued. Being well versed in Egil folklore meant that he was picky; he hated when the stories were sensationalized, when they mischaracterized the hero, or focused too heavily on his alleged *magic*. Because of that, because of the poor novelization, this story was already at a disadvantage. The real Egil was interesting enough without being fictionalized.

Egil was a phenomenon Gareth had been studying for decades: all of the peoples of Calaidia had their own cultures, their own histories, their own stories, and yet they *all* told stories of Egil. Even for all of that, there were few official records of him, and the records Gareth *did* find were contradictory, confused. Some living few from the older peoples still remembered him, but when Gareth asked, they refused to speak of him. It made Egil an interesting puzzle. At once he was the most spoken of person in the world and the least known.

While Gareth's fascination was predominantly academic, it was also an idolization that went back to his childhood. There was something about Egil. Even when you knew the man from the stories didn't exist, you wished he had. Even when the stories ended, when you had to step back and remind yourself that magic isn't real, Egil still taught you the value of hope, the strength to slay your monsters, and that magic *is* real and it's in the small things. The man from the stories was hope, kindness, compassion incarnate. And that made the truth of Histrios so much more jarring.

Gareth looked around the crowd, curious to see their reactions.

People seemed to be enjoying the show, but one stood out to Gareth: the young narrator again. He stood off to the side, watching Egil with an expression so dark it sent a chill down Gareth's spine, but that gloom fell away when the oracle's actress turned in his direction. He smiled, then went a step further and made a funny face at the stage, the kind Gareth might pull to make Ofelia laugh. The actress quickly averted her eyes, mouth turned down at the corners like she was fighting a smile.

When the young man noticed Gareth watching, he tipped his hat and bowed with a flourish, making Gareth tear his eyes away. By the time he'd refocused on the play, trying to ignore the strange chill of the young man's eyes on him, he found he had missed a portion of it. That was no matter. He'd read the novel, much as he wished he could forget it: the prince and Egil investigated the assassination plot and discovered the king's own brother conceived it. Though heartbroken over his uncle's betrayal, the prince helped Egil stop him, laying a trap for the traitor.

Egil fought the uncle with choreography that danced magnificently across the stage. At the fight's climax, the uncle stumbled; Egil held his hand out and a shower of sparks shot out from some contraption in the stage floor. Spectators in the front row jumped at the sudden light, then erupted into cheers, and beside Gareth, Ofelia squealed in delight. With the uncle's defeat, the show was over. Gareth, Isobel, and Ofelia stayed for the curtain call, but by unspoken agreement, they had reached their limits for the day.

"I'm guessing Moira won't make it for dinner?" Isobel asked as they circled back to the festival entrance.

"Nor for the indefinite future, I'd imagine," Gareth replied, "By the way, I'd meant to tell you: Prince Nochdvor is a fan of your books."

Isobel blinked, then laughed. "Oh! How'd you find *that* out?"

"It's a rather long story."

"Then let's get this one home for a nap, first. Would you mind carrying her for a while? I'm afraid she's going to fall asleep on her feet if we continue on this way."

"Of course, dear," Gareth said, scooping up Ofelia and following his wife through the crowd.

Chapter Five

Gareth's cab rolled to a stop before a squat building off the public square. Though the rain had come and gone quickly, ending before they'd even made it home from the festival, he had to take care climbing out to avoid the mud pooling over the cobblestone. His shoes were new, after all, a gift from Isobel. Unfortunately, his cab driver didn't take the same care: when her carriage wheels spun, they spat muddy rainwater all up Gareth's trousers.

"Confound it," Gareth muttered, glaring at the retreating cab before twisting to survey the damage. The white suit had, perhaps, been a mistake. Moira would be furious to see him like this, but that's what she got for summoning him at such a late hour, and with such short notice.

This building she'd invited him to reminded him of the correctional facility on Unity Island: windowless and bleak. A helpful valet opened the door for him, though, ushering him into a foyer that smelled of leather and cologne. It took Gareth back to his father's study, sitting in a corner and entertaining himself with a book while Moira and his father worked. There was no seaside view here, though, and the sleek mahogany furniture was configured into a waiting room.

A man stood behind a podium at one end; he took in the state of Gareth's suit with a sour expression. "Are you a member here, sir?" he asked. When Gareth peered over the man's shoulder, he saw a hazily lit hall full of dust particles that danced in and out of the evening light. A woman's laugh drifted from deeper inside.

It gave him an idea of where he was, at least. "This is a social club," he guessed.

"Yes, sir. If you're not already a member—"

"My sister asked me to meet her here," Gareth said. "I imagine she's on the list."

Looking doubtful, the host opened a leather-bound book. "And your sister's name?"

"Moira Ranulf."

The host stiffened. He didn't bother to consult his book. "May I see some identification?"

Gareth fished it out, then waited patiently while the host scrutinized it and handed it back with an apologetic grimace. "I'm terribly sorry, Mr. Ranulf," he said. "I didn't know to expect you. Would you, ah, like us to order a change of clothes for you?"

"That's quite all right. I don't expect to stay long."

"Then please, follow me."

The host led Gareth down the hallway behind him. Narrow windows on one side overlooked the busy street, and on the other hung portraits of serious-looking men—some sapien, some alfar, but all human. Gareth stopped at a jarringly familiar face, surprised to find his own father sneering down at them over the top of his glasses. Gareth gawked at the word "Founder" beneath the name placard.

"He never told me about this place," he said to the host, who'd slowed alongside him. "What is this?"

"The Metharow Club, founded by your father and several others as a place for humans with Unity connections to gather, unwind, and form social connections. Your sister has been a member since she was first appointed as a Representative. You are eligible for membership too, sir."

Gareth frowned. "I see."

He followed the host down a few more hallways and through a spacious lounge, empty but for a well-dressed group playing billiards in the corner. As he passed, they shot Gareth and his muddy clothes curious looks that made Gareth feel self-conscious. He was relieved when the host finally showed him into a private dining room.

"Gareth!" Moira called, waving him over. "Come in, come in."

To Gareth, the Magistrates' earlier meeting with the Nochdvors had seemed momentous, world-changing with its talk of wars and kidnappings, but he was surprised to find his sister completely at ease. She lounged in her seat, gestured for the host to fill Gareth's glass with wine while Gareth sat in the place she'd had set for him. Afterward, the host excused himself and left them alone.

"Your note came as a surprise," Gareth said while his sister drank. "I would've understood if you couldn't make time for me. I know how busy you are."

"Do you, now?" Moira asked, giving him a shrewd look. "One of my clerks mentioned you stopped by today. The fact that you're not swarming me with questions tells me you must have heard what happened."

"Heard? I—Well, I—," Gareth stammered. Sweat gathered at the back of his neck. Did she know he'd been eavesdropping? Had one of the Nochdvors mentioned it?

"Tell me, what rumors are the gossips peddling?"

Gareth sighed with relief. So she didn't know. "I've heard a few things," he said, pausing to wet his lips with the wine. It tasted expensive. "That the Prince and Princess of Alfheimr are in town, and that it might have to do with the king."

Moira hummed. Even on her best days, she looked far more than ten years Gareth's senior, her hair already gray and exhaustion lining her features. "I'm sure there's more you're not saying," she said. "You're loyal to Unity, aren't you, Gareth?"

Gareth drank more of the wine. "Of course. Why do you ask?"

Moira ignored the question, instead asking another: "And you've visited Orean before, haven't you?"

"Um," Gareth said, eloquently. He disliked discussing Orean with Moira. While Moira shared Unity's distaste for it, Gareth was fond of the little city-state. He imagined this conversation would be even worse now, after what Orean did. Under his sister's intense stare, he conceded, "We visit in the fall sometimes."

"You know it well, then?"

"Not *well*, but I know it. Moira, why are you asking me this?"

Before Moira could answer, a pair of servers entered the room carrying more wine and silver trays. Gareth belatedly realized that he'd already drained his glass.

"I know what you like, Gareth, so I took the liberty of ordering for you," Moira said while a server set a tray before him, lifting the lid to reveal a steaming steak topped with green vegetables.

"Thank you," Gareth said. He itched to get back to their conversation, but settled on a safer topic instead: "Why didn't you or father tell me about this place?"

"Don't be ridiculous. I'm sure I've invited you before."

"You haven't."

"No? It must have slipped my mind. You're here now, so what do you think? You're eligible for membership, you know."

"Humans only, Moira? It's a bit...old-fashioned." That was certainly an understatement, especially for a city like Gallonten.

Moira sighed, letting him know exactly what she thought of *that* nonsense. "In a world that's constantly changing, Gareth, it's nice to have some things stay the same."

Yes, Gareth guessed this place hadn't changed since its founding. He didn't think that was a good thing. Everything about this club and this room reminded him inextricably of his father, and that alone ensured he'd never step foot inside again. Even if it hadn't, the place's policies *would*. "I don't know, I like a bit of change."

"I don't see why you put up such a fuss about not being invited if you had no intention of joining," Moira huffed. She watched the servers leave, then said, "But let's not squabble. I have a favor to ask of you."

"Does it have to do with Orean?" Gareth asked.

"Very clever, Gareth," Moira said dryly. "Since you have it all figured out, I suppose I needn't tell you why the Nochdvors were in town. Unless you'd like to know…?"

"Please," Gareth said. Of course, he already knew, but he'd hear it from Moira, if he could. She never told him things when she could just as easily keep them to herself.

"Three days ago, the King of Alfheimr was visiting Illyon when a group of orinians massacred Illyon's leaders and absconded with its king."

Gareth didn't need to act surprised. This was the first he'd heard of a massacre. "They what?! Surely, Orean wouldn't risk—"

"And yet, surely, they did. The Nochdvors' eyewitness accounts were quite damning."

"How many died?"

"Eleven nobles and six guards. That doesn't include the king himself, of course; we hope against hope that he is still alive. Alfheimr is demanding war, of course," Moira said, in the same tone she used to discuss dinner plans. "Luckily, it's not up to them. Malong, Diomis, and I came up with a solution: we're going to send a team of diplomats to Orean to negotiate the king's return, and the young prince is going to lead it."

Gareth frowned. "*You* came up with that?"

"Smart, isn't it? It does no good to rush in and blame Orean when we don't have the facts. But if Orean has nothing to hide, then they will cooperate."

"And if they don't?"

Moira shrugged. "Then we'll have war. Rheamaren Nochdvor won't be appeased until either she has her father back or has shed enough blood to account for it."

Gareth tried to reconcile this account with the scared girl he'd seen that morning. "Why are you telling me all of this? What does this have to do with me?"

"We'd like you to be on the team, Gareth."

Gareth didn't need to act surprised this time, either. His hand slipped, his knife cutting across his plate with a loud *screech*. He stared dully at his sister. "You're joking. It may have taken you fifty years to develop a sense of humor, but you need to work on your delivery."

"I mean it. You should realize what an honor this is."

Gareth stood so fast that his chair hit the ground behind him with a *bang*. "An honor? I'm not a diplomat! I can barely even navigate Unity's conferences, let alone hostage negotiations!"

"You won't be doing the negotiations, of course. Everyone on the team will bring different experiences," Moira said. "You may not be the perfect politician, but your knowledge of Orean and its customs will be invaluable. Plus, the fact that we'd send the brother of a Unity Magistrate on this mission shows Orean we have faith they will behave civilly."

"So I'm a pawn."

"Don't be dramatic. We're extending this invitation because we have faith in you."

"If it's really an invitation, I should be able to refuse."

Moira pursed her lips. "Didn't you say you were loyal to Unity?"

"But—"

"We all have duties we must perform," Moira said, not giving Gareth a chance to argue. "I've been doing mine since father died while you've been off chasing folktales, and now it's your turn. Think of it this way: you'll be a part of the story for once, instead of just reading them in books. I know it'll be difficult leaving Ofelia, but imagine the stories you'll get to tell her—you'll prevent a war, rescue a King. You can be just like Egil."

Gareth stared at his hands, braced on the table. That *did* tempt him, if just for a moment. He wanted to be someone Ofelia could look up to, and if he had an opportunity to stop a war but passed on it out of fear, he wouldn't be. He was right to be afraid, though, wasn't he? If this was all true, if Orean really killed so many just to kidnap a king, was it a stretch to think they'd find use for a Magistrate's brother as well?

"And think how much time you'd have with Prince Nochdvor— that could be useful for your little book, couldn't it?" Moira asked. "I know what you're thinking, but I wouldn't have nominated you if it was truly dangerous. I can promise you the team will have heavy security. You'll even have your own personal guard. I need you for this, Gareth. The world needs to see how committed Unity is to protecting its people."

Gareth bit his cheek. Was this just about optics? Were Prince Nochdvor's hints about ulterior motives correct? Gareth really would be a pawn—a ploy, a publicity stunt to obfuscate those motives. Gareth was loyal to Unity, yes. He had no other way to be. But that didn't mean he was blind.

"You can think about it," Moira said when Gareth remained silent. "We still have the rest of the team to appoint, so there's no immediate rush."

"How gracious," Gareth said. Mechanically, he picked up and righted his chair. "Actually, I think I've lost my appetite."

Moira sighed. "Gareth—"

"If you want me to think about it, Moira, I need to not be looking at you. I'm going home to my wife and daughter. I'll talk to you tomorrow."

"Fine," Moira said. "Let me have the club ready a carriage."

Gareth drained the rest of his wine. It was a wine meant for sipping, and it burned his throat as it went down. "No, I think I'll walk. I need to clear my head."

"Don't be ridiculous. It's getting dark, and it's two miles to your hotel from here. Do you even know the way?" Moira called, even as Gareth backed through the door. The smell of Moira's tobacco, the same as his father's, was too sweet in here and he couldn't bear it a moment longer.

"I'll figure it out, I'm sure," he said, turning and leaving without another word. The club's long, hazy hallways passed in a blur, and soon Gareth was bursting through the doors and gasping in fresh air. The sun had set while he'd been inside, and he gazed up at the purpling sky.

He left the place on foot, relieved to swap out the grand municipal buildings for homes and shops and normal people going about their normal days. He thought he remembered the way from the cab ride over, but as he continued to walk, the homes fell away to dull brick and broken windows, the neat shops to abandoned storefronts. He told himself he needed to pass through a few unfashionable neighborhoods to reach Main Street. It was just the way. So he walked on, and after a while, he stopped noticing it. His mind was too busy circling around Unity, his sister, the Nochdvors to realize that none of this was familiar. It was only when he saw a sign that said "Now Entering Greysdale" that he finally began to panic. This was *not* the way, and now he was sure of it.

A small chimney sweep bumped into him and deposited a layer of soot onto his coat, the dusty ash standing out against the black wool. Gareth frowned at the boy, who cast too pitiable a figure to be angry with. "Do you know the way to Kramer Street?" he asked, handing the boy a coin.

The boy shook his head, mumbled his thanks, and ran off. As Gareth watched him go, he noticed two men huddled near the door of a tawdry public house, one looking Gareth's way. They'd know, surely. He worked his way over to them, but before he could say a word one hurriedly set off, knocking his shoulder into Gareth's in his haste to get away.

"You're gonna wanna check that you still have your purse," the remaining man suggested.

Gareth glanced over his shoulder to check that the man was speaking to him. There was no one else around. "Me? Why wouldn't I?"

The man coughed, clearly covering a laugh. "That fellow didn't *accidentally* slam into you," he said, holding up a hand and wriggling his finger. "Light fingers."

Gareth checked the inner pocket of his coat and breathed a sigh of relief at finding his pocketbook intact. He inched closer to his new acquaintance. "Thank you, I should've seen the trick for what it was. I was wondering—" He paused, here, to cough. The smells of perfume and booze drifting out of the public house only barely covered the stench of rot, smoke, and feces that permeated Greysdale. "Could you help me? I'm afraid I'm lost."

The man raised an eyebrow. "Are you, now?"

"I'm trying to get to Kramer Street?"

The man thought for a moment, then pointed down the street. "Go down that way and at your first chance, turn left. It'll look like an alley, but don't let that stop you. The other end opens up onto Main Street."

"Wonderful, thank you!"

Gareth followed the man's instructions, hesitating when he reached the mouth of the alley described. It was exactly the sort of place common sense told him to avoid: dark, with large objects obscuring the view to the other end. When he looked up, though, he could see the spires of a church he knew to be on Main Street. He held a handkerchief to his face to block the smell and plowed into the alley.

He'd only made it about a third of the way through, though, when a heavy hand landed on his shoulder, making him jump and hiss like a feral cat. It was only the man from before, the one who'd given him directions.

"Sorry to scare you. You dropped this, I think," the man said, hiding another smile. He held out Gareth's cigarette case, but when Gareth reached to take it, the man only pulled it closer to himself. "You should be careful walking around this place at night, sir. With your clothes and fancy way of speaking, you're asking to get robbed."

"Oh," Gareth said, uncertain.

He wanted to give the man the benefit of the doubt, but he decided such a thing was not for moments like this. While he could replace the cigarette case, the same could not be said of his life. When he turned to run, though, he found another man behind him, this one holding a knife that glittered in the moonlight. It was the other man from before, Gareth realized, the one that had bumped into him.

He'd been played. He glanced toward the mouth of the alley, but he knew no one would see them. It had been so dark from the street, the street itself too empty.

Gareth had always imagined that, being well-educated and reasonably clever, he'd be quick-thinking in emergencies. He always hated books where the hero froze at a crucial moment, but he hadn't understood then the paralyzing effects of fear, the way powerlessness chilled your bones and whistled through your blood with every beat of your heart. He understood it now, as the stranger's knife danced along the back of his neck.

"Call for help and Tag will slit your throat faster than you can piss yourself," said the man with Gareth's cigarette case.

Before Gareth could feel a fresh wave of fear at that, Tag wrenched Gareth's arms behind his back while the other slammed his knee into Gareth's groin. Gareth grunted, the air leaving his lungs in a staccato burst, and fell to the ground. He barely registered the pain of his knees hitting the hard dirt.

"Take my money, just leave me be," he gasped when his breath returned to him. He wondered, briefly, what his father would think of him begging. This was not how Ranulfs behaved, even to save their lives. Before the thought could go further, his assailant slammed his fist into Gareth's face. Gareth flew back at the blow, his head hitting alley brick. Lights burst before his eyes.

No one would see him, no one would hear him, so with shaking hands, Gareth threw his pocketbook at his assailant's feet. The man took it up with a sneer, rifling through it and pulling out Gareth's Unity identification. He held the laminated papers to the light.

"Looks like junk," Tag suggested.

When the other saw Gareth inching his way down the alley, he casually ordered, "Tag, stop him." He studied the papers more while Tag grabbed Gareth by the collar. "I dunno what it says, but that's Unity's seal, right there. I bet we can get a good price for whatever this is. Search him, see if he's hiding anything else."

It was now or never.

"*Help!*" Gareth shouted.

He thought he saw a shadow hesitate at the mouth of the alley but knew it was wishful thinking. No one could see them. He looked back at Tag in time to see a fist speeding toward his face. It came so fast he couldn't even wince: he collapsed against the wall, pain radiating as his head hit the brick, and then everything faded to black.

CHAPTER SIX

GARETH WAS OUT FOR ONLY A MOMENT, opening his eyes again to find
Tag standing over him with the knife. He came to quickly after that,
scrambling back and holding out a plaintive hand. "Don't!" he slurred.
"Please, let me live."

"Why should we?" asked the man with Gareth's cigarette case.

Gareth stared at the muddy ground, blinking back tears. "My
sister has money. She works for Unity. Spare me and she'll reward
you, but if I die, there'll be trouble."

"How do we know you're even tellin' the tru—"

The man cut off with a gasp, the glint of a blade protruding from
his chest. As it retracted, a spreading stain took its place and the man's
gasp turned into a wet gurgle. His knees buckled, but before he could
drop, a hand wrapped around his head from behind and slammed
him sideways into the wall; skull hit brick, and Gareth winced at the
horrible *crack* that followed. The man fell, leaving a stranger with a
bloodied sword standing over his body.

"Knife," Gareth mumbled from the ground. Somehow, the
stranger understood his warning: when Tag charged him, he dropped
his sword and quickly sidestepped the other man's smaller blade. He

caught Tag's forearm and twisted, graceful as a dancer, until Tag cried out and dropped the knife. This stranger moved confidently, easily, only as much as needed to get the necessary leverage.

The stranger grabbed Tag by the hair, yanked his head down, and brought his knee up until it met Tag's face. And just like that, Gareth's second assailant fell to the ground, motionless. Gareth squinted in the dark. "Did you kill him?"

"Not that one." The stranger's voice was gentler than Gareth expected. They both looked at the other's body, where blood pooled over cold cement, and the stranger added, "I try to limit myself to one murder a day."

Gareth stared at him.

"Just a joke," he said when the silence stretched on. "A poor one, maybe. Sorry. Are you all right?"

His accent was soft, the vowels round and the cadence almost songlike. Northern, Gareth thought, though thinking proved hard with the way the world tipped around him. "I feel sick," he said.

When the stranger approached, Gareth shrank back. "Come on, it's all right," the man said, holding his hands up innocently between them. "I only want to check your injuries."

"Can I trust you?"

"Sorry, but you don't have a choice." He sounded too cheerful for the words leaving his mouth, but he was right. This time, when he kneeled beside Gareth, Gareth allowed it, though he still flinched at the man's touch. "I'm looking for Kramer Street," he mumbled.

The stranger tutted. "You're quite a ways off. But it's too dark to see here—let's get out of this alley before your friend wakes," the man said. He retrieved his sword, wiping it off before slipping it into a sheath at his hip, then helped Gareth to his feet. Gareth shrugged him off and took several stumbling steps on his own, but when he fell, the man was there to catch him.

"Woozy," Gareth said.

"I bet." When the man felt confident Gareth would stay upright if he stepped away, he bent to retrieve Gareth's cigarette case and pocketbook.

"Are you going to rob me, too?" Gareth asked, watching.

The man snorted and rifled through the pocketbook, slipping Gareth's displaced identification back inside in the process. "Nah, there's not enough in there to make it worth my time." He then opened Gareth's suit-coat and tucked it into the inner pocket, giving Gareth's chest a friendly pat when he'd finished.

"Uh," Gareth said, awkwardly. "Thank...you?"

"Anytime."

Gareth squinted at the stranger. With one of his eyes swelling, he couldn't make out any features in the darkness. "Should we, erm...alert the authorities? Surely, we can't just leave them here."

He could feel the stranger's stare, even if he couldn't see it. He fidgeted, uncomfortable, when the stranger let out a disbelieving laugh. "The authorities? *Really*?"

"Is that so strange?"

"In this neighborhood, yes," the stranger said. "They're not guaranteed to come, even if we do report this. Mind if I ask your name?"

"Gareth Ranulf."

After a pause, "Not Ranulf as in the *Magistrate of Unity* Ranulf, I hope." There was something strange in the man's voice, a tension that hadn't been there before.

"My sister," Gareth said.

"Of all the rotten twists of fate," the stranger sighed. "Hold on."

And with that, he turned on his heel and left Gareth alone in the dark. Immediately, Gareth panicked. He was alone and injured, what was he to do if the man had left for good? Was he going to die in this reeking alley? He felt along the wall, grimacing at the grime under his fingers. In this state, he wouldn't even make it to the end of the alley on his own, let alone home. While he was still deciding what to do, he heard boots on gravel, and then that soft voice again. He breathed a sigh of relief as the stranger, said, "I left a message with the shopkeep next door. They'll call the cops, or they won't. Now, come on."

Gareth gratefully leaned on the man as they hobbled to the end of the alley, where they emerged onto a sparsely crowded street lit by rows of streetlamps. The man pushed Gareth onto the closest bench. "Sit. Let me look at you." He knelt in front of Gareth while Gareth shut his eyes, fighting another wave of nausea. "Atiuh and the Three, you're lucky I was following you."

"Pardon?" Gareth asked, opening his eyes again.

"I said you're lucky I found you!" the man said with an easy smile. "I'm Roman, by the way. Roman Hallisey. I'd say it's a pleasure, Mr. Ranulf, but I'm not sure the circumstances warrant it."

"Have we met before? You seem terribly familiar."

"I don't think so," Roman said. "How could I forget such a pretty face?"

"Is that some sort of jest?" Gareth reached up to touch his nose, but Roman batted his hand away.

"Don't. You're swollen and battered, but at least your nose has stopped bleeding."

"Is it broken?"

"I can't tell. I don't think so."

"And my eye? Is it bad that it's swollen like this?"

"You have a strange idea of *good* if you even have to ask. But you'll live, if that's what you mean," Roman said. "It'll stay swollen a few days, then you'll have a nasty bruise."

"You seem to know a lot about this."

"I've seen a black eye or two in my time."

Unsure how to respond, Gareth said, "Thank you for the help."

Roman patted Gareth's knee. "Of course. Anywhere else hurt? They didn't stab you or anything, did they? I assume you would've mentioned it already."

"No, they just…hit me a few times."

"Are you still dizzy?"

"No. Yes. Maybe a little," Gareth admitted.

"You might have a concussion. Or be in shock." Roman tilted his head to one side. He had wide, dark eyes, framed not only by thick lashes but by dark bags that sat underneath. Brightly, he continued, "I don't know, I'm not a doctor. How about we get you home so you can call one?"

"Please," Gareth said. He hadn't been on his feet even ten seconds, though, before he turned to the side and hurled.

Roman wrinkled his nose. "Strike that, we're going to a hospital now. C'mon, there's one on the way."

Gareth nodded, the taste of bile too fresh on his tongue to argue, and let Roman drag him down the street. Walking helped clear the nausea some, at least, and he eyed the young man's back. "Roman's an interesting name. Where's it from?" he asked, to distract himself.

"*Interesting*, huh?" Roman repeated. Gareth could hear the grin in his voice. "Thanks, I think. Technically, it's my middle name. My mother was a bit fanciful, with particular ideas about who she wanted me to be. *Romanos* is a spirit in Troasian mythology, *Ro-* meaning 'above' and *-manos* meaning all personkind, or the like," Roman said, waving his hand grandly. He seemed to make a lot of broad, effusive gestures. "She thought 'Roman' was a name for someone who'd do great things."

"And have you? Done great things, I mean."

Roman's smile fell. "That depends on how you define great, I suppose."

"I'd say saving a man's life qualifies."

"Those thieves wouldn't have killed you," Roman said. Despite his flippant tone, he looked away from Gareth, embarrassed. "Probably."

They walked in silence a moment, until Gareth asked, "Then why did you do it? I doubt anyone else would have."

Roman shrugged. "I was there; I heard you shout. I had time to investigate." He looked over at Gareth, then laughed at the man's affronted expression. "Were you expecting something more heroic? More storybook?"

"No," Gareth lied, feeling his cheeks flush. "It's just sobering to know I'm only alive because of a young man's boredom."

Roman steered Gareth away from a hole in the pavement. "Let me try again." Clearing his throat, deepening his voice, he said, "When the fearless hero Roman heard the man's calls for succor, he could not help but render aid, slaying the wrongdoers and single-handedly snatching Gareth Ranulf from death's icy grip! After all, such is a hero's duty!" Returning to his normal voice, he asked, "How was that? Better?"

Gareth hid his face behind a hand while Roman laughed at him. "I'm sorry I asked," he said. "But I'm glad you did it, anyhow."

"Anytime. Really," Roman said. He stopped walking, and Gareth followed his gaze to a squat, prison-like building. "Well, that's it."

"*That's* the hospital?" Gareth asked. It looked dirty. "Are you sure it's safe?"

"In this part of Gallonten, it's the best you're going to find."

Gareth wished he could see better. He reached up to touch his swollen eye, but Roman batted his hand away again. Gareth scowled at him.

"Are you touching just to touch, or do you need something?"

"I just...can't read the signs. I can't even tell what you look like."

"Which is why a hospital would serve you well. If it makes you feel any better, I can't tell what you look like either. Right now, you look like you spilled a bucket of red paint on your head and ran into a beehive."

"That really doesn't make me feel better."

"Then how about this: I'll read the signs for you. Realistically, they'll probably just clean you up and give you something for the pain, and at the very least, we can have them call a cab to get you home," Roman said, dragging Gareth slowly toward the doors.

"You won't—," Gareth began, only to bite his tongue.

"Won't what?"

"You won't leave me, will you?" Gareth said, embarrassed. "If I'm keeping you from anything, I understand if you—"

"I'll stay," Roman promised. Then, tone turning teasing, he asked, "Do you need me to hold your hand, too?"

"Oh, stop. Just make sure they sterilize everything," Gareth grumbled. He pushed past Roman into the building.

"Sure, but if you need stitches, I'm waiting in the hallway," Roman called, trailing behind as Gareth led the way into the surprisingly cheerful foyer. He squinted against the lights, wrinkled his nose at the sterile smell. While unpleasant, it seemed perfectly normal, as far as hospitals went. Seeing Gareth relax, Roman said, "And that's why you don't judge a dragon by the shine of their scales. Sit, I'll talk to the nurse for you."

Pain raced up Gareth's side as he slid into a seat at random. He watched Roman greet the nurses, leaning against the desk like it belonged to him. While Gareth couldn't hear what was being said, he could see well enough in the new light to make out more of his savior. Roman Hallisey seemed one of those individuals whose age was hard to place. He was old enough to be frighteningly competent, fighting like no one had Gareth had ever seen, but he also radiated a youthful exuberance. He was easily younger than Gareth's forty-two, at least, and was sapien with no signs of longer-lived heritage. If Gareth was pressed, he'd guess somewhere around thirty.

Roman wore a billowing-sleeved shirt tucked into thick sash, which he paired with straight-legged trousers and tall boots. It certainly wasn't any Gallontean custom. His hair, too, fell between the current fashions—too long to fit the close-cropped style of working men but not long enough to tuck behind his ears, a look currently sported by the upper class. It was too messy to be fashionable, at any rate. His curls seemed permanently ruffled, and Gareth understood why when he watched Roman tangle a hand through them, pushing them out of his face. Nothing about Roman was fashionable or proper, but he had the charm and natural attraction to excuse it. Again, he felt so *familiar*. The nurse nodded at something he said, then looked over to where Gareth sat. Roman beckoned him over.

"Mr. Ranulf?" the nurse asked as Gareth approached, pushing several forms and a pen across the desk toward him. "Sign these for me, please. We can take you back right away, but your friend will have to wait here."

Gareth's hand hovered above the signature line. He glanced nervously at Roman. Seeming to guess at his anxieties, Roman assured him, "I told you I'd wait, Gareth."

"Thank you. Of course, I'll compensate you for your time."

Roman raised an eyebrow. "If you're offering."

"I'm insisting."

"Even better. Now quit making the poor nurse wait on you; I'll be here when you get back. You can thank me more then, if you still feel the urge."

Gareth followed the nurse through winding halls to a barren room. While she went to the old sink in the corner, Gareth climbed onto the cold examining table. The nurse cleaned his wounds swiftly, efficiently, and passed him a small canvas bag full of ice. "For the swelling," she explained. "The doctor will be in shortly."

Once she was gone, Gareth settled back and draped the ice over his swollen eye. The lights were blessedly dim, here, but the room was too quiet. He hadn't had time to think since he'd gotten lost, but now, he had too much of it. Strangely, though, his mind didn't go to his near-death experience or surprise rescue—it went back to his conversation with Moira, to Orean and to this mission. It was horrible. He'd just watched a man die, but all he could do was worry about his own future.

A knock came at the door. Gareth started to push himself up as the doctor entered, but she stopped him with a firm hand on his shoulder. "Please, stay as you were. My name is Dr. Carthian. Can you tell me in your own words what happened tonight, Mr. Ranulf?"

Once Gareth explained, Dr. Carthian asked a series of questions about how he was feeling, where he'd been hit, and how much he could remember. His face, his stomach, the back of his head, he said. He felt fine, aside from aches and pains. He could remember his name, the date, his address. He still felt very dizzy.

"I don't think you're in shock. May I?" the doctor asked, holding her hand near Gareth's face. When Gareth nodded, she pressed her hand to his forehead and stood for a long time with her eyes closed. "I see. You have a cracked rib, a mild concussion, and swelling around your eye and nose, but that's fortunately the worst of it."

"You can tell all that from just a few questions?"

The doctor smiled and removed her hand. "I'm rosanin."

"Ah."

Rosanin were a rare class of individuals born with small, inexplicable abilities. Some had knacks for gambling, others could always point north or see people's auras. As a child, Gareth had known a young man with an exceptional green thumb. Little was known about rosanin, though. The religious claimed rosanin were blessed by the Guardians, and even with all the advancements of the last century, scientists had yet to come up with a better explanation.

Species, sex, family history—there was no predicting it. It didn't seem inherited, and it wasn't testable.

"Through touch, I can tell when a person's body is not as it should be," the doctor explained. "Many hospitals in cities have someone like me on staff. It quickens the process, saves time and effort."

"Ah," Gareth said again, more understanding this time.

The doctor smiled. "You'll be able to treat your injuries at home, Mr. Ranulf. Get plenty of rest and introduce your former activities slowly. If you have access to ice, ice your nose and eye at least four times a day. I'd also suggest—once you've healed—introducing more exercise into your routine. I sensed some concerning buildup in your arteries."

Gareth blinked. "Yes, Doctor."

"For now, I'll give you medication for the pain, but it might impair your motor functions for a few hours. You can take laudanum at home, but not until morning." While she spoke, the doctor crossed to a cabinet, retrieved a bottle from inside, and poured out a dose. When she handed it to Gareth, he nearly hurled again at the smell of it. He had to steel himself before draining the cup.

"Terrible, I know, but it'll help," she said, taking the empty cup back. "I'll have the nurse bring fresh ice. Would you prefer to wait here or in the foyer?"

"The foyer," Gareth answered easily. The sooner he could get home, the better. Isobel must be worried. He returned to the waiting room on his own, relieved to find that Roman had indeed waited. The young man sat near the door, picking at his nails, and didn't notice Gareth until he dropped into the seat next to him.

"Your face is clean!" he exclaimed.

"Yes, apparently the doctor needs to *see* the injury in order to assess it," Gareth said dryly.

"Clean him up and he's suddenly a comedian. Good one, Mr. Ranulf. Why are you sitting?

"A nurse is bringing me fresh ice," Gareth said, pulling the current bag away from his eye and shaking it so Roman could hear the slosh of water. "I've been prescribed bedrest and given medicine."

"Laudanum?" Roman asked.

Gareth shook his head.

"No?" Roman asked, studying Gareth. His face fell. "Tell me it wasn't Carujan Oil."

"I don't—"

"Clear liquid. Thick and sticky. Smells and tastes like piss."

"That sounds right," Gareth said primly. His nose wrinkled at the memory. "Is that bad? *She's* the doctor, Mr. Hallisey. I believe she knows best."

"Sure, but she didn't give much thought to the poor bastard stuck walking you home. *Carrying* you home, rather. They don't have a phone here, so we'll have to find a cab on Main Street. Are you concussed?"

"Mildly."

"Well, we'll have to walk two blocks—hopefully before that oil takes effect."

Silence fell between them while they waited for the nurse. Gareth looked around and fidgeted with his clothes and eventually asked, "Where are you from, by the way? Your accent sounds northern."

"Good ear. I grew up in Troas."

That fit into what little Gareth knew about Roman, with his mother's Troasian mythology and his own darker features. They neared the end of a bright summer, and while Gareth's skin had tanned beyond its usual pasty white, Roman's was still several shades darker. The only reason Gareth hadn't guessed Troas to start was because of the way Roman's accent had diluted, like he'd been away from home for a long time. "I had a tutor from Troas," he said. He hadn't actually meant to say it, which puzzled him.

When the nurse finally arrived to replace the ice, Gareth stood to go and found the world spinning around him. He grabbed Roman's shoulder for support; funnily, the young man didn't seem affected by the ground's rocking. He just gave Gareth an amused look and gestured grandly toward the doors, saying, "After you."

The gesture tickled at something in the back of Gareth's mind. It felt strangely familiar. Gareth mused over it as they left the hospital, but it wasn't until the next block over that it finally clicked. "Wait!"

Faster than Gareth had ever seen anyone move, Roman twirled to face him, his sword appearing in his hand between one moment and the next. He looked around, alert, then frowned at Gareth. "*What?*"

"It's you! I know who you are!"

Roman's expression darkened, and in an instant, he had become a different person, a predator instead of a savior. Gareth nearly staggered under the weight of those black eyes, fixed unblinkingly on him. Had he been in his right mind, it would have felled him. It would have *terrified* him. Under the medicine's influence, though he only let out a nervous giggle.

The sound seemed to snap Roman out of whatever he'd fallen into. The young man's sword disappeared as quickly as it had appeared. He rolled his eyes, which no longer seemed so threatening, and dragged Gareth the rest of the way across the street.

"Atiuh's name, Gareth, I thought there was trouble."

"Sorry," Gareth said, too dazed to really feel it.

"Well?" Roman asked impatiently.

"Well what?"

"You said you know me. Who do you think I am?"

"Oh! We've met, sort of," Gareth said, following Roman's lead when Roman turned down a dark side street. He didn't even question it, which worried a distant, sober part of his mind. Mostly, though, he focused on walking on ground that wouldn't stay still. "This morning, actually. You convinced me to stop for a play. Do you remember?"

Roman thought for a moment, then snapped his fingers and laughed, throwing his head back in delight. "You're the Egil scholar!"

"That's me," Gareth said proudly. "I didn't recognize you without your hat."

Roman laughed again, throwing his head back in delight. Even through his mind's haze, Gareth envied the boyishness of it. "I don't have the same excuse," he said. "I should've recognized you sooner."

"It's because I was painted red."

Roman bit his lip to keep from smiling. "Walk faster, Gareth. Call it a hunch, but I think the medicine's kicking in."

Gareth blinked up at the purple sky as they turned finally onto Main Street. A carriage rattled past, its side lanterns making him squint and avert his eyes, and it didn't stop even when Roman tried to flag it down. Gareth guessed the blood on his clothing might've had something to do with it. "Remarkably fast, this stuff. And strong, too. I hardly feel a thing," he said. Suddenly remembering the thread of their earlier conversation, he asked, "Are you one of the Webhon Players?"

Roman looked back at Gareth, trying and failing to hide his amusement. "I'm an honorary player, I suppose. I help with the opening in exchange for a place in their camp."

"I thought your opening was beautiful."

"Maybe you should stop talking for a while," Roman suggested. As they walked, Gareth had to rely on him more and more for balance.

He managed to stay quiet for a while, but they hadn't made it another full block before he asked, "How far away are we? My boots are getting dirty."

"Those boots were ruined the minute you set foot in Greysdale."

"Set *foot*. I get it." Gareth laughed. "How long to Kramer Street?"

"It's ten minutes from here, but at the rate we're going, forty."

Gareth kicked a loose stone. To his credit, Roman managed to keep a straight face, even after looking over and seeing Gareth's undignified pout. He asked, "What brought you to Greysdale, anyway? It's not the sort of place I'd expect to find such an upstanding gentleman."

"Wasn't intentional. I just don't know the city, even after all my visits."

"Visits? You're not from here?"

"No, I live in Adriad. Just outside of it."

"You came to visit your sister," Roman guessed. "For the conferences?"

Gareth nodded, then paused to peer in the window of a ladies' hat shop. He balked at how *big* some of them were. How did the ladies not fall over with those on their heads? When Roman stifled a laugh, Gareth realized he'd said it out loud. He covered his mouth with a hand.

"Atiuh help me," Roman muttered, though he was still smiling. "And how did you get so lost?"

"I tried to walk home from a meeting."

"A meeting?" Roman asked, watching Gareth out of the corner of his eye. Under different circumstances, Gareth might have noticed the sharp interest in the young man's voice. "What kind of meeting?"

"I'm…not supposed to say."

"Sure, I understand. It's not like I have anyone to tell, though," Roman said, watching Gareth out of the corner of his eye. Earnestness dripping from his every word, "I asked because…well, no offense, but you seem like you've got something on your mind. It's something to do with Unity, right? And the visiting prince?"

"Yes," Gareth admitted, worrying at his lower lip. Roman's dark eyes made him itch, just beneath the skin. "Someone's been kidnapped, and Unity's sending a diplomatic team to Orean to negotiate their return. I've been there a few times, so Moira wants me on the team. That's what the meeting was about."

Roman's eyes widened. "Diplomatic? *Unity*?" he said, tasting the word like he'd never heard it before. "That doesn't sound like them."

"And how would you know?" Gareth asked on reflex, sounding very much like his father. He could hear the condescension and hated himself for it, just a little. It made Roman stiffen, his expression shutter. Whatever sharpness Gareth had seen behind his eyes before disappeared, like a sheathed knife—hidden, but no less dangerous. "I guess I wouldn't."

"I'm sorry," Gareth said.

"No need to apologize, Mr. Ranulf," Roman said stiffly. Changing the subject, he asked, "Was that your wife and daughter with you today?"

"Yes. Isobel and Ofelia. Isobel's the most beautiful woman in the world, Mr. Hallisey. You should see her! You should come up and see her! Then you'll know."

"I saw her this morning, remember?"

"Oh. Right." Gareth sighed. "She's pregnant with our second child. I really don't want to leave her, now of all times."

"I'm sure it's no great comfort, but it sounds like Unity has things in hand. And Orean is beautiful in the fall."

"Have you been?" Gareth asked.

"Several times."

"*You* should be on the team, then, instead of me. You're much charminger than I, and you can fight, and you've been to Orean."

"You think I'm charming? I'm flattered, Gareth, but you're a married man."

If it wouldn't have given him a headache, Gareth might've rolled his eyes. "Would you go, if we could swap? Would you join the team? Hypo-*hyperothetically*."

"Absolutely not."

"Why not?"

Roman half-laughed. He looked up at the sky, weighing his answer. "Because I don't work with Unity, and I'm sure they wouldn't want to work with me."

"Why not?"

Roman turned his considering look on Gareth. "I would have leapt at this sort of opportunity, when I was young. I *did*, in fact. I won't make the same mistake again. The fact is, I don't trust Unity. I don't trust them to treat Orean fairly, and I don't trust their motives, so promise you'll keep an eye on them for me."

"I…promise."

This pulled another smile out of Roman, softer than the others. "I really wish you the best, Gareth; you seem like a nice guy. Hold onto that and don't let anyone take it from you."

"You talk older than you look," Gareth observed, the most cogent thought he could form at the moment.

"I'm fairly sure that doesn't make sense."

"It does."

Roman smiled and shook his head. "If you insist. By the way, do you recognize where we are?"

Gareth looked around. Past the slight blur, he recognized the lights and sights of Kramer Street. "Oh!"

"Should I help you to your room, or can you handle it from here?"

"I can handle it. Thank you, Mr. Hallisey. I said I'd pay you —"

"Don't worry about it, just promise you'll be more careful next time you wander around at night. Good luck with your trip, Mr. Ranulf."

With that, Roman was gone, strolling down the street and out of Gareth's life. Gareth lingered outside his hotel a few minutes longer, letting the crisp air slowly peel back the medicine's haze. He didn't want to be so out of it when he explained what happened to Isobel, so he stood and watched the—few, given the late hour—people pass by on the street.

He recognized the trio of orinians that were staying across the hall from him as they also returned to the hotel. One of them, a girl with long blonde hair, met Gareth's eye from across the street. Her smile fell—Gareth could only imagine how he must look—and she hurried after her friends.

"Kieran! Íde!" she called, catching up to them just as the hotel doors swung shut, blocking them from Gareth's view. He watched the doors long after the orinians disappeared, Roman's warning coming unbidden to his mind. *I don't trust Unity to treat the orinians fairly.* It echoed the prince's threats, the hints of *ulterior motives*. Gareth hoped they were both wrong.

They must be wrong.

CHAPTER SEVEN

"ANY FOOD FOR YOU, SIR?" a voice asked, pulling Aleksir from his thoughts. He turned from the passing crowds to find the restaurant server standing over his table.

"Nah. I told you, I'm waiting for someone."

The server shrugged. It was a doubtful motion, a *"suit yourself."* He probably thought Aleksir had been stood up, and Aleksir couldn't even blame him. Not when he'd been here for hours nursing the same suspicion, the same glass of cheap wine. If it *had* been a date, he would've stormed off ages ago, but this was for work. Standing up his boss was something people simply didn't do, so if it had happened, something must have gone horribly wrong.

As soon as he had the thought, he felt it: a strange chill, like the brush of a blade against the back of his neck. Aleksir had grown up on the streets. He knew how it felt to be watched.

He didn't immediately react. Instead, he checked his watch, fiddled with the menu, then subtly glanced around: first over the veranda tables, then down the street. There were people everywhere thanks to Gallonten's vibrant nightlife, but when Aleksir looked, no heads turned quickly away and no shapes shrank back into shadows.

Aleksir had also learned early on to trust his instincts. Complaining loudly about being stood up, he threw his napkin down and slouched off, his hands shoved in his pockets. He put on a good show; he wished Devikra could have seen it.

At the first intersection, he took off running. Maybe he was being paranoid, but his boss had enemies in this city and paranoid was always better than complacent. It was *much* better than dead. He wove through side streets and down back roads, and when he couldn't run any further, he ducked into an alley. It was a dark, dead end—his first mistake. He studied the alley's back wall for an escape route and spotted a windowsill he could haul himself onto, but the window itself was boarded shut and Aleksir hadn't the leverage needed to pry it free. He might be able to jump to the balcony above it, though.

Because he studied the shadows so closely, he noticed them shift where the roof met the sky. He hoped it was only an animal, but the longer he stared, the better he could make out a person-shaped patch of darkness outlined against the stars.

"Come down and face me!" he called, finding his courage.

A chuckle drifted down to him. Aleksir glimpsed a ghostly face, barely illuminated by the street's pale lamplight as the figure leaned forward, but just as quickly as it appeared, it was gone again. Without taking his eyes off that spot, Aleksir inched over to a dumpster and wrenched the leg off an overturned chair. The wood gave with surprising ease, and Aleksir held it aloft like a bat.

"Coward!" he called again.

Pebbles fell in answer, clanging and clattering their way to the ground. Aleksir watched them, almost missing the shadowy figure that followed them down, melting out of the shadows like he'd been borne from them. As the stranger jumped from balcony to windowsill, from windowsill to ground, his easy grace reminded Aleksir of one of those slinky toys, ceaseless and certain: fall, drop. Fall, drop.

The stranger landed on the balls of his feet, his boots making the softest of sounds when they touched down. He was a tall man, slender and lanky and sharp like a wolf. He moved like one, too, stalking toward Aleksir with a lazy, loping prowl. It struck Aleksir, in that moment, that he was the prey. With all the bravado he could muster, he asked, "You make a habit of running around on rooftops?"

"Sometimes it's the fastest way," the stranger answered, his grin too wide.

Aleksir waved his makeshift cudgel in warning. "You picked the wrong prey tonight, wolf. Come any closer and you'll get a beating."

The man's grin remained. "If I'm a wolf, what does that make you?" He paced to the side, circling Aleksir slowly. Aleksir turned with him, protecting his back, and too late he realized he'd cornered himself. At the look on his face, the man laughed. "What's the matter, little rabbit? I mean you no harm."

The lamplight seemed to seek this stranger out, like a sunflower does the suns. It illuminated a handsome face—flawless, if not for the cold smile and colder eyes. It was the kind of face Aleksir had always been jealous of, growing up, and that same feeling ate at him now. So, too, did the familiarity He thought he'd seen this person somewhere before, but when the man closer, he didn't waste time thinking about it: he swung his cudgel right at that familiar face, so swiftly the man couldn't hope to dodge.

Only, he did. He moved faster than Aleksir would've thought possible, faster than his eyes could even follow. His aim had been perfect, but somehow, he hit air and stumbled. When he tried again, the man simply stepped out of Aleksir's range, his hands clasped casually behind his back. On Aleksir's third attempt, he caught his cudgel mid-swing, halting all of Aleksir's momentum in one jarring instant. Aleksir had thrown all of his weight into the swing, so he stumbled when the wolf wrenched the wood from his hands and tossed it into the alley's shadows.

"I just said I'm not here to hurt you," the man said.

Aleksir was already looking around for another weapon. "Right."

"You're Aleksir Bardon, aren't you? I have some questions, and word is you're usually someone with answers."

Aleksir paused at that, even puffed up a little. He couldn't help himself. "I might be," he said. "An' I might have."

"Is it true you work for the Oracle of Damael?"

Aleksir paused again, a little too long. "Where'd you hear that?"

"Ah," said the man, something like pity entering his voice, "Not a rabbit, then, but a little fly caught in Devikra's web. If you're close with her, then you must know about the commotion on Unity Island today. What can you tell me about it?"

"Why should I tell you anything? Who even are you?"

The stranger stopped his pacing, his impatient back and forth. "Someone who would see Unity fall."

Great. Aleksir was trapped with a radical and a madman—a dangerous one, at that. He eyed the gap in the alleyway the man's pacing had created. Aleksir stood little chance in a fight, but he was unmatched in a race. If he could just squeeze past, he'd be free. "Why? What did Unity do to you?" he asked, hoping to distract the man. But as if guessing Aleksir's thoughts, the man took a step to the left, neatly cutting off Aleksir's escape route.

"How old are you, kid? Are you even eighteen?" he asked.

"I'm nineteen."

"And what did Devikra promise you for your service? Wealth? Power? Whatever it was, it's not worth it."

"You don't know what you're talking about," Aleksir snapped. He didn't like this man, didn't like the feverish gleam in his eyes or the way he showed all his teeth when he smiled. He didn't like being cornered. "You don't know anything about her!"

"I know her better than anyone," the man said, calm in the face of Aleksir's anger. "We worked together for a *long* time, after all."

When the man stepped forward, into the moonlight, recognition hit Aleksir like a broken chair leg to the face. He knew where he'd seen this man before: on the Oracle of Damael's desk, in a grainy tintype of a smiling man with dark eyes.

"Not possible," Aleksir breathed, his heart thudding wildly in his chest.

The man tipped his head to one side, giving that too-wide smile again. It didn't reach his eyes, not like it did in the photograph. "I thought you'd already recognized me, given your little nickname — in Adondai, they called me cù-sìth. In Gallonten, the Hound."

"You're supposed to be dead."

The man—the Northern Wolf, the hero of a thousand stories and villain of one—laughed. "I might as well be."

It was Egil.

Egil had sought Aleksir out. *Egil* knew Aleksir's name. "I can't believe it," Aleksir said, hoping the wolf wouldn't notice the way his voice wobbled. But it was *Egil,* the star of the world's greatest stories. Egil, who was known for his wit, who even Devikra called perfect. Of course he noticed.

"Still afraid of me?" he asked. "You should be. I've gone mad, haven't you heard?"

"Are you kidding?" Aleksir asked, louder than he'd intended. Egil took a surprised step back. In his excitement, Aleksir didn't even notice. "You're my hero! As a kid, I *lived* off stories about you! I probably wouldn't even be alive if not for you! See, I thought that if Egil could get off the streets and do some good, I could too. I begged Devikra to take me in, just like she did with you, and look at me now."

"Running errands for the Oracle, speaking with a dead man in an alley? Quite the step up."

"Well—"

Before Aleksir could finish that thought, Egil shoved him into the alley wall. Aleksir squawked and nearly tripped over a pile of trash, but Egil held him upright. When he pressed a finger to his lips and pointed at the sky, Aleksir looked just in time to see a dragon fly low over the alley. It was probably blue, given its size, but the lantern strapped to its belly was blinding. While he blinked against it, Egil moved closer to avoid getting caught in the light. He even *smelled* powerful, like soft cologne and smoke. He was so *cool*.

"It's just a dragon," Aleksir whispered.

"A *police* dragon," Egil whispered back, watching the last of its spiked tail vanish from sight before releasing Aleksir and stepping away. "Unity can't know I'm here, and a secret meeting in a dark alley is cause for questions, don't you think?"

"Do they know you're alive?" Aleksir asked. The various accounts of Histrios differed, but they were unanimous on two points: in Histrios, Egil went mad, and in Histrios, Egil died. Aleksir had never believed any of it. "Can't you tell Unity Histrios was just a misunderstanding? Or I'm sure Devikra would do it for you, if you asked."

Egil's lip curled. "You can't pick and choose which stories are true, Mr. Bardon. If you believe the ones that call me a hero, why not the ones that call me a villain?"

And the Egil of Histrios truly was a villain—a monster, a madman who went on a murderous rampage and had to be put down like a rabid dog by his dearest friend. No matter how much this person in front of him hissed and spat, though, Aleksir couldn't believe he was that villain. He couldn't let himself.

"You're here, aren't you? Alive? Doesn't that mean the stories kind of *have* to be wrong?"

Egil's next words chilled Aleksir down to his bones. The hero's voice was deceptively soft, his words like poison. "Don't be naïve. When they said I slaughtered their families, do you really think they misunderstood? When Unity declared me an enemy of the state, was that another *misunderstanding?*" Egil clicked his tongue. "If it helps, you can tell yourself your hero really did die that night. It's close enough to the truth."

Aleksir stubbornly shook his head.

"Ask Devikra about it, then. She knows what happened."

"Come back to Damael with me and we can do it together."

Egil laughed. "No, I'm much happier *without* her in my life. I don't know what she told you about me, but we weren't nearly as efficient together as the stories suggest."

Aleksir thought of Devikra's photograph of the softly-smiling hero. It was proof that that version of Egil had existed, that he had once been what the stories said. That version might still exist, and Aleksir wouldn't let him go so easily. "Look me in the eyes and tell me you really did all those things they say you did. Until you do, I won't believe it."

Egil looked Aleksir in the eyes. "I did it. All of it," he said, but somehow, Aleksir still didn't believe it. "Now tell me what happened with Unity today."

"But—fine. I don't know the details. You scared off my Unity contact before I could talk to them. That's why I was at that restaurant. But from what I hear, the King of Alfheimr's gone missing."

Egil's eyes widened. It was the first time Aleksir had seen him not smiling, smirking, or sneering. "Amos? How?"

"If you believe the gossips, Orean took him, and they did it with magic," Aleksir said, wiggling his fingers on the word *magic*. It was meant to be a joke, but Egil didn't laugh. Magic was a thing of stories—but then, he supposed, so was Egil. "You...you don't really have magic, do you?"

"Mm, I can call down Atiuh's powers to smite annoying teenagers who ask too many questions. Do you want a demonstration?" Egil asked, his smirk back again.

Aleksir gritted his teeth and didn't respond. Egil was Egil, but he still didn't like that smirk.

"Of course I don't have magic," Egil said. "What else can you tell me?"

"The Prince and Princess Nochdvor visited the island to talk to the Magistrates. The princess left, but Leandros Nochdvor stuck around. Does he know you're alive? He's the one who supposedly killed you, isn't he? Are you going to go after him?"

"Don't say his name," Egil spat, his hands clenching at his sides. Maybe it was a trick of the light, but the shadows in the alley seemed to gather to him, hang off his shoulders like a cloak. "Don't speak of him."

"I won't, I'm sorry," Aleksir said, eyes wide. "I don't get it. Why are you here? Why do you even care about all this, if you're so different now? Are you going to help the king?"

"Amos Nochdvor has nothing to do with me," Egil said. "I already told you why I'm here: I'm here to see Unity fall."

"What does that even mean?"

Egil tipped his head back, and for a moment, his eyes appeared entirely black. His smile was a wicked, warped version of the one from Devikra's photograph, and Aleksir took a fumbling step back. For a moment, he let himself think: what if it *was* all true? But then Egil blinked, and his eyes were normal once more. It must've just been a trick of the light. "It means that Unity is a cancer, a blight on this world, and I intend to purge it," Egil said simply. "Even if that means tearing it apart myself, brick by brick. Even if it means destroying myself in the process. Either way, I'll be doing the world a favor."

"What? No, you're wrong!" Aleksir said. He was surprised at himself, at the way his conviction echoed through the alley. It gave Egil pause; he blinked at Aleksir, his stare hard but his eyes still normal. Human.

"What makes you so sure?" Egil asked.

"Devikra," Aleksir said. When Egil scoffed, Aleksir hurried to continue: "I'm not in Gallonten because of whatever's going on with Illyon. That was just a coincidence. I'm here because the Oracle had a vision and told me to warn anyone who'd listen."

Egil held up a hand. Around him, the shadows dispersed. "I don't want to hear it."

"Too bad!" Aleksir snapped. It stunned Egil into silence, his dark eyes wide again. "I listened to you go on about Unity, so you can listen to this! Devikra says big things are coming. Bad things. It didn't make sense before, but after today, I'm starting to get it: she saw Orean on fire."

Egil frowned, faltered. "Because of Unity?" he asked.

"You know it doesn't work like that," Aleksir said. "She can't see the why, just the what. But there's more. She saw explosions in Histrios, riots in the North. She even saw red dragons in Lyryma."

Egil blinked as if coming out of a daze. "Don't be ridiculous. The red dragons have been extinct for centuries," he said.

"The Oracle is never wrong! Weird things are happening in Calaidia, weirder than alfar kings disappearing into thin air, and I don't know what Unity did to you, but we're all about to have much bigger problems!"

"We," Egil said softly. "Don't include me in your *we*. It sounds to me like Devikra will have her hands full."

"And it sounds to me like if you don't help, you're going to make everything worse!" Aleksir snapped, making Egil flinch. He didn't know what possessed him to speak to Egil this way, but now that he'd started he couldn't stop. "I'm no politician, and I know Unity has its problems, but if you think destroying it won't hurt everyone, everywhere, then you really are mad. People depend on Unity, like it or not. They could depend on you again, if you got over yourself and let them. You know what? I *don't* think you're crazy. I think you're just selfish."

Egil stared at Aleksir. The silence stretched between them, and Aleksir worried he'd gone too far. But then Egil's shoulders dropped, and the last of his cold arrogance drained out of him. "What am I supposed to do with this?" he asked. "If you're so close with Devikra, you know nothing can be done. Her visions can't be changed. It's already too late for me, for Orean."

"It's never too late," Aleksir said. "Not to stop Devikra's visions, and not for you."

"I wish I had your faith, but I've been down that path before. There's no fighting what the Oracle has seen." He smiled again, and it raised the hair on the back of Aleksir's neck. "Orean is going to burn, so the least I can do is make sure Unity burns with it."

"Egil, please—"

Egil didn't wait to hear the rest, already turning to leave. "Find Leandros Nochdvor; tell him what Devikra saw. But please, if the name Egil ever meant anything to you, don't tell him you saw me. Don't tell him what I've become."

EGIL-I

A DEAD MAN sat on the roof of a crooked old building while two suns rose over the horizon. He paid no mind to the coming dawn, that gentle medley of gold and pink, and the only sign that he felt the morning chill was the rosy flush to his cheeks. All his focus was fixed on a point in the distance, where Unity's clock tower reached into the pale sky. If he could cut it down with glares alone, it would have crumbled into the ocean long ago

When the second hand struck the hour, bells rang out over the city, interrupting the night's quiet. The sound made Egil wince and press a hand to his beating heart, as if he was trying to keep it still in his chest. With a soft *hiss*, magic flared out from his core. He'd fought hard to keep it from Aleksir Bardon, but now that he was alone, magic billowed out from him like sickly green smog, obscuring him and his rooftop and making it so he could no longer see Unity Island.

Inside the cloud of smog, his eyes turned entirely black.

He'd had years—decades—to prepare for this moment, for seeing the island again. It hadn't been enough. He'd thought he was ready to face Unity, to face this vicious, bitter city again, but now all he wanted was to flee and to forget Unity, forget the Oracle, forget Amos Nochdvor. In his defense, he hadn't expected Leandros to be here, too. That complicated things.

But in all his time alone, in all his adventures and failures and losses, he'd learned one simple truth: Unity had to fall. He'd meant what he said; he'd be doing the world a favor. Making a better future for people better than himself, people like Aleksir and Leandros. Unity had to fall, and if not by his hand, then whose?

A tremor wracked Egil's body, but he forced a deep breath. *In* and *out*, then again. Slowly, the smog dispersed and his eyes returned to normal. The magic at his core dimmed. Hand still pressed to his heart, he took another breath and felt it begin to beat again. He laughed, alone on that rooftop. He laughed, and even he could hear the edge of madness cutting through it like a blade. Aleksir was wrong about him, about all of it.

The clock quieted after the sixth bell and Egil realized how long he'd been sitting here, watching the minutes pass as night pressed into morning. Below him, the city stirred. Ahead, a dragon swept low over the city, red sunslight warm on her white scales. Twisting between church spires and weaving between buildings, she eventually made her descent toward the strip of green park along the coast and disappeared between the trees there.

Egil did not look at the clock tower again. He would have his time. He would not run, he would stay and fight and do what he'd come to do. After all, Unity's destruction was the only thing that could bring him back to life. It would fall, as would anyone that got in his way.

CHAPTER EIGHT

DURING HIS FIRST MORNING IN GALLONTEN, Leandros was ambushed. It was the third time since he'd arrived in the city; the same thing had happened to him leaving the island the day before, then again when he'd tried to go out for dinner. Disappearing for sixty years and reappearing under the most dramatic circumstances possible apparently made one something of a celebrity, and every reporter within a hundred square miles was clamoring for a feature. While Leandros could handle reporters, he couldn't handle them knowing where he slept, and this morning's offender had lain in wait for him in his own hotel lobby. Leandros had taken one look at him, a plucky, precocious boy with brownish hair and bright eyes, and walked in the other direction.

"Wait!" the boy called. "You're Leandros Nochdvor, aren't you?"

At the name *Nochdvor*, many curious eyes turned their way. Leandros ducked his head and kept walking, but he didn't stop the boy from following him, either. "How did you find me?" he asked once the boy had caught up.

"I'm good at uncovering secrets," the boy said. Then, in a loud whisper, he added, "I have a message from the oracle."

Leandros stopped abruptly, making the boy almost trip over his feet trying to stop as well. "Devikra? I haven't heard from her since…" Since Histrios. Since his self-imposed isolation. He cleared his throat. "Walk with me. Tell me everything."

The Oracle of Damael was never wrong. It was the first thing Egil had told Leandros about her, something he'd repeated again and again through their acquaintance with her. Having a handful of her prophecies dumped in his lap now, when he was less equipped to handle them than he'd ever been, made Leandros' chest ache—but whether that gripping, squeezing sensation was fear or guilt, he couldn't say. What he could saw was that this was his fault. The world was changing because *he* couldn't save his uncle. Because he'd encouraged Amos to *invite her up*. If Amos died, if Orean burned, if everything else the oracle saw came true, it would be Leandros' fault.

Leandros wanted his uncle back, but he didn't want to see anyone harmed in the rescuing of him—except, perhaps, a single orinian with glowing magic and all-black eyes.

Adding insult to injury, Aleksir Bardon proved to be something worse than a reporter: he was an Egil fan. After heaping Leandros with enough dread to last even an alfar's long lifetime, the boy had proceeded to question him about his greatest failure over and over, as if he could uncover the truth of Histrios if he was just annoying enough. Leandros finally lost him at the bridge to Unity Island, and only then because he'd sicced Unity's guards on the boy like glorified bouncers.

Then came a press conference with the Magistrates, which sank his rapidly declining mood further. His role in the conference proved to be entirely ornamental, with the Magistrates spending the allotted minutes reassuring reporters with flowery words that held no substance. By the time they concluded, they'd managed not to reveal a single detail of their actual rescue plan. And by the time Leandros reached the site of his next meeting, a half-timbered house in a quiet Gallontean neighborhood, he was tired enough for another sixty years of seclusion.

After so long in Alfheimr, he'd forgotten how to meter his energy in lively places like Gallonten. With each conversation, he spent more of it, monitoring his tone, mirroring the way people spoke here, so far from home. He'd spent so much now that he was running a deficit.

"Are you lost?" a quiet voice asked when he lingered too long at the foot of the winding drive.

Standing in the street behind Leandros was a short woman with bright red hair. Her eyebrows twitched when she saw his face, but she quickly schooled her own again behind a cold smile. "Unless you're Prince Leandros Nochdvor," she continued, "In which case, you're exactly where you're meant to be."

When she spoke, Leandros glimpsed sharp canines. Between that, her hair, and the feather-like texture that webbed across her pale skin, she was clearly maranet, the longest-lived of the human peoples. Given the gray streaks around her temples and the faint lines around her eyes, she must have been at least Amos' age.

"You have the advantage of me. You know my name, but I don't know yours," Leandros said.

Her smile eased—Leandros still couldn't call it *friendly*, but it was at least polite. "Evelyne Corscia," she said with a bow, one leg forward in the formal Alfheimr style. Surprised at the courtesy, Leandros bowed back. When Evelyne straightened again, she added, "I'll be your Head of Security for the trip to Orean."

"Pleasure," Leandros said. She wore a sword at her back and a gun at her hip; excessive, in Gallonten. If you were going to carry a weapon, it was considered polite to choose one or the other. In that sense and in others, she fit her title. She was scarred and armed, but more than that, the apathy behind her deep-set eyes unsettled him. He had to ask: "Do you work for Unity?"

"Technically," she replied, then, "We should go in, my lord. Mr. Ochoa will wonder what's keeping us."

While she started up the drive, Leandros squinted against the sunslight that crested the rooftops. Their destination stood alone on a slope, flowers and tall grasses spreading from its foundation all the way to the property's borders. It was surprisingly lovely, in this cold city. Because he was eyeing the house, he noticed a dryad peek over the second-story balcony railing before Evelyne did. The man's mossy head of hair had blended so seamlessly in among the potted flowers he'd been tending that Leandros had missed him, until that moment. "Good morning, Evelyne!" he called down. "And you must be Prince Nochdvor! Come inside, let yourselves in. I'll be right down to meet you!"

Evelyne held the door for Leandros, who had no choice but to step inside first. He just had time to glance around the foyer before the dryad breezed down the stairwell, exclaiming, "Your Highness, it's such an honor! I hope you had no trouble finding the place. I asked for accommodations on the island, of course, but what with the press conference and the news about your uncle's kidnapping hitting the papers this morning, it's bound to be crawling with reporters. The Magistrates suggested we meet somewhere quieter. My name is Eresh Ochoa, by the by. I'll be your Unity Coordinator for the foreseeable future."

He barely paused to breathe, ending the speech by sticking his hand out for Leandros to shake. Leandros blinked at him, then down at his hand, and at the last moment, Eresh snatched it back. "Oh! You don't do handshakes in Alfheimr, right? Too intimate, I think one of your Representatives said. I'm terribly sorry if I caused offense."

"You didn't," Leandros assured him.

"That's a relief. I really am a fan of you—your work. I never thought I'd have a chance to meet you in person," Eresh said. He cleared his throat awkwardly. "Please, follow me."

Eresh led Leandros and Evelyne to a sitting room, though its south-facing windows made it more like a greenhouse. The room was hot and humid—perfect for the strange flowers and trailing vines that grew along the trellised walls. While Leandros took them all in, Eresh crossed to a table at the center of the room and started sorting through stacks of folders piled atop it. Instead of sofas, plush floor cushions circled the table.

Leandros nodded at the walls. "You have quite the collection."

Eresh straightened like a flower given water. "Kind of you to notice! I was born in Lyryma forest, though I left when I was still a young thing. Most of the specimen you see here are from around Home. They're difficult to maintain in this climate, but I can be quite stubborn about getting my way."

"No one who's known you even five minutes could doubt that, Eresh," Evelyne said.

"I'll choose to take that as a compliment, Evelyne," Eresh replied. The pair's informal use of given names didn't escape Leandros.

"Who will you get to watch them while we're gone?" Leandros asked, though honestly, he didn't hear much of the dryad's reply. He was too busy watching Evelyne pace the room out of the corner of his eye. Something about her set him on edge. It wasn't as bad a feeling as that orinian woman had given him, but he still wasn't comfortable turning his back on her.

And he would never doubt those instincts again.

"I have paperwork for you both," Eresh said. "The others might come to get theirs as well, but I don't expect they'll stay long. I mostly thought we three should talk."

When Eresh passed Leandros the thickest of the folders, Leandros immediately started paging through it. "What others?" he asked.

"Our other teammates, of course. Unity's already got half the team filled. Fast, aren't they?"

"Faster than I'd expected," Leandros admitted. The impression the Magistrates had given yesterday was an ambivalent one. If they were as disinclined to act with urgency as they'd pretended, why staff the team so quickly? If they really doubted Leandros and Rhea's story about the orinian woman, why take so much caution?

It bothered Leandros. This team had been *Unity's* idea. Rhea and Leandros had both offered other suggestions, but the Magistrates had *insisted* on this team, this plan. And when Leandros wrested control of it away from them, they had been furious.

There was something strange about this plan—some angle Leandros hadn't figured out yet. It seemed Unity had ulterior motives, after all.

Eresh waved down a maid passing by the doorway while Leandros claimed one of the cushions. He had to awkwardly fold his long legs around the table to fit. "Mary, if anyone comes to the door, will you show them in? These are comfortable, aren't they, Your Highness? I once had the privilege of being admitted to the Oracle of Damael's drawing room, and it was full of cushions just like these. I told myself I'd have nothing else, from then on."

Just like that, Leandros' mood soured again. "The oracle? An honor indeed," he said.

"Quite so," Eresh agreed, not noticing Leandros' flat tone. Behind him, Evelyne raised an eyebrow, and Leandros was grateful when Eresh continued: "I suppose we should get on to business. My job for the next few weeks, Your Highness, is to handle the menial tasks associated with travel so that *you* are free to focus on bringing your uncle home. Supplies, arrangements, logistics—leave them all to me. Inside your folder, you'll find Unity's code of conduct, safety protocols, budget projections, and information on our known teammates. We'll be a small team, with five diplomats—including you and I—and a five-person security team led by Ms. Corscia."

Leandros frowned at that, the expression stopping Eresh just as he drew in a breath to continue. "So many?" Leandros asked. "This is a diplomatic mission—investigative only. Fifty percent of the team being designated security seems excessive."

"You're a very important person, Prince Nochdvor," Eresh said. "Your safety on this mission is Unity's top priority."

Leandros snorted. Flattering, but he didn't believe it. The Magistrates hadn't even offered him a guard for his stay in Gallonten, and he'd seen the looks on their faces when they'd adjourned yesterday. They'd be just as happy if he was dead. Out of curiosity, he flipped to Evelyne's entry in the folder and found it practically empty. The next security member's entry was the same. It listed a name, an age, a brief rundown of skills, and that was all. Compared to the diplomats' entries, which were several pages long each, full of experience and references, the difference was telling. Keeping his expression neutral, he said, "Unity's top priority should be rescuing the missing king. Relative to that, I mean little, and I'm more than capable of fending for myself."

"We'll do more for you than protect you, my lord," Evelyne said. She had a soft way of speaking. It sent a shiver down Leandros' spine every time she opened her mouth.

Eresh shot Evelyne an uncertain look. "Yes, well," he said, "We'll also have the brother of a Unity Magistrate on the team, and the orinians who took your uncle *did* kill more than a dozen people. I assume Unity is being cautious for both your sakes, and I can assure you, Your Highness, that Evelyne and her team are the very best Unity has to offer."

"That, I don't doubt," Leandros said, eyeing the woman in question. She met his gaze evenly, almost in challenge. Two things were becoming clear to Leandros: that Unity had suggested this investigative mission for a reason, and that that reason involved

Evelyne Corscia. He asked, "How long have you been doing this sort of thing, Ms. Corscia?"

"Longer than you've been alive, my lord," Evelyne said. Even with Leandros' experience dealing with rigid, controlled alfar, he couldn't read her at all.

"Are swords your weapon of choice?" he asked.

"I suppose."

"Did you train formally? What was the school?"

"It closed over a century ago, I'm afraid."

Leandros smiled politely. "That doesn't mean I haven't heard of it. Come, what's the name?"

Eresh watched the exchange with wide eyes. When the maid suddenly returned, a nympherai woman following behind her, he let out a relieved sigh. "Ah!" he cried, cutting the tension. "Ms. Smith!"

While the maid excused herself, the nympherai joined the small group by the table. Compared to Evelyne, who felt to Leandros like the personification of nails on a chalkboard, Ms. Smith's presence was calm and assured. Though quite short, she stood with her shoulders squared and her hands clasped behind her back, elongating the lines of her well-tailored suit. Her short hair was slicked back and her skin was spotted with opalescent scales. She didn't bow or offer to shake hands, but she gave Leandros a curt nod. "Please, call me Trin."

"You've met Evelyne already, right? And this is Prince Leandros Nochdvor. Prince Nochdvor, this is Trinity Smith. She'll be our lead negotiator," Eresh explained. "She has decades of experience in the field and has handled dozens of hostage negotiations."

"Only petty kidnappings, though. This is your first time with something of this magnitude, isn't it, Trin?" Evelyne asked. Her gentle voice made the taunt even colder.

"How fortunate I am to have you on my tactical team again, Ms. Corscia," Trin said with an unshaken smile. "Of course I haven't negotiated anything of this magnitude. If kings were frequently disappearing, that would be more of a failing on yours and Unity's parts than mine, don't you think?"

Evelyne scowled in reply.

"So, you two know each other," Leandros said. He was beginning to worry he was the only stranger in a team of old acquaintances—it would hardly be the first time. "Do you work for Unity as well, Trin?"

"Only occasionally. It's nothing to your trade agreements with the frìth, Prince Nochdvor, but when two hikers went missing in Lyryma last year, Unity brought me in to negotiate with them. I had the privilege of working with Ms. Corscia and her team then. Though I hope you won't be so eager for blood this time, Evelyne."

"Blood?" Leandros asked, eyeing Evelyne. Unbidden, he remembered the oracle's warnings of Orean on fire.

"Only a figure of speech, my lord," Evelyne said smoothly.

The reassurance didn't settle the unease gathering in Leandros' chest. "Right. And what is a tactical team in this context, exactly?"

"A specialized unit trained in combat that's called in to handle high-risk, high-stakes situations. Evelyne's team may step in if negotiations with your uncle's kidnappers fail and we need another way to extract him," Trin explained. "Hopefully, that won't be necessary. Hostile tactics are always a last resort, even if some on Evelyne's team may disagree."

They weren't only for security, then. Was it really for Leandros that Unity was sending them along? Was it really for his uncle?

"I'm not the one getting ahead of myself," Evelyne pointed out. "We don't even know who the kidnappers *are*, or if they have demands to negotiate. It's been four days with no ransom, and when it comes to information, all we have are two flawed accounts from the sole survivors. We need to launch an investigation in Illyon before we can even make contact with Orean."

It was only thanks to a lifetime of training that Leandros didn't flinch at the word *flawed*. How much of his and Rhea's testimony had Unity told her? All of it? "Flawed?" Trin asked. "Flawed how?"

Leandros made note of the question, and of Eresh's curious look. Evelyne had been told more than the others, that much was clear.

"Ask him," Evelyne said, jutting her thumb at Leandros.

"I know it may be difficult to recount, Prince Nochdvor, but if you could," Trin prompted.

"I don't mind," Leandros said. He'd expected this, had prepared a version of the story more plausible than the truth. Not a lie, but an obfuscation. He needed respect from this team, and he wouldn't get it if they all thought he'd gone mad. "We were assembled at Hampstead Hall when an orinian woman broke in and caused some sort of explosion. In the chaos, she escaped with my uncle."

"How did she cause the explosion? How did one woman carry off a grown alfar? And how did she make it back out of the estate without being seen?" Evelyne asked. The Magistrates had told her everything.

Leandros bit back his irritation, but it came out on a sigh. "I'm only telling you what I saw. Truth told, I was preoccupied with keeping myself and my cousin alive. If that makes my story flawed, then I supposed it's flawed."

The noise Evelyne made in response was doubtful at best.

"I understand. Were you and your uncle close?" Trin asked. While her tone was kinder than Evelyne's, it was analytic, not sympathetic. Leandros realized that to her—to all of them—he was worse than a stranger: he was a liability, a mystery to unravel and an obstruction in their way. It was understandable. What did they know about him? That he'd negotiated some trade agreements once, decades before most of them were even born? That he had killed the world's most famous hero? That he'd been in hiding ever since? Why should they recognize him as a leader simply because he'd talked the Magistrates into calling him one?

They knew each other, even if they disagreed on some things. They didn't know Leandros.

"As close as Alfheimr royalty can get," he answered.

"You can trust me, Prince Nochdvor," Trin said, and the condescension in it was a twist of the knife. "I'm here for you—we all are. What can you tell me about Amos that might affect how we approach Orean? Do you think he would try to escape? Is he the type to try to reason with his kidnapper?"

"Yes to the latter, no to the former. He'd know people were coming to help and wouldn't make things more difficult for them."

"Does he have a temper?"

"No." Unlike Leandros. "He's the most patient man I know."

Some of his feelings on the matter must have made it into his voice because Trin asked, "And do *you*, Prince Nochdvor?"

"Only when I feel I'm being talked down to."

Trin laughed. "My apologies, Captain. I almost forgot who I was speaking to," she said, and Leandros could make out something like respect in her voice—not quite there yet, but it could be. She addressed the gathered group: "We'll need to be patient on this mission, build trust and rapport with the hostage taker—once we identify them, as Ms. Corscia helpfully pointed out. We'll need to trust each other, too. *All* of us. Captain, if you remember anything else about that day, please tell us."

"I will," Leandros promised.

Voices drifted down the foyer, then, shortly followed by two new teammates. A tall man with the pointed ears of an alfar was the first to enter, even ahead of the maid. He threw his arm around Trin's shoulder and said, "Well, if it isn't Trin! It's been too long." Despite his ears, he spoke with a flat Gallontean accent. A patch covered one of his eyes, and the other was sleepy and half-lidded to match his lazy smile. A stern man entered behind him, though he lingered in the doorway with his arms crossed. Just from the cold detachment behind their eyes, Leandros knew which part of the team they belonged to even before Evelyne said it.

"Ivor Linde and Aaror Thomason, both my men," she supplied while Trin shrugged off Ivor's arm.

"Ah, yes! I have paperwork for you both," Eresh said, digging through his stack. "You too, Trin."

"Great," Ivor said with an eye roll. Still, he took the folders when Eresh offered them. "We can't stay; we only came for these."

"Take Will and Chia's, too," Evelyne said. At Eresh's questioning look, she explained, "Will can't make it today and Chia's out of town, but she's expected back on Thursday; we can leave for Orean then."

"That's four days from now," Leandros pointed out. "In hostage situations, delays like those can prove fatal."

"It's not ideal," Trin agreed. "Is she really needed, Ms. Corscia?"

"You know she is," Evelyne said. "Besides, Eresh still needs to finalize logistics. That will take several days on its own."

Trin sighed and gave Leandros a shrug. "If Amos is still alive at this point, statistically, the hostage takers will keep him alive longer — as long as needed for their demands to be heard."

"Then I'll defer to your expertise on the matter," Leandros said, but the words tasted bitter. He felt like a school boy again, stuck in a group project with peers who liked each other better than they liked him. He shouldn't care, but he shifted uneasily on Eresh's overpriced floor cushion. "If you don't mind, I'm going to step out for some air. It's a bit warm in here, compared to what I'm used to."

As he stood, his bruises and cuts from his jump out Hampstead Hall's window twinged—he had to fight not to wince. While no one stopped him, he felt curious eyes on his back all the way to the door, which meant he couldn't let himself limp, either.

He needed fresh air and a moment of privacy, so instead of going out the front door, he turned up the stairs, remembering Eresh's balcony. As he climbed, he told himself it was the humidity in the house, not his teammates, that made it so hard to breathe.

The cool summer air out on the balcony helped, but not enough. He paced up and down it a few times, but when it did nothing for his thundering heart, he sat cross-legged right on the balcony floor and closed his eyes, focused on his breathing. Ever since Histrios, he'd been having occasional fits like this. It would pass; he just needed to breathe.

Not for the first time since this all began, he wondered what he'd gotten himself into. He wondered what he'd gotten *Orean* into. The unknowns were adding up, and the phrase *eager for blood* had stuck in Leandros' mind from the moment Trin uttered it. He should be grateful Evelyne and her unsettling tactical team were on his side. He should be grateful they wanted to help his uncle. But he wasn't, and he still couldn't shake the suspicion that they didn't.

Paired with Devikra's visions of riots and cities on fire, Leandros began to dread this mission.

Suddenly, his sharp ears picked up the sound of the front door opening below him. "Oh. He's not out here," said a quiet voice. Evelyne.

"With any luck, he ran home to Alfheimr," came a second — Ivor. There was a soft *thump*, then, "Ow! It was a joke, Ev. What's with you? He's just a spoiled little princeling."

"Quiet," Evelyne snapped. "Do not underestimate him. He knows more than you think."

There was a heavy pause, and then Ivor asked, "About us?"

"Just keep your head down and do your job," Evelyne warned.

Leandros missed Ivor's reply under the crunch of three sets of boots passing onto gravel. Not wanting to be seen, he eased onto his back so he'd be hidden behind Eresh's numerous flowerpots. Tucking his hands behind his head, he smiled bitterly up at the passing clouds until the crunching of boots faded. Only when he was satisfied they were gone did Leandros sit up and peer over the railing, but he was surprised to find yet another person making their way *up* the drive. Yet another stranger.

On closer examination, though, Leandros realized this stranger was more familiar than the others. He pushed himself to his feet and called down, "Mr. Ranulf!"

Gareth Ranulf jumped, looking around before looking up, a sheepish grin spreading across his face when he spotted Leandros. It was, to Leandros' surprise, a face covered in bruises. "Prince Nochdvor! Yes, I'm surprised you remembered!"

Leandros leaned over the railing, resting his elbows on the painted wood. "After only a day? And after your kind gift, how could I forget? Thank you again for that; it helped me take my mind off things, if only for a little while. Don't tell me you'll be joining us in Illyon?"

"I will, in fact."

"Hold on," Leandros said, pushing away from the railing. "Let me join you downstairs."

When Gareth held a hand out to Leandros, Leandros shook it happily. "Pleasure to meet you again, sir," Gareth said. Up close, his bruises looked even worse. Curiosity gnawed at Leandros, but he held his since—he had no right to ask, and anyway, he doubted Gareth wanted to talk about it.

"Likewise. Though I must admit I'm surprised to see you here."

"Surprised my sister would put me in this position, you mean," Gareth guessed. "I'm sure I could have refused, but…ah. Well, never mind."

"Tell me," Leandros said. "If you have reservations, Mr. Ranulf, I'd like to hear them."

Gareth eyed Leandros like he didn't quite believe him, but he obliged: "I was determined to refuse Moira, but last night, I ran into three orinians who are staying at my hotel. They're young, Prince Nochdvor, and so happy. It made me worry for their sakes. I'd like to make sure Orean's treated fairly in all this." At Leandros' thoughtful silence, he hurried to add, "That's not to say that you won't, but after what you've been through, I'm sure you have some complicated feelings about the matter. I don't, so if I can help provide clarity, I'd like to."

Leandros thought again of Orean on fire. Complicated was certainly a word for Leandros' feelings. "I appreciate your honesty."

Like a peace offering, Gareth withdrew his cigarette case and held it out to Leandros. "Cigarette?"

"Please," Leandros said. He didn't make a habit of smoking, but at this point, he'd try anything to steady his nerves. He leaned in while Gareth lit the cigarette for him, then took a long drag before saying, "To tell you the truth, I'm grateful. I get tangled in my emotions easily; I'd appreciate having someone to keep me in check."

"You can count on me, Your Highness."

"And may I offer some advice?"

Gareth blinked. "Why yes, of course."

"Know that I say this out of an abundance of caution. You should warn your neighbors about what's coming. What happened to my uncle—I believe it was the work of a single individual, but Unity may not see it the same way. I don't want any innocents getting caught up in this business."

"They're just tourists. Unity wouldn't do anything to them, would they?"

"Unity is known for upholding order, not showing mercy," Leandros said. At Gareth's blank look, he explained, "If they view Orean as the enemy, then anyone *from Orean* will become the enemy.

Your neighbors could be here for any number of reasons. Maybe they're spies, maybe they're assassins. Maybe they're in league with the kidnappers."

"They most certainly are not!"

"The truth isn't the point. Do you think Unity cares about the truth? If the police, whose salaries Unity pays, care? All they need is a plausible lie, and they'll spin it." Leandros shook his head. "It's our responsibility to cut the thread before it causes harm. Have your orinians take the train to Adriad. News is always slow to reach there—if they leave today, they might beat it. Then they can catch a ride on to Orean."

"Yes, of course. I'll warn them as soon as I get home. Thank you, Prince Nochdvor. If you're right, you may have saved their lives."

Leandros shrugged, biting back the guilt that rose on his tongue like bile. It was the least he could do when he was the one leading Unity to their home, when he was the one seeking retribution and the return of his uncle at any cost. He had good intentions, *peaceful* intentions, but what use were those in matters like these? What did his intentions matter when Unity held all of the power?

Changing the subject, he asked, "Did you pass a maranet woman on your way up?"

"Ms. Corscia, right?" Gareth asked. Leandros' heart sank, but then Gareth continued: "I assumed she was part of our team, so I stopped and introduced myself."

"You weren't already acquainted?" Leandros asked, relaxing again. "I'm relieved. The rest of them seem to know each other. If I may, what was your impression or her?"

"Hm," Gareth said, a heavy sound. His sister voiced her disapproval in the same way—it must have been a family trait.

"What is it?" Leandros asked.

"We didn't speak long, but there's something off about her, don't you think? About all of them. My father had a similar air about him."

"And what sort of man was your father?"

Gareth stomped out his cigarette and didn't look at Leandros. "A cruel one."

It was no comfort to hear, even if it echoed Leandros' own impressions. He wanted to say more, to voice his theories about their tactical team, but Gareth was still the son of a Magistrate, the *brother* of a Magistrate. Leandros couldn't trust him.

From the moment he'd made his risky move with the Magistrates, asking to lead the team, he'd known he would be alone in this. Still, knowledge didn't ease loneliness.

Instead of voicing anything, he simply said, "We should get inside. Mr. Ochoa has paperwork for you."

CHAPTER NINE

BEING AN ORINIAN IN UNITY'S CAPITAL CITY was a singular experience. While Maebhe gawped at the sights and the sounds, the locals were always gawping *back*. When she caught them staring, they cleared their throats, smiled, and pointedly asked if she spoke Ellesian or if she needed directions anywhere. It was annoying, but until today, it had been harmless. Between yesterday and this morning, though, it was like the whole city had changed.

It wasn't just the man that had spat at Maebhe's feet as she left the hotel, or the pair of Gallontean police officers that followed her from place to place and thought they were being subtle. Everyone gave her a wider berth, colder stares. She hoped she was just being paranoid. This cold city made her over-analyze and overthink, again and again in a constant loop. Having her companions close helped, but because she was a good sister—the *best*, really—she'd cleared out of the hotel to give her brother and his fiancée time to themselves. That meant keeping herself entertained, alone, at the café next door. It had salty pastries and weak coffee, weaker than anything you'd find in Orean, but it also had a private patio that kept strangers' eyes off her tail and ears and birthmarks.

She ripped her pastry in half and pretended to contemplate the flaky crust, but out of the corner of her eye, she watched the two police officers lounge against the counter and whisper to the barista. Surely, though, she was just being paranoid. Surely, they'd just wanted coffee. She was trying to read the barista's lips with little luck when suddenly a man blocked them from view. Ears flattening to her head in annoyance, Maebhe looked up, ready to tell him off.

"Oh," she said instead. "It's you again."

The man fidgeted with his bowler hat. He was less bloodied than he'd been when Maebhe saw him last night, but the bruises left behind weren't pretty. Beneath them, he had a kind face—middle aged, with a full salt-and-pepper mustache. "Pardon the interruption," he said awkwardly.

"It's fine. Is your face okay? What happened?" Maebhe asked.

The man touched the bruise under his eye. "It's kind of you to ask. I ran into some trouble last night, but fortunately, a kind soul stepped in to help."

"Well, shit. I'm glad for that," Maebhe said. "Sorry I didn't say anything last night, but you looked kind of scary with all that blood and I was very drunk," Maebhe said. As soon as the words left her mouth, she regretted them. This man was religious, wasn't he? That's what the obelisk on his watch chain meant? She should probably keep her pastimes to herself.

The man was too polite to comment on it, instead fidgeting with his hat again. "I understand. Is this seat taken?" he asked.

Maebhe gestured for him to sit. "Not at all. I'm Maebhe, by the way. Please no 'Ms. Cairn' or anything like that. I can't abide it."

"Maebhe, then," the man said, sitting. "Informality for informality, I'm Gareth. I rent the rooms across from yours."

"I remember. You've got the cute kid."

"My daughter Ofelia," Gareth said with a smile that fell away quickly. "Maebhe...I'm sorry for bothering you if you're already aware of the issue, and I do realize it's none of my business, but have you heard about Illyon?"

Maebhe tilted her head to one side. "Illyon? No, what did they do?"

"I was afraid you might say that," Gareth sighed. He pulled a rolled-up newspaper out of his coat pocket and passed it to Maebhe. "You had better see this."

Maebhe read the big, blocky headline before she'd even fully unrolled the paper. "What," she said, voice falling flat. She looked up at Gareth, who only nodded at the paper for her to continue. In all caps, the headline read: AN ACT OF WAR? WHAT OREAN'S ATTACK ON ILLYON MEANS FOR THE TWO CITIES.

Aloud, Maebhe read: "Long-standing rivalries between Illyon and Orean came to a head earlier this week when King Nochdvor of Alfheimr was abducted from Illyon by orinian soldiers. Eleven Illyon officials died in the altercation and parts of the city's famous Hampstead Hall were destroyed.' Oh, gods." Maebhe glanced up at Gareth in horror before continuing. "It's unclear how Alfheimr will respond to the attack, but the king's nephew Leandros Nochdvor reported the event to Unity and remains in the city for reasons yet unknown. You may remember Prince Nochdvor from his father's scandal, blah, blah...." She skimmed the rest. "Many believe the kidnapping was an act of defiance against Unity — oh, please! As if we'd be so stupid!"

Her yelling drew the attention of nearby patrons, as well as of the barista and the police officers. She lowered her voice again before asking, "Do people actually believe this?"

Gareth hemmed, then hawed, then eventually said, "Everyone knows how the papers like to sensationalize, but I'm afraid this *is* rooted in some fact. I've spoken to Prince Nochdvor myself on the matter."

Maebhe sat back in her chair, staring at her shredded pastry without really seeing it. "Fuck," she said.

Gareth covered Maebhe's hand on the table and gave it a comforting pat. Maebhe resisted the urge to pull away. "I suspect there's some misunderstanding, but until it's sorted, it might be dangerous for you to remain in the city," he said.

"What do you mean, dangerous? We didn't do anything! It says this happened this week, right? Íde, Kieran, and I have been here for *over* a week, so we couldn't have had anything to do with it!"

"I believe you, I really do," Gareth said, "But the unfortunate truth is that people aren't always reasonable or understanding, especially when they're afraid."

Maebhe massaged her temples and said again, "Fuck. I have to tell Kieran and Íde. We'll need to pack, and...and buy new train tickets, I guess. Is it even safe for us to go back to Orean? Is Orean safe?"

"I have full faith this will be resolved peacefully," Gareth said, but his smile was troubled. "You should be safe to return home. Please, allow me to help you with the tickets. You'll have your hands full with packing, and it's the least I can do."

Maebhe stopped massaging, instead watching Gareth through narrowed eyes. "You're being so kind. Why?"

"I'm only alive now because someone took the time to show *me* kindness," he said, his hand twitching on the table as if to touch his eye again. He followed Maebhe's gaze to the police officers at the counter. "Would you like an escort back to the hotel?"

Maebhe nodded and clutched the damning newspaper to her chest, her ears pressed flat to her head. Following Gareth out, she tied her jacket around her waist to hide her tail and hoped she only imagined the way the officers pushed off from the counter as she walked past, as if to follow. With Gareth at her side, they didn't bother her, at least, and the pair made it all the way to the hotel elevator without trouble.

"Here we are," Gareth said a minute later, when the elevator dinged and they'd stepped out onto their shared floor. "I'll have the concierge leave the tickets at the front desk for you. Safe journeys, if we don't speak again, but if there's anything else I can do for you, I'm just across the hall."

"Thank you, truly," Maebhe said, shaking his hand. She waited for him to leave, then threw the door to her rooms open hard enough that it struck the wall with a *bang*. She was halfway through the entrance when she remembered why she'd left in the first place and flung her arm over her eyes, calling, "Are you decent? Can I come in?"

Maebhe heard a soft huff of laughter and the distinct sound of a page turning. "Knocking works just as well, you know," her brother called back. Not quite trusting that, Maebhe felt along the wall with her eyes still covered until she reached the point where the hall opened up into the sitting room. There, cautiously, she lowered her arm and found Kieran at the table, his feet up and his fiancée nowhere in sight.

"Where's Íde? She wouldn't like you sitting like that," Maebhe said.

"Napping," Kieran replied, not looking up from his book.

Maebhe shoved Kieran's boots off the tabletop, making him lurch forward to catch his balance. At that, he finally looked at her, his ear giving an annoyed flick. "Maebhe, *what*?"

"Read this, then come and find me," she said, throwing the newspaper at his face. Without waiting for an answer, she pushed through the living room, past the hotel's tacky velvet furniture and striped wallpaper, and didn't stop until she'd reached the balcony off the dining room. There, she stepped back into the seaside air, her arms hugged close to her body and Gallonten sprawling below her. It struck her again how alien the buildings were, how tall and new and strange. From here, she could see over them to the gray outline of Unity Island. Its silhouette reached like a gnarly, clawed hand into the sky, the clock tower a finger pointing toward the heavens.

She'd known she hated this place from the moment she laid eyes on that island. They'd toured it, their first day here, and it had convinced Maebhe that orinians and Unity just didn't mix. Every orinian grew up hearing that; every orinian knew how Unity felt about them. It was a grudge that dated all the way back to the Great War: when Runderath the Mighty slayed Tellaos and the goddess Ellaes created Unity, Orean had refused to join. Centuries had passed, but like a spurned lover, Unity had never forgiven them. It had been risky to come here on holiday, and now they were paying the price.

A few minutes later, Maebhe heard the door open behind her. "The hotel probably won't give us a refund," she said without looking.

Kieran stepped out to join her. He looked paler than he had, the thick brown birthmarks that swirled across his face bringing his pallor into sharper contrast. Anyone with orinian blood had the marks. According to old superstitions, an orinian's birthmarks reflected their soul. Maebhe had always thought that was horseshit, but that hadn't stopped her from wondering what hers and her brother's said about them—they bore identical marks, after all, reversed like a mirror image. Kieran's swept down the left half of his face, like fractal scars left by a lightning strike, and Maebhe's swept down the right.

Many things about Maebhe and Kieran were identical, unsurprising for a pair of identical twins. They shared the same wavy blond hair, the same ochre skin beneath brown birthmarks, the same wiry frames and round, gray eyes. The only difference was that Maebhe was sharper around the face, Kieran softer.

"Alfheimr wants to go to war and that's all you have to say?" Kieran asked.

Maebhe frowned at the silhouette of the clock tower, wrinkling her nose when she felt the sting of oncoming tears. She blinked them back. "Selfish, isn't it?"

Beside her, Kieran sighed. "My first thought wasn't any better. I keep wishing we'd gotten to see more of the city. So if you're selfish, I guess I am, too."

"I think we're allowed to be selfish, under the circumstances," Maebhe said. She turned to her twin and punched his arm. "But this *is* all your fault, you know."

"Ow! What? How?"

"You were the one who insisted on Gallonten, and now we're caught up in this mess!"

"Sorry, I'll make sure no one's planning any royal kidnappings before I suggest future vacation spots," Kieran said dryly.

"Or just let *me* pick. *I* wanted to go to the coast!"

"Well, then, maybe this is your fault for losing the coin flip!"

"If you want to go there, then it's Íde's fault for suggesting the coin flip in the first place."

"Fine. Truce. This is all Íde's fault."

"I'm telling her you said that."

Kieran opened his mouth and closed it, doing an excellent impression of an angry fish. "Then I'm telling her you're the one who spilled her expensive face cream!"

"She said I could try it!" Maebhe hissed, glancing nervously at the door as if Íde might be there, listening. "Does she know about all of this yet?"

Kieran nodded. "I woke her before coming out here. She's already packing."

"Almost finished, actually," Íde said from the doorway, appearing as if summoned. Though her hair was pulled up into its usual bun, long strands hung loose. She'd clearly risen from her nap in a hurry. Íde's birthmarks were thinner, lighter than Maebhe and Kieran's, barely visible against the planes of her face. From a distance, the silver patterns looked more like old scars than anything else. "We're lucky you checked the paper, Maebhe."

"I didn't, actually," Maebhe said. "The man across the hall warned me. He's getting us train tickets, too."

Kieran made a face. "The Unity fellow?"

"Is he?" Maebhe asked.

"He works for them, I think, but I'm not sure in what capacity." Kieran thought for a moment longer, then shrugged. "Should we thank him? Maybe get him a card?"

"Since we know his address, that sounds like something that can wait until we're home," Íde said, using the same patient-but-pointed voice that she used on her students. "Kieran, can I get your help inside? I can't get your suitcase off the shelf."

"Yes, of course," Kieran said. He ruffled Maebhe's hair as he passed. "Join us inside whenever you're ready, Mae."

Within an hour, the trio had crammed themselves and their things into the hotel's small elevator and were on their way out of the hotel. While stuffing her suitcase, Maebhe had cycled through emotions, finally settling on relief—relief to be going, relief that they'd soon leave Gallonten behind. Íde and Kieran had only grown more restless, though. Beside Maebhe, Íde's tail whipped anxiously back and forth, hitting Maebhe's leg in the cramped space.

"Everything will be all right, won't it?" Íde finally asked.

Kieran and Maebhe shared a look over her head. In unison, they said, "Probably."

"It drives me crazy when you two do that," Íde grumbled. "Even your *tones* matched."

"Gareth said it's probably a misunderstanding," Maebhe assured her.

"I hope so."

When the elevator lurched to a stop, Maebhe opened the cage door for her companions and followed them out, but as she did, the loose wheel on her old hand-me-down suitcase got stuck in the gap between the elevator and the floor. When it wouldn't tug free on its own, she crouched to inspect the issue. Behind her, Kieran tapped his foot impatiently.

"Maebhe," he sighed.

"Don't rush me! If I don't fix this thing now, it'll fall off halfway down the street," she said, now attempting to tighten the wheel's loose screws with the pads of her fingers. Kieran and Íde gave up, went on to front desk without her, and Maebhe switched to using her fingernail, her long hair falling into her face.

Suddenly, a sharp whistle blew, making Maebhe jump.

She'd forgotten about the officers from the café, but when she looked up, she found herself in a room full of them. Nearly a dozen clustered around the front desk—around *Kieran and Íde*, Maebhe realized with horror. Kieran met Maebhe's gaze while they secured handcuffs around his wrists. "Run, Maebhe!" he yelled.

Because she'd hung back, only one of the officers had noticed her. When he made a grab for her, Maebhe acted without thinking: she punched him in the face, feeling his nose *crack* beneath her hand. While he reeled back, she lunged for the elevator, abandoning both her suitcase and her jacket. Abandoning her brother. She slammed the cage door shut, and as the elevator lurched into motion, heading up and up, she watched a swarm of officers converge on the doors.

"Oh, gods," she gasped as the elevator climbed. The space felt even smaller than before, the walls pressing in on her while she took heaving breaths. She stumbled into the narrow hall when the elevator stopped, but she knew she was walking into a dead end. Where could she go? Back to her hotel room? And then what? The front desk would have a key, and she'd be caught within minutes.

Well, there was *one* other option. She banged on the door to Gareth's rooms, banged and banged until it finally swung open.

Before Gareth could say a word, Maebhe ducked under his arm and into the entranceway, shutting the door firmly behind them both and bolting it.

"Ms. Maebhe, what—?"

"The police," Maebhe panted, knowing how she must look, wild and panicked. "They arrested Kieran and Íde. We were trying to check out and they—they—we didn't even do anything! We were trying to leave!"

Gareth's eyes widened to match her own. "There must be some mistake. I'm sure we can reason with the officers and explain the situation."

Maebhe laughed. It sounded manic even to her own ears. "Are you joking? Gallonten's police aren't known for being reasonable, especially to outsiders. And Unity hates us. This is probably just what they wanted! Oh, gods."

"I don't know about all that," Gareth said, "But I can go and talk to them. I have some small pull here in Gallonten; they might listen to me."

"Please do," Maebhe said. "I don't know what I'd do without them."

"We'll figure this out, Ms. Maebhe. Try to make yourself comfortable while I'm gone. You're safe here. If you go ask the maid, she'll make you tea to steady your nerves."

"Tea," Maebhe said flatly. "Okay."

"I'll be back in no time," Gareth promised. After he left, Maebhe listened at the door and heard voices on the distant landing, then the sound of boots heading down stairs. They weren't coming closer, at least, so she allowed herself a deep breath and a look around. She was in a short reception hall, almost identical to the one in her suite, but reversed. Her gaze fell on a manila folder sitting on the table—it was addressed to a Mr. Gareth Ranulf and marked with Unity's seal.

Ranulf. Maebhe knew the name. One of the Magistrates was a Ranulf, wasn't he? "Gods help me," Maebhe murmured, running her finger over the golden seal.

Gareth did more than just work for Unity. He *was* Unity. One of the damned Magistrates, no less. It explained how he knew so much, how he'd "spoken to Prince Nochdvor" about the kidnapping. Had his timely warning even been a warning, or had he known that giving Maebhe the newspaper would flush them out of their rooms? Had he even bought them train tickets, or was that just a lie to make sure they didn't find their own way out of town?

Maebhe couldn't stay here.

She hurried through the suite, following a familiar path to the balcony, though she had to hide briefly to avoid the Ranulfs' maid. Once the way was clear, she eased the balcony door shut behind her, then crept to the balcony's edge to see the street below. Several police carriages blocked the building's front entrance, and there, in the middle of the mess, were Kieran and Íde. Two officers led them to the carriages while Gareth trailed behind them. He'd committed to the charade—from Maebhe's viewpoint, he made a good show of arguing with the officer.

Kieran happened to glance up as he was guided into the backseat of a carriage and Maebhe waved, watching her brother's eyes widen in surprise. "I'll save you," she mouthed desperately, but then Kieran was out of sight, Íde being guided in right behind him. Maebhe had no idea if he'd understood her, if he'd even seen.

Either way, it wouldn't change her mission.

She kicked off her shoes and clambered onto the balcony rail, wrapping her tail around it for extra balance. Then, slowly, she sank into a crouch. She couldn't think about the street behind her, about how badly it would hurt to fall. Instead, she tensed, reinforced her balance by wiggling like a cat about to pounce, then jumped to the narrow awning above the balcony door. Her body hit it with a loud *clang* and, on the street below, things went quiet. Before anyone could notice her half-hanging, legs dangling, she hauled herself up onto the awning and out of sight from the street.

Even if they did see her, even if they made it up to Gareth's suite before she was gone, she doubted they'd follow. She doubted they *could*. Unless they had a dragon with them, they couldn't keep up—no Gallonteans could climb, run, or jump like an orinian. While orinians were technically human, they had adaptations Unity humans didn't, leftover from a time when the only escape from the large predators that roamed their valley was up into the trees and into the mountains. They had extra muscles in their legs to make jumping easier, extra joints in their feet to make climbing faster. And Maebhe, who spent all her time hunting, climbing, and exploring, scrambled up the hotel's trellised wall and reached the roof in a heartbeat. There, she peered back over the edge just in time to see the final carriage door shut, Gareth now standing alone in the street.

The reality of the situation slammed into her. Vividly, she imagined falling from this height, hitting the ground and breaking bones. That was how this realization felt—the knowledge that everything had changed, nothing would ever be the same again. She covered her mouth to keep in a sob while below, carriages wheeled away one by one. She didn't want to move. She wanted to lay down and cry. If she lost sight of those carriages now, though, it was over. So Maebhe launched herself after them. She followed from the rooftops, always keeping her eyes on Kieran's carriage as she leaped from building to building. Once or twice, she nearly slipped on dewy tiles, collecting scrapes and bruises as she ran. Eventually, a monstrosity of a building blocked her path, so she cast her eyes around for the nearest fire escape. Scrambling down it, she continued her pursuit, pushing past strangers and jumping clear over a stroller.

After turning another corner, she skidded to a sudden stop, finally realizing where this road led. She watched, helplessly, as the carriage carrying Kieran and Íde crossed the bridge to Unity Island and the enemy city loomed all around her.

Chapter Ten

Roman Hallisey needed to stop caring so much. He'd wasted most of his morning worrying over his new acquaintance, which was absurd. The brother of a Unity Magistrate, who had everything he wanted and could easily get anything else, needed neither Roman's pity nor his concern. But sympathy was rarely rational, and Roman's thoughts kept drifting Gareth's way despite his best efforts.

Did he regret saving the man? No. Was he happy about doing something good for Unity? Absolutely not. Now that he knew Gareth's surname, would he save Gareth again, if given the chance? Roman shifted uncomfortably at the thought, at the inevitable answer: of course he would. Even after all Unity had done to him, after all the ways it had harmed him, he still would.

He jumped when a pair of fingers snapped in front of his face.

"Oy! Are you listening to me?"

Roman sat back. The fingers belonged to Cahrn, a large man with a dark beard and the leader of the theatrical troupe Roman had been traveling with. The man bothered Roman, but he was at least fun to bother *back*, a fact Roman took frequent advantage of.

A cloud of gloom followed Cahrn through his life, only ever

dispersing when the man stepped onto the stage. Roman could never forget his rendition of Burgess in *Only for the Roses*, a notoriously saccharine role in a notoriously tender tragedy. The Act III soliloquy, with all the raw vulnerability Cahrn had poured into it, had Roman bawling in the back row like a child. Hiding his irritation now, he smiled, batted his eyelashes, and said, "Sorry, Cahrn. I was distracted by how *dashing* you look in that costume."

Cahrn scowled and crossed his arms, though he dropped them again when the troupe's costumer, who was re-pinning his cloak hem, *tsked* disapprovingly. "This concerns your girl, so don't start with me," Cahrn said. "I passed her on my way here. She's practicing again."

"Is that a problem?" Roman asked.

"Of course it's a problem. The show is *tonight*. If she keeps pushing herself this late, she'll only tire out. Get it?"

"Yeah, I get it," Roman said, rolling his eyes. "If you need target practice the day of a battle, it's already too late for you. I don't have to be an actor to understand that much."

"Been in many battles, then?"

Roman snorted. The Webhon Players had all placed bets on what he'd been doing before he started traveling with them, he knew. While *highwayman* and *alchemist* were his favorite guesses, Cahrn's money was on soldier—and quite a lot of money it was, too. Roman had been toying with Cahrn for weeks, referencing imaginary battles and casually dropping army parlance, then walking it back if Cahrn commented on it. Somehow, the man still hadn't realized Roman was only teasing him. "It's just a metaphor, Cahrn."

Cahrn let out a breath through his nose. "Go make Dinara rest."

"I'll do my best, but you know how hard she is to reason with when she's set on something."

"Then distract her. You're better at improvisation than half my trained actors; I'm sure you can manage. It's only for a few hours."

"Are you saying I could be an actor?" Roman asked, pressing a hand to his heart. "I knew you'd ask me to join the Players if I stuck around long enough! I'm flattered, really, but I can't afford to be tied down at the mo—"

"Just go," Cahrn growled. "And make sure she's at the theater by five for hair and makeup."

Roman laughed and ducked out of the tent before Cahrn could scold him more. The walk to Dinara from here wasn't far, just through the Players' camp to the empty festival grounds. On the way, he passed Julian, the Players' fiddler, pianist, and musician of many instruments tapping at a light drum from Troas. Julian's wife nestled on the ground beside him, asleep with her back resting against his side. Further down the path, a group of Dinara's friends played footbag. Before they could spot him, Roman ducked down an alley, following a shortcut, and hopped the fence into the empty Festival Grounds. It was always strange, seeing this place when the festival was closed: the empty stages and covered booths, the open path and total quiet. Still, it meant a straight shot to the Webhon Players' stage.

He arrived there just in time to see Dinara fall.

She stood alone on the platform, dancing for the empty stands while her mentor Tabia watched. Dinara twirled, then jumped, soaring for a beautiful moment before she rolled her ankle upon landing and hit the ground *hard*. Roman broke into a run, but before he'd even reached the back row of seats, Dinara was pushing to her feet again, limping only a few paces before shaking it off.

Tabia stepped forward as well, but Dinara waved her off. "I'm all right," Roman heard her say. She rolled her ankle experimentally.

Fortunately, Tabia climbed up onto the stage anyway, kneeling and taking Dinara's ankle carefully in her hands. Dinara held Tabia's shoulder for balance and looked past her to the empty benches, her dark eyes meeting Roman's as he came down the center aisle. She was beautiful—even injured, even wearing raggedy practice clothes and covered in a sheen of sweat. She grimaced, embarrassed, and gave Roman a small wave. Roman smiled and waved back.

"It's fine, Tabia, really," Dinara said, sweeping her dark curls out of her face. Roman wondered how long they'd been out there, that Dinara was making mistakes like this. How long she'd been pushing herself in the pursuit of perfection.

"You're nervous," Tabia accused, her back still to Roman. "It's making you sloppy."

"I'm tired," Dinara corrected while Roman settled on a bench in the third row. At what was presumably a stern look from Tabia, she laughed, loud and frantic. "Fine, of course I'm nervous! I'm performing for *Unity* tonight, Tabia! What else *can* I be?"

"Confident," Tabia said, simply. "Don't think about them. Think about the story, about Edith. Would it help to hear about her again?"

Eyes wide, Dinara nodded and backed away as Tabia took the stage for herself. The older woman paused to tie her long braids behind her with a scrap of cloth, and when she finally turned toward the empty benches, she frowned upon seeing Roman there. "You shouldn't be here."

"Is it true you've met Edith, Tabia?" Roman asked in lieu of an apology. It was a common rumor among the Players, but he'd never heard it confirmed.

Tabia ignored him, instead stepping into the dance Dinara had just fumbled. When she jumped, she landed smoothly. Roman noticed Dinara flinch, noticed her drop her gaze to the ground. She'd been struggling with the role since Cahrn cast her: not because of her own skill, but because of Tabia. Edith, the spirited heroine of Cenhelm, was Tabia's legacy. From the way the Players told it, always in whispers and never when Tabia or Dinara were around, she was the one who popularized the role, who gave Cenhelm the acclaim it had amassed.

Not only had she performed it for Unity, she'd performed it for kings and queens. She'd performed it for Edith herself. It was *her* role, not Dinara's.

But mortality was a tragedy, and Tabia was getting too old to play the young ingenue. If they'd been performing for a small village off the beaten path, things would be different. Cahrn would have excused little inaccuracies. For Unity, everything had to be perfect.

"You have her heart," Tabia said, moving through the variation with ease. As she slipped deeper and deeper into character, her usual jaunty sway faded away. "But your fear is holding you back, Dinara. Edith's story is about trusting your heart and doing whatever you must to follow it, even when that's difficult."

Dinara nodded, looking miserable.

"Had Edith let fear rule her, she wouldn't have discovered the assassination plot. Ellaes wouldn't have given her the power to stop it. She wouldn't have saved Unity and, subsequently, the world." Tabia finished the dance and dipped into a bow, a smile on her generous lips. Finally, she met Roman's eye. "I have met her. Just once."

Roman moved up a row so he could hear better. "Must've been a while ago."

"Are you calling me old, boy?" Tabia asked. Roman opened his mouth to backtrack, maybe even to flirt and soften her up, but Tabia shook her head. "You wouldn't be wrong. My grandmother was a maranet; I'm even older than I look."

Dinara shot Roman a warning look. "You don't look old at all," she said.

"Sweet of you, pet, but I know it's not true."

"Did Edith talk at all about Ellaes?" Roman asked, taking advantage of Tabia's good mood while he could.

Tabia shook her head. "She called that part of the story a 'narrative embellishment.' Either it was just made up, or she had to deal with people's doubt for so long that she no longer believes it herself. But enough of this," Tabia said, holding her hands out to Dinara. Reluctantly, Dinara took them. "More practice will not do you any favors, my pet. Rest and remember: stories mean the most when *you*, the one doing the telling, are moved by them as well. Don't be so hard on yourself. Just go where Edith leads you."

Dinara nodded, a determined new gleam in her eyes. "I will. Thank you for agreeing to help me today. I'm sorry for taking up so much of your time."

"Nonsense. That's not something you ever need to apologize for."

While Dinara came down the steps toward Roman, he stood and gave her a lazy salute. "I'm glad you're done, because Cahrn sent me here to stop you—something about needing a break? You know the meaning of that word, don't you, Di?"

"Har har," Dinara said. When she held out a hand, Roman took it without hesitation. "What were you doing with Cahrn? Did you two become best friends while I wasn't looking?"

"Mm. We gossiped while I helped him braid his beard."

Dinara gasped. "Poor Cahrn! You never get the tension right."

"That shows what you know. *He* appreciated my skills."

Dinara laughed, then patted Roman's hand. "Let's go home, Roman. I'm tired."

When she turned to leave, though, Roman on her hand to stop her. "I'm not letting you walk back on that foot. Come here," he said, crouching so she could hop on his back. She laughed as she did, looping her arms around his neck. "Steady?" he asked. Dinara's curls brushed his cheek as she nodded.

"Cahrn was scolding me for not stopping *you* from practicing more, actually," Roman finally explained, heading back to camp. He cleared his throat. "And...for sneaking into camp late again."

"You'd think he'd be used to that by now," Dinara said dryly.

"Exactly!"

"How late was it this time?"

"'Early' would be a better word, I think. It was around four," Roman admitted.

"In the *morning*?" Dinara asked, going shrill in Roman's ear. He winced, veering on the path, and Dinara quickly added, "Sorry! I just—how do you even do that? If I stayed up that late then also got up as early as you do, I'd collapse. I need eight hours, minimum, or I'm grumpy all the next day."

"Believe me, I know," Roman muttered, laughing again when Dinara pinched him. "What were you thinking on stage? You made some interesting expressions."

"The usual. It's not that I don't want the role. I *really* do, I just feel so guilty. Tabia didn't even do anything wrong. She just got older."

"When you've lived past a certain age, Di, sometimes you don't mind yielding the stage."

"And I suppose you'd know, being *so* old yourself," Dinara teased.

"Ah. Maybe I wouldn't," he said. There must've been something strange in his tone because Dinara peered around his shoulder to try to see his expression. He forced a smile and a shrug. "I think Tabia is just happy for you."

"Maybe," Dinara conceded, "But I still feel bad."

"If Tabia doesn't, you shouldn't. But we're here, my lady. Shall I set you down or walk you to the door?"

Dinara wiggled to get down. "Here's fine, thank you," she said, pressing a quick kiss to the back of his neck before jumping down. The paint of her rickety trailer was chipped and cracked and you got splinters if you so much as rested your palm on the handrail, but it had carried Dinara thousands of miles. Her parents had built this trailer themselves after their marriage, and it had been with Dinara since. In that time, it had seen all of Calaidia.

Dinara turned to Roman as soon as they were inside. Standing at barely over five feet, she had to crane her neck to meet his eye. "You're going to stay for the whole show tonight, aren't you?" she asked.

"What do you mean?" Roman asked. When he tried to step closer, she held him at arm's length.

"Don't give me that; I know you've been leaving early. And the times you *do* stay, you look like you've eaten something sour the whole time. Do you really hate it that much?"

Roman winced. "It has nothing to do with you, I promise. Like I told you when Cahrn first picked the festival lineup, I just don't like that story. Tonight's show is different," he said, taking Dinara's wrist and slowly reeling her in. This time, Dinara let him.

"Are you sure it's not about Cahrn? You always leave right when he comes on."

"It's not Cahrn. It's the character he's playing," Roman said reluctantly.

Dinara frowned. "*Egil?*" she asked. It became her turn to hold on when Roman stiffened and tried to wriggle away. It was a common dance of theirs, a push-pull. "Who doesn't like Egil stories?"

Roman shrugged, his smile not meeting his eyes. "Me, I guess."

"But why?"

"It doesn't matter. And the prince—"

"What's wrong with Niko?"

"Not *Niko*, the character Niko's playing," Roman said. "I don't like him. I don't like either of them, and if I have to watch that play one more time, I really will go mad."

Dinara waited for more explanation, but when she realized it wasn't coming, she rolled her eyes. "You sound like a kid throwing a tantrum, Roman," she said. She threw her hands up, frustrated. "But fine, I'll leave it. Now, ask how my rehearsal went."

Roman blinked. "What?"

"Every day, we follow the same routine. We fight, make up, and then you ask how my rehearsal went."

"But I saw your rehearsal this time," Roman pointed out.

"Only the end of it. A humiliating end, by the way."

Roman backed toward their bed—little more than a mattress on the ground—and sat. "I wasn't aware we had a routine," he said, patting the spot next to him. When she approached, he surprised her at the last second by pulling her down onto his lap, instead. With a wolfish grin, he asked, "Is *this* part of our routine?"

Surprising him back, Dinara hiked up her skirts and straddled his hips. "Sort of. It usually comes later."

Roman gave her a coy look, up through his eyelashes in the way he knew she was weak to. "And this?"

"Wha—*Ah!*" Dinara squealed, laughter forced out of her when Roman's fingers found the ticklish spot below her ribs. She tried to bat his hands away, but he didn't let her. "*Roman!*"

Roman's own laughter stopped when Dinara launched her own attack, going for where *he* was the most ticklish: the back of his neck. He yelped and almost threw her off, and for a minute, they wrestled, Roman trying to get at Dinara and Dinara doing the same, both of them laughing until they couldn't breathe. Finally, Dinara ended the battle by pushing Roman back onto the bed and following him down. "Truce?" she asked, sitting up on her elbows so she could look down at him. This close, he could count the freckles on her warm, dark skin.

"Fine. Truce," he breathed.

"You're an ass!" Dinara said. "You know how ticklish I am."

"And it never gets old," Roman replied with a bright grin, watching her expression soften in reply. He reached up to tuck a curl behind her ear, then finally asked, "How was your rehearsal?"

It startled a laugh out of Dinara. "You cheeky thing," she said, turning her head to kiss his hand. "You know I don't like fighting with you, Roman."

"Yeah. I'm sorry."

Another kiss. "What did you do today, besides braid Cahrn's beard?"

Roman snorted. "Not much," he said, thinking again, briefly, of Gareth. "Explored north of Main Street, saved a man from being robbed, met some interesting people. Stopped in a hospital and heard some *very* interesting gossip. World-changing gossip, in fact. Have you seen the papers?"

"I—what? No, not yet," Dinara said, as if she ever might. She didn't read the papers as a rule, which was another thing they bickered over. Dinara said she didn't know what to do with the heartache the news gave her, as if ignoring problems kept them from existing, while Roman felt it was his duty to bear witness, even when—*especially* when—there was nothing he could do. "What was that about a hospital?"

"The King of Alfheimr is missing. They think Orean is trying to start a war."

Dinara's eyes widened. "What?! Why would Orean do that?"

"Who knows," Roman said. "Who can say if it's even true, or if Unity made it up. But speaking of Unity, have you seen their theater yet?"

Dinara blinked a few times at the subject change, then readjusted, used to this dizzying speed from Roman. "I got a private tour of the place yesterday, before our last rehearsal. Wait until you see it, Roman, it's beautiful! You *are* coming, aren't you? Egil's not in this one."

"I wouldn't miss it," Roman promised.

Dinara smiled down at him, dark eyes glimmering. While they were as dark as Roman's own, nearly black, hers held nothing but warmth. In contrast, Roman's were cold, unsettling, *creepy*. He'd been told it again and again: from his father, from his friends, from his mentors and enemies and acquaintances. Even Dinara, his own partner, sometimes flinched when his eyes met hers.

It happened even now. He held her gaze a beat too long and she quickly dropped her own, suddenly eager to look anywhere but at him. "Don't make faces at us this time. Cahrn was so mad about that," she tried to tease, but Roman was already withdrawing. It was an old instinct, so long engrained he couldn't stop it even if he'd wanted to.

It had been happening more with increasing frequency since they'd arrived in Gallonten. He knew it wasn't fair to Dinara. He knew she deserved him. When she kissed him, hoping to lure him back out, he shifted beneath her to slide her off.

Dinara changed tactics. She broke the kiss, twined her fingers with Roman's, and pinned his hands on either side of his head. That worked better: his eyes widened, his attention shifted back to her. Even under the full weight of his gaze, this time, she didn't flinch away. "It'll be nice to have you there," she said, as if they were still discussing the show.

Roman blinked lazily, trying to think past Dinara's hands, warmth, and weight to process the words. Dinara didn't give him the chance. She kissed him again, and when she started trailing those kisses down his jaw, he tilted his head to give her better access.

"I make no promises about the faces. When you look my way, I just can't help myself," he said, when he could find the words. He squirmed, a half-hearted attempt to break out of Dinara's grip—or get her to kiss him more—so Dinara shifted more of her weight to her hands and ducked to ghost more kisses along Roman's jaw.

"It's not that I don't appreciate this...whatever it is, Dinara," Roman breathed, "But there are things I actually needed to tell you."

"What? Why didn't you say so sooner?" Dinara asked, sitting up.

"No need to look so worried. It's just this: Cahrn says hair and makeup is at five. Also, Gemma's planning an afterparty and says attendance is mandatory. I promised her I'd ask if you were up for it."

Dinara released him. "Do you think she'll notice if we don't go?"

"You're the lead, Di."

"So?"

"It'll be fun," Roman pressed. "And knowing you, you'll spend all evening fretting over how the show went if you don't have something to distract you."

"There are other distractions than parties," Dinara tried, laying a hand meaningfully on Roman's chest.

He covered it with one of his own. "We don't have to stay the whole time."

Dinara groaned, "I'm tired, and my feet hurt."

Roman laughed and flipped their positions, Dinara squawking when he sat up and grabbed her leg. She nearly kicked him in the face, thinking he meant to tickle her again, but relaxed when he massaged her foot instead. "Do you need ice for your ankle?" he asked.

"No. It really wasn't that bad."

Roman narrowed his eyes at her. Dinara was the type to hide injuries, but she was also a terrible liar. He saw nothing but honesty in her expression—and no pain, even when he "accidentally" prodded the ankle in question. Satisfied, he returned to massaging. "I know you'll regret missing the party."

"Yeah," Dinara reluctantly agreed. She let her eyes fall shut. "Is that why you want me to go so badly?"

"I'm just too scared of Gemma not to give it a fighting effort," he said, making Dinara laugh. "Plus, if we stay, you'll fret, I'll brood, and we'll fight. Party with friends seems a better option."

Dinara hummed, then held her other foot out for Roman to massage. "But this is going to make me fall asleep."

"Nap, then. I'll wake you before five."

Sleep was taking her before he'd even finished speaking. For a moment, she looked so peaceful that Roman was tempted to join her. But Dinara's peace could never stop his own nightmares, so instead, he went to sit on the trailer stairs and enjoy the late summer sunslight.

CHAPTER ELEVEN

IF THE REST OF UNITY ISLAND WAS MERELY GRAND, its theater was the peak of opulence. Unity spared no expense in either its construction or its décor, from the red carpets to the crystal chandeliers to the painted ceilings. Everything about it was designed to be unforgettable. Gareth found it amusing, then, how often he forgot this place existed.

In his defense, he'd never been a theater man, and he rarely visited Gallonten during its late spring theatrical season. Tonight's show was an abnormality, a special treat to kick off the conference season. It was a treat for Gareth, too; he looked forward to seeing the Webhon Players again—hoped they'd start soon, in fact. He could only get away with ignoring Moira for so long, especially when she kept giving him those long, searching looks.

Finally, as the stewards went around dimming lights, Moira decided she'd had enough. She sat forward in her seat, the crinkling of her evening gown loud in the Ranulfs' private theater box. "Gareth, are you going to tell me how the meeting went or not?"

"We're not supposed to discuss it with anyone outside the team," Gareth said, as if he hadn't given Isobel a line-by-line recount as soon as he'd gotten home. His wife obviously didn't count.

"Discuss what?" Gareth and Moira's half-brother asked from the seat behind them. A self-declared "self-made man," Aldous ran several successful businesses in the north. Like a child, though, he still hated when his much-older siblings spent time together without him. When he'd learned Gareth was in town, he'd taken the first train south to join them.

"I am clearly the exception," Moira said, ignoring Aldous.

"Yes, well, maybe I don't feel like discussing *anything* with you," Gareth said, "Not unless it's about my missing neighbors."

"For the hundredth time, I don't know what you expect me to do about that. We can't control Gallonten's police."

On Gareth's other side, Isobel made a disgusted noise and leaned forward until she could glare at Moira as well. "Do you think we're fools, Moira? The Magistrates have pardoning powers. You could help those poor kids, you're simply choosing not to."

Gareth nodded along with his wife. After telling Isobel about the orinians, they'd spent all afternoon riding around the city looking for Maebhe with no luck. Gareth feared the police had gotten to her—or worse.

"Isobel," Moira sighed, but Isobel cut her off.

"I really don't want to hear another word, Moira. Not unless it's a promise to do better."

Aldous sat back in his seat, no longer wanting anything to do with the conversation. Gareth bit back a smile and laced his fingers with Isobel's. "This comes as no surprise, I'm sure, but I agree with my wife," he said. "This goes beyond your usual apathy into plain cruelty, Moira. They're only tourists. Show some mercy."

"Gareth," Moira began again, but again, Isobel shushed her.

"The show's about to begin," Isobel said. Sure enough, the audience quieted below as the orchestra struck up and the curtain lifted to reveal a bearded man in an antiquated costume.

Moira leaned over again and whispered, "If these orinians really mean so much to you, Gareth, I promise to look into it."

Gareth couldn't remember the last time she'd taken a complaint of his seriously. "Thank you. I would appreciate that."

Though she didn't look pleased about it, Moira nodded and settled back to watch the show. It was another Gareth knew, though there was no Egil in this one. It told the story of a girl named Edith Albert, the youngest daughter of a Unity Representative, who learned of a plot to assassinate a Magistrate—Gareth's ancestor, in fact. As she worked to stop it, the goddess Ellaes came to her in a vision and directed her path. But the story wasn't the only thing Gareth knew; he recognized the actress playing Edith as the Oracle of Damael from the Rinehart Festival. When he looked closer, he recognized several more of the actors: the young prince was now Edith's earnest suitor, Egil the endangered Magistrate. He wondered if Mr. Hallisey might appear again, but he ended up getting so caught in the story that he forgot to look, after a while.

When the lights went up to cue intermission, he blinked, slowly dragging himself out of the world of the story. He wanted to stay there; he didn't want to deal with his sister. Before Moira could ask him again about his meeting with Prince Nochdvor, he loudly excused himself for the restroom, the bodyguard Moira had assigned to him when she'd seen the state of his face following. Gareth spent the intermission wandering Unity's decadent halls beneath heavenly scenes of the Guardians and their champions. Gold sconces with flickering lights lined the walls between paneled mirrors, and Gareth avoided meeting his own bruised eyes in his reflection.

"This place is a little gaudy, don't you think?" a familiar voice asked when Gareth paused to admire a painting. Gareth saw its owner in the mirror first, all feline grace and sharp angles. He turned and offered his new companion a bow, one that was returned with far more grace.

"Compared to the Royal Palace in Alfheimr, I'm sure it must be," Gareth said, smiling.

Leandros Nochdvor wrinkled his nose, a small, barely-there expression. "The Palace is beautiful," Leandros agreed, but there was no warmth in it. "Your eye is already looking better."

"I have my wife's makeup and skilled hand to thank for that."

"Ah, I thought—I forgot how slowly you sapiens heal."

Gareth chucked. "I'll likely be bruised all the way to Illyon. What do you think of the show?"

"I'd debated staying home, but it makes me glad I chose to come out," Leandros said. Sensing Gareth's curiosity, he explained, "Thanks to those damned papers, reporters and other busybodies have been harassing me all day. I can barely leave my hotel."

Now that he mentioned it, Gareth felt the eyes on his back, heard the hiss of whispers pointed in their direction. He wondered how this would affect the gossip, the bereaved Prince Nochdvor greeting the Magistrate's brother like a good friend. He tutted. "People can be so entitled."

"That, at least, is something I'm used to. My uncle is a king, my mother a prima donna, my father a villain. People have always felt entitled to my time and secrets simply because they find me interesting."

"Is that why you've been, ah...out of the public eye for so long?" Gareth ventured. It was the closest he'd come to asking about Histrios, and it was as close as his courage would currently allow.

Leandros regarded Gareth out of the corner of his eyes. "Why, Mr. Ranulf, when I spoke of busybodies, I didn't realize you were one of them."

"I'm so sorry if I overstepped," Gareth said quickly. He realized afterward, by the faint quirk of Leandros' lips, that the alfar was teasing him.

Leandros laughed. It was a startling sound, musical like a pair of chimes in the wind, and it reminded Gareth of the old stories about alfar dancing on moors amidst streams of wild magic. He didn't think he'd ever heard an alfar laugh before. He must have stared too openly, because Leandros' expression quickly closed off, schooled back into something solemn and neutral.

"It's fine," he said. Gareth thought his voice sounded warmer than it had, though he still didn't answer Gareth's question, instead lowering his voice and saying, "I understand people's curiosity, honestly. The world has changed with just one headline, and the people don't even know enough to know if they should be afraid. I just wish they understood that I am, for all practical purposes, grieving."

It was easy to forget in all the politics that Leandros had lost a beloved uncle. Gareth considered Leandros' clothing: even to an event like this, the alfar wore mostly black. It could only signify mourning. Strangely, though, was that he didn't wear the plain, coarse fabrics of early-stage mourning. Instead, the lace and satin and silver incorporated into Leandros' suit implied an old loss. Gareth couldn't recall hearing of any deaths in the Alfheimr royal family in recent years. Could there be someone else he mourned?

"By the way, were you able to warn your neighbors?" Leandros asked.

Gareth winced. "Yes, but not soon enough. The Gallontean police came for them."

Leandros swore, the crass language surprising Gareth. "I should have known they might—*damn* it to hell. I'm sorry, Mr. Ranulf."

"Whatever for?"

"I should have helped you. I could have prevented this."

"Nonsense. If I couldn't do anything to stop them, you wouldn't have been able to, either," Gareth said. When Leandros met Gareth's eyes, Gareth saw fury—the same hot fury he'd seen in Leandros back at the Magistrates' chambers. But then Leandros blinked and it was gone. He'd frozen over once more. "Maybe you're right. I apologize for my outburst, Mr. Ranulf."

Gareth opened his mouth to wave him off, but then a bell rang, signaling the end of intermission. While the surrounding crowds returned to their seats, Leandros hesitated. "Would you care to get drinks after this? I'd like to discuss this further."

Maybe it did make him a busybody, but Gareth could never turn down an opportunity to study an interesting personality. And for a chance to potentially ask about Egil, too, how could he refuse? "I'd love to."

The two men walked back to the upper floors of the theater together, Leandros parting crowds with only a look. It was a peculiar effect to witness: Gareth was used to Moira's bodyguards forging a path forward, but with Leandros, it was effortless. Gareth doubted the alfar even realized he was doing it. Leandros Nochdvor simply existed in a reality all his own, like the people in his way were mere ghosts, like he was the only thing real in this entire theater. He certainly cut a striking figure, in his black damask waistcoat and slim, high-waisted trousers, the peak of fashion with a silhouette to match, but his command of attention went beyond that. Maybe it was inherited from his uncle, or maybe it came from his distinguished mother. Maybe it was something all his own.

Content with the promise of picking the alfar apart later, Gareth returned to his box, arriving just as the curtains lifted. The second act proved even better than the first. As with the other show, the Webhon Players masterfully danced the line between tragedy and comedy; Gareth cried one moment and cried from laughter the next. The effects only got more elaborate as the story progressed, particularly after Ellaes' first appearance, the Players incorporating stage tricks like metallurgy to make the goddess's magic feel real. Gareth cried again when it was over, not because it was sad, but simply because it was over.

Isobel hung on his arm afterward, staunchly ignoring Moira and leading him out of the box and down the stairs. Gareth searched for Leandros among the crowd, and it was only a prickling sensation at the back of his neck that made him turn. He didn't find Leandros there. Instead, he found another familiar face, a casual figure leaning against the far stage doors. The line of his body was tense, his muscles coiled and his wary gaze jumping over the crowd, as if he was looking for someone. He started in surprise when his eyes met Gareth's.

Without thinking, Gareth took Isobel's hand and dragged her over. "Mr. Hallisey!" he called.

Roman responded with a bright smile and a lazy wave, and Gareth whispered to Isobel as they drew closer. "Do you remember him from the festival yesterday? He's the one who saved me last night. Roman Hallisey's his name."

"What a strange coincidence," Isobel said.

"It is," Gareth agreed before adding, louder, "Good evening, Mr. Hallisey!"

"And to you, Mr. Ranulf," Roman greeted as they approached, his expression settling into something unreadable. He eyed the Unity guard that followed the Ranulfs over. "Given your troubles yesterday, I hadn't expected to see you here tonight. How's your eye?"

Gareth went to touch his cheek, a self-conscious habit he'd picked up in the last twenty-four hours, but Isobel intercepted his hand and twined their fingers together. "It could be worse. The swelling's down considerably," he said.

"I can see that. And this must be the *beautiful* Mrs. Ranulf." Roman extended a hand. When Isobel offered her own, the young man raised it to his lips and kissed it, his dark curls falling into his eyes.

Straightening again, he said, "Your husband talks about you a lot when he's drugged, did you know that?"

"I wasn't aware. I can't say I've ever drugged him."

Roman laughed. "Well, even for all his poetic waxing, he doesn't do you justice."

"Aren't you cute," Isobel said, but the considering, almost wary look she gave him didn't match the tone of her words. When Roman's gaze again darted over the crowd, she asked, "Are you waiting for someone?"

Roman's attention snapped back to her. He looked her up and down, not so quick to dismiss her, this time. "Not at all," he said with a polite smile. "Crowds just make me nervous."

"But you did such a good job engaging with the festival crowd yesterday," Isobel pushed. Gareth watched the back and forth with a frown.

"I'm touched you think so. I was just doing a favor for the troupe leader; it's not my usual scene, I can promise you," Roman said. He lit up, then, and a mischievous grin slipped onto his face. "Speaking of scenes, did you like the show? How would you two like to see something exciting?"

Gareth opened his mouth to decline, but before he could, Isobel said, "I can't speak for my husband, but you have me curious."

Roman nodded back at the stage door and opened it for them with a flourish. "Only you two, though, I'm afraid. The Players would be uncomfortable with a Unity officer back there."

"Are you certain you can invite *any* of us back?" Gareth asked.

"Very. Come, I want to introduce you to someone."

Roman ushered them through the door, the guard unhappily settling in to wait. Unlike the rest of the theatre, the backstage was messy and dark, the Webhon Players already caught up in post-show cleanup. People in dark clothing hurried back and forth carrying crates and set pieces, a frantic dance Gareth and Isobel were careful to avoid. Roman led them down a short flight of steps, stopped abruptly at the bottom ,and knocked on an unadorned door. A moment later, it opened to reveal the show's star, the young actress that played Edith. She threw her arms around Roman.

"What did you think?" she asked, cutting off with a squeal and a laugh when Roman picked her up and gave her a twirl.

"Absolutely enchanting, Dinara! You stole the show."

Dinara laughed and pulled back from the embrace, finally noticing the Ranulfs. "Oh, hello," she said breathlessly. "Roman, who are your friends?"

"Di, meet Gareth and Isobel Ranulf. Gareth, Isobel, this is Dinara Condeh."

"It's a pleasure, Ms. Condeh," Gareth said, enthusiastically shaking Dinara's hand. "Wonderful show. Your performance was so moving I nearly cried."

"Liar. You *did* cry," Isobel said.

Dinara tried to hide a laugh. "Thank you! Come in, won't you?"

Inside the dressing room, Edith's various gowns lined one wall, numerous bouquets of flowers another. Dinara dropped into her seat and regaled them all with a costume mishap that happened in the second act. She was stunning, even out of costume and clearly exhausted, with deep brown skin and curls that fell to her chin, and contrary to her bold portrayal of Edith, her manner off-stage was gentle. Gareth envied her and Roman. They had a youthful vivacity that had long escaped him—if he'd ever had it to begin with—and they were beautiful together. But seeing the young man among friends, not in a darkened alley holding a bloodied sword, felt strange. He seemed...*diminished*, somehow. Not as large as he had in the night.

"We're all going out to celebrate," Dinara said. "You two should come with."

"Would we be overdressed?" Gareth asked.

"Half the Players will be in costume," Roman assured him. "If anyone's going to stand out, it won't be you. Come, it'll be fun. There will be music and drinking and dancing."

Isobel squeezed Gareth's hand. "I told the governess not to expect us back until late," she told him.

Unable to deny his wife anything, he said, "We'd be happy to join you, then."

Roman answered with a bright, boyish smile, different from the forced one he'd used upstairs. This one lit up the room. "That's the spirit, Gareth! Wait 'till you see how the Webhon Players party. It's the only reason I'm still traveling with them, if I'm being honest."

Dinara scoffed and elbowed Roman, making him laugh again. There was something about Roman, some unidentifiable quality that made Gareth want to earn his esteem and hear more of those laughs. "I have to go find a friend, first. I need to cancel our plans," he said.

Gareth would have plenty of time to talk to Leandros in the coming weeks, he reasoned. Roman and Dinara, though, he may never see again. The Rinehart Festival was ending soon, and the Players would be gone from Gallonten.

"Bring them along!" Dinara said, adding, "If they're fun."

"I don't know him well, but I believe he could be. And I'm sure he'd be happy not to stand out for an evening—his name is Leandros Nochdvor."

"Not him," Roman said firmly, surprising everyone. The smile was gone from his face. His eyes were always strangely solemn, even when nothing else about him seemed to be, but now they were also cold. "Don't invite him."

Gareth stared at Roman, taken aback by the sudden chill. Dinara frowned as well. Under the weight of their stares, Roman shook himself, his dark expression clearing into something carefully innocent. "I mean, he's from Alfheimr. You know how they are there.

No fun. And he's…he's royalty over there, isn't he? I just don't think anywhere we go will be up to his standards."

Dinara's brows furrowed further, but if she thought Roman was hiding something—as Gareth did—she didn't comment. Gareth, too, decided not to push, though this only made him more curious about the man. He remembered the way Roman had reacted when he'd mentioned the prince at the festival yesterday, too. "I understand. I do need to find him and reschedule, though."

"I'll catch up with you outside," Roman said. He smiled and kissed Dinara on the cheek, but his eyes had gone even colder. "I think I left something at my seat."

Though there were shared looks, nobody commented as he slipped away. Dinara went with Isobel and Gareth to look for Leandros, eyeing him curiously while Gareth explained the situation; Leandros understood, as Gareth knew he would, but made Gareth promise to get drinks with him before they left Gallonten. And as promised, Roman caught up with them just as they were about to cross onto the bridge.

A short, cheerful woman with an orange pixie cut led the group of twenty or so in total to a nondescript tavern with a sign of a snarling wolf hanging above the door. Music and laughter drifted out to the street, and a warm glow streamed out the windows to greet them.

"Welcome," the woman said, gesturing grandly, "To the Hungry Hound."

A *hound*, then. Not a wolf.

The Hungry Hound was the kind of place Gareth might read about in a book: the quintessential pub, with a crackling fire, the smell of garlic and spices in the air, and music drifting gently over from the fiddler in the corner. The short woman—Gemma, he heard the Players call her—had reserved half the room for the Players and bought off the fiddler as well.

They crammed into booths and around tables, ordering drinks and dishes to share. As the evening progressed and the drinks flowed, they got the fiddler to play a lively tune and moved the tables to the sides of the room to make space for dancing. Those that didn't dance turned to telling stories—unfortunately for Gareth, that involved a few wildly incorrect Egil stories, but he reined himself in from correcting anyone. Mostly.

"That's the most preposterous thing I've ever heard," he'd told one of the Players early into the evening. "Everyone knows Egil hated Unity. He opposed them at every turn."

"That was *after* he left them. He worked for them first. Haven't you ever heard of the Hound of Unity?" the man asked.

"The Hound of Unity is a myth. I've studied Egil for ten years and I've never found anything connecting him to that character," Gareth said, meeting the player's challenging scowl with one of his own. "Besides, the hound was from the late *eleventh* century—even if Egil was maranet, he couldn't have lived that long."

Roman rolled his eyes and slid out of the booth, holding a hand out to Dinara to pull her up after him. "And with that, I'm going to dance."

"He doesn't like Egil stories," Dinara told Gareth apologetically. "Don't ask me why. He doesn't tell."

Isobel couldn't drink because of the pregnancy, so Gareth didn't either. They danced a few songs but spent the rest of their evening enjoying the company of these strange and interesting people. Roman and Dinara spent much longer on the dance floor, though as the evening wore on and they both had more to drink, their movements could be described less as dancing and more as something that wouldn't be tolerated in Gareth's usual sort of establishment.

Roman never crossed the line into drunk, though. Gareth was watching for it, hoping to even the score after Roman had seen him so high on painkillers the night before. Roman drank as much as the rest, but aside from his flushed cheeks and boundless energy, it barely seemed to touch him. Between dances, he told a few stories of his own—fantastic personal adventures that Gareth had trouble believing—and listened with rapt attention to others'. Even Gareth's, which Gareth didn't feel deserved such enthusiasm. Roman made sure the Ranulfs were always included in conversations, that they felt like old friends, and demanded that everyone have just as much fun as he was having.

When a fight broke out between one of the Players and another patron, Roman shed this enthusiasm like a mask. He stepped between them and stopped the fight so quickly Gareth wouldn't have believed his eyes if he hadn't been sober. And when both parties backed down, he slipped the mask back on and returned to Dinara's arms. If Gareth had thought this evening would give him insights into Roman Hallisey's mysteries, he'd been wrong. All he had were more questions.

Even so, he couldn't remember ever having so much fun in his life. In the early hours of the morning, he swept Isobel off her feet and carried her up into the cab bed, where she settled happily against his side with a sigh, her heels clutched in her hands. They hummed clashing melodies against the steady beat of horse hooves and carriage wheels and thought of things more pleasant than missing kings and Gareth's upcoming departure.

EGIL II

PRESENT DAY

YEAR OF UNITY 1880

TUCKED IN A SHADOWY ALCOVE BETWEEN TWO STREETLAMPS, Egil felt along the grain of a door and crowed triumphantly when he found a symbol etched into its wood. There, almost invisible against the dark stain, was *her* symbol: an open eye with a set of dragonfly wings. He'd thought the Oracle of Damael would have changed her safe houses after Histrios; what arrogance, to assume Egil wouldn't come for them.

First checking that the street was empty, he raised a leg to kick the door down. It swung suddenly open before he could, and the person on the other side shrieked and dropped their keys.

"It's *you!*" they cried, then pointed at Egil. "Wait, were you about to break in?!"

"No," Egil lied. "I came to talk to you. Did you visit Leandros?"

Aleksir Bardon crouched to retrieve his keys. Briefly, Egil could see past him into a narrow entryway with a set of stairs leading up. While it seemed to be a normal flat, Egil knew all the secrets it held. "Yeah, I talked to him. First thing this morning."

"And he listened?"

"'Course. Some people actually take the oracle's name seriously, you know. I told him all of it, except the bit about meeting you."

"And how is he?" Egil asked. When Aleksir's eyes widened, he wished he hadn't. He cleared his throat and corrected, "Don't answer that. What did he say after you told him?"

Aleksir scratched at the wispy beard on his chin. "Not much. He shooed me away when I asked him about Histrios."

When Aleksir made to step out of the safe house, Egil blocked him with his arm. "You *what*?" he hissed. "Why would you do that?"

"Because you wouldn't tell me anything!"

"That doesn't—never mention it to him again. Never even *speak* to him again. Do you understand me?"

Alarmed at the venom in Egil's voice, Aleksir took a step back and hastily nodded.

Coming here had been a mistake. Egil should have let his ghosts rest, rather than try to dig them up. But like a man prodding at a toothache, checking to see if it still hurt, he'd had to ask. Now, having confirmed that it did, he turned to leave.

"Wait!" Aleksir called after him. His voice was too loud; it grated on Egil's nerves. They were alone for now, but if Aleksir kept shouting, he was bound to attract attention. Egil didn't wait for Aleksir to lock his door, but he also made no attempt to stop the boy from catching up. "Are you seriously going, just like that? I thought I'd never see you again."

"You should be so lucky. Now stop following me."

"But I have more information for you!" Aleksir said. When Egil didn't immediately shoo him away, Aleksir took his silence for curiosity and grinned. "I'm running late for a meeting. If you walk with me, I'll tell you what I know on the way."

Devikra's visions had always been like a drug: as soon as Egil knew a little, he needed to know more. And so, against his better judgment, he fell into step beside the Oracle's errand-boy and pointed down the street. "You have until that streetlamp to convince me not to leave."

The street was quiet, the cobblestone and dark storefronts lit by the city's new electric carbon arc lamps. The white light they produced was cold compared to the lamplight pouring out of second- and third-floor windows, occasionally filtering through the cracks between the drawn curtains. Unlike Aleksir, Egil eyed every shadow with suspicion. This city could be dangerous at night, and Aleksir made himself an easy target. The boy almost tripped over his feet several times, too busy watching Egil with a look that came uncomfortably close to awe to watch where he was walking.

"I met with Devikra's Unity contact, the one you scared off last night," he said, "And I found out what Unity's planning. They're—"

"Sending a team to Orean to investigate King Nochdvor's disappearance," Egil finished. So this wasn't about Devikra's visions at all. "Your deadline is almost here. Tell me something I don't already know, and be quick."

Aleksir grinned from ear to ear and spun to walk backward so he could face Egil as he talked. "I should've guessed—no one can keep anything from Egil! You know your Prince Nochdvor is leading the team, then, yeah?"

Egil frowned. He had not known. "He agreed to that?"

"This was all his idea, far as I can tell," Aleksir said. Glancing back and finding his lamppost close, the rest came out in a rush. "How about this: there's more to those magic rumors than I thought."

"I'm listening."

"Apparently, the King of Alfheimr was abducted out of a tower full of people, all of them dead now except for the prince and princess.

The only way out was down a single set of stairs. People saw a single orinian go up, which Unity is keeping hush-hush, and no one saw her come back down. That's not even getting into the explosion."

"Explosion?" Egil asked. The lamp post came and went.

"It killed everyone. Charred the flesh right off those nobles' bones and shook all of Illyon. The amount of firepower that orinian would've had to smuggle in there...no one knows how she did it, and that's why they're saying it's magic."

"How did the prince and princess survive?"

"The prince threw them both out the window in the nick of time," Aleksir said, his smile growing wider the longer he kept pace with Egil's interrogation.

"And what's the prince saying happened?"

"Dunno. He's being as tight-lipped as Unity. My contact is on his team and even *they* haven't been told everything."

The two of them turned onto a bright, noisy street full of taverns and lights and people. Though no one paid them any mind, Egil kept quiet, waiting until the lights and laughter had faded back into darkness and quiet to ask, "If your contact is on the team, have they noticed any shady characters among their teammates? Anyone that stood out to them?"

"What do you mean by shady?"

"Just...suspicious. They'd likely have a connection to Unity. Details in their resumes wouldn't line up. They could have impressive, unexplained skillsets. Evasive natures, disarming charm. I can't get more specific—something would just feel off."

"I can ask. Why? Who're you looking for?"

"Have you heard of the Enforcers?"

Aleskir shook his head. "What's an Enf—"

Egil shushed Aleksir. "Gods, boy, you're trying to join the game and don't even know the most important players? You're in over your head. Ask your Oracle about them. She knows."

"But Devikra never tells me anything," Aleksir whined.

"And?" Egil asked, smirking at Aleksir. Last night, he'd noticed how Aleksir reacted to his smirks—the flash of irritation that crossed the boy's face without fail. He had a temper, and a great deal of pride, too. The more Egil could stir those embers, stoke them into a fire, the faster he could burn down Aleksir's idol worship and dance in the smoke. "Don't you have somewhere to be? What am I, your mother? Your assistant, that I have to keep your appointments for you?"

Aleksir's cheeks flushed, but he ducked his head and hurried on. Egil followed him down a side street, then over a fence into a park he knew well. It was a popular meeting place in Gallonten among individuals who wished to go unnoticed: popular, but not too popular. Maintained, but not monitored. Dense, with foliage that formed quiet, obscure paths. Best of all, because of its location in Greysdale, Gallonten's police paid it little mind. As he and Aleksir walked between the dark trees, the only sounds were the occasional crunch of early-fallen leaves beneath their boots and distant church bells. They walked until they came upon a pond, moonlight glittering off its surface and a dragon crouching at its bank. She lifted her head and turned when they approached.

At the painfully awkward wave Aleksir gave her, Egil had to bite his tongue to keep from laughing. Devikra's standards really had changed, over the decades. In his day, she'd had strict policies governing meetings between her agents. Not only had Aleksir broken them by inviting Egil along, he'd failed to check the perimeter for eavesdroppers. While Aleksir sidled up to the dragon, Egil sank back into the shadows to do on the boy's behalf.

"Nice weather we're having," Aleksir said.

"The Guardians have blessed us," the dragon agreed. Unlike Aleksir, *she* followed protocol. Though the exact wording had changed over the years, Egil recognized the start of a passcode.

"May Ellaes continue to do so," Aleksir said, finishing the code.

"Who is your friend?" the dragon asked. A dragon's vocal cords were incapable of whispering, so her rumbling voice carried through the park. All the more reason to check the perimeter.

"He's–" Aleksir jumped when Egil suddenly appeared beside him and shot him a warning look. "Uh. He's all right. He's with me."

Egil smiled at the dragon, hands clasped behind his back. "Just a trainee. Happy to be here."

She seemed to accept it, fortunately for them both. "I have a letter from Our Lady in my bag," she told Aleksir, lowering one shoulder so Aleksir could reach the bag strapped to her scaly side. "If you have any to return to her, put them in the front pouch."

So that's what this was. A delivery. To require an in-person trade-off, though, that letter must contain something interesting indeed. Aleksir climbed up and made the exchange quickly, but as he tucked his own letter in the dragon's bag, Egil asked, "Did you mention me in there?"

Aleksir froze. "Um..."

"It's fine. I'll be gone from here before Dev can do anything about it." The nickname slipped out unconsciously, and when both Aleksir and the dragon turned to gawp at him, Egil winced. That woman didn't deserve nicknames, not from him. "I'm leaving," he announced, then turned and walked away.

"Wait!" Aleksir called. Like the last time, Egil didn't wait. He was over the fence and back in the city proper by the time Aleksir finally caught up, nearly falling from the fence in his haste.

"Does she really let you call her Dev?" Aleksir asked as he jogged after Egil. "I thought only Wil could call her that."

Egil ignored him and snatched the unopened letter from Devikra out of Aleksir's hands. When Aleksir made a grab for it, Egil simply held it far over his head. He had half a foot on the kid, and Aleksir seemed to realize he'd never get it back just by jumping. He settled for glaring at Egil instead. "Let me read it," Egil said. "If Devikra's written about any new visions, I want to know."

As if to catch Egil by surprise, Aleksir suddenly jumped for the letter. Egil easily stepped out of reach, laughing and waving the letter around just to mock him.

"C'mon. She'll kill me. You know she will," Aleksir reasoned.

"Don't be dramatic. At worst, she'll pull you from the field and tell you how disappointed she is."

Aleksir whined. "I *hate* disappointing her."

"Let me read this and I'll tell you about the Enforcers."

Aleksir paused, weighing his idolization for Egil against his worship of Devikra. He looked between the letter and Egil's face, back and forth. "And Histrios, too?"

"Absolutely not. Do not try to bargain with me."

Aleksir grimaced. "Fine, fine. But I have to tell her you read it."

"Fine," Egil agreed, finally unfolding the letter. The familiar handwriting startled him; if Devikra was writing to this boy personally, he must be deep in her circle of trust. He walked as he read, Aleksir following his winding path back to the safe house without complaint.

Its contents were utterly useless. No new visions. Nothing interesting, except: "So that's the name of your Unity contact."

Aleksir swore and snatched the letter out of Egil's hand. This time, Egil let him. "Please don't contact him," Aleksir begged. When Egil made no promises, he said, "Ugh, she really is going to kill me. Tell me about these Enforcers, then—you owe me that much."

"I'll tell you commensurate with the information I got from that letter."

Aleksir's pout turned into a glare. "That wasn't the deal!"

Egil laughed, tapped the tip of Aleksir's nose, and said, "Too bad." If he couldn't use the boy's temper to alienate him, he'd use the madness. It tended to alienate people quickly. "The Enforcers are similar to Dev's agents, but before that, they're soldiers. The deadliest soldiers you'll ever meet, trained to do anything Unity asks of them. They'll have their hands in this mess, one way or another."

Aleksir clearly waited for more, but Egil stopped there, noticing something strange down the alley he'd stopped in front of. Without giving Aleksir any warning, he turned down it.

"Huh? Egil?" Aleksir asked, following.

Gallonten's streets were full of the downtrodden and houseless. It was, unfortunately, a common occurrence to glance down alleys and spot small encampments, though Gallonten's police came down on them hard when they found them. Several feet ahead sat a small, shoddy shelter tucked alongside a dumpster. Sticking out of it was a pair of bare feet and, more notably, the tip of a tail. As Egil neared the makeshift shelter, both the tail and feet disappeared inside. Egil knocked on the wood twice. "I'm not with the police. I won't hurt you," he called, far gentler than he'd ever spoken to Aleksir. "You're orinian, aren't you?"

A long pause answered Egil's question, then a messy head of hair peeked out from the shelter. It belonged to a girl, barely older than Aleksir. When she saw they didn't wear uniforms, the tension in his shoulders eased, though she bared her teeth at them all the same. "Go away. Leave me alone."

"I will if that's what you want," Egil said, crouching, "But you have to know Gallonten's not safe for you."

"No shit," the girl said. Aleksir frowned and opened his mouth, probably to do something stupid like defend Egil's honor, but Egil held a hand up to silence him.

"What do you need? Money? A ride out of town? How can I help you?" he asked.

"You can't. I need my brother back."

"What happened to him?" When she didn't answer, Egil ignored the feel of Aleksir's eyes on his back and pressed, "Neither of us will know if I can help or not unless you tell me. Give it a chance."

"Who do you think you are, Egil? Unless you can break onto Unity Island and free prisoners, there's no point."

Aleksir chose that moment to jump in. His eyes were brimming with excitement, and Egil felt all the work he'd done disillusioning the kid fade into oblivion. "He is, actually! And he can! You'd be lucky to have his help!"

"Shut *up*, Aleksir," Egil hissed.

But the damage was already done. The girl looked between Egil and Aleksir, her expression closing off. "Great. You're crazy. Just so you know, I was the star boxer on my college team. If you try anything, I'll punch you."

Egil crept back from the shelter, giving the girl more space. In her, he saw a fellow victim of Unity, another life blackened by their cursed touch. This girl was why Unity needed to be destroyed. "Ignore him. We work for the Oracle of Damael," he said, brushing his dark hair aside to reveal the mark tattooed under his ear: an open eye and a set of dragonfly wings. After a beat, Aleksir did the same. "You know what the tattoo means, right?"

Eyes wide, the girl nodded. She leaned out of her shelter to see it better. The Oracle's purple ink could never be replicated, the pigment produced only in Damael and the ink made with secrets guarded by her temple. It bothered Egil, sometimes, knowing that he was forever branded with Devikra's mark, but he couldn't regret getting it, either. Not when it did him good, in moments like these. "Your brother—did they arrest him?"

Another nod.

"After the king's kidnapping?"

"Yes," the girl said, voice barely a whisper.

"If he's on the island, I know how to get him back," Egil said, watching hope reignite behind the girl's gray eyes. It made him uneasy. He wasn't a hero anymore, so playing at one felt wrong. But the words came too easily to his tongue, even half-forgotten as they were; he was speaking them before he could stop himself. "I know you have no reason to trust me, but at least trust that this is better than waiting for the police to find you. The oracle has a safe house near here. I'm afraid I can't come with you, but Aleksir will help."

"What!" Aleksir said, biting his tongue when Egil threw a cold look at him over his shoulder.

"Why? Why would you—why help me at all?" the girl asked.

Egil smiled at her, as warmly as it could manage. That wasn't much, but it was enough to make the girl tentatively smile back. "What's your name?"

"Maebhe Cairn."

"Well, Ms. Cairn, I help because it's my job. It's what the oracle does," he said, the oracle's name bitter on his tongue. To Aleksir, he said, "Take her back to Dev's place. In the morning, go to the Rinehart Festival Grounds. Find the camp east of it and ask for a man named Roman Hallisey. He'll help."

"What if he won't?" Maebhe asked, her long, cow-like ears pressed flat to her head.

"He will," Egil promised her. He shrugged out of his cloak and passed it to Maebhe. "Hide your ears and tail with this."

"Thank you," she breathed.

"Who's Roman Hallisey?" Aleksir whispered while she shrugged it on.

"He was an Enforcer," Egil said, standing again. "In fact, he was once the strongest of them."

Chapter Twelve

The morning following Dinara's Unity performance promised a beautiful day. Beams of sunslight streamed through the trailer's windows and an easy breeze rattled the chimes in the doorway. Outside, the sky was cloudless, clear for the suns' tandem trek across its blue and gold expanse. It was too bad Dinara was too hungover to appreciate it.

She rolled to face Roman. The fact that he was still here, in bed, meant he must be feeling it as well—normally, he was awake and gone before Dinara had even stirred. Without so much as opening his eyes, he mumbled, "Go back to sleep."

Dinara tried to laugh, then groaned when it made her head throb. "Oh. Ow. I feel gross."

"You know what'd help with that? More sleep."

Dinara squinted at him. "Do I remember you leaving in the middle of the night?"

Realizing she wasn't about to let him rest, Roman buried his face in his pillow. "Couldn't sleep," he said, muffled. "Walked around a bit."

No wonder he was still here. With how exhausted he must be, she should let him sleep. She should also try going back to sleep herself, as he suggested, but the sunlight through the windows wouldn't let her. "I'm hungry. Something greasy sounds good, doesn't it? Would you make something?" When he ignored her, she prodded his side. "We could do something fun, afterward."

At that, Roman finally cracked an eye open. Dark bags sat underneath them, but that was nothing new. "Like what?"

"An adventure. It doesn't matter, as long as we do it together."

Roman yawned and stretched like a lazy house cat. As he settled back into the mattress, he tried pulling Dinara to him, but she laughed and squirmed away. If she fell into that trap now, she'd never escape. Roman's body always radiated warmth, perfect for curling into and falling asleep against, but since they'd arrived in Gallonten, she'd been seeing him less and less. She'd like to spend this time with him doing something other than sleeping.

"Roman, I'm finally free of Edith! We should celebrate!"

"We celebrated plenty last night."

"Not in all the ways I would have liked," Dinara cooed, running her fingers meaningfully down to his waistband, loving the way his cheeks flushed in response. Between his tossing and turning and the morning's humidity, his curls were all mussed. Dinara loved seeing him like this, soft and unguarded. She said a quick thanks to Atiuh for the opportunity.

Roman caught her hand before it could trail any lower. "Make up your mind," he accused, though his smile was fond. "What happened to breakfast?"

"That can wait, don't you think?"

"And your adventure?"

"Forget it. Let's stay in."

Roman laughed. "But now I want to know what you had in mind."

"Ugh." Dinara quickly wracked her brain for something. As she looked around the room, her gaze fell on an opera mask hanging on the wall: a token from her first leading role. "I've got an idea. Do you remember what you said the first time you saw our costume trailer?"

"...No," Roman admitted, after a moment's thought.

Dinara rolled her eyes. "Your memory is really awful sometimes, Roman. You said you wanted to take one of the demon masks somewhere and play tricks on strangers."

Roman was silent for so long Dinara almost accused him of falling back asleep, but then a slow, mischievous smile spread across his face. "That doesn't sound like something I'd say, does it?"

Dinara gave him a flat look.

"Wouldn't you get in trouble?" he asked.

"With Cahrn? That's never stopped us before. Besides, he owes me after making me take Tabia's role. If he catches us, we can just say we were advertising and he'll have no choice but to accept it."

Roman felt around the bedside table until he found Dinara's watch. A small furrow appeared between his brows when he saw the time, but it was gone before Dinara could even comment, buried under a yawn. "It's a compelling proposition. Let's discuss this adventure of yours more while I cook."

Two hours later found them outside Dinara's trailer, costume crates open all around them. Explaining their mission to the costuming assistant had started badly, but Roman had complimented the taurel she was pressing and they'd bonded over the language of flowers—something Dinara didn't realize he even knew—and she'd agreed to look the other way. She'd even let them haul the crates back to Dinara's trailer, at Roman's insistence.

"What about this one?" Roman asked for the twelfth time. He pulled on a flat, wooden mask depicting an open-mouthed face. Dinara snorted when she saw it.

"If you're looking to scare people, that won't do. It's sky blue, Roman. It's *smiling*."

"It's snarling!"

"It's from one of our children's shows."

Roman's hands dropped from where he'd been holding them up like claws. The mask tipped to one side as he tilted his head. "The general public doesn't know that, do they? It could be scary if you weren't expecting it."

Dinara, who'd had a mask picked out for half an hour while Roman flitted between options, pulled hers on. It had a long, wrinkled snout and protrusive brows that formed shadows around the eyes. She took a step back, into the path, so Roman could see it better. "But it's nothing like mine."

Roman stared from behind his mask. "You might scare people *too* well with that one, Di. We want light mischief, not full-blown terror."

Before Dinara could respond, a blur with blonde hair rounded the corner and collided with her. As they hit the ground in a tangle of limbs, Dinara shrieked and the blur muttered strings of curses. When they managed to detangle themselves, Dinara saw that it was just a girl. An *orinian* girl. What was an orinian doing *here*? Dinara opened her mouth to ask, but at the sight of her mask, the girl shrieked in return.

"Wait, it's only a costume!" Roman said. Dinara scrambled to lift the mask so the girl could see.

The girl fell back on her ass in the dirt with a winded huff. "Oh," she said, punched-out. Before she could say anything else, a whistle sounded down the street.

Seeing the fearful look the girl cast in its direction, Roman didn't hesitate. He kicked the ends of the girl's cloak so they covered her tail, grabbed a helmet out of the closest crate, and dropped it onto her head. Only moments later, before the girl even had time to react, four men on horseback turned onto the path, their badges and helmets easily identifying them as Gallontean police. The girl tensed, but Roman subtly held out a hand, urging her to be still.

"What is this? What's with the masks?" one of the approaching officers called.

Roman lifted his mask and Dinara noticed the orinian girl give a startled jolt. "Officers," Roman greeted cheerfully. "Surely, you know where you are? This is the Webhon Players' camp; we're a traveling troupe from Adondai. Five shows a week at the Rinehart Festival and one for Unity, in fact, just last night."

That got the officers to lift their hands from the clubs at their sides, at least. Dinara pushed herself to her feet; she didn't know what Roman was doing, but she trusted him. For now, she'd play along. "We were taking stock of some old costumes," she said. "Is there a problem, officers?"

"We heard screams," another officer said, watching them through narrowed eyes.

"Ah, sorry to be a bother. A spider leapt out when Ms. Condeh opened a crate, she isn't fond of the little creatures. Rest assured, I've since eliminated the threat," Roman said with a winning smile. Dinara looked down at her feet, as if ashamed. The officers seemed to buy it.

"Please keep it down in the future," said the first officer. "Since you've been out here, did anyone suspicious come through here?"

Roman casually positioned himself in front of the orinian. "Suspicious how?"

"We're looking for an orinian fugitive. She's very dangerous."

While Dinara twitched at the word "dangerous," Roman didn't so much as blink. "I did see someone running toward the festival grounds. Now that you mention it, they might've had a tail," he said.

Without so much as a thank you, the officers took off again. Roman watched them go with a dark expression, but he'd brightened by the time he turned back to his companions. "There. That'll keep them busy."

"Are you sure about this? Is this safe?" Dinara asked Roman. The officers were long gone, but she still whispered.

Roman gestured at the orinian, who still sat on the ground with the helmet over her head, watching them. "She clearly needs help."

"They called her dangerous!"

"I'm right here," the girl pointed out, her voice muffled by papier-mâché.

"She's an orinian in Unity's capital city; it's not hard to figure out what happened. Be charitable," Roman said, making Dinara's cheeks heat up. She felt like a child, scolded for misbehaving, and she was relieved when Roman turned his attention back to the girl. He laughed when he finally got a look at the helmet he'd given her. It was round, painted like a baby's head with rosy cheeks and a single curl on its forehead. "That thing's scarier than both of our masks combined, Di. What show is that for?"

"Roman," Dinara chided.

"Roman...Hallisey?" the girl suddenly asked.

"You know him? Roman, do you know her? Is that why you did all of this? If you'd said so from the start—"

"I don't need to know her to hate Gallonten's cops," Roman said brightly. When the girl started to lift her helmet, he stopped her. "Not here. You're not going to hurt either of us, right?"

The girl violently shook her head, the helmet rocking.

"There. See?" he asked Dinara. "She means no harm. Now, let's all get acquainted. You know my name, and this is Dinara Condeh. You are...?"

"Um," the orinian said, staring at Roman. Only her eyes were visible behind the helmet, wide and unblinking. When Roman held a hand out, though, she let him pull her up. "Maebhe."

"Maebhe..." Dinara repeated thoughtfully. She gasped. "You're Gareth and Isobel's missing orinian! When I saw your tail, I wondered...but what a coincidence! Maebhe Cairn, right?"

"What's this?" Roman asked, brows furrowed.

"The Ranulfs told me about her last night. I was so drunk at that point, I nearly forgot. You might've been somewhere else, Roman."

Dinara was so excited that she didn't notice Maebhe backing slowly away. Roman noticed, though, and caught the girl by the wrist before she could get far. "Where are you going?" he asked.

Maebhe tried to pry his hand free, frowning when she couldn't get so much as a finger to budge. "I appreciate the help, but I really shouldn't have come here."

"But the Ranulfs will be so happy to hear you're okay! They've been looking everywhere for you," Dinara said.

Maebhe struggled harder against Roman's grip. "All the more reason for me to go."

"What? Why? They only want to help!"

At that, Maebhe stilled. Satisfied she wouldn't run, Roman released her. "Let us get you some food and a change of clothes. We've got bacon, eggs, and toast inside. You can decide what you want to do once you've eaten."

Maebhe's stomach decided for her, choosing that moment to grumble loudly. Her tail swished beneath her cloak, which was slightly too long for her. "I don't eat meat," she said. "But...I'll take the toast and eggs."

While Roman stuffed the costumes back into the crates, Dinara coaxed Maebhe into the trailer, served up food, and drew her a bath. Aside from her cloak, the girl's clothes were a mess—dirty, wrinkled, torn. She also, inexplicably, didn't have shoes. What she *did* have was nearly a foot on the petite Dinara, so they had to give her a set of Roman's things, instead.

Finally, when the costumes were back in the costume trailer and Maebhe sat on Dinara's mattress with wet hair, too-long trousers, and jam on her fingers, she began to open up.

"We had bad luck on our way here and ran into that group of officers near the festival grounds. There were even more of them, to start, but the boy helping me drew their attention to give me a chance to run," she said, briefly meeting Roman's gaze before settling on Dinara, instead. "I hope he's safe."

"Let's worry about *you*, first," Roman said. "It sounds like that's what he would've wanted."

Dinara stared at him. They were dealing with police and fugitives, but he didn't seem shaken at all. He'd lied to the police like it was nothing. The fact that Maebhe had been coming here, looking for *him*, specifically, also didn't seem to surprise him in the slightest. "But who was he?" she asked. "Why'd he bring you *here*? How did you know Roman's name?"

Maebhe glanced at Roman again, quickly and then away. "His name was Aleksir. I met him and...his friend last night. They said Roman could help me save my brother," she explained. When Roman didn't object, she added, "I don't know how much Gareth told you, but my brother and his fiancée were arrested. I, um, thought Gareth was working with Unity, so I ran from him. Isn't he a Magistrate?"

Roman shook his head. "Just the brother of one. He's naive, but a decent fellow overall. If he already knows you and wants to help, we should start with him. Getting your family free through the proper channels would be ideal, and he might have some pull."

Dinara didn't want to know what *improper* channels might look like. Truth told, she didn't want to know anything more about this situation at all. "Roman, this is bigger than us. Maybe we should just take her to Gareth, let him help instead."

"It's bigger than *you*, Di," Roman said, again with that tone—neither unkind nor condescending, more like the gentle scolding an elder might give to a child. But they were the same age, for Atiuh's sake! Dinara snapped her mouth shut and glared at him, but he crouched in front of Maebhe and didn't see.

"If you want my help, you need to tell me everything. Start from the beginning," he ordered. And so Maebhe obeyed, starting with her family's arrival in Gallonten, covering their arrest the day before and the way she tracked the police back to Unity Island, ending with that morning's adventure with the boy named Aleksir. It sounded like the beginning of a story, a show the players might put on.

"The Oracle of Damael," Dinara breathed, forgetting to be angry. What would one of the oracle's agents know about *Roman*? "Are you sure they worked for her? Really?"

Maebhe shrugged. "They had the tattoo."

"Tattoo?" Dinara asked.

Maebhe brightened, pointing to her long ear. A line of delicate gold earrings hung off it. "Don't you know the stories? The oracle's agents all have her symbol tattooed behind her ear, because their lady hears all. If you see the purple ink, you can trust them."

"The pigment can only be made in Damael," Roman explained, not meeting Dinara's eye. To Maebhe, he explained, "Di is from the north. The oracle's agents rarely make it up that far, so they don't have much cause to discuss her."

Dinara was staring at him again. "Roman, *you* have a purple symbol tattooed behind your ear."

Roman winced. He had the gall to look surprised that Dinara knew, as if she hadn't seen every inch of him. And as if it would free him from the conversation, he covered the spot with his hand. That explained how this Aleksir knew him—or knew *of* him, at the least. Dinara couldn't believe it. An agent of the Oracle? Her Roman? The players liked to speculate about his past, inventing all kinds of outlandish theories, but this really was *too* fantastical.

Maebhe watched them through her long bangs. Cautiously, she asked, "So you work for her, too? Did you ever meet Egil?"

Roman scoffed. "Hm? How old do you think I am?"

Maebhe stuck her tongue out in answer, clearly an instinctual response to his tone. "Aleksir seemed convinced that Egil's alive."

Briefly, very briefly, Roman stilled. Then, he laughed. "Did he? And you believed that?"

Maebhe shrugged. "Not really. Either way, he and his friend seemed confident you could help me, so I chose to trust him. Did I waste my time?"

Roman let out a slow breath. "You didn't," he said.

He said it so confidently, so seriously, that for a moment Dinara didn't even recognize the man before her. Where was her sweet, silly Roman, who flirted and teased and joked? Their trailer, normally so roomy, felt too small to hold the magnitude of this stranger. She *would* believe this person knew the oracle. She'd even believe he knew Egil.

But it was *Roman*. Wasn't it? In the end, she forced herself to look away. "Your story matches Gareth's, so I have to believe it, but I don't understand what's happening," she said. "What does Unity think one girl is going to do?"

"Protest, fight, spy, sabotage," Roman said, ticking off possibilities on his fingers. When he looked at her, she had to fight not to shudder. His eyes were a flat black, colder than Dinara had ever seen them. They pierced through her and past her, somehow making her feel both seen and invisible at once. "Realistically, they don't think she's going to do anything, they just don't want her or her family *here*—because having her here reminds Gallonteans that orinians are people, too."

Maebhe's lip wobbled. Seeing it, Roman blinked, his dark eyes softening, refocusing. By the time he opened his mouth to ask if she was okay, Maebhe had begun to cry.

"Look what you did!" Dinara accused, hurrying to sit beside Maebhe on the bed.

Though she tried to hold it back, Maebhe was a messy crier, and the harder she fought it the messier she got, blotchy and snotty and wet. Horrified, Dinara rubbed her back in soothing circles and Roman scrambled for a handkerchief. "Come now, Ms. Cairn," Roman said gently. "I'll help you and your family. Please don't cry."

"I'm not doing it on purpose!" Maebhe said, crying even harder. She scrubbed at her face. "But...call me Maebhe."

"Maebhe," Roman agreed. Desperately, he asked, "Would you like more toast?"

Maebhe nodded. And it seemed to help, too. She sat beside Dinara, sadly nibbling on toast and occasionally hiccupping as her tears dried.

"Roman, what about Unity?" Dinara asked.

"Kono ta'hy lehah," she said, switching to Sheman so Maebhe wouldn't be able to understand. She wouldn't give the girl any more cause to cry, if she could help it, but she had to voice her concerns.

Roman switched as well, though his own phrasing was halting and messy. "They'll only kill me if they catch me. But they have to catch me." He frowned. "How would I say that as a...*conditional*?" he asked, switching back to the standardized Ellesian for the word "conditional."

"You want to ask me about *grammar*? Now? Roman, I don't care if you work for the Oracle of Damael. You can't smuggle fugitives out of the capital city, whether they're innocent or not. Unity will stop you."

Roman shrugged. "They can try."

"What is *wrong* with you?" Dinara hissed. "Who are you?"

Roman shook his head and switched back to Ellesian for good. "Dinara, I'm not asking you to join me, but I *will* get Maebhe and her family home."

"Tell me something true," Dinara said, still in Sheman. "Tell me one honest thing and I'll help."

Roman regarded her for a long moment. Dinara thought that was pity in the set of his brow, but there was nothing at all in his flat black eyes. "I know you're worried," he said, "But I have the skill to do this. That is the truth."

Dinara released the breath she'd been holding. "Fine," she said.

"Let's visit Gareth," Roman said, turning to Maebhe. "If we're lucky, he can use those family connections of his to free Kieran and Íde. If not, I know another way."

"Visit? Don't you have his phone number?" Dinara asked.

"No, but I know where they're staying. If we go now —"

"*I* have their phone number," Dinara said. "Isobel gave it to me last night."

Roman blinked, and then his expression thawed. His smile was almost the one Dinara remembered. "I could kiss you, Di! Maebhe, give us an hour. The phone's across camp, but Dinara and I will be back as soon as we can."

"O-okay," Maebhe said, but they were already gone, Roman dragging Dinara off faster than she could keep up. To the now-empty trailer, Maebhe announced, "I'll just wait here, then."

Chapter Thirteen

Maebhe didn't know how long she waited, but it was definitely more than an hour. It was at least long enough to snoop around the trailer, get bored, take a nap, then uncover and start perusing a book on acting she'd found. Seeing Roman and Dinara's long faces when they returned, she raised an eyebrow at them from the bed. "No luck?" she asked.

Roman sighed and flopped onto the open spot beside her, Maebhe yelping in surprise as the mattress bounced. He'd been so cheerful when he left; he must have suffered indeed in the time since. "Magistrate Ranulf won't budge," he said, voice muffled. "Gareth's been trying to get your family released since they were first taken, but he's had no luck."

"We learned some useful information, though," Dinara said from the doorway. She lingered there, as unwilling to come inside as she'd been to tangle herself in Maebhe's problems. Not that Maebhe blamed her. But where Roman was difficult to read, with his fluctuating moods and guarded smiles, Dinara was easy. Her eyes kept sliding over to Roman, emotions flurrying through them: concern, worry, fear. It was all because of Maebhe, and she couldn't help but feel guilty.

"Your brother and his fiancée were detained on charges of conspiring against Unity. They're being held on the island," Roman explained, rolling onto his back and staring at the ceiling. "It's nice to know where they are, but it doesn't actually help us get them back."

"Still, they're alive! That must be a relief," Dinara said with an encouraging smile. Maebhe didn't much feel like smiling back, but Dinara had been so kind, it felt like the least she could do.

"Unfortunately, 'on the island' almost certainly means 'in Unity's prison,' which is impossible to break into. With no Magistrate's brother to ease the way for us, that poses a challenge," Roman said.

"So what do we do? You're not suggesting we give up?" Maebhe asked.

Roman shook his head. "I said impossible to *break* into. I know a secret way. I can walk us straight in, but it'll be dangerous."

Dinara opened her mouth, then shut it just as quickly, biting her lip, and Maebhe guessed Roman hadn't explained anything more to her in their time away.

"Let's go," Roman said. "Maebhe, put that cloak back on. We're going to visit an old friend of mine."

Roman led them north, deeper into Gallonten. Maebhe should've been suspicious of their direction—*away* from Unity Island, instead of toward—but she was in too deep to question her choices now. For her, anxiety ran in a limited supply, and she'd used it all up crying and worrying about Kieran and Íde. So when this strange man, all secrets one moment and smiles the next, had given her the first glimmer of hope she'd felt since Kieran was taken, she decided she would trust him. Even if it led to her death, she would trust him. And she'd keep his secrets, too—a favor for a favor.

What else could she do? Strike off alone again? Not likely.

Beside her, Dinara had less faith. Her eyes never left Roman's back, though instead of voicing the concerns that were clearly ready to bubble out of her, she followed along quietly. Roman wove through shortcuts and turned down hidden paths like someone who'd lived in Gallonten his whole life, managing to avoid all the major roads in the process. As they went on, Maebhe questioned less and less that Roman might know what he was doing.

Finally, they ended up in a quiet neighborhood—middle class, if Maebhe had to guess, though the architecture here was so different from that in Orean—filled with rows of tightly-packed, near-identical brick houses.

"Where are we going?" Dinara finally asked, keeping her voice to a whisper.

"I know a smuggler who lives near here. He can get anyone onto the island, only..." Roman trailed off, wrinkling his nose. "Ah, forget it. I just hope neither of you have sensitive noses."

Being an orinian, of course, Maebhe *did*. Before she could ask what he meant, he stopped in front of one of the houses, this one utterly indistinguishable from the others. It could have just as easily belonged to a doctor or a merchant as a smuggler. With its curtains drawn shut, Maebhe couldn't peek inside.

"If Ivey's not home, we'll break in and wait," Roman said.

"Break in?" Dinara squeaked.

"Trust me, he's not the type to mind."

While Maebhe and Dinara lingered at the gate, Roman knocked twice, the bass knocker creaking in protest. He paused, then knocked three more times. Only upon the fifth knock, the door flew open to reveal an older, disheveled-looking man with a full beard and wild eyes. His hair, which stuck in every direction, was the sort of seashell-gray that implied it had once been a bright, vivid red.

Roman opened his mouth to speak, but the man cut him off, saying, "Code's changed." With that, he slammed the door in Roman's face. Roman glanced sheepishly back at Maebhe and Dinara, then knocked again, more insistently. This time, when the door opened, the man was grinning. "Only kidding, Aim! It's great to see you alive, my friend!"

"Alive?" Maebhe asked, at the same time Dinara asked, "Aim?"

Roman stood at least a foot taller than this stranger, but that didn't stop the man from dragging Roman into a hug. Roman squawked indignantly, struggled, and finally gave in, his whole face scrunching up as he wrinkled his nose. It was…cute. Maebhe hadn't been sure when they first met, but she thought now that Roman couldn't be much older than her.

"Roman? What's going on?" Dinara asked.

"Roman?" the man repeated, pulling away to look Roman up and down. Holding Roman's shoulders, he then peered around him to study Dinara. When his gaze finally landed on Maebhe's cloaked form, curiosity ignited behind his eyes. He pushed Roman aside, toward the open door. "Come in, come in."

Maebhe understood what Roman meant about sensitive noses immediately upon crossing the threshold. Beneath the smell of cigars and old furniture was something wet and rotten. It was overwhelmingly foul. Though Dinara seemed not to notice, Roman gave Maebhe a knowing look. Maebhe flushed and stepped inside so the smuggler could shut the door behind her. It was lucky that she still wore the hood. Her ears, the most expressive part of her, were pressed flat to her head, drawn back in distaste.

Her voice, she could at least keep even. "This is…nice," she said. She didn't want to offend the man whose help she desperately needed.

It was true, though, if you could get past the smell. This smuggler had eclectic taste, his front rooms filled with all sorts of strange collections—mounted rifles, pinned butterflies, framed photos and other ephemera. The decor was patterned and bright, giving the place a homey feel. Maebhe lowered her hood as she looked around, and the smuggler regarded her with even more interest now that it was off. "An orinian," he said. "I might have known. Here, I'd hoped this was a social call, Aim."

"Sorry," Roman said, not sounding particularly apologetic.

"And you're a maranet, aren't you?" Maebhe asked. She'd never met one in person; they were rare, even here in Gallonten. In addition to being a mostly northern people, their long lives meant they didn't have the same drive to reproduce as the other human peoples. It kept their population low.

When the smuggler grinned, he revealed a double set of sharp-tipped canines. "The name's Ivey."

"Ivey...?" Dinara asked.

"Just Ivey."

"This is Maebhe Cairn and Dinara Condeh," Roman said.

"Let me guess: Ms. Maebhe needs a swift exit out of Gallonten."

"Nothing gets past you," Roman said with a smile. He wandered into the dimly lit sitting room, and they all followed him without question, as if it was *his* house. Even Ivey. Though the street-facing curtains were shut, several lamps throughout the room gave them enough to see by. "Before that, we need to use your tunnels."

"Tunnels?" Dinara asked.

Ivey frowned. "What for? If the route is unfamiliar to me, I'll require time to map it for you." He spoke formally, Maebhe noticed, like a character from an old book.

"You won't. It's the same route we used last time."

"Last time? Surely, you can't mean..." Ivey trailed off, then crossed his arms. "Wait just a moment, now. I've heard such stories about you that you wouldn't believe, and it had been my belief that I'd never see you again. Now here you are, healthy and hale and not even a day older, besides, claiming you want to go back to *that* place? I'm owed some explanations, I think."

"You're not the only one," Dinara said, crossing her arms as well. "What do you mean, 'last time?' How do you and Ivey know each other? Does this have to do with the Oracle?"

Maebhe took a definitive step *back* from the conversation, instead wandering over to Ivey's pinned butterflies to separate herself from it as obviously as possible. He had an impressive collection. She recognized at least one specimen, gold and spotted, from the mountain forests behind Orean. She wished she was there, not here. None of this was fair.

"I'll explain everything to both of you," she heard Roman say, "But only when this is all over."

Ivey folded first, rocking back on his heels and heaving a sigh. "Very well. I'll grant you access to my tunnels, but only on the condition you dine with me afterward. You promised last time, too, right before you fled Gallonten with Unity's Enforcers at your heels. I know you better now, you rascal, and won't let you slip away again. I'm an old man; I demand my time to reminisce."

"You had to flee Gallonten? What is he talking about?"

"Dinner is yours, as long as you pay," Roman told Ivey. He perched on the arm of Ivey's sofa and told Dinara, "Ivey helped me out of a toxic workplace. That's all. About the tunnels, there's a web of them running under the city—sewage tunnels, underdrains, even some old smuggling routes that predate Unity's founding. They're impossible to navigate if you don't know what you're doing, but Ivey was one of the original contractors on the project almost three hundred years ago, when they were first expanding Gallonten's infrastructure."

"Over three hundred years now, Aim," Ivey interrupted. "Quite a bit over."

"Really? I didn't realize," Roman said, eyes wide. He shook his head. "The point is, Ivey knows a path to Unity's prison."

"Aim, to get to the prison from my tunnels, you'll have to—"

"I know. It won't be a problem," Roman said sharply. When Maebhe met Roman's eye, though, he winked and gave a cheerful smile. It was about as real, Maebhe suspected, as the "orinian" glassware Ivey had displayed on his shelf: convincing until you spotted the inconsistencies in the pattern.

Ivey rocked back on his heels again. "I know you love your swords, but you should bring a gun, too. They'll all have them. I have one I can lend you."

Roman wrinkled his nose, but nodded. Beside Maebhe, Dinara looked ill. When Ivey left the room, Maebhe pressed down on Dinara's shoulder until the girl took the hint and dropped onto the sofa behind her, her skirts fanning out over the patterned fabric. As she laid back and closed her eyes, Maebhe decided to turn the conversation away from firepower. "Why does he call you Aim?" she asked.

"It's just an old nickname."

"How many names do you *have*?"

At that, Roman's lips quirked. "A few."

"A few?" Dinara asked, opening her eyes again. "Why do I only know the one?"

"It just...never came up?" Roman said.

Pivoting again, Maebhe asked, "How long will this take? Will we be able to get Kieran and Íde back today?"

"We?" Roman asked. "You're not going."

"What! You can't mean to go alone?" Maebhe asked.

Dinara stood again in a flurry of fabric. "Roman, you can't!"

"I'm not taking either of you with me. If we run into trouble, what will you do?"

"I can fire a gun," Maebhe said, jutting her chin out. "My brother taught me."

To her surprise, Roman didn't immediately turn her down.

Instead, he looked her up and down, considering. "Are you a good shot?" he asked.

"Decent. And I'm a good runner, too. If there's trouble, believe me when I say I'll just leave it to you."

At that, Roman's smile actually reached his cold eyes, making them seem somehow warmer. It was possibly the first real smile Maebhe had seen from him. "Fine, but only because I'll need help identifying your brother when I find him."

Maebhe nodded, glad she hadn't mentioned that said brother was an identical twin.

"And what about me?" Dinara asked. "You can't stop me from coming. If you leave me here all alone, I'll worry myself sick. Roman, please."

Roman sighed. "If I let you join, you stay down in the tunnels. No going up to the island with us. Agreed?"

Dinara nodded.

When Ivey returned, it was with a whole armful of supplies: a revolver, a canvas pouch with spare bullets, a pocket lantern, a rope, a crowbar. He passed Roman the gun and kept the rest for himself, tucking everything but the lantern into a satchel at his side. While Roman passed the revolver to Maebhe, Ivey delivered instructions: "While we're down there, it is *imperative* that you memorize the route to the best of your abilities. If we get separated, or if anything happens to me, you'll need to be able to return on your own. While we're down there, do not speak needlessly. Sound carries in the tunnels, and despite Roman's glowing praise, I am not the only one who knows these routes."

"If we do meet anyone, run. Leave them to me," Roman added.

"With pleasure," Ivey said. "I hope you don't mind, but I plan on staying in the tunnels this time. I'm not as young as I once was."

"I was going to ask you to stay back, anyway. Dinara will be waiting with you," Roman said. He clapped his hands together, then looked over their mismatched group. "Shall we?"

The entrance to Ivey's tunnels, it turned out, was disguised as an old cistern in his basement. Maebhe expected water when Ivey first lifted the hatch, but the inside was hollow, a hole at the bottom leading deeper into darkness. More of that smell oozed out. It was impossible *not* to smell it, now, and even Dinara wrinkled her nose. Maebhe guessed, "That leads to the sewage tunnels?"

"Am I going to need a bath after this?" Dinara asked.

"It's not too late to stay back," Roman offered. In answer, Dinara scoffed and dug around in her pockets until she found a strip of cloth, then used it to tie her hair back. After a moment's thought, she pulled out a second and passed it to Maebhe.

"Thanks!" Maebhe said cheerfully, piling her long hair into a messy bun atop her head.

"It's not so bad, once you've grown accustomed. We'll move out of the sewage tunnels quickly," Ivey said while Roman swung his legs over the side of the cistern and dropped in.

The thin bar of the lantern's light fell on the entrance at the bottom, just large enough for a single person to fit through, and Maebhe glimpsed the first prongs of a ladder leading down. Roman took the lantern from Ivey, looping the handle around his wrist before starting his descent.

Due to the cistern's size, Maebhe had to wait for Roman to climb down before she and Ivey could follow. Dinara, small enough to squeeze in next to them, brought up the rear. She, Maebhe, and Ivey leaned over the hole to watch Roman climb and saw the faint glimmer of light hitting water at the bottom.

"Shit, that smells," Maebhe complained, plugging her nose.

"Your word choice might be more fitting than you intended," Ivey said. With a good-natured pat on Maebhe's shoulder, he started his own climb down. The joke startled a laugh out of Maebhe. It struck her, finally, that these tunnels would lead to Kieran and Íde. For that, she'd wade through as much shit as she had to.

"If I can handle Kieran after he takes his boots off, I can handle this," she said, mostly for Dinara's benefit. The girl had been looking uncertain, but Maebhe's comment at least made her crack a smile. Before Dinara could lose courage, Maebhe asked, "After you?"

One at a time, they descended the ladder. It was almost exactly as Maebhe expected—narrow, dark, smelly—but the one pleasant surprise was that she didn't have to walk through shit, after all. A dry sidewalk ran parallel to dark water Maebhe tried not to look at closely. Trickles of natural light reached them, too, so that they didn't have to rely entirely on the lantern.

"I'm going to be sick," Dinara mumbled.

"If you need to throw up, rest assured it won't be the worst thing to have gone into this water," Roman said cheerfully, earning a chuckle from Ivey.

"Not helpful, Roman."

Maebhe laughed, too, but when the sound echoed, her ears pressed flat to her head. She remembered what Ivey said about silence. They all seemed to, after that, and it settled heavily between them. Together, they pressed onward, following Roman's lead just as they had on the walk to Ivey's.

To Maebhe, it felt like hours had passed before the tunnels changed, one flowing into another: the ceilings stretched higher, the water deepened, flowed faster as more trickles from branching tunnels converged. Then Ivey redirected them, turned them down a narrow path—so narrow that Maebhe had to turn sideways, inching through while holding her cloak so Dinara wouldn't step on it from behind. In that tunnel, the path tilted downhill, the texture of the walls changed. Smooth, vaguely slimy brick changed to rough stone that caught on

Maebhe's clothing. It reminded her of cave exploration; if she closed her eyes and ignored the smell, she could imagine she was exploring the cave systems outside Orean, Kieran right behind her.

Then they came out the other side and found themselves in a new tunnel system entirely. The tiled walls struck Maebhe as old, depicting some sprawling pattern she could only see a fraction of at a time. It was the darkest it had been since they started their journey, no more diffused sunslight to keep them on their path, so Maebhe grabbed Dinara's hand and the back of Ivey's jacket. She'd almost grabbed Roman, instead, but something stopped her at the last moment. For some reason, even facing the darkness felt easier than touching him.

"We're under the bridge, in the old smuggling tunnels," Roman whispered. "If we're going to run into anyone else, it's going to be here. Remember what I said back at the house: leave them to me."

"How did they build this?" Maebhe whispered back. "Aren't we underwater?"

"Dragons. Negotiating those contracts was a chore, let me tell you," Ivey answered.

Dragons. Maebhe gave a wistful sigh. "I didn't get to talk to a single dragon on this trip. I was ready for it, too; I took draconic in school. I can understand 'how are you' and 'the washrooms are that way' and even 'please get off my tail.'"

Ahead of them, Roman snorted, but Dinara gave Maebhe's hand a light squeeze. "This must be so hard. I'm sure all of this will blow over quickly. War will never really happen. I'm sure of it."

Maebhe wasn't. Still, she smiled at Dinara, even if Dinara couldn't see it. When Roman and Ivey kept quiet, Maebhe chose to believe it didn't mean anything. It wasn't that they disagreed, they were just focused. That was all.

Before long, the tunnel climbed gradually upward. Water re-entered the tunnel at some point, too now flowing past their ankles.

This water was clean, too—Maebhe guessed they were in the storm drains under the island, now. The hints of sunslight that streamed down through grates above confirmed it.

"Are you sure you can do this, Aim?" Ivey asked, just enough light hitting his face to reveal the concerned set of his jaw.

"I've done it before."

"That's not what I asked. Last time—"

"Don't remind me," Roman interrupted. His voice was harsh, cutting above the rushing water like a blade. He laughed, then, as if to soften it. "Don't worry, Ivey. This time will be different."

Ivey nodded. "Then all that's left is to find you a way up."

CHAPTER FOURTEEN

THE TUNNELS CONTINUED TO CONTRACT as they walked, eventually reaching a point where Maebhe and Roman had to stoop to avoid hitting their heads. Despite that, Maebhe didn't feel claustrophobic; sunslight splashed off the walls ahead, though the curve of the tunnel blocked Maebhe's view of its source.

Roman explained their route as they walked. "Picture Unity Island as a crescent. At one end is the courthouse and clock tower, at the other Unity's prison. The bridge connects at the innermost curve of the crescent," he said. In the dim light, Maebhe could just make out him mapping the curves with his free hand while he spoke, the other still bearing the lantern. "The further you get from the clock tower, the fewer buildings you'll find. All that surrounds the prison in the north are fields and watchtowers, so there's no way to approach from ground-level without being seen."

"So we're approaching them from...not ground level?" Maebhe asked.

Roman smiled at her as they passed under a grate, streaks of sunslight flashing over his features. Maebhe wondered why he kept whispering—what was above their heads right now? Some important

Unity building or another? When she'd toured the island with Kieran and Íde, she'd been shocked at how many there were. She couldn't even guess at what they were all for.

"Good catch," Roman said. "The prison itself is made up of several buildings—administrative offices, inmate housing, the cafeteria and laundry facilities, and so on. In the complex, there's also barracks. The Unity soldiers who live inside come and go at odd hours and can't always use the public bridge. Three guesses which route they take."

He'd stumbled strangely over the word *soldier*, as if he'd meant to use a different one and swapped it out at the last second. Unable to stop herself, Maebhe glanced over her shoulder, half-expecting to see one of these "soldiers" lurking in the shadows.

"So if you take their path to the barracks, you can get from there to the prison," Dinara guessed, not sounding pleased about any of it. "That's what you're getting at?"

"Exactly. The barracks connect to the main block via a skyway, so that's our access point," Roman said, pretending not to notice Dinara's tone. When they passed under another grate and that brief flash of sunslight came again, though, Maebhe noticed his furrowed brow.

"I thought Unity didn't have a standing army," Maebhe pointed out. "You just call on the armies of the nations pledged to you. I learned about that in school."

"They're not an army, they're just...fighters. Very strong ones," Roman said.

"Whatever they are, how is marching through their *barracks* in any way a good idea?" Dinara asked. "What will you do if they catch you?"

"Fight back, I suppose."

Beside Maebhe, Ivey murmured something fervently under his breath. It sounded suspiciously to Maebhe like a prayer.

"Fight the strong fighters?" Dinara clarified. "That's your plan?"

"Don't make it sound so dire. They're strong, not unbeatable," Roman said, clearly trying to convince himself as much as he was Dinara. "At this time of day, there should only be a few of them around. If we're lucky, the rest are out on missions or attending to business."

Missions, he said, like they were spies of some kind. *Fight*, he said, like Maebhe could do any such thing.

"This is going to be dangerous," she said. Logically, she'd known that from the start. But if the smuggler who defied Unity for a living was nervous, touching each on a string of beads while he prayed under his breath, if *Roman* was nervous, with all Maebhe knew about him—then she was afraid.

"Yes," Roman said, simply. Those splashes of sunslight had turned to a steady stream now, steeping them in it, but shadows cut across Roman's face. His brows were drawn together, casting shadows that made him look like a different person entirely.

When they rounded a final bend, Maebhe held up a hand to shield her eyes, suddenly confronted with the pale, blinding sky. Past a gated drainage pipe was the sea and its horizon, storm water running past their ankles to empty into the sea ahead.

"Here we are. Ivey?" Roman asked.

Rifling through his bag, Ivey withdrew a small roll of tools and passed it to Roman. While Roman withdrew two long, narrow needles and turned his attention to the lock on the gate, Maebhe pressed herself against its bars, trying to see directly below them. What she found was a five-foot drop to a beach, where a rocky stream actually carried the water to the sea. Suddenly, the lock clicked and the door Maebhe was leaning against gave. She nearly fell, but Roman caught one of the bars, keeping the door shut before she could plunge headfirst into the stream she'd been trying to see. She laughed breathlessly. "Ah, sorry."

With a snort, Roman passed his lantern to Dinara, who took it with the same disapproving frown she'd been wearing since she saw the lock-picking tools, and held his hand out for Ivey's satchel. "Wait here for us. If we're not back in two hours, leave. Don't look for us."

"As you wish," Ivey agreed.

"How can you say that?" Dinara asked. "What am I supposed to do if you just disappear?"

Roman sighed. "Try Gareth. If we're caught, he might be able to help Maebhe, at least," he said. Before Dinara could argue, he kissed her cheek and then was gone, hopping down to the beach and carrying on without waiting for Maebhe to catch up.

Maebhe tried for an encouraging smile. "I'm sure we'll be fine. He seems to know what he's doing."

"As if that's not worrying in its own way," Dinara sighed.

Unsure what more she could say, Maebhe patted Dinara's shoulder and jumped down as well, landing far less smoothly than Roman had and almost losing her balance on the slippery rocks. She heard the gate creak shut behind her.

"We'll keep this way unlocked," Ivey called, as loud as he dared. "Be quick, before any Enforcers pass through."

Roman waved over his shoulder as Maebhe picked through the water after him. She craned her neck as she went; the two of them walked along a sheer cliff face, bracketed on the other side by the endless sea. "Where are we?" she asked. From here, though, she couldn't see the mainland, and that told her enough.

"The outside of the crescent," Roman confirmed. He pointed behind them. "The clock tower is that way, which means we're headed in the right direction."

Maebhe looked back the way he pointed, but she couldn't see any sign of the tower—just rock and sky. Obviously, he'd been this way before, enough times to have the route memorized. "These soldiers—

or Enforcers, was it? How do you know about them?" Maebhe asked. It was the only explanation that made sense.

She thought she saw Roman wince. "I was one of them, once."

"That's the workplace Ivey helped you escape?"

"Hm. Clever," Roman said. "Exactly right. Once you become an Enforcer, you can't exactly quit, but Ivey helped me get away."

"And now you're back."

"Now I'm back," Roman agreed. "Put your hood up, Maebhe."

Maebhe scrambled to cover her ears again, though onlookers from above were unlikely. With the cliff's magnitude, you'd have to be standing toes to the edge, looking straight down, to spot them. Even so, they kept as close to the rocks as they could, staying in the cliff's shadows.

"You said that if they catch us, Gareth might be able to help *me*," she said, eager to keep the conversation going. "No hope for you, then?"

Roman laughed humorlessly. "If they catch us, I won't be alive for Gareth to help."

"Those sound like bad colleagues," Maebhe said. She gave him a sly look, then added, "But all that makes sense, if you really are—"

"Watch it," Roman warned, shooting her a knowing look back. "I know where you're going with that. My price for helping you, Maebhe Cairn, is that you ask no more questions."

Maebhe bit her lip. She managed to keep quiet for about ten seconds, then asked, "No more questions at *all*? Not even about the prison? Or our plan for getting Kieran and Íde? What if there's something I need to know for our mission?"

"Is there?" Roman asked.

"Why doesn't Dinara know about any of this? Aren't you together?"

"That has *nothing* to do with our mission," Roman pointed out.

"Then tell me more about the Enforcers. I can tell you're afraid of them. Should I be worried?"

"I am afraid of them," Roman admitted, his voice soft, "But you don't have to be. As long as you stay behind me, I'll keep you safe."

Maebhe believed him. She thought maybe she shouldn't, but she did. Back in Orean, they had their own stories. They had their own heroes. Roman fit so naturally among them that it was natural, too, for Maebhe to put her faith in him. It was like following a familiar script, coloring within bold lines — of course it was easy.

"I'll tell you this about the Enforcers: they're Unity's best kept secret, and they'll go to great lengths to *keep* it secret. They'd kill you for even knowing they exist."

"Seems like they'd kill me just for being orinian, too."

Roman sighed. "You may be right."

"Can I ask one last question? No more prying into secrets, I promise."

"That was a question," Roman pointed out, lips twitching when Maebhe rolled her eyes. "Fine. But if I don't like it, I'm not answering."

"Your prerogative. I was just wondering...why are you *really* helping me? It would've been easy for you to just leave me where you found me. You didn't *have* to help."

Roman sighed. "To tell you the truth, I didn't want to. I hate this feeling — the weight of someone else's trust in my hands, the heavy steps out of safety and into danger. And I hate knowing that if I fail, I'm failing both of us. It's terrifying, and you're right: the coward's choice would be easier. The coward's choice is *always* easier, but it's also the one they want us to make — everyone out there looking to hurt us. As long as I'm alive, I won't give them the satisfaction. So I did have to help, in a way — for both me and for you, and for a future without *them*," he said. "Besides, regret weighs heavier than fear, and I know which choice lets me sleep at night."

Maebhe dropped her gaze, watching the sand shift and cling to her wet boots. "I understand," she said. She didn't, not really, but she'd never had to make the selfless choice or fight enemies like this. Rescuing Kieran and Íde was the closest she'd come, but it was still Roman doing all the work, and it was as much for herself as for them.

As they circled the island, the strip of beach narrowed until they could no longer walk side by side. Maebhe, who kept looking up at the cliff's face as they went, waded more than once into the water by accident. To distract herself from *why* they were here, she'd turned to focusing on where they were, as if this was just another tour. It struck her how excellent this spot would be for cliff diving. The water was deep, free of visible obstacles, the cliff jutting out above to provide a good jumping point. If she had to guess, she'd call it seventy feet: less than her record, but pushing her comfort range.

She loved the rush of adrenaline, the fear of falling. It certainly beat what she felt now, this knotted and tangled terror. It was wilder, freer. The anticipation made it worse. She thought it just might kill her until finally, a sinister-looking gray building appeared over the cliff's crest. It grew and grew until it loomed high above them. Ears flat to her head, Maebhe asked, "We're breaking into *that*?"

"*That* is the cafeteria," Roman corrected. "The main block is behind it."

They rounded a sharp bend and moved into the inner curve of the island's crescent. Maebhe could see the mainland in the distance, now, and Unity's bridge arching over the water. Looking up at it from below, it seemed much larger. "How do we get from down here to up there? Are we supposed to scale the wall?"

"You'll see," was all Roman said. His hand never strayed far from his sword, now.

And she did. Just before the strip of beach ended entirely, they came upon a narrow opening in the rock, hidden behind sharp outcroppings. Maebhe grimaced when she saw it, but reluctantly followed Roman into the creepy cave. To her surprise, she found that it wasn't so creepy on the inside, after all. Lit from above by orangeish industrial lights, the walls were smooth, the cave clearly man-made. She and Roman stepped up onto dry cement and toward a rusty service elevator built into the far wall.

Roman frowned at it. "That wasn't here in my day."

"Really? It looks ancient."

Roman hummed. Instead of the elevator, he made for the stone steps beside it. They appeared to climb up without end—for at least seventy feet, if Maebhe had to guess. "Is there a reason we're not taking the elevator?"

"That thing looks loud enough to alert the entire island to our presence," Roman whispered. "We don't know who might be waiting at the top."

Cowed, Maebhe followed him without further complaint, ears still flat to her head. After a climb that seemed to last ages, the stairs led to a tidy cellar, the cellar to another short flight of stairs that ended in a closed door. Roman stopped at the bottom of those stairs, his hands clenching into fists and unclenching at his sides. Unsure what else to do, Maebhe waited several paces back, watching him with wide eyes.

"I'm sorry," he said finally, with a short, self-deprecating laugh. "It's been some time since I was last here."

"Take your time," Maebhe said, trying to sound encouraging. While she'd never been good with vulnerable emotions, either expressing *or* witnessing them, she wanted to help him for all that he was helping her.

Roman squeezed his eyes shut. By the time he opened them again, the vulnerability was gone. He rolled his shoulders, gestured for Maebhe to wait, then started up the stairs alone. Maebhe watched as he eased the door open, peered cautiously around it. Her tail lashed back and forth behind her, the suspense too much.

Then Roman was gone, leaving Maebhe alone, and this commonplace cellar suddenly felt much scarier. Maebhe waited thirty whole seconds, counting in her head, before deciding she couldn't wait any longer. She hurried up the stairs, boots quiet on the old stone, and mirrored Roman's earlier position, peering cautiously around the door just in time to see Roman ease a body to the ground. He cushioned the woman's head as he laid her down; some comfort, as it meant she must be alive.

Maebhe knew killing might be required—had known it more from the look in Roman's cold eyes than anything he'd said—but she didn't want to *see* it. She didn't even want to know about it. Maybe that was selfish, expecting Roman to kill for her while she looked the other way.

She crept slowly into the room, trying to see the girl's face. She was just that: a girl with sweet features, barely twenty and dressed in a utilitarian vest-trousers combination. A perfectly normal-looking person. Now that Maebhe considered it, *everything* about this place looked normal. Too normal. She eyed the bland common room, plainly furnished and lit by narrow windows. The strangest thing was the table before Roman, which sat full of half-assembled weapons. The girl must have been standing at it when Roman snuck up on her.

Maebhe watched him while he watched the girl at his feet. He slowly drew his sword, inch by inch.

Maebhe knew he intended to kill her, and she was struck by the urge to stop him—or at the very least, to stand by his side while he did it. Staying back was the coward's choice, and Roman had already made the selfless one to come here for *her*. Whatever else happened, he shouldn't have to face it alone.

On her next step into the room, though, the floor creaked. It was barely audible, even to her own ears, but Roman whirled to face her, his sword drawn between one moment and the next. His wild expression eased when he saw Maebhe, but then his eyes widened. "Maebhe!"

Maebhe didn't need the warning; her ears had picked up the telltale *swish* of fabric behind her. She dove forward on instinct, hitting the ground and rolling while Roman leaped over her. She heard the *clang* of metal striking metal, and by the time Maebhe got her bearing and spun around, Roman was facing off against a tall, broad man with dark mutton chops, their swords locked.

Aside from the sword in his hand, this man was also utterly unassuming. Uncannily so. If Maebhe had passed him in the street, she would've thought him some sort of workman—not a spy or an assassin, or whatever else the Enforcers may be. Just who were these people?

"Who in the hells are you?" the man asked, looking between Maebhe and Roman with what Maebhe would call *mild irritation*, as if they were ants in a kitchen. His gaze flicked from Maebhe's ears to her birthmarks to her tail, cataloguing her orinian features.

Roman laughed and shoved at their crossed blades, the strength behind it forcing the man back a step. His eyes widened. Grinning and brandishing his sword, Roman said, "If you were smart, you'd keep your eyes on me. You're far too outmatched to get distracted in this fight."

CHAPTER FIFTEEN

WHEN ROMAN FINALLY ATTACKED, alarm quickly swept away the Enforcer's irritation. He could barely keep up with Roman, could barely block each new swing in time. It wasn't that he moved slowly. On the contrary, he moved faster, than anyone Maebhe had ever seen, almost too fast for her eyes to follow. Roman just moved faster.

Despite her various athletic pursuits, Maebhe knew little about fighting. Kieran had taught her basic self-defense, but watching this was like a farm boy with a plow horse judging the worldwide dressage finals.

When Roman attacked, the Enforcer dodged. When the Enforcer dodged, Roman feinted, spun, and swung, each clash of steel a sharp staccato, a squeal of metal. Roman struck the first blow, and Maebhe only knew it from the Enforcer's grunt of pain and the crimson that bloomed across his thigh when they broke apart. He favored his uninjured leg, after that, as that crimson stain spread down his leg and soaked into the rug beneath them. They both stepped in and out of it as they fought, tracking blood across the florals. Maebhe felt ill watching it—as ill as the Enforcer looked. Sweat dotted his brow, panic and pain sank into the lines around his eyes. When he stumbled,

Roman caught him with a heave kick that sent him flying into the table of weapons, which splintered and collapsed under his weight.

Maebhe scrambled out of the way in time, but when she reached back and her fingers brushed warm skin, she yelped. Behind her was the Enforcer girl Roman had knocked unconscious. For a horrifying moment, Maebhe thought the girl had awoken, but her chest rose and fell as steady as before, steady amidst the chaos. This close, Maebhe noticed something strange on the girl's wrist: a fresh brand, a swirling loop with a sword running through it.

"Are you all right?" Roman asked, making Maebhe turn back around.

Why was he worrying about *her*? In the time he spent asking, his opponent scrambled to his feet. Roman had wasted his advantage just to make sure she was unharmed. "Fine!" Maebhe said, quickly.

Then the Enforcer attacked, and Roman could no longer talk. Belatedly remembering the gun from Ivey, Maebhe drew it and trained it on the two men but had to lower it again only seconds later. They were moving too fast. She couldn't risk hitting Roman by mistake.

Finally pressing an opening, the Enforcer tackled Roman, catching him by the waist and making him drop his sword in his surprise. By the time they'd hit the ground, though, Roman had flipped their positions. Straddling the man, he threw a punch that *cracked* when it struck the man's jaw. Roman swung again and again, the Enforcer struggling to buck him off until eventually, his struggling stopped. Even then, Roman didn't stop hitting.

Maebhe pushed to her feet. "Roman, stop! Don't kill him!" she cried. If she'd ever thought she could be okay with killing, she was wrong. She didn't want anyone to die here—not for her, not for Kieran, not for Íde. She knew that, now.

Roman froze, his arm drawn back to deliver another blow.

"Maebhe," he said, breathlessly. His head was bowed, his curls falling to hide his eyes. "If you knew the things he'd done in Unity's name, you'd be thanking me. I'm doing the world a favor."

"Why do you get to decide that? Why do you get a second chance and he doesn't? If someone had killed *you*, back when you still worked for them, there would've been no one alive today willing to help *me*. So wasn't it good that you lived?"

Roman sat back, stunned, and dropped his arm. He stared at his bloody hands, avoiding her gaze. "We should keep moving, anyway," he said, finally. When he looked up at her, Maebhe took an step back. Had his eyes always been so large? She remembered them being striking, but something seemed different. It was like both pupils and iris had blown wider, the cold black fixed on Maebhe, reflecting her face. Maybe that's all it was—her own fear, her frightened expression, presented for her so clearly.

Before she could offer him a hand, he brushed her aside and hauled himself up. Maebhe looked away while he wiped his hands on a handkerchief, then his bloody boots on the rug so they wouldn't leave a trail. He stepped over the Enforcer's body, bloody but still breathing, and nodded at Maebhe. Together, they hurried through the common room, down a hall, and into a barren stairwell.

It was a good thing Dinara hadn't come, Maebhe thought as they climbed. Good for Dinara and Roman, both, and for any future they might still have together. As if he was reading her thoughts, Roman looked back at her. His eyes were normal, Maebhe noticed. It must have been a trick of the light, before. "I have an answer to your earlier question."

Maebhe looked at him, but his expression gave nothing away. "Yeah? Which one?"

"About Dinara. She...pushes. Right where it hurts. You've probably figured this out already, but I don't like remembering my time with Unity, let alone talking about it. Dinara thinks all wounds can be healed by talking."

"I get it," Maebhe said. This time, she did. She had her own past that she hated to remember. "Kieran's the same way. When I wouldn't talk to him about our parents' death, he found Íde. Someone who listens. But I...well, anyway, if this is your way of asking me not to tell her, I won't."

Roman sighed, and there was no mistaking the relief in it. "Thank you."

"I should be the one thanking *you*," Maebhe pointed out. When he made a face, she quickly added, "You can't stop me. *Thank you.*"

Roman snorted. For all his talk of words not healing wounds, his step seemed lighter now that he'd spilled some of his secrets. "Hold your hands behind your back, like they're tied," he said, face settling back into a serious mask.

Before Maebhe could ask why, they rounded a corner, pushed through a door, and were greeted by a sudden breeze and the open sky. This must be the bridge connecting the barracks to the prison. It was a short walk to the imposing stone building, and Maebhe's tail gave a nervous swish at the sight. But when she spotted the guard at the opposite door, she did as Roman said, just in time for him to spot *them*. He tensed and drew his rifle, but Roman strode confidently forward, dragging Maebhe by the upper arm as if she was a prisoner. Maebhe couldn't help peering over the edge as they went, eyeing the blue-green water that stretched beneath them.

Once they were closer, Roman tugged up a sleeve and revealed a brand on his wrist, the same as the Enforcer girl's but older, Roman's scar dark, healed, and settled into his skin. The guard relaxed at the sight, returning his rifle to his side and nodding.

"Where are the other orinians being kept?" Roman asked, tone haughty.

"This floor, block six, sir," the guard said, his eyes trained deferentially on the ground. Maebhe hoped he wouldn't notice the blood spattered on Roman's boots, but then, maybe that was a common sight when it came to these Enforcers. Maebhe doubted this guard's fearful respect was merely a matter of rank.

She didn't protest when Roman grabbed her arm again and dragged her into the prison, conveniently blocking the view of her unbound wrists with his body as he did. He released her as soon as they were inside, shot her a cheery wink, and started down a hallway seemingly at random. Compared to his demeanor back in those barracks, he'd lightened considerably, practically cheerful. In contrast, Maebhe slunk along quietly behind him. The normalcy of those barracks had lulled her into a sense of comfort; even with the fighting, she'd been able to forget where they were. Now, there was no forgetting. Stone floors, cold brick walls, and iron-barred cells surrounded her on all sides. This was nothing like Orean's cramped, underfunded prison, which she'd toured when briefly considering a criminal justice major. Even without Unity's crest stamped onto every flat surface, a prison of this magnitude could belong to no one else.

They passed cell after cell. Each contained a rickety bunk, a sink, a toilet, and little else—even including occupants. Most of the cells were empty, but passing the ones that weren't, Maebhe ducked her head before she could make eye contact, guilt eating at her.

"Why...?" she whispered.

"Why is it so empty?" Roman finished. "Unity's prison is only meant to be a short intermission for prisoners awaiting sentencing, execution, or transfer to a more permanent placement. The only exceptions are for those who've committed crimes with no prevailing jurisdiction, like maritime crime or crimes against Unity."

Before Maebhe could respond, Roman dragged her into a shadowy alcove. They stood pressed to the wall, side by side, until the jingle of keys Roman had heard faded into the distance. Fortunately, the rest of the way was clear. It was as they passed down the next row of cells that they heard an incredulous voice call, "*Maebhe*?"

"Kieran!" Maebhe cried, forgetting to keep quiet. She rushed to Kieran's cell, Kieran meeting her at its iron bars. She was so happy to see him she could cry. His eyes flicked to Roman and narrowed, then widened again when Roman pulled out Ivey's lock-picking kit.

"Where's Íde?" Maebhe asked.

"Here," another voice called from across the aisle.

"Maebhe, why did you come here? *How* did you come here?" Kieran whispered. "This is reckless, even for you."

"Scold me later," Maebhe said as Roman got the cell door open. He unlocked Íde's even faster, now used to the arrangement of the pins, and soon Maebhe was hugging them both at once. They were grimy and dirty, Íde's dress torn and Kieran's jaw bruised, but they were *alive*.

"A jailbreak in Unity's prison?" asked a deep, unfamiliar voice. "What loyal friends you have."

Maebhe jumped, half-drawing Ivey's gun, but they were still alone in the hallway. There were no guards to be seen. Looking around, she realized the voice came from the hulking figure crouched in the corner of the cell beside Kieran's.

"Drys!" Kieran said. He gave Roman a plaintive look. "Could you...?"

Roman was already at the door, working the lock.

"Drys was here when we were brought in," Kieran explained. "There were others, too, but they...I don't know what happened to them. We're the only ones left."

Roman pushed the door open, but when the figure made no move to rise, he slipped inside and crouched beside them, using his tools again to unlock the manacles around the stranger's wrists. While he worked, Kieran sidled closer to Maebhe. "Mae, who is this guy?" he asked. His whisper was loud in the quiet hall, and Maebhe flicked an ear. "Where'd you find him? Why's he so good with thieves' tools?"

Maebhe shushed him. In the cell, the lock clicked and the figure rose. Maebhe had thought their silhouette too large to be human, and she was right: when Drys stretched, a pair of wings unfurled behind them. Maebhe tried not to stare. She'd never met one of the fae before.

"Thank you," the faerie told Roman. "I owe you a great debt."

Evidently knowing a thing or two about the fae, Roman didn't argue, only inclined his head in acknowledgement. When the faerie stepped out of the cell, into the light, Maebhe gasped. They cut an impressive figure, all willowy curves, corded muscle, and silky dark hair, but the gasp was for their injuries. Cuts ran along their wrists where the manacles dug in, and bruises covered their bare shoulders. Worst of all was the state of their wings. The feathers looked yellowish, but it was hard to tell their true color behind the filth, dried blood, and matted feathers.

Drys, standing tall despite their injuries, arched an eyebrow at Maebhe. The dark purple bags under their eyes should've lessened the look's intensity, but Maebhe shivered all the same. She squared her shoulders, stuck a hand out. "Call me Maebhe. I'm Kieran's sister."

"Drys Homeborn," Drys countered, shaking her hand. A smile played at the corner of their lips. "That's a lovely name, Maybe."

"May-*vuh*," Maebhe corrected.

"And who are you?" Kieran finally asked Roman.

"Don't look at him like that! He just saved you!" Maebhe hissed, elbowing him.

"It's understandable. I *am* awfully good at thieves' tools," Roman said. Kieran flushed when he realized Roman had heard, but Roman ignored Kieran's mumbled apologies and dropped into a hasty bow. "Roman Hallisey, at your service. I'd introduce myself further, but we should leave that for when we're off this damned island. Let's go, quick."

And with that, Roman and Maebhe hurried the group back the way they'd came, the others dutifully following. When they neared the bridge, Roman said, "Maebhe, get Ivey's revolver ready."

"She has a *revolver*?" Kieran asked. "She's never shot a revolver in her life!"

"Just because I haven't doesn't mean I can't. I know the theory," Maebhe sniffed. "And I've fired dad's hunting rifle."

Roman gave her a stern look. "Give the gun to your brother."

Maebhe sighed and passed Kieran the revolver.

Of course, they wouldn't make it past the guard on the bridge so easily a second time. Not with the size of their new group. When the guard saw them, Roman held a finger to his lips. Somehow, that simple action was enough to freeze the guard in place, staying his tongue so quickly he choked on his own saliva. Maebhe suspected it was thanks to the brand on Roman's wrist, peeking out from under his sleeve cuff.

"Speak," Roman warned, voice low, "And my friend shoots. Or worse, I'll kill you myself. You don't want that."

The guard must have agreed, because he stayed miraculously silent while Roman used a length of rope from Ivey's bag to bind him to the iron sconce protruding from the prison-side wall. Their luck couldn't last forever, though, and neither could the guard's silence. They'd only made it halfway across the bridge when duty finally outweighed fear and the guard started shouting for help. Roman swore and broke into a run, and the others followed suit.

They passed back through the doors and over to the stairwell, but before they could even start down it, Maebhe flung an arm out to stop them. In the silence, they all heard what Maebhe's sensitive ears had caught first: several sets of footsteps hurrying *up* toward them. "What do we do?" Maebhe asked, her long ears pricking toward the sound.

"Get back to the bridge," Roman said, his tone leaving no room for questions.

Back in the salty air, a second guard had arrived from the prison side to untie the first. Both groups froze momentarily, and then the new guard scrambled for his gun. Kieran was faster, though; he aimed the revolver and called, "Step away with your hands up!"

The guard hastily obeyed, his hands held above his head.

"Why did we turn around? Do we go back through the prison?" Kieran asked Roman.

Roman shook his head. "A group this size? We'd be caught before we even reached the front doors. The barracks are the only way out, but I can't protect you all in that wide stairwell. This position will be easier to defend. Just make sure we're not ambushed on the prison side."

Maebhe peered over the low brick wall, down to the water. Maybe the barracks weren't the *only* way. "Drys, can you fly? How many can you carry?"

Drys grimaced, but said, "Yes, but with my wings like this, only one at a time."

"Take Íde down to the beach," Maebhe said, pointing over the wall, "Then come back up for us. If you can carry all of us, Roman only has to stall, not beat them."

Drys' grimace grew, looking over the four of them, but they only sighed and promised, "I will try." With that, they scooped Íde into their arms and launched them both into the open air, the snap of their wings accompanied by the rushing wind and Íde's screams. Kieran's eyes widened, watching his fiancée go, but he resisted the urge to run to the wall and watch, his gun still steadily trained on the guards.

Just then, the barracks-side door flew open and three people stepped onto the bridge. One was the Enforcer from their earlier fight, his face ghastly but his spite keeping him on his feet. His leg had been wrapped in a makeshift tourniquet, and he'd recovered his sword. The second was a towering dryad, the third, leading the group, was a woman with vivid red hair and feather-textured skin. After spending time with Ivey, Maebhe recognized her as maranet. She stopped abruptly, her eyes widening when she saw Roman. Though already pale, she seemed to go paler at the sight of him.

"You," she breathed. "That's impossible."

"If you think so, then let's call me a figment of your imagination and let me pass," Roman said with a grin. She clearly knew him, but if *he* recognized *her*, he gave no indication.

The woman bared her teeth at him, revealing two sets of sharp fangs. Before she could respond, the Enforcer from before pushed past in a rage, even as she tried grabbing his arm to stop him. This time, there was no great fight. Roman dodged the man's messy swing and grabbed his arm, using his own momentum to carry him into a spin that launched him over the side of the bridge. He screamed as he fell, and Maebhe knew she would never forget the sound.

Trying to take advantage of the chaos, the guard on the prison-side raised his rifle, but Kieran fired a warning shot at his feet. "Drop it!" Kieran called. "Over the wall, or I shoot!"

The guard obediently threw his rifle over the side, right after Roman's Enforcer. When Kieran lowered his gun again, though, the guard launched himself through the door into the prison, the heavy door slamming shut behind him before Kieran could get another shot off. He was gone, and it could only be to get reinforcements. Who knew how quickly they'd arrive.

Kieran swore and took a step as if to follow, but Maebhe grabbed his arm. "Just wait for Drys!"

On the other side of the bridge, the maranet woman also sprang into action. She drew the sword strapped to her back and surged forward, as fast as lightning. Roman raised his own sword to meet her, but instead of charging *him*, she ducked past and headed for Maebhe instead. Only Roman's speed saved Maebhe; he shifted his weight and launched himself at the woman, slamming her shoulder-first into the bridge wall and nearly making her drop her sword over the edge. She grunted in pain, but between one moment and the next, a knife appeared in her free hand. Roman had to push away fast to avoid its blade.

Fast as he was, though, he couldn't dodge it entirely. He flung himself to the opposite wall, but he was grimacing by the time he hit it, the cream of his shirt sleeve rapidly turning vivid red. The woman followed him, slashing with her knife, a snarl on her face. Roman dodged each time, but when she brought the blade down in a clean arc toward his heart, he only had time to raise a hand against it. It pierced through his palm to the other side, but the sacrifice at least stopped the knife's progress: it stuck in his hand with the tip less than an inch from his chest. Gasping, Roman used the leverage to wrench the knife from the woman's hand, his expression twisting even further with pain.

"Roman!" Maebhe cried.

The woman retreated several steps, as if to give Roman time to recover. Maebhe thought it odd, but then the woman clicked her tongue disappointedly and said, "The last time we met, you didn't fight back. I see you're holding back this time, too. Why won't you give it your all?"

Roman smiled as he pulled the blade out of his hand. It wasn't one of his cheerful, fake smiles; it was dark and twisted and made Maebhe shiver. "If I gave it my all, Bellona, you'd be dead in seconds."

"It's *Evelyne*!" the woman snapped, charging him again.

Maebhe couldn't watch. He was only injured because of her, because this *Evelyne* knew that Maebhe was a weakness to exploit. She peered nervously over the wall just as Drys reappeared, their wings causing a gust of wind that blew her hair back.

It was then the maranet realized what they were doing, how they planned to escape. She whipped around to shout at her remaining comrade, "Gather as many as you can and get down to the beach!"

The dryad nodded and turned to run back into the barracks.

"No, you don't!" Roman threw the knife, and Maebhe watched it spin as if in slow-motion. It hit its target, sinking deep into the dryad's shoulder and making him stumble, but he managed to push through the door anyway and disappeared from sight.

With reinforcements coming from both ends, they were officially out of time.

"Get Kieran!" Maebhe shouted at Drys. "Don't worry about me. I'll make my own way down!"

"What does *that* mean?" Kieran asked, but Maebhe was already climbing onto the wall. Behind her, Roman and the maranet woman were circling each other, but seeing this, they both paused to stare.

Maebhe met Roman's gaze. With the orinians out of his way, he wouldn't have to hold back. Roman seemed to understand her plan, because he nodded. "Go! Don't wait for me," he called.

Maebhe's heart clenched. Despite the fear running through her in violent tremors, she nodded back. "Good luck."

"Maebhe, wait—," Kieran started.

But there was no time. She steadied herself and jumped, hearing Kieran shout her name as the sea rose up to greet her.

CHAPTER SIXTEEN

WHILE DRYS AND KIERAN FOLLOWED MAEBHE OVER THE EDGE, Evelyne only watched, stunned. Roman knew she wasn't used to her quarry escaping so easily, especially in so spectacular a fashion. He knew something else, too: that in her mind, as long as she killed *him*, nothing else mattered. So he made sure that by the time she turned back to face him, he was already gone, the prison door slamming shut behind him as he fled.

"Coward!" she shouted. Then, just as he'd hoped, she charged after him.

While Roman fled, Maebhe hit the water. She'd imagined her death a million ways as she fell, but after all of that, it was a smooth entry. She'd pointed her toes and engaged her core thanks to instinct and old-engrained muscle memory, following all the steps she took when cliff diving back home. She could only than *luck*, though, for not hitting any of the rocks that waited at the bottom. And while she'd accounted for everything else, she hadn't accounted for the water's temperature.

It was *freezing*.

Pressure closed around her while her muscles tensed and locked against the numbing cold. It took all her strength to move them, her limbs dragging and her heart pounding as she pushed slowly toward the surface, swimming on and on until she thought she'd never breathe again. She'd die here, so close to freedom but stuck in Unity's shadow. And after the show she'd just put on, how *embarrassing* would that be?

She broke the surface of the water only for the waves to push her back down. She couldn't even feel the cold anymore. She couldn't feel *anything*, but she forced her muscles to carry her up again. This time, she managed several great, heaving breaths, then took a moment to orient herself, spinning until the cliff loomed above her. She spotted Kieran and Íde's forms on the beach, waiting and waving.

Kieran was crying when she finally hauled her sopping form out of the water and waddled over to them. The wind was almost worse than the water had been; between it and her wet clothes, she couldn't stop shivering. While Kieran fussed and checked her for injuries, Drys removed their jacket and draped it over her shoulders. "I'm surprised you're still alive," they said. Full of adrenaline and gratitude, Maebhe only grinned.

Beside them, Íde's ears twitched toward the elevator cave. "They're coming. Can you run, Maebhe?"

Maebhe knew she had no choice. She staggered, at first, her limbs stiff, but the sight of the Enforcers finally spilling onto the beach spurred her on. Together, the orinians were quick and Drys had the advantage of flight. Though Maebhe's entire body burned, the Enforcers had fallen far behind by the time their group reached the drain.

"Ivey!" Maebhe shouted.

The gate swung open and a grizzled, grayish head peeked out. Ivey stretched out his hand, catching Maebhe's when she ran and jumped and hauling her surprisingly easily up into the drain. He was stronger than he looked. "Aim?" he asked her. When Maebhe only shook her head, he nodded, expression grim, and turned to help the others. Íde and Kieran were next. Dinara and Maebhe swapped places, Dinara helping Ivey while Maebhe squatted in place and shivered.

In the end, the Enforcers reached them just as Ivey crammed his crowbar into the gate's lock, jamming it from the inside. Maebhe stuck her tongue out at the Enforcers on the beach below, but yelped and ducked further into the tunnel when one of them drew a gun.

"Go," Ivey urged, and Maebhe didn't hesitate to obey. They'd had enough of a break that she could run again, the stitch in her lungs from the long sprint not so sharp anymore.

"Where's Roman?" Dinara asked suddenly, making Maebhe trip over her own feet. When no one answered, she stopped, dug her heels in, and repeated, "Maebhe. Where's Roman?"

"He told us to go on without him," Maebhe admitted.

Dinara drew in a sharp breath. They'd stopped under a manhole, and the filtering light illuminated her horrified expression. "And you listened?!" She turned to Ivey. "We're under the regular part of the island now, right? Let me up."

"Ms. Condeh, you can't—"

"Let me up!" Dinara repeated. "I won't cause any trouble. I won't go to the prison. I just want to see what's happening up there."

Seeing that glint in her eye, Ivey rocked back on his heels. Maebhe was beginning to recognize that as a sign he was about to give in, so Maebhe decided for him, standing up on the tips of her toes to lift the manhole cover, then twining her fingers together and holding them low so Dinara could step up for a boost. "I'll come with you," she offered.

"You're soaking wet, clearly freezing, and you're an *orinian*. Don't be silly, Maebhe. Get somewhere safe—that's what Roman wanted, right?" Dinara asked.

Unable to trust her own voice, Maebhe nodded. Her extremities were still numb, but she certainly felt the sting of tears behind her eyes. "Good luck."

"Thank you," Dinara said. She stepped up onto Maebhe's hand, then squeaked when Maebhe hauled her up. She peeked the top of her head out first, making sure no one was around before pulling herself up and through.

Looking at the buildings all around her, Dinara gave a start when she realized where she'd ended up: in an alley behind the theater, of all places. Frantic bells rang somewhere in the distance, and Dinara partially slid the cover back on the manhole with her boot before setting out in search of information.

She'd never seen the island in such a state of chaos. People were in an uproar, running from building to building or gathering in large, frantic groups. Dinara passed one woman wailing about escaped murderers, then a man assuring everyone that the warning bells were a routine drill. No one had any information. Certainly, no one mentioned a dark-eyed young man who may or may not have broken into the prison. Unity guards patrolled the streets, their rifles resting on their shoulders, but whenever Dinara tried to ask them any questions, they simply told her not to worry and to get inside.

The people apparently took that to mean "Get to the courthouse." They all flowed in that direction, only Dinara pushing against them like a salmon swimming upstream. When that became too conspicuous, she ducked into an alley and continued on by weaving between buildings. It was in one of these back alleys that she rounded a corner and collided bodily with someone—a *sturdy* someone who let out a familiar-sounding "*oof.*"

Dinara stumbled back, more dazed at the voice than the actual collision. "Roman!" she cried.

Roman clapped a hand over her mouth and pressed a finger to his lips, Dinara going cross-eyed to look at his tie, which had been tied tightly around his palm. She then noticed his sleeve, stained a vibrant red. A bruise was blossoming along his cheekbone, too, but his eyes twinkled when he smiled at her. "It's all right, it's all right. It's not as bad as it looks," he whispered, not removing his uninjured hand from her mouth. "Di, what are you *doing here?*"

He lifted his hand just enough for her to answer, "I had to find you. Roman, you're bleeding!"

Maybe it was the tears pooling in her eyes, but he didn't scold her, only sighed. "Not all of it is mine. I'm okay, see?" he said gently. He moved his uninjured hand to her arm, gave it a gentle squeeze. "Did you come up through one of the grates? Where?"

"Back at the theater," Dinara whispered.

Roman nodded and took her hand, leading her back the way she'd come. Now that he was here, now that he'd taken the lead, her fear melted away. He seemed so sure of himself—how could she be afraid? They wove slowly through the streets, Roman peering around every corner before pressing on, keeping them to alleys and avoiding the bigger Unity buildings—with their dark, inscrutable windows— entirely. They'd have to cross Central Avenue to get to the theater eventually, though, and Roman seemed to realize it would be easier to do so here on the outskirts than close to the courthouse.

They waited for a break in foot traffic, made sure no guards were around, then dashed across the street together, Dinara taking the lead. But when she felt Roman's hand slip from hers, she looked back.

She had never seen that expression on his face before.

He'd frozen halfway across the street, staring at something down the path. Dinara followed his gaze to a tall alfar man standing on the steps of a nearby building. He was certainly handsome—tall, blond, and broad-shouldered, but he had a stern look to him, with pale eyes and wicked scar curving up one cheek. Dinara looked at Roman again, feeling something uneasy churning in her stomach.

"Roman," she urged. At that, Roman finally moved again, shaking his head and slipping into the next alley. Dinara lingered, though, and looking back at that alfar once more—only to find him looking her way, brow furrowed. Uneasy, she swallowed and ran after Roman.

She had questions, endless questions, but they'd have to wait a little longer. She tugged Roman down the path she'd come from, then to the partially-covered manhole. He nudged it aside with his foot, but before either of them could climb down, a woman called, "Stop!"

A maranet woman with red hair stood at the end of the alley, her face twisted with fury. Guards flanked her on either side, and Dinara's heart hammered to the beat of their steps as they approached. Before she could ask Roman what they should do, he suddenly grabbed her from behind. She heard a *click,* then felt cold metal press to her temple. The woman froze, holding up a hand to halt the guards as well.

"Good choice," Roman called from behind Dinara, his voice cold. "What would the Magistrates say if you got a civilian killed?"

The woman's eyes narrowed. "You won't shoot. It's not your style."

Roman laughed, his breath warm against Dinara's neck. It wasn't his usual laugh; it was sharp, cruel. For a terrible moment, she wondered: *would* he shoot?

"You don't know a thing about me," Roman said to the woman, echoing Dinara's own thoughts. But then he drew Dinara closer, his hand on her arm gentling, and whispered "Trust me," so soft that only she would hear. How could Dinara have doubted him?

She pretended to struggle as he backed them toward the grate. When he reached it, he shoved her suddenly forward and made her stumble into the maranet woman, who caught and steadied her with surprisingly strong arms. And while the woman's hands were occupied, Roman made his escape.

"Shit!" the woman swore, passing Dinara off to one of the guards and running to the drain. She didn't bother climbing down herself, just stomped her foot and repeated, "*Shit!*"

"Should we go after him?" one of the guards asked.

"And trap yourself with *him* in a narrow tunnel? That would be as good as suicide," the woman said. She stomped over to Dinara, her green eyes furious. "Where was he going?"

Dinara fell back a step, holding her hands up between them. "I—I don't know," she said.

"Who are you? What were you doing back here? Were you helping him?"

"Ms. Corscia, that's enough," a new voice said. Dinara and this woman—Ms. Corscia—turned to the newcomer, who stood calmly at the alley's mouth. The guards parted for him as he approached, and Dinara saw it was the alfar from before, the one with the scar on his face. "What is going on here?"

"With all due respect, Captain Nochdvor, this is official Unity business. I'd thank you not to interfere," Ms. Corscia said through gritted teeth.

"Normally, I wouldn't, but I'm curious what reason Unity has for accosting the actress it so widely celebrated just last night."

The maranet's brows twitched. "What?" she asked.

"The show last night—this woman played the lead. We *are* outside the theater," the man pointed out, stopping beside Dinara, "The day after the Webhon Players' performance here, no less. If you're asking why this woman is here, now, I'd say that's reason enough."

"You're certain you're not mistaken, Your Highness?" one of the guards asked.

Your Highness. Dinara tried to remember who that honorific applied to. If "Majesty" was the king or queen, then "Highness" was a prince. Dinara felt her soul escaping her body. She had no idea she'd been performing for royalty. The prince inclined his head in a nod. "I saw the show myself. I could hardly confuse the show's star."

"He's right. I saw it as well," the other guard volunteered.

Ignoring him, the maranet woman narrowed her eyes at the prince. "I know what you're trying to do," she said, jamming a finger at his chest. "Where were you these last two hours?"

The alfar blinked, seemingly surprised to find himself suddenly the suspect of an unknown crime. "Meeting with the Magistrates. Enlighten me, Ms. Corscia; what am I doing?"

Evelyne stepped in closer. She was much shorter than the prince; she shouldn't have been as terrifying as she was. "If you continue to get in Unity's way, *Captain*, we will not be merciful."

The alfar laughed humorlessly. He leaned down, lowered his voice so the guards wouldn't hear. But Dinara, beside them, still could. "We both know my fate is sealed," he said. "Are you offering me a choice between a quick or a painful death?"

Instead of answering, the woman only pushed past him, signaling for her guards to follow. Once they were gone, the alfar sighed. He did a poor job of hiding his emotions, unlike other alfar, and his expression was troubled. He used his boot to close the storm drain. "I wouldn't recommend going that way again, lest you rouse her suspicion further," he said, casually.

Dinara had suspected as much, but now she had it confirmed: he knew she wasn't here for the theater. He even knew about the tunnels. He'd only been covering for her. But why?

"Thank you," she said, her voice coming out as only a whisper.

The alfar nodded. "That person who was with you just now," he started, carefully, "Who was he?"

"I really don't know," Dinara said. In a way, she was being honest. If she were to be even more honest, she didn't want him to know.

"Ah," the alfar said. Though he tried to hide it, Dinara could see his disappointment. "You'd better be on your way. The bridge security will be flooded with people leaving, which makes this a good time to slip away."

Dinara nodded, murmured quick thanks, and fled.

———

By the time she finally made it back to Ivey's, over an hour of waiting at Unity's congested security checkpoint later, her fear had faded and left only disquiet. Unity, which Dinara had always believed to be good, was rounding up orinians without cause. Roman, her sweet traveling companion, not only worked for the Oracle of Damael, he seemed to be a longstanding enemy of Unity. The people were talking about war, and if things like *this* kept happening, the talk might turn true. It was all more than she knew what to do with.

She knocked at Ivey's door, remembering only after that Roman had done a special pattern for it. But before she could try again, the door flew open anyway. There was Roman, immediately pulling her into a hug. It was all she'd wanted all day, but now she stiffened and pushed him away, reminded of the cold bite of steel against her temple. His expression fell, and even after everything she'd learned about him that day, it still made her heart twist with guilt.

"I'm so sorry, Di," he said in a rush. "That woman—I've known her for a long time, and she never forgets a face. She saw you with me, so making you a hostage was the only way to keep you from being implicated. The gun wasn't actually loaded, I promise."

Some of the tension in Dinara's chest eased, but not enough. "I understand. That alfar we saw—he helped me get out of trouble," she said. She mentioned him as a test, one that yielded results: Roman stiffened, his expression smoothing to something so neutral it could only be fake. Unable to stop herself, she asked, "Did you know he's a prince?"

"I'm not even sure who you mean," Roman said, stepping aside to let her in. Dinara's heart clenched all over again.

As she stepped inside, Maebhe popped her head into the foyer. She wore a large wool blanket around her shoulders, her long hair still damp. "You're back! If you hadn't shown up soon, I was sure Roman would march right back to the island to rescue you."

Dinara smiled at her. "I'm glad you're safe. Are any of you injured?"

Maebhe shook her head. "Only Roman, but Ivey patched him up. You'd think stitches couldn't be worse than being stabbed through the hand, but the way Roman whined about it, you'd never know."

Roman wrinkled his nose and waved a bandaged hand. The bruise around his eye deepened to a dark purple, but beyond that, he seemed hale and whole. He'd even changed into something less blood-stained, but Dinara still followed Maebhe into the sitting room so she wouldn't have to look at him. There, she found their escapees, Maebhe's brother fast asleep on the other's shoulder. Maebhe, blanket and all, shuffled over to their sofa and curled up on the dark-haired orinian's other side.

"Wasn't there another one?" Dinara asked. She'd been distracted with the escape, but it would have been impossible not to notice the faerie with the group.

"Drys is bathing. Their wings were in a state," Roman answered, leaning in the doorway behind her. "I was about to go buy supplies for their journey, while we wait."

From his writing desk in the corner, Ivey looked up, mouth pulling into a wide frown. "My dear fellow, *you* mustn't go anywhere. Not after that show you put on today," he said. "The entire city will be looking for you, not to mention the Enforcers. Tell me what you need and I'll go."

"I'll help," Dinara offered. She'd been so eager to get back to Ivey's, but now she couldn't wait to leave.

"We can't pay you back," the dark-haired orinian said. She was short and delicate, different from the twins all the way down to her birthmarks.

Roman waved a hand, already taking out his pocketbook and passing Ivey a few laminate bills. "Don't worry about it. Ivey, do you have pen and paper? I can make a list."

Once they had their shopping list in hand, Dinara and Ivey departed. They spent half the walk in silence, the awkwardness building between them until Ivey finally asked, "So, pardon my asking, but are you and Aim...?"

"We're close," Dinara said. She didn't have a better word for what she and Roman were, especially not now. A night together had turned into friendship had turned into more, leaving Dinara confused. "Why do you call him Aim?"

Ivey started like a rabbit. "Why do *you* call him *Roman*?"

"That's his name."

"And Aim is his nickname."

"But what does it mean? It doesn't make sense."

"Must nicknames make sense?"

"Generally, yes. They at least have stories," Dinara argued. Ivey hurried toward the large general store at the end of the block, as if he could escape her questions.

"If you must know, the nickname comes from his skill at the game of darts," he said with the air of a man picking a story out of a hat and committing to it. "He never misses the bullseye."

Dinara frowned after him, having to jog a few steps to keep up. The door nearly swung shut in her face after Ivey refused to hold it for her. "Why was he on the island before? Why did he need to flee? What was his old job? I know you know."

"Ms. Condeh, please. It's not my place," Ivey said. "In my line of work, I hear many people's secrets. They trust me because I *keep* those secrets, and I pride myself on that reputation."

Dinara sighed, looking around while Ivey passed the shopping list to the attendant. Strangers passed by the gritty windows, oblivious to the chaos on Unity Island, to Orean's struggle, to the storm in Dinara's mind. Their thoughts weren't occupied by smugglers, spies, and secrets. They lived normal lives, and they seemed happy for it.

"I will say this," Ivey began, watching the attendant flit across the store while gathering their things. "I consider Roman a dear friend, and I imagine I've known him for longer than anyone else alive. Even so, I know only a fraction of his story—only what he *had* to tell me. I doubt anyone in the world knows all of it."

"Oh," Dinara said.

"But he obviously cares for you. He's changed tremendously since I saw him last. He was...in a bad way, then. It would've taken someone special to draw him out."

Dinara stared at Ivey. "It wasn't *me*," she said. "He was like this when I met him."

"Oh," Ivey said, scratching his nose. "Ah, well. He obviously cares about you, all the same."

"Maybe," Dinara said.

Loaded down with bags and parcels, they arrived back at Ivey's house to find Kieran awake and Drys sitting among them, their gold wings almost sparkling except for the few bandaged spots. Dinara and Ivey dumped the parcels on the dining table. "Here we are. Food, travel gear, and a change of clothes for each of you," Ivey said, sorting through the various packages.

"Is this enough food to last us to Orean?" Maebhe asked doubtfully.

"No, but it'll last you to Home," Roman answered.

"Home?" Íde asked, eyes widening. "Isn't that in —"

"Lyryma Forest," Drys finished.

"There's no way we can go through Lyryma," Kieran said.

Lyryma Forest, the vast tangle of wood south of Gallonten, was a dangerous place to travel. This danger came not just from the terrain, but from the impossible flora and fauna as well. If you were not born to the wood, if you did not already know its secrets, it may well kill you. Orean alone had so many stories and superstitions about the old wood that no orinian with any sense would go near it.

"You can't travel in the open, especially not after today's escape. Unity will have warrants matching your descriptions sent to all major towns by the end of the day," Roman explained. "But cut through Lyryma Forest and not only will you avoid Unity roads, you'll reach Orean faster."

Íde bit her lip. "The extra time would be wonderful, but we'd never last —"

"It's safe if you have a guide, and I'm calling in a favor. Drys Homeborn, will you see these three safely to Orean for me?" Roman asked.

Drys' lips quirked into a smile, and they bowed. "A debt owed, a debt repaid. Consider it done."

"Good. Ivey, I need that paper again. I have a letter to write."

While Roman sat down at Ivey's desk, Ivey addressed the orinians: "There's still enough light that I can get you out of Gallonten today, but if I were you, I wouldn't head into those woods until morning."

Kieran still looked vaguely ill at the idea of approaching the forest at all, let alone at night, but he nodded. "The sooner we can get out of here, the better I'm sure we'll all feel."

"What did Unity want with you?" Maebhe asked her twin. "Unity, I mean."

"Good question," Kieran answered. "I wish I knew."

"There started friendly," Íde said. "We weren't even in cells, originally. We were in some kind of common room. They gave us food and said that all of this was for our safety, and I almost believed it. But when they found out Kieran works for the city guard, they locked us up and started asking questions we couldn't answer."

"What kinds of questions?" Maebhe asked.

"Whether we were here under orders, what kind of defenses Orean has, what we might want with the alfar king. I don't think they knew the meaning of the word 'vacation,'" Kieran said. "Then they went off the rails completely and started asking about magic."

"Magic?" Roman asked sharply, looking up. "What about it?"

Kieran shrugged. "Just whether I'd seen anything inexplicable, working for the king. They dropped it when I made it clear I didn't know what they were talking about."

Roman frowned to himself, then resumed writing, more furiously this time. When he finished, he fanned the paper so the ink would dry faster. "There's a reason they asked. Apparently, Amos Nochdvor was abducted under strange, inexplicable circumstances. Unity's plan is to send a team to Orean to dig deeper."

"How do you know that?" Dinara asked.

"I've been listening," Roman answered, unhelpfully.

"What's in the letter?" Maebhe asked.

Roman looked between her and Dinara, exasperated. "So many questions. If Orean is going to be forced to play this game, your king needs to know the key players," he said, stuffing the letter in an envelope. "This explains everything I know—and suspect—about the situation. Give it to King Riordan; hopefully, it'll help him plan his strategy. Do *not* open it yourselves."

Once the letter was sealed, Roman passed it to Maebhe. Maebhe, knowing she'd lose it in a day, passed it to Íde.

"We should be going," Ivey said, though he eyed the envelope with open curiosity.

"Don't you want to come back into the sewers with us?" Maebhe asked with a small smile. "It's such a lovely walk! And to be honest, we'd all feel safer having you with us."

Roman laughed. "You'll be perfectly safe, and besides, there are things I still need to do here. But if you meet someone named Senga in Lyryma, give her my best."

Drys started. "Senga? You've been to Home?"

"Many times. The frìth took me in when I had nowhere else to go—including after Ivey helped me out of Gallonten, in fact."

Maebhe looked Roman up and down, her expression turning serious. "And if you see Aleksir, give him my thanks. And tell him I believe him about his friend."

Roman's smile faded. "I will."

"This is goodbye, then. I don't know what we would've done without you," Kieran said, shaking Roman and Dinara's hands. While Roman saw them down to Ivey's cistern, Dinara waited at the front door. They left together, afterward, and while Dinara basked in the sunslight and the quiet, she said, "I can't wait to get home."

Roman nodded his agreement, but when Dinara started down the street, he didn't follow. "I'll meet you there. I have a few things I need to do."

Dinara stopped. "Are you serious?"

"Sometimes," Roman said, expression unreadable. Not that Dinara had ever been able to read him, apparently. "Right now, yes."

"What could you *possibly* have to do? Shouldn't you be staying out of trouble?"

Roman shifted his weight from one foot to the other, grimacing slightly. "Aleksir—the boy that helped Maebhe find us. I'd like to make sure he didn't end up in a jail cell somewhere."

"Why is that *your* job? Haven't you done enough today?"

"I won't cause trouble," Roman said calmly, talking to her like he was soothing a startled cat. "There won't be any risk. I just want to find him. And I did promise Ivey dinner, after."

"Ugh," Dinara said. There was no invitation for her to join for dinner, she noticed. When she pushed past him, he made no move to follow. "Fine. See you at home, then."

Roman's answering smile was sad. "I'll see you."

CHAPTER SEVENTEEN

ROMAN WANDERED THROUGH A SILENT FOREST. Above him, the overcast sky stretched through leafless branches that shot like lightning into its gray expanse. Roman followed the line of those branches down to their scraggly blue trunks, nothing like the trees around Gallonten. He knew them well, though. He knew this wood, knew this path. Worst of all, he knew where it led.

Beneath him, dead leaves lined the trail under a dusting of snow, autumn's life wrung from this wood by winter's icy grip. Roman's breath clouded in front of him in bursts, but he couldn't feel the cold. Still, he pulled his coat reflexively tighter as he continued down the path, heading toward the last place in the world he wanted to go. This dream compelled him on, an invisible thread reeling him in like a fish on a line.

Before he was ready for it, a dark shape loomed out of the fog. It solidified into a lonely cabin, one made from the same dark blue wood as the forest: the wood of the ibal tree, found only in Troas. The cabin stood as Roman had last seen it, its windows boarded shut and its door broken off the hinges. It tipped precariously to one side, and the messily thatched roof had begun to collapse inward.

Roman stepped into the clearing. No grass grew on the frozen ground that led up to the cabin. Nothing lived in this cold place, not anymore. Roman took another step toward the door, but a movement glimpsed out of the corner of his eye—the rustle of a skirt, the wave of a hand—stopped him. When he turned, all he saw was trees, their sickly shapes affording little coverage for anyone hoping to hide.

Someone laughed behind him and he spun again, this time finding a figure on the porch. She raised a hand to beckon him closer, but Roman couldn't move.

"Catalina," he breathed.

Catalina Rosario smiled. Or rather, this distorted dream version of her did. Roman had forgotten his own mother's face so long ago that what had once been a world-shattering revelation had simply become a fact of life. The Catalina of his dreams, the Catalina that stood on the porch, was a blur, her features warping and transforming whenever he looked away. Only two things remained constant: her voice, always close to laughter, and his eyes, far lighter than his own. They were the honey-sweet tones of sunshine streaming through a bottle of whiskey.

"Amaimon!" she called, no longer looking at Roman. Roman started at the sound of his birth name; it had been a *long* time since he'd heard it, but Catalina wasn't speaking to him. She ran down the steps, past Roman, and scooped a child into her arms. The child stared at Roman over his mother's shoulder, golden eyes boring into Roman's black ones.

Catalina's clothes were all wrong, Roman noticed. His sleeping mind had put her in a modern Gallontean gown, all dark wool and structured drapery, but in life, she'd always worn traditional Corinidan dress. Even years after leaving her home and family to live with Roman's father, years in cold, subdued Troas, she wore off-shoulder bodices, bright colors, and flowing skirts whenever the weather permitted.

"Well?" she asked, leaning back to examine her child's face. The Corinish word, asked in a language nearly dead in Calaidia, had bittersweet nostalgia rising in Roman like bile. "Amaimon Roman Rosario, didn't you miss your mother?"

"Yes," the boy said seriously. "Don't go away again."

Catalina laughed and made no promises. She often went on trips, ostensibly across the sea to visit family, but she never brought Roman with. "When you're older," she used to say, when he asked. "Can I make it up to you, sweet child?" she said now, to the boy in her arms.

Amaimon considered this. "Tell me a story."

"As you command," Catalina said, wide eyes dancing with laughter. The boy seemed to know he was being made fun of and squirmed to be put down. "Hush. Be still, now. Must you be so serious, love? I'll tell you your story."

The pair faced Roman now, oblivious to his presence. Roman remembered dozens of moments like this. His mother knew many stories for someone her age, more than Roman knew even today, and she was good at telling them. She spoke to Amaimon softly, sweetly, using her free hand to make grand gestures, and Amaimon wore the same blank-faced expression he'd started with. Catalina was right; Roman had always been a serious child. He'd learned to stop taking life seriously when doing so just made him want to end it.

"I want to be like him," Roman's younger self said. "Like the hero in the story."

Roman gave an amused snort at the same time as Catalina. "Don't be foolish," she said, teasing her son with a tap to the tip of his nose. "You can be better than that. Never settle for less, love."

When Catalina and Amaimon started toward the open doorway, Roman braced himself for what came next. He'd had this dream enough times to have it memorized, enough times that he'd grown numb to it. This was where it all fell apart.

Next, a person would step out onto the porch, their features all shrouded in shadow except for the snakeskin boots on their feet.

Next, they would attack, and Catalina would fall.

Next, he'd watch his mother—or this dream approximation of her—die all over again.

This time, none of that happened. This time, pain crashed into Roman like a freight train. He grunted and fell to his knees, caught entirely off guard. Fire scorched his insides, his heart pumping the burning heat through his body with every one of its beats. It seared across his ribcage, trying to escape.

This was only a *dream*. He shouldn't feel *anything*. He certainly shouldn't be doubled over in agony, unable to move or breathe. How could this feel so real?

Distantly, he heard the dream carrying on without him: Catalina screamed. Amaimon cried. A warbled, distorted voice shouted. For once, Roman couldn't pay it any mind.

Then, as suddenly as it began, the pain vanished. Roman stayed on the ground, folded in on himself and fighting to catch his breath, for a moment longer.

"Wake *up*," he hissed, his breath clouding in front of him.

Of course, it wouldn't be that easy. When the waking world still evaded him, he pushed himself up on shaky arms and saw that the scene had changed: the sky darkened, black ribbons of something *alive* and *writhing* shivering through the air. Some old memory tugged at Roman's consciousness at the sight, urging him to remember.

He was distracted, though, by what lay before him. It wasn't his dream-mother lying dead at the bottom of the stairs. That, he'd seen before. It was the man who knelt beside her, his hands covered in blood.

"Get lost," Roman snapped without thinking. We winced as he stood, a hand over his heart as if that would stop the burn.

Egil tipped his head to one side. "I can't leave you. I never will. What did you do to her?" he asked, looking down at Catalina.

"Do? I was a little busy, over here," Roman said. He looked around. He'd dreamed the same dream for years and years; he knew the script, so why did it change now? What else could he alter? He was supposed to stay at Catalina's side until he woke, but this time, he stormed past her into the house, hearing Egil pick himself up and follow. He didn't know what he expected to find—some lingering sign of the figure with the snakeskin boots, maybe.

Those boots were all he could remember from that day, beyond the sight of his mother lying dead in the grass. He used to think that if he could just remember the person's face, the hollow ache in his chest would subside. It was a child's dream, an attempt to make sense of a traumatic event.

Inside, he found only darkness, cobwebs, and an interior he wasn't convinced truly belonged to this house he'd grown up in, a place half-remembered in the way of dreams. Something told him he should keep looking, though. He'd forgotten something, and he might find it here, in these cobwebs of his memory.

"I don't know what you expected," Egil said from somewhere behind him. In the kitchen, Roman looked out the broken windows into the darkened forest. He watched mist swirl through the trees.

"Are you running again?" Egil asked, when he didn't respond. Egil heaved. "How very like you. I thought we were done with that."

Roman wanted to keep searching, but he couldn't. Not with Egil whispering in his ear. Angry, hurting, Roman drew his sword and spun to attack, but he froze mid-swing when he found a red-headed maranet woman standing behind him of Egil. She looked down her nose at him, her expression dripping with contempt.

"Not going to do it?" she asked. When he didn't move, she stepped up to his blade, letting it rest against her pale neck. "I hope you do a better job of killing me than I did of you."

Carefully, Roman withdrew the sword and returned it to his sheath. "I won't hurt you," he said.

Evelyne Corscia sneered. "Always afraid to do what it takes. Keep it up and you'll never find her."

"Find who?" Roman asked, but Evelyne didn't answer. He followed her gaze to something over his shoulder: outside the wide window, between the trees, a pair of glowing crimson eyes and a twisted smile faded back into the mist.

Roman sat up, the bedsheet tangled around his limbs making him panic until he realized where he was: in a trailer in Gallonten, thousands of miles away from Troas and his childhood home. He reached for the other side of the bed, for the warmth of a companion to reassure him he was there, that this place was real, but he was alone.

At that realization, Roman fell apart. As if it might stop the shivering, as if it might protect his raw edges, he wrapped his arms around himself. He felt exposed, like a ripped-off scab after this horrible day, after that dream cut him to shreds and left the pieces to flutter in the wind. He still felt echoes of that dream pain, rasping in his lungs when he drew a breath. He dug a thumb into his injured palm, wincing at the bite of it. It was a reminder: *this* pain was real. The dream was not.

In time, when the shaking subsided and only the pain in his hand remained, Roman scrubbed at his eyes. He didn't know when these tears began to fall, but he knew he'd made a mess of himself. He wanted to find Dinara, but not in this state. Only once he'd pieced himself back together did he stand, hearing a *thump* from above just as he was about to leave the trailer. Outside, he climbed onto the trailer's handrail, then up to the roof. Sure enough, there Dinara sat, her knees hugged to her chest and the moon hanging large and bright behind her like a frame.

"Star gazing, Di? You could've invited me along," he said, keeping his tone light and hoping it was too dark for her to notice his red and puffy eyes.

She turned at the sound of his voice, expression still unguarded. In it, Roman saw all of her thoughts and fears and doubts laid bare. If he could see all of that, with the moon shining so brightly above him, he knew there was no hiding his own sorry state. "What are you doing awake?" she asked.

Roman made his way along the roof to sit beside her. "I'm always awake at strange hours of the night. You know that."

"I didn't wake you?"

"You didn't wake me."

Dinara reached up to touch his still-damp cheek. "You had one of your nightmares again," she guessed, letting her hand fall when Roman leaned out of her touch.

"I'm fine," he said reflexively. In the face of all his lies, though, he owed Dinara some truth. He *wanted* to tell her some truth. He wanted to tell her about his mother, about how she haunts him and has haunted him since childhood. He wanted to tell her about Unity, about Egil, about the Oracle of Damael. About all the people he'd trusted and hurt and lost, and worse, all the people who'd wrongly trusted *him*. But if he said any more, he might cry again, so he shrugged instead. "I'd ask you why you're up, but I think I already know."

Dinara looked away, the moonlight catching on her curls.

"You're thinking about today?" he pressed.

"Yesterday, technically," Dinara said, looking up at the sky. "It's morning."

"Yesterday, then."

Dinara sighed. "I'm thinking about a lot of things," she said, pointedly. It was clear she wanted Roman to offer something up first.

"I don't mean to be evasive."

"Evasive is putting it mildly, Roman! I feel like I'm worlds away from knowing you. Why won't you just let me *know you*?"

Roman followed her gaze to the stars. He tracked the constellations until the warning tingle behind his eyes subsided. "You know me better than almost anyone else."

"That's not comforting. It's *sad*."

"Maybe," Roman agreed, feeling a familiar loneliness creep in. "Dinara, if you really want to know, I can—"

"Tell me about last time," Dinara said, not even waiting for him to finish. "When you had to flee Gallonten."

Roman's mouth snapped shut. While Dinara waited for him to continue, he stared out over the quiet camp, lost in thought. Eventually, he said, "I worked for Unity, but not by choice. While they never put me in a cage or a cell, I still couldn't leave."

"Why not?"

"An easy question to ask, but not to answer. It was psychological, mostly. They beat me down, taught me not to dream of freedom. I was supposed to be grateful—they saved me from the gallows, and because of that, they felt I belonged to them." He watched Dinara, cataloging the changes in her expression when he said, "I had killed someone."

There was fear there, in her eyes, and Roman knew with utter certainty that they wouldn't make it to morning. Not together.

"It was an accident," he added, as if that changed anything. Digging into the haze of old memories, he continued, "I was friendless and homeless, and I came to Gallonten naively thinking I could find a job, maybe save enough to finish my education. I had no idea what I was walking into, and the police then were even worse than they are now. A week into my stay, a group of them accosted me while I was trying to find somewhere to sleep. They were beating me, and I just reacted. I was so sure they were going to kill me. I killed one, wounded two others, and was arrested immediately after."

Ignoring Dinara's horrified expression, he continued, "Then Unity recruited me, promised everything I'd ever wanted. I stayed with them a long time, until I learned to hate them and everything they stood for. When I met Ivey by chance, I convinced him to help me. The rest is history."

"History," Dinara repeated. "What about the Oracle of Damael? How does she fit into this?"

"Dinara," Roman said, gently, "This isn't a world you want to be a part of."

Dinara sighed. "Maybe you're right." Tears swam in her eyes, but her cheeks were dry and her voice was even as she asked, "Where does that leave us, Roman? If you can't tell me about yourself and I can't hear it? I've always felt like there was something missing, between us. Something you were holding back. I thought *I* could draw it out, but yesterday, you were more yourself than I've ever seen you. If you can't be that with me..."

Roman rubbed his eyes. He was tired. "I know. You deserve better."

"Maybe. But so do you."

Roman wasn't so sure.

"You're welcome to travel with us," Dinara said, though her heart clearly wasn't in it. "You're part of the family. That won't change."

"No, I need to stay here," Roman said, making it easier for them both. Now that the festival was wrapping up, the Players would soon be leaving Gallontena. When he smiled at her, it was almost genuine. "When the Players leave, what will you do? Where will you go?"

Dinara frowned, surprised at the question. She'd probably thought to stay with the Players, like she'd always done, but Roman saw the question ignite possibilities behind her eyes. "I don't know," she said, as surprised at her answer as she'd been at the question. "Maybe I'll try something new."

"Whatever you do, you'll be great."

"What about you? After today, everyone will be looking for you. Isn't Gallonten the last place you should be?"

"I'm tired of running," Roman said. He owed Dinara some truth, after all. It was easier to give it now that he needn't fear her reaction, now that the worst had happened. He rested his chin on his knee and stared up at the sky. "When I worked for Unity, the things I did for them shattered me. You've glimpsed the broken pieces, but you've no idea how bad it really was. Even after years, I'm a badly patched vase one shove away from breaking all over again. But all this time, I've been so focused on not letting them hurt me that I missed them doing the same harm to others. Much as I want to tear Unity apart, brick by brick, I need to help Orean first."

"Be careful, Roman," Dinara breathed.

"I will," Roman promised. Raising her hand to his lips, he kissed her for the last time. "I won't be able to sleep anymore tonight, anyways, so I'll leave you be. I'll come back for my things tomorrow."

"Okay," Dinara tried to say, but no sound came out. "Goodbye, Roman."

Roman didn't bother climbing down from the trailer, just jumped, landing easily on the balls of his feet. As he walked away, an echo of his dream pain returned, like a fire burning over his heart. He embraced it, let it wash over him.

EGIL III

DURING EGIL'S FIRST VISIT TO DAMAEL, he limped into the city with the setting suns, having to fight against a sea of farmers and tradesmen leaving after a long day at market. He hadn't expected the crowds, but perhaps he should have. Damael was currently the safest city in the Ejeran province, the rest of it still reeling from the dissolution of an empire that had ruled since the Great War. While the empire's scraps made desperate bids for control, quelling rebellions and establishing outposts, opportunity-seekers took advantage of the chaos to steal and fight and kill.

Even Unity's grip on the province had crumbled. For the first time in over 1700 years, lawlessness reigned.

It was because of that lawlessness that Egil had come. He was drawn to pitiful places and powerless people, and he'd thought to help where he could. Instead, he'd arrived at the same time as Unity's reinforcements and barely escaped with his life. That was why his first steps into Damael were slow and staggering, why a bruise bloomed along his jaw and a scarf was wrapped tightly around his thigh, slowing the flow of blood from a wound he hadn't had time to stitch up.

He needed to find a place to hide and nurse his wounds, but he found Damael's streets far too quiet. He disliked quiet. His thoughts were too loud, and he needed them drowned out. More than that, though, he always stood out in quiet places, and he couldn't afford to do so now, not with Unity's Enforcers on his trail.

He wandered the city until he found the loudest pocket of it, a district where strangers passed by in large, merry groups, where music and sweet perfume drifted out of questionable establishments, and where patrons of taverns and opium dens and dance halls leaned out from balconies, calling drunkenly into the night. It was loud and colorful and, most of all, fearless. And why *should* the people of Damael have any fear? Their oracle told them all would be well. Egil wasn't so optimistic. He rented a room at a middling inn, busy but not flashy, and immediately retreated upstairs. Only hours later, when his wounds were tended, hunger clawed at him, and he could no longer stand the company of his own thoughts did he venture back down.

The common room was nearly full, strangers sitting in groups around mismatched tables. Warm firelight flickered over their faces and all the golden oak built into the walls, bathing the place in an orange glow. Egil's attention was drawn to a group at the bar, the man at the center sharing local gossip in a loud voice. A woman in red hung off his arm. When Egil paused to listen, she met his gaze and a shiver ran down his spine, surprising him. He ducked his head and hurried over to an empty table in the corner.

That people could be so at ease in a time like this was because of the city's strange figurehead, the Oracle of Damael. This oracle was not a fortune teller, reading fates in cards and bones, not a rosanin with an unusual gift, but a true oracle ordained by the church and consulted by empire, rebellion, and Unity alike. While the empire had ruled the province since the Great War, the oracle had ruled her city for even longer. Intrigued as Egil was, he had no time to investigate. By morning, the Enforcers would be here and he would be gone.

He jolted to attention when someone fell into the seat across from him, the knife at his thigh halfway out of its sheath before he recognized the red crepe fabric of the woman from the bar. She was nympherai—fae, Egil guessed, though she lacked the telltale wings. A thick white braid draped over her shoulder and a glittering pattern twisted over her bronze skin like dancing flames.

"You're new here," she slurred, batting all-white eyelashes.

"Is it that obvious?"

The woman gave a breathless laugh and tucked her long bangs behind a pointed ear. "No, but I'd remember a face like yours."

"It'll be better for you if you don't."

"Remember you? Lucky you, then. After all that wine, I won't remember anything by tomorrow." She leaned in, her heavy ears swaying with the movement. Egil expected the smell of booze to follow, but it never did. "Will you give me your name? We can make it a trade: mine's Dev."

It was a very fae introduction. Having just come from Lyryma, Egil felt right at home. "Egil."

Dev gasped, her dark eyes widening. "The Hound of Unity himself, here in Damael."

Egil stiffened. "How do you know that name?"

"Everyone knows that name. They just don't know *Egil* belongs to it," Dev said.

"But you do," Egil said. Beneath the table, he eased his knife out of its sheath.

"I've heard rumors about you, Hound. For example, I've heard that you also have magic. Is it true? Can you show me?"

"Only if you tell me why you came here looking for me."

"What makes you think I—" Swiftly, Egil drew his knife and drove it into the table—right into the space between Dev's first finger and thumb. She squawked and yanked her hand to her chest, cradling it there. "What is wrong with you?! You could've stabbed me!"

"The *Hound of Unity* doesn't miss," Egil hissed, pulling his knife out of the wood. "Call me that again and the next one goes into your hand."

Dev bared her teeth into a snarl. "You—"

"Wow. That was the first real reaction I've seen from you all evening," Egil said cheerfully, pointing his knife at her. "No more pretending. now. You knew who I was the moment our eyes met. Somehow, you even knew to find me here. If you're ready to talk like adults, tell me how."

Dev sighed and straightened in her seat, her languid slouch replaced in an instant by cold authority. She draped an arm over the back of the booth and asked, "What gave me away?"

"I can always tell good acting from bad. Yours may be good, but it's still *acting*."

Dev smiled. It was sharp, predatory, and nothing like the saccharine one from before. "Is it so hard to believe I came over because I find you attractive?"

"I'm covered in dirt and blood, I haven't slept under a roof in a week, and I'm long overdue for a bath. Yes, it's hard to believe. Especially when I'm being hunted."

"By the Enforcers, I presume?" Dev asked. She said the name so casually, fearlessly. Enforcer was a name sensible people whispered. "Aren't you worried I'm with them?"

"No," Egil said.

"Oh?" Dev asked, raising an elegant eyebrow. "Should I feel insulted?"

"I can always recognize an Enforcer by their eyes," Egil said, ducking his head slightly to meet Dev's. They were dark and warm. "The things they do for Unity makes them hollow. Their eyes are always cold, empty."

"Like yours?" Dev asked. "The Hound was the best of them once, wasn't he?"

"I was the first, and maybe once, I was the best." Egil tipped his head to one side, letting the candlelight fall on the blossoming bruise on his jaw. "But the student has since surpassed the master."

"Oh." Dev leaned in to examine it. For a moment, Egil thought he saw anger flash across her features, between the candles' flickering. "A gift from someone you knew?"

"My former apprentice," Egil said. "Are you really here to chat about Unity, Dev? Do you prefer Dev, or should I call you Oracle?"

Devikra laughed. "From you, still Dev," she said. "I was wondering how long it would take you."

"In my defense, I've lost quite a lot of blood today," Egil said, matching her smile. "To what do I owe the honor? Unless Devikra, the famed Oracle of Damael, finds herself inns in Damael's pleasure district often."

"Only when she has visions of promising young men dying in them. The Enforcers are coming for you, and sooner than you think," she said plainly, making Egil's stomach twist. He kept his smile carefully in place.

"I've escaped them before."

"Not this time. Not tonight. You should know the oracle's visions are never wrong," Devikra said. Egil wasn't sure if he believed her, but he wouldn't risk it, either. He scanned the room, already planning a quick escape, but Devikra halted his thoughts with her offer: "Come back with me. They won't find you at my temple. I'm feeling generous, so I'll even lend you use of my guest room and bathtub."

Egil narrowed his eyes. "The Oracle works with Unity. How do I know you won't turn me over to them?"

"I consult with Unity because it would be bad business not to. It would be just as silly to turn you over to them when I could employ you instead, so come back with me and listen to my offer. That's all I want in exchange for my hospitality," Devikra said. She reached out, placing her hand over Egil's, and Egil couldn't bring himself to pull away. "Besides, I have a vested interest in keeping you alive. Don't ask me more, because I can't tell you."

Across the room, a glass shattered on the ground. Egil jumped at the sound, and Devikra said, "Decide quick, Hound: this is the start of the vision. Will you come with me or not?"

Egil met her warm gaze. To his surprise, he found he wanted to trust her, if only to have someone to trust. He'd been alone for so long. Warmth flowed from her hand on his, and he couldn't remember when he'd last been touched so gently.

He nodded.

Devikra had already planned an escape: out the back, a messenger dragon waited to bear them to safety. He bowed when he saw them, cheating one shoulder down so Devikra and Egil could climb onto his back. Egil winced as the movement jarred his leg, but he didn't have much time to think about it before the dragon was off, cutting higher and higher into the sky and treating Egil to an aerial view of Damael.

It was bigger than he'd realized, with a massive temple situated right at its heart, and he leaned over as far as he dared to watch the city pass by below. Devikra glanced back at him only once, smiling at the awe on his face.

"My city," she called over the warm night air whistling past their ears. "I hope you like it."

Eventually, the dragon made a circling descent right into the Temple of Ellaes Egil had seen before. It was a brightly colored building inlaid with gold and surrounded by high walls. As he climbed to solid ground, he craned his neck to admire the statue of the goddess that stood in this courtyard, with her enigmatic smile and dragonfly's wings spread in invitation.

Ellaes, the patron goddess of the nympherai. He hadn't realized the oracle made her home in one of her temples.

"All of the oracle's work is to honor Her," Devikra explained, as if guessing his thoughts.

Devikra led him around the building, then down a hidden staircase. The door at the bottom swung open before she'd even reached it, hold by an alfar woman with long ears and close-cropped hair. She glanced over Egil curiously before dropping into a curtsy.

"My handmaiden, Wilhara," Devikra told Egil, skipping the last few steps to where Wilhara waited. "Did anyone notice I was gone?"

Wilhara answered with another curtsy, then stepped aside to let them in. "All was quiet."

"Thank you for watching the place, dearest. I know you don't like being left alone," Devikra said to the girl, dropping her voice low. Egil looked away, not sure he was supposed to hear.

The room beyond was wide and comfortable, lit by a smattering of candles and a lively fire in the stone fireplace. Near it, so many pillows were piled up that Egil could barely see the sofas beneath them. A corridor at the back led deeper inside, the faint smell of incense wafting through. "I'm sure someone noticed our arrival," Devikra said, heading for that corridor. "Wait here; they don't like me leaving unannounced, so I have to go smooth some ruffled feathers."

Once she was gone, Wilhara dismissed Egil entirely and sat near the fire, on a cushion on the floor. She pulled a large book into her lap and didn't so much as glance up at Egil again. He paced the room a few times, looking around, then finally wandered to the sofa across from Wilhara, foregoing it at the last moment to join her on the ground. When he winced at the movement, Wilhara looked up, watching his mouth and not his eyes. "You're hurt," she said, more fact than question. "The Enforcers found you on the road today."

The Enforcers again, mentioned so casually. "Does everyone here know about them?"

Wilhara dropped her gaze. "The oracle has seen them many times."

"She tells you what she sees?" Egil guessed, subconsciously lowering his voice to match Wil's soft tone. She relaxed, at that, looking back up at him.

"Dev tells me everything."

"I see," Egil said. Wilhara tugged nervously at the fabrics of her skirt, jostling the book on her lap enough that he could see the pages of a sketchbook covered in charcoal. "What are you drawing?"

"I don't know yet."

"Do you mind if I watch?"

Wilhara bit her lip, considering, then shook her head. When she drew again, her eyes were distant, her hand seeming to move across the page without conscious thought. Egil felt content to watch in silence, enjoying the rare peace of the moment.

"She must like you. She never works with other people present," Devikra said. Her appearance didn't startle Egil—he'd heard her coming down the hall—but he tensed at the sound of a voice coming from so close behind him. He fought the old urge to turn, so his back wouldn't be to her.

"Works?" he asked.

Devikra didn't explain further, coming around the sofa and sprawling out on the one behind Wilhara. Her head tipped back, her eyes closed, she asked, "How much do you know about my operation here?"

"I know you take appointments and that people ask you about their futures," Egil said.

"There's much more to it, though I do try to keep the rest quiet. If the general populace knew everything, they might think of me as...well, not a *false* prophet, but perhaps a disingenuous one. The oracle's visions predict the future. That much is true, but the visions are only flashes without context. There's no controlling what's seen or when. I'm sure you can imagine how inconvenient that is, seeing only fleeting glimpses of such a great world." She looked over at him. Same as back at the inn, he found it difficult to look away from her dark eyes.

"For a long time," she continued, "I struggled with how to use this gift. The visions would predict terrible things, and I didn't know enough to be able to interpret them, to recognize what was happening—not until after they came to pass. I've come to realize I can't save the world unless I see and know as much of it as possible. The more I see, the better I can recognize what the visions predict. I found you today because an acolyte knew the tavern when I described it—goddess knows how. That's not my business. I send agents across the world, have them listen and report back to me. I consult with world leaders and put names to faces. If they ever appear in the oracle's visions, I will know them. Such is my business. It's a business based in the collection of knowledge."

"This is your offer? You want me to be a spy?" Egil guessed.

"Atiuh above, no. I imagine you've had enough of that."

"Then what do you want from me?"

"There's another step in the process, one that comes after the visions. If I can interpret them quickly enough, I can soften the damage. If a vision shows a house burning, while I can't stop the fire, I can evacuate the building before the match is even set. But I'm only one woman, and I can't be everywhere at once. I need help."

"Why me?" Egil asked. "Knowing who I am? What I've done?"

"It's *because* of your work for Unity that I'm interested in you,"

Devikra said with a smile. She sat up and leaned forward, her eyes bright. "In all the world, there is only one information network better than my own: the Enforcers. And you used to lead them! I won't make you do what they did. I want you to help, not hurt. That, and you remind me of someone very dear to me."

Wilhara looked up at that, searching Egil's face closely. When Egil met her eye, she ducked her head.

"What do you say? If you work with me, I can make you a hero," Devikra said.

Egil dropped his gaze to the woven rug, tracing the interlocking pattern with his eyes while he thought. He'd done terrible things for Unity. No matter how much he wanted to, he could never fully atone, but that wouldn't stop him from trying. He wanted the Hound dead. He wanted *Egil* to be someone who does good. He wanted, so desperately, to be a hero.

"Count me in."

———

PRESENT DAY

YEAR OF UNITY 1880

Aleksir jumped at a sudden *clang* in the darkness. Light flooded the hallway beyond his cell as a door was opened, and Aleksir hastily stood when he heard footsteps headed his way. He may be cold and hungry, dirty and disheveled from his day spent in the county jailhouse, but damn it all, he still had his pride.

The constable who'd been on duty all day stopped at his cell door, his wide mouth pulled into an ugly frown. "You've got friends in high places, kid," he grumbled. "You're lucky."

Aleksir's breath caught. Had Devikra sent someone to rescue him? So quickly? Glad as he was to get out, a part of him hoped she'd never learn of this. She'd almost certainly pull him from the field for causing so much trouble.

Then another voice spoke. It wasn't Devikra's. "And *you're* lucky he's in one piece. If you'd hurt him, I would've been very unhappy."

The speaker stopped in front of Aleksir's cell, his black eyes unusually bright and his dark curls falling into his face. His smile was softer than Aleksir had yet seen it, forming two perfect dimples on his cheeks. He snapped his fingers, an impatient gesture that was directed at the constable. "Well?"

The constable scrambled to unlock the cell door.

"Eg—" Aleksir breathed, but Egil held a finger to his lips. His hand was heavily bandaged, Aleksir noticed.

"Come on, kid," Egil said, once the door was unlocked. "We're leaving."

Aleksir didn't hesitate, shooting the constable a glare as he scurried past. "How?" he asked Egil, once they were out of earshot.

"I called in a favor," Egil said, simply. He glanced at Aleksir as they walked, and after a moment, ruffled Aleksir's hair. "You did well today."

Aleksir almost tripped over his own feet. It was almost alarming, how quickly tears sprung to his eyes at the compliment. "You... really?"

"I wouldn't have said it if I didn't mean it."

Aleksir scrubbed at his eyes while slowly, a smile spread across his face. By the time they left the jail, there was a new spring in his step. "What about Maebhe? Did your friend get her family back?"

"He did," Egil said. "They should be on their way back to Orean, by now."

Chapter Eighteen

Far beyond Gallonten's walls, three orinians, a faerie, and a maranet emerged from a wide storm drain onto the shore of a lagoon. The lagoon's dark water reflected the overcast sky above, but when rain began to fall, first with a drop and then with a downpour, that image fractured into a thousand pieces.

"I'd only just dried," Maebhe whined. Beside her, Kieran frowned and pulled his jacket up over his head.

"The storm drains'll be flooded, soon enough. I'll have to go back over land," Ivey complained as well, squinting up at the sky.

He certainly hadn't dressed for cold, biting rain, and Maebhe found herself shrugging out of her borrowed cloak. "Do you want this?" she asked, but Ivey hurried to stop her.

"Don't give that up for me, Ms. Cairn. An hour or two of discomfort is nothing to the journey you all have ahead of you."

When he started up the hill, the others trailed after while Maebhe ran ahead, stopping at the top to blink owlishly down at the plains. It was bright, despite the rain and despite the storm clouds, but maybe that was just her eyes, used to darkness after so long underground.

From where Maebhe stood, the Gallontean plains sloped gently downward and away, their tall grasses bisected by the Unity Road. Small towns and settlements sat scattered along it, as far as she could see, and somewhere beyond it all, Lyryma waited.

Maebhe looked to the north, toward Gallonten's silhouette on the horizon. From here, she could just make out the spired peak of Unity's clock tower and a single dusk-soaked sun past a break in the clouds. It fell on the city, giving it a sinister red cast.

"I didn't realize we'd gotten so far," she said. Her curls clung to her head, rain-damp, and made her look smaller.

"We have a long way to go yet," Drys said. "If we want to reach Lyryma this week, we'll need to cover more ground tonight."

Ivey pointed to a small cluster of lights far down the road. "I know a farmer who'll give you a dry place to sleep. He lives on the far side of that town; look for a barn with a blue and gold barn quilt, but don't let anyone else see you."

They said their goodbyes at the side of the road, Ivey returning to Gallonten while the others started their journey south. It was a long walk, longer than it had seemed from the hill, and they didn't reach the barn Ivey mentioned until late into the evening. By then, they were all tired, sore, wet, and irritable. After some bickering, Kieran and Íde went ahead to the farmhouse while Drys and Maebhe stayed back; Drys couldn't risk venturing into sight with their wings, and Maebhe couldn't maintain pleasant conversation.

When Kieran and Íde returned, Íde carried keys to the barn and a large pot of soup for them to share and Kieran carried an armful of blankets. His eyes were suspiciously red-rimmed, and at Maebhe's questioning look, he sniffed, "They were very kind."

It wasn't exactly a *comfortable* night's sleep for Maebhe, laying on a bed of damp hay with Íde's feet in her face, but it beat sleeping in the rain. And in the morning, the farmer's wife woke them early, offering them a ride to the Lyryma Forest.

Maebhe elbowed her twin. "You should cry on people more often, if this is what it gets us," she whispered.

She spent her morning sprawled in the back of a wide wagon, her head pillowed on Drys' soft wings while she listened to Kieran and Íde chat with their driver. In the late afternoon, they reached a branch where the road split around Lyryma Forest. One branch led east, circling toward the coastal Unity city of Adriad, and the other west, toward the Alfheimr province. There was no road through the wood, and for good reason.

The farmer's wife stopped her wagon there, in the shadow of Lyryma's trees. "You're sure you want to go that way?" she asked.

Maebhe eyed the trees as she hopped to the ground. From here, they looked like any old trees, nothing scary or supernatural about them. Maybe the stories were wrong again. If Egil could still be alive, then Lyryma could be friendly.

"I'm afraid we don't have much choice," Kieran said, shaking the woman's hand. "Thank you for bringing us this far."

She gave Kieran's cheek a fond pat, and Maebhe fought the urge to roll her eyes. Her twin had always been popular among a certain crowd. "Be careful in those woods!" the woman called in a final, ominous parting.

Maebhe waved her goodbyes along with the rest, but turning her back on Lyryma made her shiver. She almost expected the trees to have moved when she turned around again, but they looked exactly as they had before: simple, unassuming, even *pretty*. There was little green left among them, their leaves changed instead to yellow and orange and the occasional crimson. The wind rustled through them while Maebhe waited for someone else to take the lead. No one did. Looking over, she found them all eyeing the forest with the same unease—all but Drys, who gave her a cheeky wink.

"I don't know about this," Íde said, echoing Maebhe's thoughts.

"It's just a forest," Kieran said. It was a poor front; Maebhe could tell he was the most afraid of all of them. "Drys, tell them they're being ridiculous."

"They're wise to fear Lyryma," Drys said, unhelpfully.

Kieran scoffed. Like Maebhe, spite had a way of spurring him into motion, so he straightened his shoulders and marched into the trees without another word.

"Are you going after him, then?" Maebhe asked Íde. "Because I won't if you won't."

"He's *your* brother."

"And your fiancé."

When Kieran had passed almost entirely into shadow, he turned and waved his arms at his companions. "Look!" he called. "I entered the forest and nothing bad happened!"

Maebhe pointed at Kieran and *screamed*. "Kieran, behind you!"

Kieran moved faster than Maebhe thought him able, whirling so frantically that he slipped and landed flat on his tail. Maebhe couldn't help it; she doubled over laughing, and Drys joined in. Even Íde fought a smile. It took Kieran a moment to realize he'd been tricked, and when he did, he picked himself up and angrily brushed the dirt off his pants. Maebhe could hear him cursing from where she stood.

"You should be ashamed of yourselves! You—" He cut off abruptly, something dragging him into the forest and out of sight.

Íde ran after him first. Maebhe was right at her heels, quickly overtaking her and darting between the trees—only to scramble to stop when Kieran jumped out from behind a tree crying, "Boo!" She had time only to scream before colliding with him. He fell, she tripped over him, and they both landed face-first in the mud.

"You *ass*!" Maebhe shrieked. She tackled Kieran just as he'd started to pull himself back up, easily catching him in a headlock while he laughed too hard to defend himself. She shoved him into the mud, ignoring his muffled protests, and only released him when Íde arrived.

Íde was normally the one to pull Maebhe off him, but this time, she flicked him on the forehead.

"What have I told you about including me in your pranks?"

"Not to do it," Maebhe said smugly, sitting on her haunches in the mud.

"Don't you dare," Íde warned her. "You started this."

"I quite like you all," Drys said, catching up to them with a massive grin plastered across their face.

Maebhe wiped the mud off her face and glared at Kieran. As dignified as he could manage, half-covered in mud himself, Kieran said, "Don't look at me like that. I got you into the forest, didn't I?"

Loath as she was to admit it, he was right. All four of them had safely entered Lyryma forest, and as Kieran said, nothing bad had happened. It was strange, though. As normal as the forest had looked from the outside, inside, it was as if it had doubled, tripled in scale: Maebhe couldn't see the tops of the trees from where she kneeled, but the roots that twisted over the ground were almost as wide as she was. She thought of all the stories she'd heard growing up about orinians vanishing in the woods, about monsters the size of houses and magics that stole your soul and changed you into something unrecognizable.

Well. It was too late to turn back.

Once Maebhe and Kieran had picked themselves up, they pressed on. The deeper they journeyed, the more the trees' canopies blocked the sunlight, the more the air around them warmed, the more the humidity clung to their hair and skin. Maebhe had to roll up Egil's muddied cloak and secure it to her pack. She didn't understand how, but this climate was completely different from Gallonten north of it and Orean south. It defied all reason and science.

Ahead of the perplexed orinians, Drys sighed contentedly and stretched their wings, the only one unbothered by the changing weather. Maebhe watched the light dance across their golden feathers and let it distract her.

"Drys, what did you do to get locked up?" she called. In yesterday's chaos, it hadn't occurred to her to ask sooner. She didn't *think* she'd been traveling with a murderer, but it was best to check.

Kieran elbowed her. "Don't be rude."

"As if you didn't already ask," Maebhe hissed, elbowing back.

"I didn't!"

"I don't mind," Drys said magnanimously. "I killed a Unity representative."

Kieran and Maebhe stopped slapping at each other and stared, wide-eyed. "Really?" Íde asked.

Drys scoffed. "No. I flew too near Gallonten. Unity thought I was stealing secrets and sent a police dragon after me."

"Oh," Maebhe said.

"You sound disappointed, my dear May-*vuh*. Would you rather I'd killed someone?" they teased. Not waiting for an answer, they laughed and shook out their wings. "It's good to be back. It'll be even better to return to Home."

"You've said that a few times, now. Don't you mean return *home*?" Kieran asked.

"*To* Home," Drys repeated. "Home has many names, but we use this one with outsiders because it gives you the best understanding of what Home *is*. You could also call it a city, or a hub. Or what do you call Orean? A city-state? Millions of nympherai make their homes in this forest, scattered to the winds, but during the dangerous seasons we all return to Home."

"Dangerous seasons," Íde echoed. "What does that mean?"

"Lyryma doesn't follow winter, spring, or summer like the outside world. It has its own cycles, and during some of those cycles, we need the extra strength that numbers provide," Drys said. The concerned look the orinians shared didn't escape them, and they chuckled. "Don't you believe your own stories? When we say this forest is magic, it's not superstition, and it's not exaggeration. We have science and reason, too, but we still say this forest is impossible. But I don't need to lecture—you'll see, soon enough."

Maebhe realized something, then. "Are there frìth in Home?"

"Of course. Have you never met one?"

"Never," Maebhe said, shaking her head. "Until yesterday, I'd never even met a faerie."

"Hmm. We used to visit Orean, on occasion, but I can't remember if that was two, twenty, or two-hundred years ago."

"You don't *remember*?" Maebhe asked. For the first time, it struck her that Drys might be older than they looked. She'd only ever been around orinians; she'd forgotten how wonderful and diverse the world was. "Did frìth visit Orean, too?"

"Not since the current king took reign, at least," Kieran answered.

"A word of advice, then: they're very different from humans. The frìth of Home are the oldest people alive today, some of them even older than Lyryma itself," Drys said. "That affects how they move through the world. Be patient with them; they don't understand how little time you or I have, by comparison."

Ears pressed to her head, Maebhe craned her neck, the trees seeming to stretch on without end. She couldn't imagine anything older than them.

"They also won't hear of the outside world unless it's on their terms," Drys continued. "So I wouldn't mention this kidnapping and war business."

"But—," Kieran started. At a warning look from Drys, he shut his mouth again. "Understood."

"No arguments from you, Ms. Maebhe?" they asked, turning to walk backwards so they could face her. Maebhe's eyes widened. Instead of answering, she cried, "Look out!" just as Drys backed into a tree.

With an *oof* and a dazed step forward, Drys twisted to look up at the tree trunk in surprise. None of them had noticed it there moments before. It was as if it had materialized out of the foliage, its gnarled, coarse bark covered in strange blue drawings. As Maebhe stepped forward, trying to get a better look at the drawings, the tree trunk—the crooked, *furry* tree trunk—moved back. It picked itself right off the ground and jumped back several feet, a cloven hoof bigger than Drys' head striking the ground with a thud.

With growing horror, Maebhe lifted her gaze.

It wasn't a tree trunk at all. It was a *leg*.

Chapter Nineteen

A FLAT, ALIEN FACE EMERGED from between the branches and leaves as the leg's owner bent to examine Drys. Yelping, Drys stumbled back into Maebhe, stepping on her foot in the process. Alarmed by the noise, the creature straightened, disappearing back into the foliage. After a long, tense moment where neither party moved, the creature pulled one of the branches aside and looked down at them again. They all stared at each other, Maebhe with an armful of faerie wings, the creature with its free hand on its chest in an affronted gesture, and Íde and Kieran watching from the back with open mouths.

"What—," Maebhe squeaked. But no, that would be rude. "Um. *Who* are you?"

Before the creature could respond, Drys' feathers puffed indignantly. "Leileas, you startled me!"

The creature's face scrunched up as she bared her teeth at Drys. It took Maebhe a moment to realize she was smiling. "I hardly recognized you, Drys. You have been gone so long," she said. Her voice was softer than Maebhe expected.

Drys huffed. "Don't be sarcastic, Leileas. I haven't been gone four months; that's nothing to your kind."

Leileas was covered in shaggy brown fur dappled with white spots. Her legs were like a goat's, the same shape as some of the other nympherai Maebhe had seen in Gallonten. Her face was like a deer's without the snout, with a wide forehead that blended into a flat nose. There was something almost *cute* in the twitch of it and flutter of her eyelashes, which had to be longer than Maebhe's entire hand.

Even as Leileas met Maebhe's gaze, two of the creature's ears swiveled away from the group, picking up something in the forest that the orinians couldn't hear. They were similar in shape to an orinian's, long and round like a cow's, but she had three on each side, each weighed down by a collection of small earrings. A pair of twisting horns sat atop her head.

Leileas must be frìth. Maebhe had seen drawings in dusty old sketchbooks, but those never accounted for scale.

"You two...know each other?" Íde asked.

"Leileas is a friend from Home," Drys said.

"Are you bringing them there?" Leileas asked. "Why?"

"Just a stop on the way to Orean. They need to get through the forest quickly, so I'm guiding them," Drys said. At Leileas' inquisitive head tilt, they explained, "I'm repaying a debt."

Leileas nodded and eyed the orinians. Maebhe fidgeted under her stare, her large black eyes reminded her of Roman's—seeing her, seeing *through* her, making her feel for a moment like she mattered in the grand plot of the world. "You trust them?" Leileas asked.

"Enough for them to see the way to Home? Of course," Drys said. "They're orinians, Leileas. Unity hates them almost as much as they do us. They won't harm Home."

Leileas' ears all perked up at once. "Orinians!" She squatted to examine them all closer, branches snapping as she went down. Even crouching, she was big as a shed. "I've never met an orinian. Forgive me. I thought you were of Unity."

"If you ever wonder in the future, orinians are the only ones with tails," Maebhe added, grabbing Kieran's and holding it out for inspection. He slapped her hand away.

"They've never met any frìth, either," Drys supplied.

"You will meet many in Home," Leileas said, standing again. Pointing at the path behind her with her chin, she turned and pressed into the wood, making a trail through the brush. Drys didn't hesitate to follow, but the others did, all staring after Leileas with awe. Over her shoulder, she called, "Come. Orean is a long journey—a week, with no complications."

"Complications?" Kieran asked, finally hurrying to follow and dragging Íde along with. Not eager to be left behind, Maebhe jogged after them.

"The forest is dangerous, especially for little ones. Even more so than usual, of late," Leileas said, her voice like wind through the ancient trees. When she ducked out of the way of a branch, a bird flew out of it to perch on her shoulder, remaining there as Leileas kept walking. Her ears twitched when the bird chirped, but she didn't otherwise react. "While Drys can get you through safely, safety requires caution. That caution may slow you down."

"I suppose it's still faster than going around would have been," Kieran sighed. "There would've been no taking the train, anyway."

Though she tipped her head curiously at the word *train*, Leileas didn't ask. "What are your names?"

"Maebhe," Maebhe said, pointing to herself. "And this is Kieran and Íde. It's nice to meet you."

"What do your tattoos mean?"

Subconsciously, Maebhe touched her birthmarks. Leileas had tattoos of her own; while her neck, chest, and inner thighs were covered in fur, other parts were covered in hard, bark-like armor—shins, arms, shoulders, back. Blue drawings were etched across the armor, depicting strange creatures—big cats with three heads, elk with twisted faces, and more. Swirling, intertwining borders ran between them.

"They're not tattoos," Kieran answered. "We're born with these."

Leileas' tufty brows drew into something like a frown. "I was under the assumption that humans tattooed themselves, too. Don't they?"

"Some. Some orinians do, too, to accentuate their birthmarks. Or to cover them," Íde said. She held her arm out in front of her, looking at the scratch-like markings on her hand and exposed wrist. While the others were turned away, Kieran took her hand and kissed it.

"Do yours mean something?" Maebhe asked.

Mirroring Íde's position, Leileas looked over her own arm disinterestedly. "Some, not all. This one was my first hunt. I wanted to remember it, even a thousand years from now," she said, pointing to the three-headed cat on her shoulder.

The journey passed in pleasant conversation, Leileas quietly inquisitive about the orinians and Orean. She knew more than Maebhe would have expected about the outside world; when she asked, Leileas said it was because of the fae. While frìth never left the wood, the fae could get away with doing so. Now and then, they checked on the state of things outside and reported them back to Home. After the old human traditions, they jokingly called it "setting out to seek their fortunes."

It was what Drys had been doing when they'd been caught by Unity. From Leileas' teasing about it, Maebhe learned it was only Drys' second excursion, and that made Drys quite young for one of the fae. From Drys' teasing reply, she got the sense that Leileas, too, was considered young.

After a full day of walking, they reached the hidden city of Home. Maebhe ached from the exertion, but when she saw Home, she forgot her pain. If magic really existed in Lyryma, it existed here. She'd expected a towering city like Orean or Gallonten, but instead, Home was built deep into a canyon. The trees cut off abruptly at the canyon's edge, where the grassy forest floor changed into a steep, muddy slope. Dreamy layers of mist hung over the city, but from where she stood, Maebhe could still make out the size of how *massive* it was. Bigger than Gallonten, bigger than Orean. Bigger than both combined, probably.

Below them, Home fit snugly in its nook, as colorful and lively as the forest rooted around it. The brick buildings were covered in the moss and flowering vines of hundreds of years of growth.

"How many frìth live here?" Íde asked, voice stained with awe. A river ran through Home, bisecting the old buildings. The grander of these ran along the river's bank, and at the center of the city, Maebhe could make out a swath of green.

"Less than you would think. Less than there are orinians in Orean."

"But it's so big," Maebhe said.

"It's busier during the dangerous seasons, but most of these buildings have sat empty since the Great War. Our population still hasn't recovered," Leileas explained.

Íde bit her lip. "I'm sorry."

Leileas shrugged. "I wasn't alive to see it."

The way she said that made Maebhe wonder... "But others were? Are there really frìth that were alive during the Great War?"

"Oh, yes. There are five or six of them still, though only Muir and Senga are in Home today."

"But that was almost two thousand years ago!" Kieran said. Of the human peoples, not even maranet could reach a thousand. While Maebhe marveled over this revelation, she followed Leileas along the canyon edge to a stone staircase leading down into the city. As far as she could tell, it was the only accessible entrance from this side. It was also, she noticed with dread, frìth-sized. Each step would be a jump for them.

Kieran groaned at the sight.

It was then Maebhe noticed the melodies drifting up to them from the streets below, impossibly complex. Maebhe felt them calling her.

"Try not to listen," Leileas told the orinians. "Drys, will you fly ahead and tell Muir and Senga to expect visitors?"

"Of course. I'll see you all at the bottom," Drys said with a lazy salute and an unsympathetic smile. With that, they spread their wings and took off, leaving the others to start their slow descent. Leileas waited patiently for the orinians after each step, apparently in no rush to reach the bottom.

"Drys likes you," she said conversationally. "That's a lucky thing. If a faerie dislikes you, they'll make you miserable. And if they don't care, that's even worse. Who is their debt to?"

"A friend of ours. He broke us out of—" Kieran bit his tongue when he remembered Drys' advice. "Well, he got us out of some trouble."

Leileas only nodded.

At the bottom of the stairs stood a statue even taller than their frìth friend. It depicted a woman in an elegant, draping gown, a thousand small flames etched into her skin and a pair of dragonfly wings flaring out on either side of her. Her stone gaze seemed to settle directly on Maebhe. While Kieran and Íde caught their breath, Maebhe approached her, eyeing the flames on her skin, the marble vines crawling up her dress. "Ellaes?" she guessed.

"Yes," Leileas said approvingly. "As Atuos is the patron Guardian of your people, Ellaes is ours. She created this forest for us during the Great War to keep us safe from the outside world."

As they continued on, Maebhe glanced back at the goddess, watching her fade back into the mist.

Leileas led them into the heart of the city, through winding streets, past houses more plant than brick, and to the river they'd seen from above. Somehow, the industrialization of the outside world had not touched Home. There was no electricity here, no factories, no lanterns or carriages. Above the trees surrounding the canyon, the air was clean, without a hint of smog.

"This Muir and Senga we're meeting," Kieran started as they walked, "They're the ones you mentioned earlier?"

Leileas nodded. "The current leaders of Home," she said. Noticing their nervous looks, she said, "You have nothing to fear from them. If you feign interest in their stories, they will love you."

Maebhe laughed. "Our Nana's the same way."

"I'm sure there'll be no need to feign anything," Íde said warmly.

They turned another corner to find a small crowd gathered in an open, grassy field—the green Maebhe had seen from above. Drys stood between two frìth even larger than Leileas, one with Leileas' red fur and the other with the same twist to their horns. Leileas inclined her head respectfully as they reached the group. The orinians, unsure of how to act, dropped into awkward bows, half-hidden behind Leileas.

"Welcome, little ones," the red-furred frìth said, crouching to examine them. "Drys was just informing us of thy arrival."

"Hello," Íde said, when the twins were too stunned to speak. "We're sorry to intrude so suddenly."

These two frìth, older than Unity, older than the forest, older than even the Great War, bared their teeth in those strange frìth smiles. "Thy people are always welcome in Home," the other said. "But Drys warned us of thy hurry. I pray there is no trouble?"

Seeing Drys' expression tighten, Maebhe said, "No trouble. We're just feeling homesick."

Given the frith's curious head tilt, Maebhe guessed it wasn't a problem they frequently experienced. "Well," said the red-furred frith in her thick, curling accent, "We shall help thee forget thy homesickness, at least for tonight."

That night, Home threw a party for the orinians complete with music, drinking, and dancing. It was more of what Maebhe had expected from Home, given the stories she'd heard: melodies that soothed and stoked, wine that danced on the tongue. None of the orinians were ever able to figure out where the music was coming from, even after Kieran and Maebhe made a game of it. It came from everywhere at once, from above and below, in front and behind. It was unlike anything they'd heard before.

There were dozens of frith and even more fae present, spread across the grassy field at the center of Home. Watching the frith dance was a delight in itself; they twirled and stepped to the music like their strange legs had been made for it, weaving between each other in patterns too complex for the orinians to follow.

"We're being rude," Íde announced, standing. They'd been sitting off to the side for most of the evening, watching but not participating, talking only to those who talked to them first, even if that number was quite high. Maebhe was on her third glass of wine. "They threw this party for us; we must try to enjoy it. Kieran, dance with me." She held her slender hand out, pulling Kieran to his feet when he took it. He dipped into a gallant bow, wobbling a little from the wine, and let Íde drag him away.

"I'm coming for you, next!" Íde called back to Maebhe.

"No, she's probably not!" Kieran added, pulling Íde to his side and making her laugh.

"I'll just sit here alone, then," Maebhe grumbled. "Who would want to dance with them, anyway?"

She was only alone for a minute. Leileas squatted beside her, balled up so she and Maebhe were almost on the same level. "You seem upset, little one. Do you not like parties?"

"I don't feel like celebrating right now. Thank you for arranging this, though."

Leileas nodded, accepting the explanation without question. "The fae did most of it. Our good neighbors seize every opportunity to celebrate, and now they have outsiders to perform for. I'd offer to dance with you, but I'm afraid I'd crush you. I take after Muir when it comes to dancing."

Maebhe looked over to where the old frìth was twirling and hopping about and giggled. "As funny as that would be, I like living."

Leileas laughed as well, her furry nose wrinkling.

"Wait. What do you mean, *take after*?"

"Muir and Senga are my parents," Leileas said. She dropped onto the ground fully, spreading her long, hoofed legs out in front of her. "They are pleased to meet you, little one. They've always liked orinians."

"Really? I feel like we're intruding. You've all been very welcoming, but Home feels so private."

"You could not intrude here. You're orinians. You're like us, so you're welcome. We outsiders must stick together, just as Unity's people stick together. One day, we may need to come to each other's aid."

"Do you really believe that?"

Leileas frowned, tufty eyebrows jutting out. "Of course."

Maebhe inched closer to the frìth. Alcohol making her mind tip and twirl like Muir's dancing, she said, "There's a reason I don't feel like dancing. And why we're in such a hurry to get home. My people are in trouble."

Leileas nodded slowly. "Drys warned you not to tell? My

people…they are not very receptive to news of the world outside, but if it needs to be said, little one, then say it."

Maebhe did. She told Leileas everything. She told her about the alfar king, Kieran and Íde's arrest, the war-mongering newspapers, and their escape from Unity. Leileas remained expressionless throughout.

"I must tell Senga," Leileas said when she'd finished, moving to get up.

Maebhe stopped her with a hand on her arm, surprised at the softness of her fur. "Don't. Let them have this party. Let them have tonight."

After studying Maebhe for a moment, Leileas nodded. "Morning, then. But rest assured, Maebhe Cairn: we frìth will help you." They fell into silence after that, Maebhe watching Kieran and Íde dance. They looked so happy. Maebhe wrapped her arms around herself.

Drys chose that moment to join them, sitting on Maebhe's other side and holding something out to her. Maebhe took it and examined it. It was a chain of pink flowers, tied to form a circle. "What—"

"It's a crown. You wear it on your head, like so." Drys took it back and placed it atop Maebhe's head.

Maebhe couldn't help but laugh, adjusting the flower crown. "This is for me? But what about you?"

"I made one for myself, too, of course," Drys said, pulling out a second crown and placing it on their own head. The golden flowers matched the feathers in their wings. "I would've made one for you, Leileas, dear, but I don't think there are enough flowers in all of Home."

Maebhe laughed. Drys stood and held out a hand. "Dance with me, May-*vuh*."

It may have been the wine, but Maebhe found herself agreeing.

Chapter Twenty

Gareth hurried down the hall, wrapping his dressing gown tighter around himself and cursing whoever was pounding on his door so early in the morning. Isobel, Ofelia, and the servants still slept, but if this visitor kept at it, they wouldn't for long.

Normally, Gareth was the last to rise, but he was just finishing a forced all-nighter. Well, perhaps not *forced*—he'd procrastinated spectacularly on some team readings and now had less than eight hours to finish them. He opened the door, ready to tell his visitor he had an important meeting to prepare for and no time to waste indulging rude guests, but the person was pushing his way inside before Gareth could get even a word out.

"I beg your—why, Mr. Hallisey!"

"Hello, Gareth!" Roman said with one of his bright, boyish grins. Despite already standing in the foyer, he asked, "Mind if I come in?"

"You may as well," Gareth huffed, shutting the door behind him. When he turned to look at the young man, all the admonitions he'd been readying died on his tongue. That smile of Roman's was *off* somehow. Or maybe it was his eyes. They were too wild, the black irises too large, the dark circles beneath them even darker than usual.

"Atiuh's name, Roman. Are you all right?"

"Hmm? Just fine," Roman said, with a smile even less convincing than the last.

For a moment, they just stared at each other, and then Gareth cleared his throat. "Well, don't apologize for waking me, or anything," he teased.

Roman looked down at Gareth's velvety dressing gown. "Oh. Sorry?"

"Do you have any idea what time it is?"

"I thought it was morning," Roman said, rubbing his eyes. Gareth hadn't realized the effect the young man's stare had on his nerves until it was hidden behind his hands.

"It is. *Early* morning."

It took Roman a moment to understand, and his eyes widened when he realized his mistake. "Shit! I am sorry, Gareth," he said, finally sounding himself again. "One of the suns is up, and I didn't think about it beyond that. Hit me over the head and send me on my way; I can bother you at a more reasonable time."

"It's quite all right, Roman. It's always a pleasure to see you, and besides, I was already awake. I was only teasing, before," Gareth assured him. Team readings be damned. He had a friend who needed him. "Come upstairs, why don't you? I have some work to do, but you can keep me company."

Gareth led an unusually subdued Roman up to his sitting room. Apart from the slivers of pale sunslight peeking around the edges of the curtains, a small electric lamp on Gareth's cluttered writing desk was the only source of light in the room. Roman took careful steps inside ahead of Gareth, his hand trailing along the back of the sofa as he went. The slow, predatory movement gave Gareth an uneasy feeling, the small hairs at the back of his neck standing on end.

"You don't seem yourself, son," Gareth observed.

Roman said, "That's funny, because I feel more myself than I have in a long time." He shrugged, his smile not reaching his eyes. "I'm sorry if I seem strange. I didn't get much sleep last night."

"That's all right," Gareth said, though he didn't like that smile. He'd spoken to Roman on the phone only a few hours ago, and he hadn't been…like this. "Did something happen?"

Roman blinked, then looked away. He shrugged. "A lot, actually. Dinara and I decided to go our separate ways."

"What?! You seemed so close the other day! What happened?"

"*Seemed* is the right word for it," Roman said. "The truth is that we're not as compatible as we had hoped, and in the end, it was a mutual decision. While I'm sad, I'm not heartbroken."

Gareth gave the young man's shoulder an awkward pat. Almost imperceptibly, Roman flinched at the touch. "If you need to talk about it, I'll listen. But give me a moment," Gareth said, gesturing back at his desk. "I have one report to finish before I can take a break."

"Of course," Roman said, eyeing Gareth's desk with a spark of his former curiosity.

While Gareth sat back down to work, Roman wandered to the bookshelves behind him. He tried to ignore the *slide* of cloth-bound books being pulled from shelves, the rustle of pages, but when Roman made a soft, contemptuous sound, Gareth had to turn to look. Roman held one of Gareth's earliest publications, an anthology on mythological figures and their lasting impact. Unsurprisingly, Gareth had written his chapter about Egil.

"It's only been sixty years since Histrios; that's no time at all," Roman said. "I wouldn't call Egil mythological.

No time at all? Gareth gave Roman a sidelong look. "Though it's true that I would classify Egil more as a folk hero than a mythological one, technically, the defining criteria of mythology has less to do with time and more to do with how a story has shaped a culture's belief systems. If you look back far enough, Egil stories have roots in many cultural origins. Especially if you view him as a son of Atuos—"

Roman shut the book with an audible *thump*. "Well, you know him best. I'll take your word for it," he said.

Gareth squinted, trying to interpret Roman's tone. He wasn't sure what he'd said wrong, but he felt the need to defend his credentials. "I've been studying him for twenty years," he pointed out. "I do, in fact, know a thing or two about him."

Roman laughed, but the mocking tilt to it seemed to be directed more toward himself than Gareth. "Somehow, I forgot that about you. Atiuh only knows how I managed *that*. Have you ever met anyone who knew him?"

When Gareth only squinted harder, Roman seemed to realize Gareth had misinterpreted the question. "I'm really just curious," he quickly clarified. "I'm not trying to challenge your expertise."

To hear it said so plainly, Gareth felt foolish. "I've had a few short interviews, but people who knew him *well* are hard to find. And when I do find them, they often won't talk about him. In Damael, no one wants to cross their Oracle. In Alfheimr, they only sneer—as much as alfar ever sneer, anyway. I think everyone else has been threatened by Unity." Gareth chuckled. "I asked Magistrate Diomis about him at a Yuletide Party once and I was half sure the nympherai would have me banned from the premises for it. If only I could go to Home—I'm sure I'd have luck there."

Roman nodded and perched on the arm of Gareth's sofa. "What about Prince Nochdvor?"

"I haven't worked myself up to asking him, just yet. You know the stories. Despite their friendship, it was Prince Nochdvor who shot Egil in Histrios when Egil lost control."

Roman watched Gareth closely, his black eyes glittering in the low lamplight. "Are you afraid that if you ask him, he'll tell you the stories about Histrios are true? What if Egil wasn't the hero you've written about all these years?"

Gareth fidgeted. It was hard not to shy away from those eyes of Roman's when they saw so easily through to his greatest fears. "I think that's unlikely."

"Why?"

"None of the stories we tell about Egil are, strictly speaking, *true*," Gareth said, gesturing to his bookshelves. "They're full of embellishments and exaggerations. Some are total fabrication. If you study a subject long enough, though, you'll see a pattern in the stories. It's in that pattern where you'll find the truth. By all accounts, in every story, Egil loved this world and the people in it. Everything he did, he did it for them. That's why the stories about Histrios fall flat, and it's more nuanced than just 'Egil is good' or 'Egil is bad.' *No one* is all good or all bad. Did you know Prince Nochdvor dresses only in black? He's in mourning, and I suspect he has been for sixty years."

Whatever Roman expected Gareth to say, it clearly wasn't that. His eyes widened. "What?"

"That's a *long* time in mourning, even for an alfar. It says a lot about the kind of man Egil must've been, don't you think? He's not the only one whose life Egil touched. That's why, even if Egil *did* go mad in the end, and even if the prince confirms it, that doesn't mean Egil wasn't a hero. All I can do is look at what I know, that Egil was someone who tried to do the right thing, and have faith in that."

Roman slid off the arm onto the couch cushion, flopped onto his back, and stared dully up at Gareth's ceiling. "What did doing the right thing ever get him?"

"I can't speak for him, but I know what it got *me*," Gareth said, earning himself a curious look from Roman. "When I was young, my nanny gifted me a book of Egil stories. It was thanks to her, and certainly not my parents, that I learned to love the world and people around me, and it was thanks to those stories that I found my courage. I've tried to live every day holding to Egil's values, and now I'm teaching them to Ofelia, as well. And when our son is born, I'll teach him, too. It's the nature of kindness to bloom and spread, but the unfortunate truth is that we rarely see the results of the seeds we sow. And so we return to the importance of faith: faith that, at the end of each day, the world will grow just a little bit better."

Gareth only had time to see Roman's brows furrow before the young man slung his arms over his eyes, hiding them. "I wish I could have that kind of faith."

"Having faith isn't a wish, it's a choice. Does this have something to do with Ms. Condeh?" Gareth asked gently.

"Well...maybe. Traveling with her was easy, but cowardly, too. Now that I don't have the excuse of traveling with her, I don't know what to do." When Gareth approached, Roman peeked briefly out from under his arm, his eyes suspiciously red-rimmed.

"You're a bright, charming young man with excellent prospects," Gareth assured him. "You have plenty of options."

Roman's mouth twisted into a wry smile. After a moment and a suspicious sniffle, he sat up, the couch cushion leaving his hair mussed. "Options, yes, but which of them is *right*? How did your Egil of myth and folklore always know the right thing to do?"

"I imagine he followed his heart," Gareth said. It was his turn now to perch on the arm of the couch. From this angle, his young visitor looked especially pitiful. Perhaps that was why Gareth said what he said next. "I hate to drag you into this, but if you're truly at a loss for what to do, you would be welcome to join us on the mission to Illyon."

Roman stared at Gareth. "What?"

"I know what you're thinking. Why would you want to, right? If you come with, I think you could do some real good."

"No," Roman interrupted. "I meant, can you *do* that? Invite me? Do you have the authority?"

"Ah," Gareth said. "Yes and no. Ultimately, I'll have to run it by Moira, but Unity has allowed me a guard, and I just got word last night that the fellow I'd previously chosen can no longer join us. So I have my pick, and you *have* already saved my life once."

"What happened to the last guy?"

"I'm not sure," Gareth admitted. "Apparently, he's 'no longer fit for duty,' whatever that means."

Hearing this, Roman's expression turned complicated.

"I know working for Unity is not ideal for you, but it would be nice to have you along," Gareth said, guessing at the meaning for it.

Silence stretched between them while Roman thought. Finally, he heaved a heavy sigh. "Okay," he said. "I'll do it, if you can get your sister's blessing."

"That's wonderful!" Gareth clapped his hands together. "Don't you worry about Moira; I'm sure I can bully her into agreeing, since she forced me into this mess in the first place. Do you have any questions? Anything I can say to allay your concerns?"

"There is one thing I'm curious about," Roman began, looking innocently up at Gareth. "I've heard so many rumors about what happened. People keep mentioning *magic*—do you know why? Is there really magic involved?"

It was a reasonable thing to be apprehensive about, Gareth supposed—the accounts in the newspaper were getting more outlandish by the day. Explosions, magical teleportation, sleeping spells. "No one's mentioned it on the official record, or in any of our meetings," Gareth said. And that was true. Even Moria had kept tight-lipped when Gareth had questioned her. But he remembered that day on the island, listening to Leandros and Rheamaren Nochdvor argue with the Magistrates through closed doors. "That said, I do believe the Nochdvors saw something strange that day."

"So Leandros knows," Roman sighed, defeated. And there it was again—Roman's casual use of the prince's given name, just like that day at the theater. "I guess I'll have to talk to him."

"If you're planning on joining the team, I would think so."

He'd suspected as much, but Gareth felt certain now that Roman and Leandros knew each other. He opened his mouth to ask about it, but then Roman interrupted by waving Gareth back toward his desk. "I know you have work to do, Gareth. I feel much better now, so you needn't waste any more time with me. I'll be quiet as a church mouse."

True to his word, Roman quieted after that, but even after returning to his desk Gareth could feel those dark eyes on his back. He skimmed hastily through the last few reports, turning when he was done only to find Roman curled up on the couch, asleep. Gareth smiled and draped a blanket over Roman before heading upstairs to try to get some sleep of his own.

———

Roman woke much later on a sofa that was too short for him, his feet hanging absurdly off the edge. A muscle in his back gave a sharp protest when he sat up, and he buried his head in his hands with a groan, blocking the bright sunslight. He was far too old to be passing out on random couches.

It took him a moment to remember where he was, and with it came all the memories from the night before. He didn't want to think about any of it—not Dinara, not his dreams, not Unity. So instead, he peered around Gareth's sitting room, then down at himself. At some point, a knitted blanket had been draped over him.

He shouldn't have come here. He didn't know why he had. As long as he was here, though...

He crossed over to Gareth's desk and picked through the papers strewn across it. Most had CONFIDENTIAL stamped across them, but Roman ignored the warning, picking up a page up to study it.

"You're up," a voice came from behind Roman. Quietly, subtly folding the roster and slipping it into his vest pocket, Roman turned to find a maid standing in the doorway, regarding him with curiosity. When she realized she was staring, she dropped into a hasty curtsy. "The Ranulfs are taking breakfast out on the balcony; they've asked that you join them."

"Thank you," Roman said. "Which way is that?"

"Down the hall and to the right, through the dining room. Would you like me to show you?"

"That won't be necessary," Roman said. Following her directions, he turned down a cheerfully-decorated hallway and found an alfar man lounging against the wall, looking bored. An eyepatch covered one eye, his reddish-brown hair flopping into the other, but Roman stopped short when their gazes met. He could always tell an Enforcer by the empty look in their eyes.

The man looked Roman up and down and asked, "Got any weapons on you?"

Roman raised an eyebrow, then both of his arms, doing a slow turn to show that he was unarmed. Satisfied, the man nodded Roman into the dining room. Roman didn't so much as breathe as he passed. A part of him was sure the alfar would attack, but instead, he just picked idly at his nails.

The dining room itself was empty, a flute-like laugh drifted in through the open balcony doors. Isobel. Roman followed the sound to find all three Ranulfs and a stranger sitting around a table, the white ends of its tablecloth snapping and fluttering in the fall breeze. While he'd never met the human Magistrate, he'd known as soon as he saw that Enforcer in the hallway that he would find her here.

"Good morning!" Gareth called. He sat facing Roman, his back to the rooftops of Gallonten. Beyond him sat Unity Island and the blue horizon, streaks of color dancing through the sky above it. It was rare that Gallonten wasn't lost under a blanket of smog. Roman had thought he was past finding beauty in this crooked city, but suddenly, he was struck by it.

"Morning," he greeted. He had no desire to dine with a Magistrate, but for such a view, he'd plug his nose against the bitter taste. "I don't want to intrude—"

"It's a good thing you're not, then," Isobel said cheerfully. Sitting beside Gareth, she gestured at the open seat across from her—next to the Magistrate. "Join us. Help yourself to some breakfast."

"I didn't want to wake you; it seemed like you needed the sleep," Gareth said. "Moira, this is Roman Hallisey, the one I was telling you about. Roman, this is my sister, Moira Ranulf."

Moira's eyes trailed over Roman's face—the dark bags under his eyes, his mussed hair—and then his clothes—well made, but worn and out of style by several decades. Her assessment ended with his scarred, calloused hands, and Roman tugged his sleeve down so she wouldn't see the brand on his wrist.

"Pleasure," she said flatly.

"Likewise," Roman said, matching her tone. In agreeing to Gareth's guard idea, he'd foolishly hoped he wouldn't have to meet with any Magistrates personally. Had Gareth already told her about his offer? From Moira's cold look, Roman had to assume the answer was yes. With a sigh, he took a seat beside her.

The table was piled high with more food than five people could comfortably eat: plates of rolls, bowls of fruit, warm ham and a pot of rich, bitter coffee Roman could smell from where he sat. He felt a little out of place, though he couldn't tell if it was the luxury or the familial domesticity. Both were foreign to him.

"And of course, this is our daughter Ofelia," Isobel said. "Ofelia, say hello to Mr. Hallisey. He's a friend of your father's."

Ofelia stared at him. "How d'you do," she murmured through a mouthful of potatoes.

"It's a pleasure to meet you, Ofelia," Roman said seriously. "I like your dress."

Ofelia muttered something else that could've been a "thank you."

"She looks just like you, Isobel," Roman observed.

"Fortunately for her," Gareth agreed.

"She has Gareth's curls," Isobel said, tucking a lock of dark hair behind Ofelia's ear. Ofelia and Roman's eyes both went to Gareth's bald head.

"I *choose* to shave it, you know," Gareth said stiffly.

Isobel made a sound that could have been a cough. "Gareth told me what happened with Dinara," she said, watching Roman for signs of unease. "You're welcome to stay with us a while, if you need a place. We have a spare room."

Roman stared at her and, when Gareth nodded his agreement, at Gareth. "I..." was all he managed before having to stop. There was a strange lump in his throat. He'd resigned himself to cheap inns at best, the oracle's safe house at worst. "That's very kind of you."

"Think nothing of it," Gareth said with a smile. His eyes crinkled at the corners, lines left there by a lifetime of smiling. "Consider it my thanks to you for saving my life."

Moira looked up from her plate. "I beg your pardon?"

"Didn't I say? Roman's the one who saved me the night I was mugged. That was how we first met."

The Magistrate studied Roman anew, her gaze more calculating this time. It was a familiar look, especially found in the eyes of a Unity Magistrate—like a man eyeing up a painting he was thinking to buy. It was a look that reminded Roman of past pain, of a long line of Magistrates who'd hurt and used him and felt no remorse. He had no doubt Moira would do the same, if given the chance.

She would not get that chance.

"You have my thanks, Mr. Hallisey," Moira said, her tone warmer now. "Gareth mentioned the invitation he extended to you. Have you done any guard work before?"

"I've been traveling with the Webhon Players for two years in that capacity."

"Ah! The Webhon Players," Moira said. "That was an excellent show they put on, the other night. It's a pity we had to close the theater after the break-in."

Gareth choked on his food and started coughing into his elbow. "The *what*?" he asked, when he could.

"It was in the papers this morning, darling," Isobel said. "The island was locked down yesterday afternoon after some intruders somehow got past the bridge. I meant to ask you about that, Moira. You can't really believe orinian terrorists were behind this."

"Terrorists?" Gareth repeated.

"That's what the papers are saying," Isobel explained.

"I'm not at liberty to discuss it," Moira said stiffly.

Isobel wouldn't be dissuaded. She clicked her tongue. "It just strikes me as extremely unlikely. How did they get onto the island? How did they even get into *Gallonten*? Hasn't the city been closed to orinians since the Nochdvors arrived? What were they trying to accomplish?"

"I don't see why you're getting so emotional about this," Moira said.

If Roman hadn't already been keeping his head down for this conversation, he would have done so at Isobel's answering fury. "*Emotional*? I'm just trying to understand the facts, Moira. You know, the proof you need before you can call something true. Did anyone see the intruders? Where did the papers get their information? Is Unity going to release a statement, or—?"

"There will be no statement. Gareth, will you pass the butter?"

Gareth picked up the butter tray but didn't immediately hand it over. "What about our neighbors? They won't be punished for this, will they? You know they're innocent, Moira."

"As a matter of fact," Moira said, "Your *innocent* orinians broke out of their cells and escaped with the criminals responsible."

Isobel sat back, stunned. "They escaped?"

Gareth's eyes found Roman's across the table. Roman knew he was putting together the pieces: yesterday morning, he and Dinara had called Gareth asking about the orinians that were arrested. Later that same day, those orinians were broken out of prison. Whether or not Gareth suspected Roman's involvement, though, he said nothing.

"I will remind you both that those orinians are fugitives and they are to be considered dangerous," Moira said. "If they show their faces here, or if you learn anything—"

"We would tell you right away, of course," Isobel said. Though her voice was sweet, her smile was sharp.

"Were any of the people involved caught?" Gareth asked.

"Not yet, but I have faith they will be," Moira said.

Roman kept waiting for Gareth to blame him, but it never came. Instead, Ofelia interrupted, loudly declaring that she wanted to go play, and the tension cracked like ice. Isobel laughed and stood with some difficulty, sidling around the table with her hand on her stomach. She scooped Ofelia up. "I'm going to take Ofelia up to her governess. I'll be right back."

Moira watched her go, then asked Gareth, "How far along is she now?"

"Almost five months."

"How time flies."

"It does. I hope I don't miss the birth," Gareth said. If it weren't for his frigid expression, the comment could have seemed offhanded. For a moment, Gareth looked just like his sister; it was a side of the man Roman hadn't seen before. But Gareth softened again on a sigh. "Do you have to make everything so difficult, Moira? Isobel is just trying to understand what happened."

This had the tread of a well-worn argument, and Roman watched with fascination. That Gareth and Isobel would try to sway Moira at all surprised him; that she wouldn't listen even to her own family did not. Gareth said that people weren't just good or bad. Roman used to believe that, too. He used to believe that the Magistrates had good in them—families they loved, values they stood for, people they respected. Too late, he learned they knew none of it. No love, no values, no respect. One day, he would at least like to teach them fear.

Roman considered the stories of Histrios people liked to tell, of a tragic hero turned feral and the dear friend who shot him to save him from becoming a monster. Leandros was the hero of that story, not Egil.

The truth was this: Roman wouldn't have cared if the Magistrates *did* have good in them, for all the harm they'd done to this world. They deserved to be put down, just as they'd tried to put down Egil.

He rolled up his sleeves and rested his elbow on the table, flashing the brand that marked him as one of Unity's own Enforcers. Moira went still when she noticed it, the color draining from her face.

"Is something wrong, Magistrate?" Roman asked innocently, licking the jam off his knife. It was blunt, meant only for spreading butter, but she would know that in his hands, it was the deadliest weapon. That *he* was a weapon, all because of the Magistrates that came before her.

"Moira?" Gareth echoed, watching his sister with concern.

Moira's eyes darted toward the door, as if she was contemplating running—or calling for her Enforcer. Roman smiled again, silently daring her to try it. Her eyes dropped to his knife, and she quickly lied to save her own life. "Not at all. I'm quite all right," she said.

Abruptly, she stood. "Unfortunately, though, I just remembered something important I must do on the island. Give my apologies to Isobel, Gareth...Mr. Hallisey."

Roman's smile fell. He watched Gareth watch her flee, the man's brows knitted in confusion, and all he felt was pity. Moira Ranulf had just abandoned her baby brother to what she thought was a ruthless killer, and Gareth didn't even realize it.

"That was odd," Gareth said, returning to his breakfast. He glanced at Roman across the table and frowned. "Ouch. That must have been painful—what happened?"

For a moment, Roman thought Gareth meant the brand, but then he realized Gareth was looking at the other arm—at a fresh pink scar on the back of his hand. "Oh, this?" Roman asked, holding his hand up to the light. The scar was mirrored on his palm, too, where the blade had pierced right through his hand. The wound had fully closed, the skin knit back together. He considered it for a moment, then said, "It was a cooking accident."

Chapter Twenty-One

Leandros watched Ivor Linde, the alfar from Unity's security team, flick a folded triangle of paper across the table toward Trin. Without even looking Ivor's way, Trin swept it to the floor. It was so absurdly childish Leandros almost couldn't believe what he was seeing.

While he wasn't listening to his coordinator's logistics report either, he at least gave Eresh the courtesy of hiding it. He should have felt guilty, but these meetings—safe on the island, with Unity on their best behavior—were his only moments of peace. On top of the Magistrates overworking him, trying to push him to quit before they even left Gallonten, the reporters who kept finding and following him were making him paranoid. He had enemies. His family had enemies. The number of people who wanted him dead in this city increased every day, and he couldn't afford to let down his guard anywhere but here. Here, with Unity's Enforcers sitting before him, he at least didn't have to worry about them stabbing him in the back.

He rubbed his tired eyes and bit back a sigh.

Of the gathered team, Trin seemed to be the only one paying attention. Evelyne was in a foul mood, her arm in a sling following yesterday's break-in. Gareth frowned at the wall, tapping his pen against his empty notebook. Cathwright, a white dragon and a barrister, sat in the corner and picked at her claws. Aside from Ivor, the rest of the security team hadn't even bothered to show up.

It wasn't hard to guess what took them away. If yesterday's attack involved the prison, then it likely also involved the barracks hidden within. Leandros had known what his security team was from the moment he met them, of course. You couldn't travel with Egil for any length of time *without* learning about the Enforcers, and Leandros knew even more than most. He watched Evelyne thoughtfully, not looking away even when she met his gaze. Five Enforcers, all for what was meant to be a diplomatic mission. At first, he'd thought Unity appointed them all just to kill him—to free them of a pest—but he was beginning to realize that they were serious about going to Orean. So what were they after?

"And that covers meal planning," Eresh said. Turning to the chalkboard behind him, Leandros' Unity Coordinator crossed out another item on his agenda—only six of eight, after they'd already been in this cramped room for well over two hours. "If you have questions about anything I've covered up to this point, please consult your travel guide. You'll find emergency protocols at the front and an index at the back. For our route, we'll be traveling around Lyryma Forest on the western Unity Road, stopping in Lyryma to perform a full investigation before we make contact with Orean."

"Eresh, c'mon. We already know an orinian did it. We just don't know which one," Ivor said, tipping lazily back in his chair. "And that, Illyon won't tell us. Why waste time poking around there?"

"Because this mission is about rescuing my uncle, not charging into Orean and starting a war," Leandros said coldly. "If there's anything to be learned from an investigation, it will be worth it."

Ivor looked Leandros up and down with his good eye, seeming almost bored. "Then have your investigation, but expect your uncle to be dead before we ever make it to Orean, *Your Highness.*"

He loved to emphasize Leandros' title, loved to imply that he'd been given and had not earned his position on the team. Calmly, Leandros leaned down to pick something up. He would not give Ivor the satisfaction of getting angry. "As Ms. Smith has said multiple times, if the king is still alive by the time we reach Illyon, he'll still be alive when we leave it. I understand struggling with the dense information being presented to you, Mr. Linde, but you seem so fixated on Ms. Smith that I thought you would have at least listened to *her*. Or maybe your attention span is simply more suited for children's games?" he asked, holding out the paper Ivor had flicked across the table. "I believe this belongs to you."

The feet of Ivor's chair hit the ground with a *thud* as he reached to take the paper back. He grinned, and Leandros' first thought was how unbecoming the expression was on an alfar. His second was chagrin—he had many reasons to dislike Ivor, but escaping Alfheimr's rigid rules of expression wasn't one of them. Ivor spun the little triangle of paper on the table and said, "I do love games, but that's not *all* my attention span is good for. It's good for fighting, too. It's good for violence."

"How unfortunate, then, that you've been assigned to a peaceful mission. Perhaps Ms. Corscia should speak with the Magistrates and have you replaced," Leandros said.

"You use pretty words, Your Highness, but we all know you'll do anything to get your uncle back," Ivor said, leaning in. "We see the hunger you just can't hide. It's okay. Embrace it. We're all here to support you, after all. That's what Trin likes to say, isn't it? So point and tell us where to strike, and we'll strike."

"Leave me out of this, Linde," Trin said coldly.

Leandros' hands clenched into fists beneath the table, where Ivor and Evelyne couldn't see. Normally, this was where Evelyne intervened—she allowed Ivor his little insults, then pretended to rein him when he went too far. This time, she kept quiet, so Leandros said, "I appreciate the sentiment, Mr. Linde, but that won't be necessary. If you'd like to support me, you and your peers can refer to me as *Captain* for the remained of the journey."

"Of course. For as long as you're with us, *Captain*," Evelyne agreed. While her tone was polite, her words sent a shiver down Leandros' spine. He couldn't forget yesterday's threats. He knew he needed to stop goading them, but he couldn't leave the insults be.

"Ah, Ms. Corscia, that reminds me—I noticed McDermott and Thomason are missing today. Are they investigating yesterday's attack on the island? Haven't you found the culprits yet?" he asked.

Evelyne's expression darkened. "You—*You* have some nerve saying that to me, of all people."

It matched the accusations she'd made yesterday. "I really don't follow," Leandros said. Why *him*, of all people?

"Didn't anyone tell you? McDermott's dead," Ivor supplied. "He was killed in yesterday's attack."

Gareth tuned into the conversation at that, sucking in a sharp breath. "Killed? Moira only told me he was indisposed, not that he'd bloody died!" It was the most he'd spoken the whole meeting.

While Leandros still wondered what that had to do with *him*, Evelyne stood, slamming her hands on the table as she did. Despite her next words, she looked only at Leandros while she spoke. "This is an excellent time to remind everyone here that if you know anything about yesterday's attack, it is your duty to report that to Unity. Failure to do so is nothing less than treason."

Leandros blinked. He thought she'd been upset because he intervened with that young actress. She couldn't really think he knew anything about the attack?

"Really, Evelyne. The captain was with me almost all day yesterday, except when he went to meet with the Magistrates," Eresh said, unexpectedly coming to Leandros' defense. "Certainly well past the time that the break-in occurred."

"Yes, what exactly are you accusing Captain Nochdvor of, Ms. Corscia?" Trin asked.

Finding all eyes on her, Evelyne paused to take a steadying breath. "Nothing, of course," she said flatly. "It was only a reminder."

"A reminder I dare say none of us needed," Cathwright rumbled, eyeing not Leandros, but Evelyne and Ivor suspiciously.

"My apologies, then, for repeating useless information," Evelyne gritted out. "Eresh, are you finished? As Captain Nochdvor pointed out, Mr. Linde and I still have a fugitive to catch."

Eresh looked back at his chalkboard, which had two agenda items still unchecked. "I suppose? If you miss anything important, I'll catch up with you this evening."

"Then Ivor and I will be excusing ourselves."

"Wait! One more thing. Chia—our final team member," Eresh began. "When are we to expect her?"

Evelyne shrugged. "Soon. When I see her, I'll tell her to come find you." And with that, she swept out of the room with Ivor at her heels, neither of them so much as glancing Leandros' way again. Leandros sighed. He was in far over his head.

After Eresh officially concluded the meeting, Gareth sidled up to Leandros. "I have a complaint, Captain," he said, waiting until Leandros looked up from packing his bag before adding, "We're leaving Gallonten in two days and have yet to get those drinks."

"Ah. That would be because you stood me up at the theater," Leandros replied.

The joking smile fell from Gareth's face, his eyes widening almost comically. "Well, I—"

"I'm only joking, Mr. Ranulf," Leandros said, feeling an

unexpected pang of homesickness. Any alfar would have seen the teasing for what it was. "As I told you then, I understand. Plans change."

"Oh! Yes, I see. You're too kind," Gareth said. "I didn't know they taught you how to do that in Alfheimr. Joke, that is."

Despite himself, Leandros' lips twitched up into a smile. The ending of that meeting—and Ivor's expression as he stormed out behind Evelyne—had significantly lightened his mood. "They don't, of course. The capital even has laws against humor. Tease the wrong person and you'll end up on the gallows," he joked some more. "Fortunately for you, we're not in the capital. Would you be free for drinks this evening?"

"I can't tonight. My wife and I attend the evening service at St. John's. Tomorrow?"

"I could make the time." Leandros paused, then, remembering something. "About Will McDermott—I know he was to be your personal guard. Has your sister mentioned getting you a replacement?"

"She has, in fact. I recommended a friend of mine for the job."

Leandros was surprised by this. A friend—did that mean this replacement wouldn't be an Enforcer? Going from five to four Enforcers on his team would be a significant improvement. Gareth continued, "But speaking of, I could use your advice. This is all theoretical, of course."

"Of course," Leandros agreed, wary.

"If you suspected you knew something about yesterday's attack, or at least suspected you might know someone involved, what would you do?"

It was the last thing Leandros expected to hear from Gareth Ranulf, brother of a Unity Magistrate. Was this a trick? Had Evelyne put him up to it? Deciding to give Gareth the benefit of the doubt, he asked, "Do I trust this person?"

"Yes," Gareth answered after a moment's thought. "But when Ms. Corscia said—"

"Do you trust Ms. Corscia?"

"I barely know Ms. Corscia."

"Then you have your answer. If you say you trust this person, Mr. Ranulf, then *trust them.*"

After a moment's consideration, Gareth nodded. "Yes, you might be on to something."

"I'm sorry to interrupt," Eresh said, joining them. Looking around, Leandros realized the others had left, only the three of them remaining in the room. "Captain, we have a meeting with the Magistrates in fifteen minutes. We should be on our way if we're to make it to the courthouse in time."

"Do you mind if I walk with you?" Gareth asked. "The truth is, Mr. Nochdvor, there's one other thing I've been wanting to ask you about."

Leandros nodded, gesturing for Eresh to lead the way, and Gareth fell into step beside him. After Eresh's pestering, the Magistrates had finally granted them a dedicated meeting space on the island, in the bowels of one of the under-used administrative buildings. All for the sake of secrecy, they said. While it was a step up from Eresh's home, it still meant a long walk to the courthouse.

"This is a question of a more personal nature, if that's all right," Gareth hedged, watching carefully for Leandros' reaction. When Leandros didn't give him any, he ventured, "You...knew Egil, didn't you?"

Ahead of them, Eresh nearly tripped over his own feet. He glanced back, eyes wide, to watch Leandros' reaction as well. Leandros felt vaguely offended. Did he really seem so volatile? Or was it fragility, instead? He gave a wry smile, and both of his companions relaxed. "I was wondering when you'd ask," he said. Seeing Gareth's eyes widen, he added, "You're one of the most prolific folklorists on the continent, Mr. Ranulf; did you really think I wouldn't know your work? And if I hadn't before, it's in the biographies Mr. Ochoa prepared."

"I—well, I suppose I'd forgotten about those. When you say that you know my work, do you mean to say that you've…?"

"Read it?" Leandros finished. "Almost everything you've written on the subject of Egil, in fact. My cousin brought one of your early papers to my attention, some decades back, and I've been following your career with interest since."

Gareth's mouth fell open in surprise, amusing Leandros. After a moment of stammering, he managed, "Oh, how embarrassing. If I'd known *you* were—I apologize for any factual inaccuracies. I work mostly with Unity records and secondary sources."

"Factual inaccuracies don't bother me, Mr. Ranulf. I know you already know the answer to this, but yes. I knew him."

"What was he to you, exactly?" Gareth asked Leandros. Eresh slowed to walk beside them, three to the cobblestone paths of Unity Island. He didn't speak, only listened, his notes and folders clutched to his chest like an eager schoolboy.

That was a harder question to answer. In the end, Leandros went with a vast oversimplification. "He was my dearest friend."

"Then in Histrios, why…?" Gareth asked, trailing off.

Leandros had expected this question, too, though not so early into the conversation. He felt his mood begin to sour. "I'm sure you've heard. He changed," he answered flatly. It was the same response he'd given anyone who'd asked over the decades.

"I'd be interested in hearing the full story, if you'll tell it."

"Me too!" Eresh chimed in.

Leandros was not his uncle; he was not adept at holding court. That, and he didn't trust either of these men enough to tell them the truth. "Maybe someday," he said, in the end. The fall breeze rustled through the late-blooming taurel, making the blue flowers sway along the path. "Not here."

Though Gareth visibly deflated, he nodded, gracious despite the rejection. "May I ask just one more question? What was he like? Histrios aside, was he everything the stories say?"

It was hardly just one question, and they both knew it. Leandros tipped his head to one side, weighing his response. He considered the Egil of stories: fearless, courageous, compassionate. "No," he said, finally. "He wasn't fearless."

Gareth waited for more, but Leandros had nothing more to say. Silently, they followed Eresh up the steps to the courthouse, Unity's clock tower looming behind them. When Eresh held the door, Leandros passed through first, though he had to stop before he collided with someone. Not just someone—an orinian, standing right in the middle of Unity's courthouse.

His stop was so abrupt that Gareth nearly ran into his back, and Eresh into Gareth's.

The last time Leandros collided with an orinian, he hadn't been able to tear his eyes away from her. This time was much the same, though for a very different reason: this person in front of him had a very peculiar sense of style.

Having worn mourning blacks for the better part of six decades, Leandros paid little mind to the latest styles. He knew the silhouettes that suited him and appreciated the elegance of black-on-black embellishments, but even he knew how démodé this woman was. She wore a threadbare collegiate sweater at least twice her size and paired it with a long, vibrant green skirt decked in glittering lace, bells, and glass buttons. Her long dark hair was piled atop her head, and jagged birthmarks cut like lightning across her face.

Eresh peered around Gareth and Leandros. When he saw her, he cried, "Chia! You're back early!"

Chia? Then this must be their final teammate, Eftychia O'Neill. Eftychia waved at Eresh, her entire face lighting up, then pushed up her sleeve and extended a small hand toward Leandros. Leandros noticed a brand on her wrist, one he was well acquainted with. "Pleasure to meet you, Captain Mourning Dove."

Leandros twitched at the nickname. "Nochdvor," he corrected as he shook her hand.

"It's just a game she plays," Eresh explained—not quietly enough to keep Eftychia from hearing, but at least enough that she could pretend she hadn't.

"I like nicknames," Eftychia said with a shrug, stepping aside to let Leandros pass, then following him through the echoing hall. It was busier here; they would have had to fight to get to the stairwell, but Leandros and Eftychia together drew attention, and onlookers were quick to step out of their way. Somewhere nearby, Leandros heard the shutter of a camera. More reporters.

Unnoticing or uncaring, Eftychia continued, "I also like animals! Dear Eresh is just upset because I've dubbed him a weasel." She gave an exaggerated eye roll, then laughed brightly at herself. "I said squirrel first, Eresh, but you didn't like that either!"

"And I'm a mourning dove?" Leandros asked, frowning.

"No. I was just trying that one out, but it doesn't fit. You do have a gentle sort of sadness about you, though," Eftychia said, not noticing Leandros' frown deepen. "I'll keep trying. We'll have plenty of time for it on the journey, after all. There's no better way to pick people apart and learn what makes them tick than to travel with them over a great distance. Don't you think?"

Leandros gave her a sidelong look, but her expression remained sweet and open. "I suppose."

"I'm very sorry to have made you all wait, by the by. I meant to be back last week, but there were complications," she said. As an

Enforcer, she had probably been out on a mission. Leandros shuddered to think what those "complications" might have been. "Have you been enjoying Gallonten in the meantime, Captain?"

"I haven't seen much of it," Leandros admitted. "My days have been spent here on the island."

And he hadn't dared go anywhere except back and forth from his hotel, too concerned about the eyes he felt following him everywhere he went. He hadn't seen who they belonged to, but he hadn't needed to. At best, they were reporters. Most likely, they were Enforcers. At worst, they glowed with crimson magic.

"I was hoping you'd say that! Please, let me show you the city!" Eftychia chirped, the bells on her skirt jingling as she gave a little skip. "I simply *can't* let you out of my sight until I've figured out your nickname, anyway."

"You're going to have to," Eresh said, checking his watch. "We have a meeting with the Magistrates to get to and you're not invited."

Leandros was surprised by Eftychia's offer. This had to be a trap. He couldn't trust her, but his loneliness sometimes overwhelmed his reason, and he'd been sorely missing the company of people. There was a bitter, ugly beast inside Leandros that didn't take abandonment or rejection well, and it had been pacing in its cage since he'd arrived in Gallonten. Gareth standing him up for drinks hadn't helped.

"Tomorrow?" he asked. He was awarded with a brilliant smile from Eftychia. He'd be foolish to go anywhere with an Enforcer alone, so he added, "Mr. Ochoa, Mr. Ranulf, would you care to join?"

"I'd be delighted," Gareth said, making Leandros smile approvingly. If Eftychia had intended this to be a trap, she couldn't try anything with the brother of a Magistrate present.

Eresh shifted his weight from one foot to the other. "I'm really very busy."

"Eresh, you simply *must* come!" Eftychia said, grabbing Eresh's arm and hanging off it. She had a willowy frame and was nearly as tall as the dryad.

"We have no meetings scheduled, for once. I see no reason you shouldn't come along," Leandros pointed out. "Let's just not meet too early in the morning."

"Do you not like mornings?" Eftychia asked. "Oh, let me think. What kind of animal doesn't like mornings?"

"Sloths," Eresh suggested, smugly.

"Hush, weasel," Leandros replied. He stopped at the top of the stairs, where the hallway branched into three, and the others followed his lead.

"Eresh, you're coming," Eftychia said, making the decision for him. "Let's all meet on the bridge at nine o'clock tomorrow."

Eresh rolled his eyes but smiled. "Very well, but only if you promise to read all the files I've sent over before then. Now, we really must be going."

"Have a good meeting, Eresh! It was a pleasure meeting you, Captain Leopard! I'll see all three of you tomorrow! Nine o'clock, and don't you forget!"

"I wouldn't mind if that one stuck," Leandros said, even as Eresh started down the tallest of the three hallways, toward Magistrate Malong's office.

"No, it's still not right. I'm getting closer, though," Eftychia said, giving him one more goodbye wave before flouncing away.

"She's a strange one," Eresh said when Leandros caught up with him. "A bit childish, at times, but a quick fighter. Don't worry, Captain, she'll make an excellent addition to the security team."

"I wasn't worried," Leandros said. Not about that, at least. He turned to watch Eftychia's dark hair and vibrant skirt disappear into the crowd. Above her, over the grand foyer of Unity's courthouse, hung a wide window. Through it, the dark silhouette of Unity's prison and barracks sat on the clear horizon.

CHAPTER TWENTY-TWO

GARETH SWEPT INTO THE PARLOR for the fourth time in as many minutes, immediately dropping onto his hands and knees to peer under the furniture. "Has anyone seen my green cravat?" he called. When Isobel's reply came from closer than he'd expected, he jumped, hitting his head on the bottom of the sofa.

"I have it," she said. She stood behind him, tie in hand. "You left it sitting out; I think Wyndie was just trying to tidy up."

"Ah, thoughtful girl. Is she up with Ofelia?"

"I told you; she has the night off," Isobel said reproachfully.

"Sorry, Bel, I've had a lot on my mind. Where's Ofelia, then?"

"She should be down soon. She wanted to put her shoes on all by herself. She was quite insistent," Isobel said. She put on a pair of dangling earrings, their glittering green catching in the light whenever she turned her head. Her dress was a similar shade, though not half as elegant as the one she'd worn to the Webhon Players' performance, with less lace and a smaller bustle. Gareth found he liked it better. "Will Roman join us? Did you invite him?" she asked.

Gareth laughed, remembering the look on Roman's face when Gareth had invited him to *church*. "I did. I think he would have accepted just to be polite, but a messenger from Unity came and swept him away."

"He really will be joining the team, then?"

"Moira hasn't outright said no, which is a promising sign. I'm sure there's some sort of interview process that must be followed, though."

Ofelia pranced in, then, whining about how her shoes hurt. Isobel took her hand and led her over to the couch. "That's because you put them on the wrong feet, silly girl. Let your father fix them for you."

Gareth smiled at the two of them, feeling his chest constrict. He would really miss them. "How pretty you look in your new dress, Ofelia," he said, kneeling in front of his daughter and pulling her shoes off one at a time. "How old are you now? Twenty?"

"No, I'm five!"

"What? *Five*?" Gareth exclaimed. "I simply don't believe that. You look much too grown up to be only five."

"I am! Momma, tell him!"

"It's true," Isobel said. She managed not to laugh, but Gareth could see the threat of it in her smile. "She's only five, but she's *almost* six."

"Oh, almost six. That explains it, then." Having fixed the shoes, Gareth stood. "Are you ladies ready to go? I know Ofelia doesn't want to miss the songs."

The Ranulfs shared their rented carriage with the Carols, another family renting in the same building. As the driver spurred the carriage into motion, leading them off down the bumpy streets, one of the Carols complimented Ofelia's dress. After Isobel made Ofelia—suddenly turned shy—say thank you, Isobel returned the compliment by telling the Carol women how handsome their sons looked in their new finery. And that was all the conversation that passed on the short ride to their destination. Before Gareth knew it, the driver was pulling to a stop on the busy street. Gareth climbed out first and offered each of the women a hand out, but the Carol boys were content to jump without assistance, one of them landing in mud and ruining his shiny shoes. Gareth caught Ofelia before she could follow their example.

Before them, the pointed spires of St. John's stood dark against the dusky sky. Lights poured out through its stained glass and shone down on the congregation that poured in. As Gareth and Isobel walked arm in arm, Ofelia winding through the crowd ahead of them, Gareth waited for the familiar peace of an evening church service to descend. For the first time in his life, though, it didn't come. This Gallontean church might be louder and colder than the one back home, but even it usually gave him *some* sort of calm. Tonight, he couldn't find it beneath thoughts of missing kings and Unity missions.

Ms. O'Neill's arrival in Gallonten had shaken him; she hadn't been expected until Thursday. He'd thought he had more time.

They found an open pew in the sanctuary, the seating all arranged in a half circle around a metal obelisk pointing to the sky. The obelisk was meant to represent Atiuh, though every sect of Atiuhism had different representations of what they thought he looked like. Sometimes he was human, or nymph, or dragon, and then others, he was something more fantastical. The Gallontean church didn't give him a shape. Gallonten was too diverse a city—this way, no one argued about which species Atiuh belonged to, even if they all secretly believed it was their own.

The service began, and by the time the hymnal singing was done, Ofelia had stopped paying attention. She had a great deal of patience for a five-year-old, but even she had a limit. So did Gareth, and more so than usual of late. His mind kept drifting, and something about the way the preacher spoke on *kindness* and *faith* made Gareth feel ill. He stayed silent throughout the service, on their way back to the carriage, and even on the ride home. He was grateful for the Carols' presence, as it meant Isobel could do nothing but shoot him worried looks. If she asked him what was wrong, he wouldn't know how to answer.

"Will you put Ofelia to bed, Gareth?" Isobel asked as the carriage rolled to a final stop in front of their building. The girl had fallen asleep on the ride, lulled by the rocking of the carriage and the warmth of her parents on either side of her. During the transition from carriage to bedroom, she woke just enough to wrap her arms sleepily around Gareth's shoulders and then help him get her into a sleeping gown. He sat with her and took all the small pins and clips out of her hair, singing an old hymn under his breath as he did. Ofelia piped in sleepily where she knew the words.

"Momma says you're leaving," Ofelia said, while he hummed.

Gareth almost dropped the hairbrush in his hand. "Yes," he said. "For a little while."

"How long?"

Gareth struggled to speak past the lump in his throat. He remembered all the times he'd had this exact conversation with his own father, all the times he'd been consoled with later-broken promises. He never thought he'd do the same to his own child. "Not long at all, love. Soon, you and your mother will go back home, and I'll be there with you before you know it."

"When are you going?"

"Very soon." Too soon.

"You'll bring me back a present, won't you?"

"Of course," Gareth said, laughing past the cold dread pooling in his chest. "I always do."

Ofelia fell asleep while Gareth was brushing her hair. He wrapped her blankets around her, blew out the lamp burning on the table, and backed out of the room, not letting her sleeping form out of his sight until the door clicked shut. He rested his forehead against the cool wood and tried not to think about the danger of the upcoming mission.

Eventually, Gareth returned to his and Isobel's room and found Isobel still getting ready for bed. "I think I lost my brooch back at the church," she said when she saw him. "The one from your mother."

"Shall I go look for it?" Gareth asked, jumping at the opportunity. Anything to save him from thinking about the lies he'd just told his daughter.

Isobel gave him a concerned look, the same she'd given him in the carriage. "You don't have to do it tonight."

"No, no, it's fine. I need to get some fresh air. Besides, there's another service tomorrow morning—someone will surely find it and take it if I wait."

"If you don't mind, then," Isobel said, clearly not buying it. "Thank you, Gareth."

On his way back down to the kitchen, Gareth passed the room they'd had prepared for Roman. The door stood open, the room inside dark. Roman's meager possessions sat on the bed, their owner still out despite the late hour.

This time, Gareth walked to the church. Only a few blocks had come and gone before he reached the cathedral, the splendid lights from inside now dim. The first door he tried was locked, as were the second and third. Only the fourth and last of the church's doors opened when Gareth pulled the handle. Slipping inside, Gareth finally felt an echo of that peace he'd been looking for earlier. He wandered through the halls, quiet and filled with the solemnity of night and hollow space. Gareth had never realized how large the church was, how high its ceilings were. It was usually too packed with people to notice much beyond the crowd. Only one or two lamps were lit to guide the way, and with the sharp architecture, shadows pooled at every corner.

Being here alone made Gareth feel small, insignificant. He found it strangely comforting. At the doors to the sanctuary, he paused to admire yet another thing about this place he'd never really noticed before: the statues above the three sanctuary doors.

Above the largest of the three was a statue of a feathered black dragon, his wings stretching above and over the statues on either side of him. His mouth hung open in a snarl, rows of intricately carved teeth grinning down at Gareth. To his right stood a red statue of a nympherai woman made from fire. She held a hand toward the dragon, as did the statue on the dragon's other side—a human man, tall and proud in a full suit of armor, the kind popular during the Great War. All three of Atiuh's Guardians, created to protect this world and now protecting his sanctuary.

Gareth stared at Tellaos and the dragon stared back.

The scriptures said that millions of years ago, Atiuh spun the world into being. In one corner of one continent in the vast universe Atiuh created, he made life. He made life in plants, in trees and in flowers, but that was not enough. He then made life in animals, in small insects and massive Misenean beasts that stood taller than mountains, but even that was not enough. From them, then, Atiuh created the first intelligent life.

He made three kinds of people: humans, nympherai, and dragons. Over time—thousands and thousands of years—the people grew and changed, and Atiuh changed the world to accommodate them. He spread them across the land, gave them the space they needed to adapt. The various peoples were born—sapien, alfar, maranet, orinian. Dryad, fae, frìth. Dragons of red, blue, and white. Then, Atiuh again made life from nothing.

Some say it was because of his mortals' flaws, that they were not enough for Atiuh in the same way his animals and plants weren't enough. But the more popular teaching, the one Gareth preferred, was that he simply loved his creations so much that he wanted to ensure they were always protected. He made three more beings, these incapable of dying or aging. Three beings, each a patron of one of his species. Human Atuos, nympherai Ellaes, and the great serpent Tellaos. Each of these, Atiuh gave a fractured piece of his magic.

For a time, the Guardians watched over Calaidia, but Tellaos grew resentful of the job he'd been given and the people he'd been made to protect. He started the Great War with manipulation and tricks as an act of defiance against Atiuh.

Or so the story went, anyway.

Gareth pushed through Tellaos' door and into the sanctuary, following the aisle past rows of pews to where his family had been sitting. He caught a glimpse of green almost immediately—there was the brooch, nestled against the leg of a pew. He grabbed it and turned to go, but his gaze caught on the obelisk at the center of the room.

Without consciously willing his feet forward, Gareth climbed the steps toward it. He touched the metal, feeling its smooth texture beneath his fingers. It was cold, and Gareth felt no peace. He didn't know why he'd expected anything different.

Voice echoing in the hollow space, he said, "Atiuh, if you're listening—"

He stopped. *If*, he'd said. When had it become an if?

He continued, "I could do with your blessing right now. Bring me safely home from this journey, back to my daughter and wife. It's silly, but I'm scared that I—" He cut off again with a sigh. "I'm being selfish. We could *all* use your blessing—everyone on the team, everyone in Orean, and King Nochdvor, wherever he is."

Gareth withdrew his hand from the obelisk, the weight of his fears settling heavily on him. Newspapers pushing war, scheming governments, diplomatic teams with more soldiers than diplomats. It was too much. It pushed Gareth to his knees. "Things are terrible here, Atiuh. There may be a war, and our leaders are..." Gareth stopped himself before he could speak any treasonous thoughts out loud. "Help us solve this problem in Orean before it gets worse."

He rested his forehead against the cool metal. He didn't expect a response. He didn't expect a miracle. But the hollow *nothingness* that he got made him feel foolish. He sat back and stared at the idol, and still, nothing answered.

Eventually, the soft cadence of voices drifted in from outside the sanctuary doors. Gareth wiped his eyes, clearing away tears he hadn't noticed forming, and made a hasty retreat, slipping out a side door before he was caught in here after dark. He followed the winding hallways of the church and didn't stop until he was back in the street.

When he reached his flat and found he still hadn't recovered, he ducked around the gated veranda of the café next door and slipped into the alley between the two buildings. He lit a cigarette, not ready to go inside, but a familiar voice stopped him cold before he could ever raise it to his lips.

"Just tea for me, and toast if you have it. Anything for you, Hallisey? My treat."

Gareth looked around, but he was alone in the alley. The voice must've come from the other side of the high wooden fence.

"I'm all right, thanks." Another familiar voice. Noticing a small gap between the planks, not more than an inch wide, Gareth shuffled toward it.

"Ah, right. You had dinner with my brother and his family, didn't you?" That was Moira, her proud voice muffled but unmistakable. Gareth put out his cigarette. The proper thing to do would be to announce his presence. Not doing so would be a betrayal of both his friend and his sister. But then, he also didn't want to startle them unnecessarily.

Guiltily, he looked through the hole in the fence just in time to see Roman drop into the seat across from Moira. They sat at a small bistro table, in shadow and well apart from the other patrons.

"I was surprised you asked to meet me here," Roman said, emphasizing *here* and not *asked to meet*. And it was strange, when Gareth thought about it. Moira liked grand, formal venues. She used Unity's splendor as a tool, both to boast and belittle. To invite Roman to this private café must have meant she wanted secrecy.

"As surprised as I was to see that brand on your wrist this morning," Moira replied. In trying to blend in, she had dressed plainly —the plainest Gareth had ever seen her. He could only see her side profile from his position, but he could tell her face was set in its pleasant politician's smile.

Roman held his hand up to the café's lights and examined his wrist. There, Gareth could see a patch of dark brown skin that might have been a scar—or a brand, as Moira said. "Oh, this? I've had it for ages."

"I'm not convinced it's real. If you had really been an Enforcer, I would remember you."

It was obvious to Gareth that Moira was baiting him, trying to get him to voluntarily give up information. Roman seemed to know it, too, his smile turning sharp. "You've only been a Magistrate for twenty years. What would you know?"

Gareth pressed himself to the fence, trying to angle himself so he could see them both at once. What was Roman saying? That he'd been an Enforcer—whatever that was—for longer than Moira had been a Magistrate? His first instinct was to brush it off as impossible, but it did echo something Roman had said to him that morning: *it's only been sixty years since Histrios. That's no time at all.* Gareth had thought Roman was sapien, younger than him, but he should have known better than to assume.

Moira tapped her fingers against the table, the only sign that Roman's answer unsettled her. "I would still know about you. Any Enforcers who leave Unity are watched."

"And mysteriously turn up dead not long after, right?" Roman asked with a wry smile. "Where are Diomis and Malong? Didn't you ask either of them about me?" When Moira hesitated for a beat too long, Roman sat forward. Sounding almost gleeful, he asked, "You didn't, did you? Why not? Want to keep me as your little secret? A rogue Enforcer tucked in your back pocket?"

Moira scoffed and looked away, so Gareth could no longer see her face. He had to strain to make out her next words. "I invited you here to discuss your application to be my brother's guard. That's nothing the others need concern themselves with."

"And what do you think of my application, Magistrate?"

"You would have to be mad to think I'd let you anywhere near this mission."

Roman threw back his head and laughed. To anyone watching, it would seem as if Moira had told a particularly funny joke. "Maybe I am mad. You wouldn't be the first one to call me that."

"You're going to attract attention," Moira scolded. She watched Roman more warily, after that outburst. "I'm going to be frank with you, Hallisey. Given the circumstances of this meeting and your... unique insight into Unity's workings, I like to think we've reached a certain level of candor, you and I. So tell me plainly: were you the one behind yesterday's attack on the island?"

Gareth held his breath, but Roman only asked, "So you're saying that because I know Unity's secrets, I should tell you mine?"

"I'm saying we can be honest with each other."

"Give me something interesting, then, and maybe I'll do the same," Roman said. The cruel tilt to his smile was new to Gareth.

"This is not a negotiation," Moira said. "Why did you do it?"

And with that, the smile fell, leaving only the cruelty. "You know why. You had no right to hold those orinians."

"I find it hard to believe you went to such lengths—storming the barracks, risking arrest and rediscovery—just for a city guard and a simple schoolteacher. Did they know something?"

Roman sighed. "That's the problem with you Magistrates. You want so badly to pull the strings, but you don't even understand the people you're trying to make puppets out of. Until you learn basic compassion, you never will."

"I understand enough," Moira snarled, pounding her fist on the table and making Gareth jump. Realizing what she'd done a moment later, she smoothed her hair, took a deep breath, and then smiled. That, somehow, was even more alarming than her outburst had been. "For example, I understand you have someone you care about—a promising young actress named Dinara Condeh. And speaking of Ms. Condeh, I noticed something strange in yesterday's logbooks. Her name is recorded leaving the island but not entering it. Unusual, don't you think?"

When Roman only glared, she continued, "You may think your employment history makes you untouchable, Mr. Hallisey, but Ms. Condeh is not. One of our Enforcers *died* yesterday. Two others are seriously wounded. The people are demanding answers, and a discrepancy like this is all we need to launch a full investigation into Ms. Condeh."

"If you're the one who noticed this logbook discrepancy, what's stopping me from killing you here and letting the secret die with us? We've already established you haven't mentioned me to the other Magistrates so I'd guess you haven't mentioned Ms. Condeh, either," Roman said. When Moira smirked, he said, "Oh, I know all about your shadow, the Enforcer on the roof. I know how sharp her shooting is, too, and I'm faster. Shall we test it?"

"Don't do anything foolish, Hallisey," Moira warned.

"I could say the same for you. Threatening the people I care about—that's very foolish."

Gareth had never seen Roman like this, so angry and steely-eyed. In this moment, he really believed Roman capable of harming Moira. Should he intervene? Or would that only put *himself* in trouble?

Moira said, "Perhaps I was too hasty with my threats. Ms. Condeh seems like a sweet girl. I don't want to see her wrapped up in this either, but you threatened *my* family first, infiltrating brunch the way you did."

"I would never threaten Gareth or Isobel!" Roman objected. "Believe it or not, Magistrate, my presence at brunch had nothing to do with you."

"You expect me to believe that?"

Roman folded his arms. "Do or don't. I'm done trying to convince your kind of anything."

"This leaves us at an impasse, then, Mr. Hallisey. Perhaps we can make a deal as equals: if you answer my questions, I'll pull some strings and ensure neither you nor Ms. Condeh are ever implicated in yesterday's attack."

Roman narrowed his eyes at her. "Ask your questions, then, but if you ever break your word, there will be consequences."

Moira nodded and sipped her tea, unbothered. "Understood. First question: who are you?"

"Not that one. Ask another."

Moira set her cup back in the saucer with a loud *clink*, her expression turning grim. "How did you get away from the Enforcers?"

"I faked my death. How else?" Roman asked with a shrug. "Like you said, anyone who leaves alive is watched. Now ask me something interesting, Magistrate."

"Were you behind King Nochdvor's disappearance?"

Gareth's breath caught, and he didn't let it out again until Roman smiled and said, "I can see why you'd think so, but no. I'm as curious about that as you are."

"That's why you want to join this mission?" Moira asked, buttering her toast. How she could be so casual, Gareth didn't know.

"I also want to make sure *you* don't start a war in Orean."

"Is that what you think Unity is after? *War?*" Moira asked. As closely as he was watching Roman, Gareth noticed uncertainty flicker across his face. Moira missed it, continuing, "I think you have the wrong idea about us, Mr. Hallisey. You seem to have a great deal of hostility toward us, but we only want to keep peace."

"When someone wants to keep things exactly as they are, it's often more a sign of oppression than benevolence," Roman countered.

Moira considered this, then offered no rebuttal. Instead, she asked, "What are your intentions toward my brother?"

At that, Roman rolled his eyes. "I already told you, I *like* Gareth. I'm *friends* with him."

Despite the intensity of the situation and everything being said that he didn't understand, Gareth felt relief at that, at least. If it had all been a lie, well. He didn't know what he would have done.

"And yet you used him to get an invitation to the team," Morris said.

"No, I didn't! Whether or not you believe it, he and I share some values. I had no thoughts at all about joining the team before *he* invited me this morning."

"Then what are you doing in Gallonten?"

"Traveling with the Webhon Players. Is that allowed, Magistrate? Or do I need your permission?" Roman mocked. "Let me ask *you* a question. How much does Gareth know about all this—about the Enforcers?"

Moira laughed, sharp and short. "Nothing at all. Could you imagine?"

Roman said. "Oh, I think I could." He lifted his eyes to the fence behind Moira and looked right at Gareth.

Gareth flung himself away from it, his heart beating wildly in his chest. He stood there for what felt like ages, listening to his heartbeat slow in his ears, before he convinced himself Roman *couldn't* have seen him. The hole was too small. He was too far.

"Well...all I have for you," Gareth heard Moira say, more muddled now that he'd moved away from the fence. He inched back toward it, this time avoiding the hole between the planks. "I think it would be in your best interest to leave Gallonten—and my brother's life—as soon as possible. I agreed to pardon your past crimes, Hallisey, but having a rogue Enforcer stay in my city is another matter. If you continue to loiter, I may need to take action."

There was a pause while Roman considered the warning. "And about yesterday? And Dinara?"

"You have my word neither you nor Ms. Condeh will take any of the blame for yesterday's proceedings."

Something about the way she said it had Gareth pressing his eye to the hole again. Roman, he saw, had also gone tense. "Then who will?" he asked—slowly, as if afraid of the answer.

Moira took a casual sip of her tea and said, "We Magistrates already have a plan in place. You needn't concern yourself with it."

"If you're framing someone else for something I did, I think I do."

"*Someone* needs to take the blame, Mr. Hallisey. If this crime goes unpunished for much longer, people will begin to lose faith in Unity. We need to act swiftly."

"I'll ask you again, Magistrate: who are you framing?"

"Such a crude word. He's hardly innocent, himself."

"So it's a he. Knowing you lot, you'll be trying to kill two birds with one stone, get rid of somebody who's in your way." He sat back, thinking. "They'll be friendless, probably, easy to frame. Some sort of public figure."

Gareth figured it out before Roman did. "No," he whispered

before he could stop himself, dread swelling in him like a balloon filled too far.

Roman's expression, too, had turned grim. "Tell me it's not Leandros Nochdvor," he said.

"Perhaps you understand Unity better than I thought," Moira said, painfully casually. Her tone was in stark contrast with the horror Gareth felt, with the anger in Roman's eyes. "If you think about it, he's the perfect target: people are already primed to hate him after Histrios and his father's failed coup. His own people *already* hate him, his silly cousin aside. And now, inexplicably, he and Rheamaren were the sole survivors of an attack that killed everyone else present. Then he happens to be on the island the day of this attack, as well? His only alibi is me, Malong, and Diomis, and we're all in agreement. It seems Leandros Nochdvor never made it to the meeting with us yesterday afternoon. He could have gone anywhere instead." She smiled, shrugged. "The crime falling under Unity's jurisdiction only makes everything easier."

"And if you fail to find Amos, you can blame his disappearance on Leandros, too," Roman guessed, "Saving you credibility."

Moira smiled, pleased with herself. "Precisely."

"Why?" Roman asked. There was something in his expression Gareth hadn't seen before: an upward tilt to his eyebrows, a wildness around his eyes. Desperation. "Is it just that you want control of the team?"

"That, and he insulted us. No one gets away with that."

Gareth listened for more, but at that moment, a door opened further down the alley, warm light from the café spilling out over the pavement. Before whoever opened it could step out, Gareth fled.

On the other side of the fence, Roman watched Gareth's distinct patent leather shoes turn and leave. Slowly, he stood, laying his hands on the table as he did. He looked down at this Magistrate, so very like every Magistrate that came before her. "Hear this, then," he began. "I think you're a pathetic, slimy piece of shit. You're also a fool. I've told you that insulting people I care about is a mistake, but you haven't realized your biggest one. Magistrate, who do you think I am?"

Moira puffed up indignantly at the insults, anger turning her face red. "How should I know? You wouldn't answer my—"

"You don't need me to tell you. There's only one Enforcer who could have truly escaped Unity, only one who could have faked his own death. Who am I, Magistrate?"

Now, Moira had gone pale, all the color drained from her face. "That's not possible."

"What's the meaning of madness, Magistrate? Is it not seeing the world as it truly is? Is it rejecting the reality that's in front of your own eyes? If so, then maybe *I'm* not the mad one between us. Prove me wrong. Say my name."

"Evelyne would have warned us—"

Roman hummed and looked toward the roof, where he knew Evelyne Corscia was watching, waiting to pull the trigger at a signal from Moira. It must have been killing her to wait. "Ah, yes. Evelyne. Do you know who trained her to shoot, Magistrate?"

"Egil," Moira breathed.

Roman clapped politely. "Very good, Magistrate! And who am I?"

Moira hesitated, then repeated, "Egil."

"Now that you know that, tell me: who is my closest friend in this world?"

Moira gripped the arms of her chair until her knuckles turned white. "Leandros Nochdvor. But in Histrios, he—"

"I didn't ask for your commentary," Roman interrupted. "And I won't let you succeed in framing him. Oh, by the way," he said, tone brightening as he turned to leave, "Your brother overheard this whole conversation through the fence. I know he's struck up quite the friendship with the prince; I'd wager Leandros knows all about your little plan by tomorrow. Would you like to take that bet?"

"That's not possible—"

Roman tutted. "I guess there really is no reasoning with madness. You have a nice night, Magistrate," he said, turning and walking away before Moira could speak even one more word.

EGIL IV

PRESENT DAY

YEAR OF UNITY 1880

ROMAN CROSSED AN ABANDONED WHARF, lost to his thoughts while the tide lapped at the quay. Moira Ranulf's smug expression haunted him, as did the knowledge that his friend was in trouble—if he still had any right to call Leandros such. He kicked a rock, watched it land in the dark water with a rippling *splash*. In the stillness, even that seemed loud.

Did Leandros know what was coming for him? What he'd gotten himself into? Was there anything Roman could even do about it?

Noticing a tingling in his arms, he raised a hand to find it faintly aglow, the veins criss-crossing the back of it shining the brilliant red-white of light passing through skin. It spread slowly up his veins, up his arms, and from experience, he knew what came next: his eyes would turn all black.

Roman clenched his hand into a fist. Of all the Egil stories he'd heard, he hated the ones about magic the most. They treated magic like a gift; in reality, it was a curse. He'd felt the magic watching him since he left Dinara, breathing down his neck and waiting for its chance to take over. As he'd done a dozen times since then, he pushed it back and waited for the glow to fade.

Maybe there was nothing he could do about Leandros, but there were things he could try. He stopped outside of a rickety old building, its shape and the faded sign above its doors suggesting it might have once been a pub or a restaurant. The sign read "The Broken Pisto," an L at the end of the last word half-fallen, dangling on the backboard.

Broken was a fitting term for this place. Cracks ran along the dull façade, and the glass windows, which had been boarded from within, were full of shattered panes divided by rotting muntins. No lamplight drifted out from inside, and no streetlamps were around to light the place from without. It was only thanks to the full moon, hanging high above the water behind him, that Roman could read the sign at all.

When he tried the handle, the door opened easily and silently, without the creaking groan you'd expect from hinges left to rust. The inside, though, was exactly what you'd expect: the pub floor was coated in layers of dust, the tables and chairs covered with coarse cloth. Broken glass and furniture lay strewn about, but when he studied the floor, Roman saw a path through the debris toward a door at the back. When he listened, he heard something other than the lapping waves: distant music and distant voices.

The place was empty but for a burly nymph behind the bar, who eyed Roman as he shut the door behind himself. "We're closed," the man said, as if that wasn't obvious from simply looking about.

"I'm an old regular," Roman said.

For a moment, he thought he might be turned away, but then the man held a black object out. "Fine. Take this. You'd be stupid to go down without it."

Roman crossed to the bar. The object turned out to be a mask, one that covered only the eyes and left the nose and mouth visible.

"Thanks," Roman said, sliding it on. He crossed to the back door he'd seen, which led to a step of stone stairs. Those stairs then led down to a darkened landing with a single, heavy door. Roman paused there to tug up his hood, further obscuring his identity, before pushing through.

The music and voices, which before had been muffled, burst free at the door's opening. A soulful piano tune echoed up the stairwell, followed by a man's laughter. Through the door was a world of crystal, leather, mahogany and velvet. Masked strangers filled the bar-lounge and cigar smoke drifted on the air, set aglow by the ornate amber oil lamps hanging above the low tables. At the bar, straight ahead, an impressive selection of liquor bottles were displayed along the wall.

Roman lingered in the doorway, taking it all in and making sure the white-haired bartender's back was turned before he slipped into the dining room, which was separated from the bar by a half-wall. With his view of the bar blocked by a thick support column, Roman lowered his hood again.

Few in Gallonten knew about the Broken Pistol, the only place in the city the law—and *Unity*—couldn't reach. That wasn't to say the Broken Pistol itself was lawless; it had its own social mores, ones that its community strictly enforced. If you already belonged to that community, you would be welcome in the Broken Pistol. If you were *invited* by someone within it, you would be welcome in the Broken Pistol. Unless you were desperate, you did not invite yourself here; such a misstep could result in your body being found floating in the pier, robbed to its undergarments.

Over the decades, it had become a sanctuary for the elite of Gallonten's underworld, and that meant it was full of powerful people who hated Unity almost as much as Roman did. While Roman moved between their tables, he collected dirty looks—they didn't realize, yet, that he was one of them.

Roman dropped into the open seat across from a man in a vivid blue butterfly mask. All around, the masks were more ornate than Roman's; his own marked him as an outsider, he knew. "Long time, no see," he said, ignoring all the eyes turned his way.

Recognizing Roman's accent, that distinct mix of Troasian and Gallontean, the man laughed. Two pairs of sharp canines glinted in the low light. "Graced with your presence twice in one week! Color me surprised, my friend; you usually drift away on the changing winds, here and gone in an instant. A pleasure to see you again, Aim."

The eyes that had been watching turned away, appeased. Roman may be a stranger to them, but he knew Ivey. And Ivey, who had frequented the Broken Pistol since its grand opening, would make sure Roman understood its values: discretion and prudence. Roman found it more amusing, than anything—he'd attended the grand opening, too, right beside Ivey. It continually surprised him how much people could forget in sixty short years.

Roman waved over one of the servers that stood ready. While the young man that approached had an affable smile, he wore a pistol at one hip and a dagger at the other. Insurance, in case of disturbances. Roman returned his smile. "Just wine for me. Whatever you have open. Ivey, can I treat you?"

"I'll have the same," Ivey said, though he still had some left in his current glass. Secretly, Roman was relieved. A single meal from the Broken Pistol would have depleted his meager savings.

"I hope you didn't come here for me," Ivey said, swirling the wine in his glass. "If I were you, I'd much rather stay home with my beautiful girl than sit in a cold basement with an old man."

"If *you're* old, what does that make me?" Roman muttered. "I'm here to speak with Thane, actually."

Ivey's gaze cut sharply up toward Roman. "Have you seen him yet? He's changed since you disappeared."

"I can imagine. I saw his hair," Roman said, glancing over his shoulder. That column still stood between himself and the bar, hiding the bartender from view. "I'm here on business. Also, she's not my girl anymore. Not after yesterday."

Ivey winced. "Terribly sorry, Aim."

"But not, I think, surprised," Roman said, watching Ivey shrug. "The orinians made it out okay?"

"Of course; I would have told you if they hadn't. If all went well after our parting, they'll be in Home by now. You're still keeping a low profile, I hope?"

"More or less. I almost joined Unity's mission to Orean," he said, "But I had an interview with Magistrate Ranulf tonight and I think I blew it at the last moment. Too bad."

Ivey stared at Roman for a long moment, then burst out laughing. It was infectious, and after a moment, even Roman had to laugh at the absurdity of it. "Only you—," Ivey began, pausing to wipe his eyes, shamelessly lifting his mask to do so. Everyone knew Ivey's face here, anyway. No one who wanted to see the Pistol again would lay a finger on him. "Only *you* could attack Unity one day and then interview with a Magistrate the next. It's good to see you haven't lost your magic, even after all this time."

As if sensing it had been mentioned, Roman's magic gave a twinge. It felt like a spiritual cramp, an ache in his heart. Ivey sat forward, expression turning serious. "I must ask, Aim: what are you doing here? You've been dead to the world for nearly a century only to return now, of all times. What in the heavens brought you back?"

The server reappeared with two glasses, then, and Roman was grateful for it. As soon as the wine was set down, he took a larger swig than the vintage warranted. "I'm not back," he said, more bitterly than he'd intended. As far as anyone was concerned—as far as *he* was concerned—he was still dead. Histrios had damaged him in ways he couldn't admit, even to an old friend. "I won't be until Unity is destroyed."

Ivey raised a single reddish-white eyebrow. "And that's what you want?"

Yes, he wanted it. He wanted it *desperately*. He'd never wanted anything *more*, not in his very long life—not death, not companionship, not freedom. He wanted Unity gone. He wanted to travel without watching for Enforcers over his shoulder. He wanted to make new friends without keeping all that he was a secret. He wanted to love without putting those who love *him* in danger. He wanted to live again. Unable to voice any of that, though, he simply nodded.

Ivey didn't seem surprised by this answer, either, but he tapped his fingers against the table thoughtfully. They were wrinkled, gnarled, while Roman's were still soft and youthful. Sometimes he wished his hands looked like Ivey's. "If I may: how will you accomplish it? It's not as if you can simply kill the Magistrates. A Representative will just be promoted to take their place."

"Then I'll all kill the Representatives. The Enforcers, too," Roman said, simply. "I'll wipe out the Representatives' entire bloodlines, if I must."

"I thought you left Unity to escape that life. The Egil I knew was never a killer," Ivey said sternly, watching Roman over the rim of his glass. The butterfly mask reminded Roman of Ivey's house, his walls filled with dozens and dozens of trapped creatures, caught and killed and cataloged. It wasn't as if Ivey killed all of the specimens himself, but a shiver still ran down Roman's spine.

He sighed and drank more of his wine. It was an excellent merlot, the flavors layered and complex, and Roman distantly wondered how much it would cost him. "I don't suppose you have any suggestions?"

"Governments only have power when people believe in them," Ivey said, simply. "Martyrdom *unites* people; it does not alienate them.

It seems to me the people already have too much blind trust in Unity, these days. What of this mess with Amos Nochdvor?"

Roman blinked. "What about it?"

"We all know that Unity is scheming," Ivey said, gesturing around the Pistol. "Ms. Cairn and her family knew it, too. But the general populace does not. If Unity says they intend to rescue the king, then in the people's minds, that is what Unity will do. Perhaps things would change if they saw the truth."

"I see what you're getting at."

"It's only the start, but it is *a* start. Who's better poised to reveal Unity's crimes than Egil?"

Roman shook his head. "No one will take my word for it, after Histrios. I'm a madman, remember? If I'd made it onto that team, I could've gathered evidence. Whatever they're after in Orean, I could've stopped them."

Thoughtfully, Ivey asked, "How's your relationship with the young prince, these days?"

Seeing Roman's grimace, he quickly said, "Never mind, then. I have faith you'll find your evidence, one way or another. You've always been resourceful. But on the subject of your prince, I would be remiss not to ask...you're aware of the bounty on him, yes?"

Roman stared dully at him. "Bounty?"

Ivey leaned in, and Roman matched the movement. "I heard the Wu sisters discussing it the other night," the maranet said, inclining his head toward the two women playing cards at the next table. Roman knew them by name; they had a dozen grand burglaries accredited to them and a combined bounty of nearly two hundred triems on their heads. "There's a twenty triem offer on him from the Golden Rose."

"That's not so much," Roman said, though he wasn't sure. "They want him dead?"

Ivey shrugged. "They want him gone."

"I'm not familiar with the Golden Rose. Who are they?"

"A new anarchist group, very anti-Unity. Their name's a reference to the Great War, to some scholars by the same name who protested Unity's creation."

Roman bit his lip. On any other day, he'd probably get along with them. "What do they have against Leandros?"

"What do you think?" Ivey asked, pointedly.

Roman sighed. Leandros led a Unity team, now. He worked for Unity. Roman wasn't pleased about it himself, and he knew Leandros better than anyone.

"But that's not all," Ivey said. "There's a second bounty, and this one *does* want him dead. I didn't hear how much, but from context, I gather it's outrageous. Ask Thane about it when you go up."

"Is it from Unity?"

Ivey clicked his tongue. He didn't seem surprised that Unity, too, would wish Leandros harm, even despite their purported partnership. "You know how Thane gets about his business; anonymity's the word. I only know the other's from the Golden Rose because they do their business here, out of the Pistol."

Roman drained the last of his wine and pushed to his feet. "I'd better get this over with."

"Best of luck," Ivey said, toasting with his glass.

Roman reluctantly circled the room and found Than occupied with helping another patron. He settled at the opposite end of the bar to wait, idly wondering whether Thane would recognize him. His hair was shorter than when they'd last met, though he knew that even behind a mask, his eyes might give him away.

When Thane finally turned to him, his expression was cool. There was no glint of recognition, but Thane had always been unbeatable in poker.

"I don't think we've been introduced," Thane said as he approached, holding out a hand even more weathered than Ivey's. Roman shook it but instantly regretted it when Thane wrenched his hand forward, turning it over to reveal the brand on his wrist. The old bartender bared his teeth, revealing sharp canines just like Ivey's. "Your kind's not welcome here."

Thane's hair had faded, but his strength hadn't; Roman winced, then tried to smile in the way the bartender used to like. "And here I thought I was the exception."

Thane released Roman's hand as if he'd been burned, and Roman took a moment to rub his wrist. He expected the usual—*that's not possible*, or *you're supposed to be dead*. Instead, Thane surprised him by barking out a laugh and saying, "*You*. You have some nerve coming here. More than a few of my patrons would kill you themselves, if they knew you were alive."

Roman rested his elbows on the counter and tried to look innocent. "You wouldn't let any of them hurt me, Thane."

"Where do you think you are? I'll let anyone do anything to you in here, for the right price. Maybe I'll get in line myself." Thane owned the Broken Pistol now, but before that, he'd been a mercenary. Even Roman would've shuddered to make an enemy of him, then. Probably still would.

"It's good to see you," Roman said.

"Yeah, yeah," Thane said. "I knew you weren't dead."

"Well, it was a close thing."

"No thanks to your pet alfar. I told you keeping him around would only cause trouble, and now he's gone straight, I hear. At least *you* haven't, if you're still coming around here."

"I could never," Roman said, pressing a hand to his heart. "But I'm glad you brought him up. Your grandfather mentioned something about a bounty?"

Thane pulled a heavy leather book out from under the bar, retrieved a pair of spectacles from his waistcoat pocket, and flipped through yellowing pages, each filled margin to margin with his cramped writing. This book was part of the Broken Pistol's draw: a meticulous ledger of open bounties and private jobs, available to anyone who knew to ask.

"There," Thane said, pointing to a recent entry. "A twenty triem offer from—"

"The Golden Rose, yeah. I meant the other one."

Thane made a disgruntled noise. "Guess I'm going to have to remind the old man about the Pistol's gossiping policy."

"How much is it?"

"Three hundred triems."

Roman swore. He left Leandros alone for half a century and he'd somehow ended up with a *three hundred triem* bounty on his head? Who had he pissed off so badly? Money like that was enough to tempt anyone. He'd have to keep a closer eye on Leandros going forward. "Who placed it?"

"An anonymous guarantor," Thane said, shutting the book.

"Won't you tell an old friend?"

Thane repeated his familiar barking laugh. "Is that what we are?"

"I certainly thought so," Roman said. They had been, once—sometimes more, when Roman's visits to the Broken Pistol coincided with periods where they were both unattached. That was back when Thane's hair was still red and Roman's life had some meaning.

"I can't believe you went white before Ivey. You've grown old," Roman observed, reaching out to touch Thane's hair. It stuck out in every direction, just like his grandfather's. Roman knew there were eyes on them, weighing how familiarly Roman interacted with the Pistol's frightening owner; he wouldn't have risked touching an irritable Thane unless he had something to gain from it.

Thane batted his hand away, but there was no anger in the gesture. "That's no way to get what you want," he said. Then, he added, "You haven't."

"I never do."

Thane gave Roman a hard look, then sighed and caved, first glancing around to see if anyone was within earshot. "I'll tell you this: the bounty's been around for as long as you've been dead. I don't know what happened in Histrios an' I don't want to, but afterward, Unity went around telling everyone Nochdvor killed you to save the city. It really boosted his reputation, and the Alfheimr Council didn't like that much."

"*Alfheimr?*" Roman asked. Dread seeped into his veins and made them glow.

This didn't surprise Roman. The truth was, Alfheimr's Council had despised Leandros since his father's failed coup, since he ran away with Egil and refused to be an easy pawn for them. But this meant that Leandros had made enemies of the Golden Rose, the Magistrates of Unity, *and* Alfheimr itself—not to mention whoever had kidnapped Amos, lying wait in Orean.

Leandros was clever, but with enemies like those, he was as good as dead.

"He's been locked away in the palace for decades. There's no getting in that place uninvited, so no one bothered taking the bounty up," Thane explained. "Since he came to Gallonten, though, all out in the open, there's been interest. That's all I'll say, but if memory serves, Nochdvor's capable of taking care of himself."

Roman hated the word *capable*. Lots of people were capable until they made a mistake. He looked down at his hands, finally noticing how bright they'd grown. Normally, this was where he withdrew, pushed down the darkness inside him. For the first time, though, he decided to embrace it. He needed it, so he let it spread.

Thane hadn't noticed, but it was only a matter of time. As evenly as he could, Roman asked, "Mind if I make an announcement?"

"Normally, I'd make you pay for that," Thane said, as if Roman didn't know the Broken Pistol's biggest rule: if you caused a scene, you paid for it—literally. It worked as an effective deterrent, as Thane's rates were high, and he had ways of collecting.

Roman grimaced. "I can't afford it."

"Whatever you say, you know it'll be everywhere by morning."

"I'm counting on it," Roman said. The Pistol's no gossiping rule only went so far, and everyone in this room was influential in Gallonten, in one way or another.

Again, Thane sighed. "For old times' sake, then, I'll allow it. Just this once."

Roman saw the exact moment Thane noticed his hands, the man's expression shifting to alarm, but Roman was already turning away. Wordlessly, he stepped up to the half-wall separating the bar from the common room and climbed onto it. There, he waited until he had everyone's attention. When the pianist in the corner faltered, everyone else followed, dozens of masked faces turning toward Roman. The silence felt familiar, after his time with the Webhon Players. He knew just how long to wait to make them squirm.

He'd been feeling too heroic, these last few days—Aleksir Bardon and Maebhe Cairn had drawn it out of him. But watching the patrons' faces as he removed his mask, their annoyance and distrust turning quickly to horror, he remembered what he truly was. He knew what they were seeing: his face etched with glowing veins, making him look as though he wept ichor, and a pair of all-black eyes. He gave them a moment to look their fill.

The Wu Sisters dropped their cards. Ivey set down his drink. Thane stared, mouth hanging open, and then Egil asked: "Did you miss me?"

As with every time before, the shadows draped off him, pooled around him like a cape until he felt more shadow than man. Somewhere in the back of his mind, he knew he'd let the transformation go far enough. It was time to stop. This *thing* inside him fed on his helplessness and fear, and he had too much of that inside him tonight. But he pushed those feelings away to focus on the scene before him.

Of course, no one answered him.

"I'm the one who attacked Unity Island yesterday," he said, holding his hands up and spreading them wide, letting everyone see how they glowed. "I'd like you all to send them a message from me: tell them I'm coming for them. Tell the world that Egil has returned."

Roman turned to jump down, then thought better of it. On a whim, he added, "And for anyone seeking the bounty on Prince Nochdvor's head, know that you'll have to go through me to get it."

After that, Roman left without so much as looking Thane or Ivey's ways again. He was too unsettled by the magic, too unmoored. By tomorrow, all of Gallonten would know Egil was here, Egil was behind the attack on Unity Island. Grimly, Roman smiled to himself. They'd have trouble blaming Leandros for it, now.

Out in the fresh air, Roman stumbled down the dock, his limbs feeling too heavy and too light all at once. He wasn't sure where he ended and the shadows began; they flocked to him, crowded around him, and he knew if he wasn't careful, they would smother him. If he wasn't careful, he could lose himself in them forever.

He'd never let the transformation go this far. For a moment, he feared he couldn't pull himself back. But as his pulse slowed and he remembered how to breathe, the glow faded from his veins. Finally, the suffocating fear that this time would be it, that he'd traded his humanity away to this darkness for good, lifted from his chest and allowed him to sensation again.

No one was around to see Roman stand on the docks and take great, heaving breaths as he fought the darkness inside of him.

No one was around to see Roman fall to his knees and heave into the murky water, half as much blood coming up as bile.

No one was around to see Egil wrap his arms around himself, holding himself together as best as he could while he shook and shivered and waited for the shadows to bleed out of him.

Chapter Twenty-Three

Back home, Maebhe spent all her free time exploring the forests and valleys around Orean. She was a hunter, a runner, a climber, and a swimmer, but even with everything she put her body through on a regular basis, even with all her strength and stamina, it seemed she had no tolerance for fae wine.

That might have stung her pride, if she could think past the pounding in her head, so she lied and told herself this throbbing ache was from jumping off a building into uneasy waters. She knew what it really was, though: a hangover. And that thought led to more pressing concerns: first, that she couldn't remember much of the previous night. Second, that she didn't know where she was.

She lay on the ground, enveloped in a warm quilt. Unable and unwilling to move just yet, she relied on the sounds around her for clues. Birds sang. Kieran snored nearby. Beyond a closed door, feathers rustled and feet shuffled.

Finally, Maebhe flopped onto her back and opened her eyes. The ceiling was high, higher than she could reach if she jumped. Higher than she could reach if she stood on Kieran's shoulder and *then* jumped, and that gave her her best clue yet: this was one of the massive frìth houses they'd passed on their way into Home, made of the same clay brick and climbing vines. She sprawled at the foot of a bed wide enough for someone with a wingspan to sleep on comfortably, but not long enough for a frìth, and that gave her another clue: the fae. When she sat up, she saw Kieran and Íde's sleeping forms curled up on the mattress.

Before she could puzzle through anything else, the bedroom door slammed open. The room flooded with sunslight, haloing the tall figure standing in the door's frame. Maebhe groaned and covered her eyes.

"Good morning!" came a deep voice, far too loud and far too cheerful for a morning like this.

"Why are you so loud?" Maebhe asked. She uncovered her eyes to massage her temples but regretted it when sunslight colored the back of her eyelids. Even that was too bright.

"The better to wake you, dear, though I see you were already up," Drys said.

On the bed, Íde sat up and blinked blearily at them. She looked around the room, then down at Kieran, who'd slept through Drys' arrival.

"You're going to have to be much louder than that if you want to wake him," Maebhe told Drys. Nodding, the faerie drew a breath as if to yell, but Maebhe hurried to stop them: "Don't! Please. My head."

"Mine too," Íde sighed. She passed her hands across her face, then tried to flatten some of her bedhead.

"Our wine has that effect, especially on humans," Drys said, not sounding particularly sympathetic. "I should have warned you."

"You should have," Íde agreed.

Drys' impish expression faded into something more serious. "I'm not here to torture you needlessly, I'll have you know. The elders of Home are meeting to discuss what Maebhe told Leileas last night."

"What I told Leileas..." Maebhe echoed. When she said it out loud, she uncovered a hazy memory of a conversation with the gentle frìth. "Oh, fuck! I told her everything. I'm sorry, Drys. I know you said not to."

"What's done is done. As I predicted, they're not pleased with the news. For those of them that already hate outsiders, this is vindication." Seeing Íde and Maebhe exchange wary looks, Drys sighed and said, "Yes, *outsiders* includes orinians. You aren't Unity, but your forebears still committed terrible violence during the Great War. To you, it was so far back you don't see it as being connected to you, but the elders of Home lived that war. It's fresh in their memory, and they're not wrong to remember it. Their children are not wrong to remember it, either, when they see the effects of it every day here in Home. Trust is not a right, and it's *your* responsibility to prove you are not your ancestors.

"That said," Drys added, "All meetings in Home are public. Muir and Senga, at least, would be happy to see you there, taking an interest in Home's politics."

"Yes, please. We should wake Kieran. He'd want to be there, too," Maebhe said. Unfortunately, though, that was easier to say than do. Between them, they spent the next ten minutes prodding, pleading, and eventually jumping on Kieran until he was awake as well, rubbing sleep from his eyes as Drys led the way outside.

Home was calmer in the morning, quieter. A layer of dew blanketed the ground and above, around, the trees of the forest were still. Back home, Maebhe had to journey far into the mountains to taste air this clean. Orean was no industrial force, but Illyon was; it tainted the valley and the sky above both cities. On the walk, Drys gave what advice they could. Receiving advice from a faerie, however, was a difficult thing: they didn't explain anything they said and half of what they *did* say contradicted itself.

"These meetings have a tradition of lazy beginnings," they explained. "Don't rush them or get impatient. Commit their songs and stories to memory, enough that you could repeat them back. Remember who they belong to or you'll offend them all. A song is a sacred thing. It's your honor to hear it, but their honor to share it. These cancel each other out, so don't offer additional thanks or you'll offend the sharer. Do *not* clap. Speak your mind if you must, but don't speak over anyone and don't interrupt. Always acknowledge the point of the person who spoke before you."

"Right," Maebhe said, glancing at Kieran to see how he was handling the information. He stared down at his feet as he walked, nodding to himself like he understood, but Maebhe could tell that he didn't. She felt a little better for it.

Drys pursed their lips. "If you can't remember that, just be your darling, charming selves. I'm sure it'll work out fine for you." Their voice was light, but they shot a stern look back at the trio. "You're lucky my people rarely attend these meetings. They'd be less forgiving of social missteps."

They led the orinians to the same field they'd danced in the night before. All signs of the revelries had been cleared away, and in the morning light, Maebhe noticed how strange the field was. A ring of toadstools enclosed it in a perfect circle, the long grass within not just green, but turquoise and purple, too.

At the center, two dozen frìth lounged around baskets and trays of food. It looked more like a picnic than a meeting, but Drys stepped carefully over the line of toadstools and approached the group, so Maebhe and the others followed. As they did, a frìth with horns nearly as long as Maebhe's body looked their way, his black eyebrows drawing low over blue eyes and his lips pulling back to show his teeth. While Maebhe was far from an expert at reading frìth expressions, she didn't think it was a smile.

"Good morning! How do our guests find themselves, after last night?" Senga called to the newcomers as the frìth all shifted to widen the circle. Senga's voice was rougher than her daughter's and her fur grayer around the eyes, but sitting beside Leileas, they looked as identical as Maebhe and Kieran. Muir sat on Leileas' other side with a tall instrument like a twisted harp propped in his lap.

"Wholly changed, thank you," Kieran said, offering a wobbly bow. Maebhe watched him with horror, realizing too late why he'd been so amiable on the walk over: he was still drunk from the night before. Íde winced, coming to the same conclusion.

The words made Muir smile, though, as he passed the instrument to Leileas. "Sit, please. Help thyselves to food. I'm afraid thou hast missed the start, but there is much still to hear. Leileas?"

Leileas nodded, adjusted the instrument in her lap, and began to play. Maebhe's legs gave out as she sat, the song quite literally sweeping her off her feet. Leileas' fingers danced across the strings in intricate loops, pulling from the instrument a surprisingly sweet song. Though there were no words, it felt like bright suns in early morning and a breeze billowing through tall grass. It was over far too soon.

Maebhe raised her hands to clap but remembered Drys' advice in time, changing the direction of the movement to brush her hair out of her face instead. Beside her, Drys nodded approvingly as Leileas passed the instrument to Senga, who began a song of her own. So it continued, only a few frìth passing the instrument without playing. They sang songs of merriment, sorrow, hope. Songs with stories, songs with feelings. Songs about everything and nothing. It was different from the music they'd made last night, music that had been made with only one purpose: to encourage dancing. This was so much more.

By the time the instrument reached Drys, Maebhe had half a dozen melodies swimming through her mind, some wordless, others not. Some simple, others impossible. Despite Drys' warning, there was no remembering them all. Maebhe was the kind to stand on a bar and join a hearty drinking song, but complexity like this...she drowned in it. The faces around the circle, too, were too similar to her untrained eye. She couldn't say who sang what. She felt vaguely dizzy.

Drys passed the instrument to Maebhe without playing. It was lighter than she expected, the wood warm in her hands as she passed it to Kieran. Before she could hand it off, Muir interrupted with: "Did Drys explain the rules to thee? If thou dost not share a song, thou mayest not speak until the meeting is done."

Maebhe froze. "What if I have no songs to share?"

"Everyone has a song."

Maebhe wracked her mind for a song that wasn't horribly inappropriate for the situation. "Maebhe can't sing," Kieran provided.

Maebhe elbowed him and hissed, "Shut *up*."

In return, Kieran gave her a wounded look. "No. You obviously don't have a song. *I* do. Give me the thing."

"No," Maebhe said, holding the instrument closer. "What do you mean, you have a song?"

Kieran wordlessly held his hand out for the instrument.

"Does Maebhe know it, too?" Leileas asked. To Muir and Senga, she said, "They are twins—born at the same time. They should be allowed to sing together."

Muir nodded. "In that case, thou mayest share. If thou dost not know the hearpe, thy voice is enough."

Maebhe didn't think her arms would be long enough to play that thing even if she *did* know how to. She met Kieran's eyes. Without waiting for Maebhe to catch on, Kieran began to sing:

> *Under pink morning suns,*
> *I made my way to you.*

Maebhe winced. She should have seen this coming. Of course

Kieran—*especially* a drunk Kieran—would choose that song. Taking a shaky breath, she joined on the next line.

> *The road was lone, my pack was heavy.*
> *For you, o'er land I flew.*
> *To see your smile, I'd run again.*
> *To hear you laugh, my love, I'd fly.*
> *And though I may be gone again,*
> *You'll see me soon, ere springtime's end.*

Kieran let Maebhe carry the melody, his light voice spinning harmonies around her that she hadn't known him capable of. In all the times their mother had sung this to them, her voice had never wavered the way Maebhe's did now. When they finished, Maebhe closed her eyes. In her memory, she was in her parents' arms again, holding them after they'd returned from one of their trips. They were singing to her, their voices soft and gentle and fond, and Maebhe's heart was breaking with their loss all over again. Wordlessly, Kieran took the hearpe from her and passed it to Íde.

"That was beautiful," Senga said gently. "It is a lovely thing, sharing songs. It is a way to share joy and wonder and knowledge...as well as memories, emotions."

Maebhe nodded and wiped her eyes, opening them in time to see Íde pass the hearpe on without singing. She reached over Kieran to take Maebhe's hand, and Maebhe held it as tightly as she wished she'd held her mother's on that final morning.

Eventually, the hearpe reached the frìth with the long horns that Maebhe had noticed earlier. He strummed a few thoughtful notes, and in a voice deeper than the lowest point of Home's canyon, said with a sharp smile, "I have a song about an orinian. For our guests."

He strummed a cascade of flowing notes that reminded Maebhe
of a waterfall and sang:

> *Lady Luighseach, Lyryma bound*
> *Bathed in black night beneath the moon*
> *and sang sweetly songs from her home.*
> *Nearby, beneath the nightdark trees*
> *a dragon drank, but drawn by strains that*
> *like a lark, Luighseach sang*
> *he treaded 'tween the trees to her.*
> *Unknowning now how near he lurked,*
> *our Lady lingered in her lapping pond.*
> *O'er crystalline calm he called to her:*
> *he meant no malice, meant only to hear.*
> *And Luighseach laughed, allowed him near,*
> *unafraid and unabashed. Each unable to resist*
> *the other, they offered out secrets and sighs,*
> *and softly spoke while two suns rose.*
> *Orean opposed our lady's flight*
> *and searched swiftly for signs and tracks.*
> *Bewitched by her beauly and bound by budding love,*
> *the wyrm withdrew to the woods with*
> *Luighseach to live in Lyryma for good.*
> *But forgetting this forest is full of darkness,*
> *the lovers lost themselves in Lyryma's night.*
> *It sank to their souls, sundered their hearts.*
> *It tore apart their—*

"*Enough*, Galam!" Leileas interrupted.

Galam's fingers stopped abruptly on the strings with a *twang*, and
all the frìth in the circle turned to Leileas. Her voice was a snarl, her

teeth were bared. All six of her ears were pressed flat to her head.

"You interrupt my song?" Galam asked, sounding more amused than insulted. Still, an uneasy wave swept through the assembled frìth. Maebhe watched, wide-eyed.

"I do. You insult our guests. They have all the forest to travel through yet, and you are trying to frighten them," Leileas accused.

"She is right," another in the circle said. "We all know how the song ends. Galam knows his choice is inappropriate."

A few others murmured agreement. Maebhe looked at Drys, wanting to ask how the song ends, but they shook their head.

"Enough," Senga said. She gave Galam a sharp look, again looking very much like her daughter. "I believe no one here would intentionally slight our guests, but Galam, thy song is finished. It does not do to speak of the darkness of the forest, not with all we have seen in it, of late."

Drys leaned toward Maebhe. Quiet as a breath, they said, "Ask what she means."

"Why don't you do it?" Maebhe hissed back.

"I didn't sing, remember?"

"But I don't want to be rude—"

"What do you mean?" Kieran asked, shooting Drys and Maebhe a quick, exasperated look. "What have you seen?"

Muir shook his head, and Senga looked away. Even Galam seemed cowed, his ears lying flat and his hands tightly gripping the hearpe. It was Leileas who finally answered. "The forest has been restless," she said. "There's something evil lurking at its heart, a plague we cannot find. An illness we cannot root out. There are strange creatures here, new monsters and ill omens."

"Do not worry, little ones," Muir said. "The path to Orean skirts around the heart of the forest. The danger is lesser, there."

"Lesser," Kieran repeated.

"We will speak of this no more," Muir announced. "To speak of dark things is to invite them in, and I will not bring that upon Home. Galam, pass the hearpe along and let us finish our sharing."

Galam did. Though the remaining few frìth played, their songs lacked the earlier spirit, more a chore to hurry through and less a celebration. It ended again with Muir, who laid the hearpe beside him. Maebhe expected the meeting to begin then, and maybe it did, but it still felt nothing like a meeting. She learned about how someone named Taran asked to court Mael Muire, and Mael Muire's father disapproved of the match. Another frìth named Alpin was heard arguing with his mother about joining the hunt. Leileas caught her first shaari, whatever that was.

It reminded Maebhe of her older aunts, when they got together for tea. Always gossiping and bragging over snacks. They would never *call* it gossiping or bragging, of course.

With an irritated look in the orinians' direction, as if he hated they were even there to hear it, Galam talked about his home village, how the crops were doing well but hunting had grown dangerous. Others asked about this frìth or that faerie, and he answered. He told them he'd be returning home at the end of the week, so if anyone had any gifts or letters they'd like him to take, they should get them to him before then. At that point, the frìth beside Muir said she'd found limneberries south of Home and was making a tincture for them. He should take a jar back with him. Someone suggested she send some with the orinians as well.

It carried on like that—a lot more nothing, but Maebhe remembered Drys' advice about lazy starts and made herself wait. Even when frìth started rising to leave, she bit her tongue. It began with Galam, of course: he frowned at the orinians as he passed them by, others following at his heels. But as they left, Kieran blurted, "Wait, what about Unity?"

Galam paused. "We do not wish to talk about Unity."

"I don't care what you *wish*," Kieran said. It was so unlike him, so bold that Maebhe could only stare. "I don't *want* Unity poking around my city, but they're probably on their way there now!"

"So you say."

"What's that supposed to mean?" Kieran asked, struggling to keep his voice even.

"Kieran," Íde warned.

"We wouldn't lie about that," Maebhe tried. "I promise."

Galam ignored her. "You may be allowed to speak in our circles, but you are not from Home. I am. I adjourn this meeting."

"Can he do that?" Maebhe asked Drys in a whisper.

It was Muir who answered. "A meeting requires twenty-four frìth to be present. If Galam leaves, we will not have enough."

And then Galam was gone, making the circle that much smaller. It wasn't until he was well out of earshot that Senga explained further. "Forgive him," she said. "Like many of us, Galam is wary and frightened of Unity. He is worried about thy story, and worry makes him hostile."

"But you can't just ignore things you're worried about!" Kieran tried, probably loud enough for Galam to hear. Maebhe remembered reading about how good a frìth's hearing was in some old textbook.

"That is what Lyryma is for. That is why Ellaes made this forest for us to begin with. During the Great War, the other peoples of this world nearly destroyed us, just as they did the red dragons. When our killers joined together under the guise of peace-making, forming Unity, our Guardian helped us hide."

"And we have been in these woods for so long, little ones," Muir said in a gentle voice. "We are used to confronting problems at our own pace. Thy news came as a surprise, and we are not yet ready to discuss it."

"When *will* you be ready?" Kieran asked.

"That is hard to say. When it becomes urgent. When we have fixed the problems in our own forest. When we know more. Kieran, thou art our guest and we shall not insult thee, but Galam is right. This is too large a matter to take thee at thy word. We will look into the truth of what thou sayest about this Unity mission, and when we do, *then* we shall speak on it more."

"We understand," Maebhe said, before Kieran could argue, "But I won't apologize for telling you about it. I'm glad you know, just so you can be wary. We don't know what Unity wants from us. Our friend thought there might be more to it than the missing King."

"I hope they mean thee no harm, and I am sorry we cannot be of more assistance," Senga said. She hesitated, then added, "If Unity's intentions prove foul and thy king requests our help directly, that would be a different matter."

It was a hint. One she shouldn't have given, based on Muir's warning look. Maebhe nodded and did her best to keep the hope off her face. "Thank you."

"Enough of this, for now," Muir said. "Truthfully, we hoped thou wouldst spend the morning regaling us with stories from Orean."

"Stories?" Maebhe asked, glancing nervously at her companions. "I'm not sure we have any that are interesting enough for—" *Someone as old as you,* she'd been about to say. Would that be rude?

Before she could decide, Drys waved a hand. Now that the meeting had adjourned, they apparently could speak again. "Interesting doesn't matter. You have the advantage of novelty. Trust me, the frith will take any story that's *new*, if it means they don't have to listen to the same old ones again and again."

"It's true," Muir said, sounding pleased. He sighed dreamily. "Ah, when Egil lived here, we had new stories every night. It was the liveliest our meetings have ever been."

Maebhe sat forward. "Egil lived here?"

Beside her, Kieran snorted. "Since when have you cared so much about Egil?"

Maebhe ignored him. "He's the one who saved us from Unity," she told Muir. "And Drys, too! Oh, I completely forgot—Senga, he says hello."

Kieran stared at her, wide eyed. Senga stirred, too, her ears back with surprise. Finally, she smiled. "Is that so? Little ones, it seems thy story is *very* interesting, after all."

CHAPTER TWENTY-FOUR

LEANDROS GLANCED OVER HIS SHOULDER, unable to shake the sense of *wrongness* that followed him—a sense not just of being watched, but of being hunted. The feeling on its own didn't surprise him, but the persistence of it did. Everywhere he went in Gallonten, it followed. Even switching hotels hadn't been enough to shake it.

At least his new hotel was close to the island, a straight shot down a busy thoroughfare. It shortened the time spent in-between, exposed to the world. Leandros had never been particularly cautious in his youth. He'd never worried after his own safety, but it was no longer just *his* safety on the line. This paranoia didn't suit him, but if he died now, he had little faith Unity would continue the search for Amos.

He wished circumstances were different. He wished he could experience more of Gallonten. Everywhere he looked, people lived their lives and openly expressed their enjoyment of it. A man told stories to his friends, his movements animated. A woman broke out in bright, unrestrained laughter. A group rode by on horseback, calling out fond nicknames. There was so much *feeling* here: joy, humor, excitement, love. Leandros wanted to immerse himself in it wholly.

He recalled a story that had broken in Alfheimr a few years back. A previously healthy woman, the widow of a former Alfheim Council Member, died only months after her husband. In the weeks leading up to her death, she had gone blind and her voice had left her. When the postmortem revealed caustic damage to her airways and lungs, the city cried murder, but an investigation quickly uncovered the true culprit: the widow's mourning veil.

The veil had had been made of the stiff black crape that had recently come into vogue, a fabric that was colored and treated with substances that stained her skin and filled her lungs with toxins — hematoxylin, bichromate of potash, and copper chloride. The saddest part of the story was that the unfortunate woman had known it was the veil causing her slow decay. Proper mourning was expected of her, and so she had mourned her husband to the last.

These days, Alfheimr's rules, his own grief, and his family's hopes covered Leandros like that veil. With every breath, he inhaled poison. He could not see a way out from this life.

Near the bridge to Unity Island, a frantic movement caught his eye. It was Eftychia O'Neill, sitting cross-legged on the fieldstone wall and waving at him. As Leandros approached, she patted the spot beside her. While he didn't climb up to sit, he did lean against it. His mother would pitch a fit to see him leaning so casually in such a public place.

"Hello, Captain!" Eftychia greeted.

"Good morning, Ms. O'Neill."

"Eftychia," the orinian corrected. Then, "Actually, just Chia."

"You seem in good cheer this morning," Leandros said. He wondered if she was capable of being anything else.

Today, Chia wore a wide-brimmed straw hat decked with flowers and a similar sweater-skirt combination as the day before. None of it matched. She beamed at him. "I am indeed. Yesterday, my bosses gave me a terrible job. I hadn't wanted to do it, and then just this morning, they told me I no longer have to. That would put anyone in good cheer, don't you think?"

Leandros couldn't help but feel concerned. Eftychia was an Enforcer; her "bosses" could only be the Magistrates, and Leandros suspected that "job" certainly didn't refer to paperwork.

"What were you thinking about just now?" Chia asked.

"Just when?"

"When you stood across the square. You look sad when you think no one's watching, I've noticed," she said. This was only their second meeting that *he* knew of; to make such a perceptive observation, Leandros wondered how long she must have been watching. "That's why I called you a mourning dove yesterday. They're named that because of their calls, you know. Very mournful, just like your clothes."

Leandros considered this, then answered, "I was thinking about how easily love lost can ruin an adventuring spirit."

"Love lost? Do tell," Chia said, leaning in.

"You asked what I was thinking, and that's all you'll get."

"How cruel," Chia sighed, though she brightened again almost immediately. "Hello, Eresh! Oh, what's wrong with you?"

Leandros looked over just as the dryad joined them, wide-eyed and out of breath. He clutched a newspaper to his chest. "Captain!" he panted. "Have you seen the papers?"

"No," Leandros said, dread sinking through him like a heavy stone through water. He held a hand out. "Let me see."

Eresh's fingers tightened around the paper. "Captain—"

"Mr. Ochoa."

With a grimace, Eresh handed the paper over. At first, Leandros thought it must be a joke. He read the headline again and again, but he couldn't get past the first two words, big and bold and spelling out: EGIL RETURNS.

The dryad hurried to explain, "Several witnesses saw him, Captain. He told them exactly who he was and used his magic to prove it. He wanted them to send a message to Unity."

"What was the message?" Leandros asked.

Eresh swallowed nervously. "That he was the one behind the break-in on the island. And that he was coming for them."

The world around Leandros felt distant, like he was falling deeper inside himself. "It's an imposter. Someone is only pretending to be him."

Chia peered over his shoulder to read the paper. "Oh," she said. She didn't sound particularly surprised, and that made the heavy stone of dread settle right in Leandros' gut, kicking up silt and sand. Did Unity know something he didn't?

He thought back to the day of the break-in. That afternoon, he thought he'd seen someone that almost looked like—but no. It was impossible. He'd held Egil's lifeless body in his arms. This was a lie, and hoping would only hurt him.

"Who else could break onto Unity Island?" Eresh asked. Then, studying Leandros' face, "Do you want us to cancel today's plans?"

The question, along with the gentle way it was phrased, annoyed Leandros. He opened his mouth to lash out, to free the anger that always waited to break out, but then Gareth arrived in much the same state as Eresh had: disheveled and out of breath. His waistcoat was off by one button, Leandros noticed, and his hat sat askew.

"Prince Nochdvor, good morning. Can we speak privately?" he gasped.

Another flicker of irritation.

"Is this about the papers?" Leandros asked. "I've already seen them."

"The papers? No, I overslept this morning and didn't have a chance to read them. Why? What did they say?"

"Oh dear," Eresh said, sharing a look with Chia.

With a hand on his shoulder, Leandros steered Gareth away from the other two and onto the bridge, far enough to get away from the crowds. "What is it, then?" he asked.

Gareth removed his hat and fidgeted with it while he explained, "I overheard something terrible last night, Captain. I feel it's my duty to warn you, relations to the other parties be damned. My sister was meeting with a friend—the one I put forward for the guard position, you remember. I hope you won't think less of me for this confession, but I admit I was eavesdropping. I know it's wrong, but I couldn't resist. It's a terrible habit I—"

"On with it, Ranulf. What did you hear?" Leandros said, manners forgotten in his urgency.

"They want to frame you for the break-in on the island," Gareth blurted. "The Magistrates want you out of the way, and they said that if they can't find your uncle, they'll blame you for that, too."

Leandros took a step back, putting some space between himself and his emotions. What Gareth said made sense. It fit with the Unity Leandros knew. Even so, his hands shook, his heart raced in his chest, and his ears rang. "Is that all?" he asked.

"I know, it's horrib—ah? What do you mean, *is that all?*"

Leandros had been sure Unity would kill him for his threats on the island that day, but in a way, this was better. For days now, he'd been locking every door, checking every shadow, sleeping with a gun under his pillow. He never would have admitted it out loud, but he had only planned to survive long enough to rescue his uncle. After that, as long as he succeeded in that, he would've let them have him.

This, though. This changed things. If Unity wasn't planning on killing him, then it could only mean that they needed him alive.

Yes, it was possible that the Magistrates still intended him for the gallows. Before that, though, he'd go to trial, and he was a *Prince of*

Alfheimr. The whole world would be watching—was that not the perfect opportunity for Leandros to tell the world everything he knew? If they wanted him silenced, wouldn't it be easier to simply kill him? They certainly had the means.

"It seems strange, doesn't it? Framing me, instead of killing me?" Leandros asked, more to himself than Gareth. Gareth looked horrified.

The timing of this bothered Leandros, too. One of the Magistrates happened to share this plan on the same day Egil returned from the grave, claiming full responsibility for the break-in? It would be just like Egil, making himself a martyr to save someone else. Maybe those papers were right.

"Who did you say your sister was talking to?" he asked.

"A new friend of mine. He just split with his partner, so he's been staying with me as he gets re-settled. I put his name forward when the guard position opened because—"

"His name, Mr. Ranulf."

Gareth fidgeted with his hat again. He looked guilty as he said, "Hallisey. Roman Hallisey."

Roman Hallisey. Though Leandros kept a straight face, inside, he was falling and falling and falling away. "I see."

"You know him, don't you?" Gareth asked, watching Leandros like he was waiting for him to break. Little did he know that Leandros already had. Little did he know that Leandros was gone, floating somewhere outside his body, completely unmoored. "Who is he to you, Captain?"

"Describe him for me," Leandros demanded, ignoring Gareth's question. He could barely hear it, anyway, past the racing of his own heart. There was still a chance this was an imposter. He had to believe this was just an imposter.

Gareth blinked. "Ah...about this tall," he said, holding a hand just above the top of his own head. "Curly hair, strikingly dark eyes."

It was no imposter, but Leandros didn't understand—why hadn't Egil come back to him? "What did he have to say about your sister's plan?" he asked.

"I didn't hear the end of the conversation, I'm afraid."

Leandros leaned back against the stone wall, his legs no longer able to support him. "How long has he been in Gallonten? Do you know?"

"At least as long as the Rinehart Festival has been running. His partner was one of the Webhon Players."

Leandros closed his eyes. He knew exactly which one. He saw the actress's face perfectly in his mind, gentle and lovely. So *that* was why she'd been on the island that day. And the man with her, the one he'd glimpsed only briefly, the one who had *run* from him, really had been Egil. Leandros was a fool.

He laughed suddenly, startling Gareth. Leandros barely recognized his own voice, not with all the bitterness in it. "It's incredible, Mr. Ranulf, that you asked me so much about Egil when, all this time, you've had him living under your own roof."

Gareth started. "I beg your pardon?"

Leandros shoved the newspaper at him. Without waiting for him to read it, barely waiting for him to take it, he made his way back to Eresh and Chia.

"Oh, Chia, please be careful not to fall," Eresh said as Leandros approached. The dryad was peering over the wall, down at the steep rocks that led to crashing waves. When he noticed the alfar, he straightened. "Everything all right, Captain?"

"Perfectly. Where to first, Ms. O'Neill?" Leandros asked. He must have controlled his tone well enough, because Eresh relaxed and Chia smiled.

"I was thinking of taking you through my favorite park. Is that acceptable, Captain Adder?"

"*Adder?*" Leandros asked, but Chia was already wrinkling her nose and shaking her head.

"I saw the bottom of your tattoo and thought I'd try it out, but it definitely doesn't fit."

Leandros looked down at his wrist. At least today, his sleeve fully hid the tattoo that twisted up his forearm. He eyed her warily. It seemed she really had been watching him. Of the Enforcers, only she'd tried to befriend him, and that alone made her suspicious. He wondered if the "job" she'd mentioned earlier involved Unity's plan to frame him, a plan now made pointless by Egil's dramatic return.

He wondered where that left him. Safe from being framed, at least for now. It would be unwise to rely on speculation, but Leandros was beginning to suspect Unity wanted him alive. If true, being at an Enforcer's side was probably the safest place in the world.

"Wherever you want to go is acceptable to me," Leandros said, smiling at Chia. She smiled brightly back.

Once Gareth rejoined them, Leandros ignored the man's attempts to catch his eye and followed Chia across the square. She linked her arm with his, and he allowed it because it meant Gareth and Eresh had to walk behind them on the sidewalk. Leandros really didn't want to look at Gareth, right now. He didn't want the reminder of Egil.

"How much do you know about Gallonten, Captain?" Chia asked, looking up at him from beneath long eyelashes.

Leandros didn't notice. "Academically? A little. Practically? Much less. I've been here before, but only for short stays."

"Then you may know that we stand in the historic downtown," she said, gesturing broadly. "When Gallonteans first settled on the water, Unity was still part of the city. That building over there, the post office, was one of the first Unity buildings. It was only much later, when Unity had outgrown the city, that it moved to the island. Ah! Here we are."

At that last part, she turned them toward a vividly green park. It was full of others out for promenades, getting the last out of the warm weather and their summer walking ensembles. Again, Leandros and Eftychia together collected attention, so Chia leaned in, her dark hair draping over his shoulder. "Captain, since I'm being such an excellent guide, may I ask you a few questions? I'd like to get to know you better so I can find you a nickname that fits."

Leandros raised an eyebrow. "Very well, but only a few."

"Too subjective!" Chia protested. "I can stretch a few to four or five. May I ask you five questions?"

"Three."

"Very storybook," she said, sounding pleased. She reached up, almost touching his face but stopping at the last moment. "Where did you get that scar? It looks very heroic."

Leandros touched his cheek self-consciously. "I'm sorry to disappoint, then. I got it in a bar fight."

Chia laughed and clapped her hands together, delighted.

"Really?" Eresh asked from behind them. "I didn't think you even had those in Alfheimr—fights, not bars. I assume there are bars everywhere."

"There are fights everywhere, too. This was from my first," Leandros said. He'd tried to stay out of it, but a swing meant for Egil had missed and struck Leandros instead. Egil was the one who'd started the fight, who'd chosen the bar. Leandros had been angry at the time, but Egil was also the one who'd stitched him up afterward, who'd taken him to his favorite opera in apology, who'd taught him to defend himself so it never happened again.

Was he teaching that actress, now, too?

"May I ask you a question in return?" Leandros asked Chia. The orinian narrowed her eyes but nodded. "How did you end up in Gallonten?"

"I've never even been to Orean, if that's what you're asking. I grew up here. My turn: what scares you the most?"

Leandros didn't for one moment consider giving an honest answer. "Red dragons. My father used to tell my cousin and I terrifying stories about them."

"How traumatic!" Chia said. She took his hand and pressed it to her heart. "Don't you worry: I'll defend you from any we meet on the journey. From your father's stories, too."

As gently as he could, Leandros removed his hand. "There's no need for that. My father was executed for treason a long time ago."

Chia clapped a hand over her mouth.

"It's all right," Leandros assured her.

"What happened?" she asked tentatively. Frantically, she waved her hands between them. "No, don't answer that! That wasn't one of my questions!"

"It's a matter of public record, so I won't count it. He wanted the throne, tried to kill his own brother for it, and gave little thought to the lifetime of pain he was inflicting on his son in the process." Leandros shrugged. "But there's a novel based on the story; I'm sure Mr. Ranulf could tell you more."

Gareth jumped at being suddenly addressed. "I—well, yes. It's an Egil story. I'm familiar." It was as if being given permission to speak had restored his confidence because he suddenly blurted, "Prince Nochdvor, how could Egil be back? Did you not kill him in Histrios?"

Beside Leandros, Chia went conspicuously quiet, watching the alfar for his response. Leandros neatly side-stepped the question. "Aren't you the Egil scholar? I'd expect you to know the stories."

"Damn the stories! The stories are clearly lies!" Gareth said. He stopped walking, and Leandros turned to face him. Anger flickered behind Gareth's eyes, the most Leandros had ever seen from the man. Still, that flicker was nothing to Leandros' raging inferno.

"Are you calling *me* a liar?" he asked calmly. He hoped Gareth recognized the warning in his voice for what it was, like a blistering doorknob warned of a blaze on the other side of a door.

"How could you be a liar if you haven't *said anything*?" Gareth asked. "Prince Nochdvor, please. You disappeared and made the world take Unity's word for what happened. Now, Egil's back. Will you hide away for another sixty years before you tell us the truth?"

Leandros stepped up to Gareth, until Gareth had to crane his neck to meet Leandros' eye. "You want the truth, Mr. Ranulf? I held Egil in my arms as he bled out. I felt the *moment* his heart stopped. If I did hide, it wasn't because of people like you, demanding answers they don't deserve. It was because I was in mourning. If Egil's death was a lie, I was made more the fool than anyone, so watch where you direct your frustrations."

Gareth fell back a step, eyes wide. "I didn't know."

"No, you didn't," Leandros said. He turned on his heel and stormed away, not waiting for the others to catch up. Chia kept pace with him; she gave his arm a comforting pat. "A lion cub," she said. It felt like a peace offering. "That's what you are. You'll grow into your roar soon, I think."

His anger reduced to a simmer, Leandros almost smiled. "I feel like I should be offended, but I suppose it's better than a weasel."

"Hey!" Eresh said from behind them. "Chia, *please* pick a different one for me."

"Have you ever seen a weasel, Eresh? They're so cute! Just like you."

Chia and Eresh's bickering gave Leandros time and space to get himself under control—and to stop thinking about Egil. Or to try, at least.

"Oh," Eresh said suddenly. He eyed the park exit with a peculiar expression, and Leandros followed his gaze to an unusual tree with white bark—not spotted like a birch or chipped like a sycamore, but a uniform bleached-bone white. While the surrounding trees were still in varying stages of green and orange and hadn't yet dropped their leaves, this one was already bare. It stretched over the walking path, bending on swollen joints.

"A candlewood tree? Here?" Gareth asked. When the others shot him looks, he explained, "There's an orchard of them near my home in Adriad. We pass them whenever we head into town."

"You know what they are?" Eresh asked, surprised. "Most humans don't."

Gareth nodded, his lips pressed into a thin line. Beside Leandros, Chia stifled a yawn and looked around the park, clearly uninterested. "What is it?" Leandros asked.

"A grave—a grave marker, technically. In a way, it's also a womb," Eresh answered. "When a nymph dies, we're buried in the ground, much like humans. Unlike humans, though, a candlewood tree grows over us. It stands for a decade or so until it one day blooms. When it drops its last flower, an infant sings its way out of the trunk. That's why we view death so differently from the rest of you. From death comes life."

"There's a whole orchard of these?" Chia asked, tuning back in. "A field of dead nymphs?"

"And what is a cemetery?" Eresh countered. "It can be traumatic for a young nymph, singing their way out of a tree to find themselves completely alone. You never really recover from it, and I should know. When we keep them together, we can watch for blooms and be there when the nymph emerges. From the look of it, this one is fairly new. I do hope someone's monitoring it."

"I'm sure they are. The fact that the groundskeeper hasn't cut it down means they must know what it is," Chia said.

Eresh winced at the words *cut it down* but nodded, nervously running his hands over his mossy head. "I'm sure you're right."

"Come! Let's continue the tour," Chia said, skipping ahead. The others followed, passing out of the park and deeper into Gallonten. While Eresh pointed out historical buildings and unique architecture, Chia's portion of the tour was more personal, filled with things like "Here's where I got in my first fight!" and "This is the best bakery in the whole world." It worked to distract Leandros, at least until the orinian looked over her shoulder and asked, "Lion cub, are you aware you're being followed?"

"Captain," Leandros tried to correct. It was better than the other Enforcers insisting on *Your Highness* and *Prince Nochdvor*, though.

"What do you mean, being followed?" Eresh asked, his voice rising an octave.

"I meant what I said. There are two of them: a human with a brownish beard and another with a wide-brimmed hat. They're not very good; I caught sight of them three whole times, once at the bridge, once in the park, and again just now," Chia mused.

Leandros was surprised she'd said anything. He'd noticed them as well but assumed they belonged to Unity. If Chia didn't know about them, though, that couldn't be the case. He frowned, concerned.

"So you didn't know?"

"I knew. They've been around all week," he told her. He'd seen them this morning, on his way out of his hotel. "It's not always the same two—sometimes they're in different pairings, like they're taking shifts."

"What! Lion cub, why didn't you tell the Magistrates?" Chia asked. When Leandros only gave her a *look* in reply, she gave him a knowing look back and sighed. "Oh, that's fair. It's not us, though, I promise."

Leandros believed her. He was beginning to understand that Eftychia O'Neill was not a dishonest person, but only because she knew the truth was often the more discomfiting option. "But who would be following the Captain?" Eresh asked. He kept looking back to see if he could spot the men in question.

"And why?" Gareth asked, more thoughtfully.

Chia ignored both of them except to say, "Stop it, Eresh. You'll give away that we saw them." She asked Leandros, "Do you know if they're violent?"

"They're certainly armed. I've been careful not to go anywhere alone since I first noticed them, so I can't say for sure."

"Do you know who they might be?"

Leandros shook his head. They could be anyone: fans of Egil's, angry about Histrios. Someone from Alfheimr who wants me out of the picture. Someone who hates Unity and doesn't want them to succeed." A chilling thought occurred to him. "They could work for the woman who took my uncle." Even as he said it, though, he doubted it. That woman didn't strike him as someone who works well with others.

Chia considered this, then said, "There's a little pedestrian mall near here that's been closed for construction. What do you say we go there next? Just you and me, this time?"

That Leandros would consider going anywhere alone with an Enforcer was foolish, but he guessed Chia's plan—goad them into attacking, and then: "You want to set a trap?"

Chia smile broadly. "I want to teach them not to mess with Unity's things."

A shiver ran down Leandros' spine. He knew that should have bothered him more than it did. "Let's go."

"Eftychia! Your Highness! This—this is absurd!" Eresh said.

"I have to agree. Is this wise?" Gareth asked. "Whoever this is could be dangerous. Captain, maybe we could get—"

"Think carefully before you finish that sentence, Mr. Ranulf," Leandros warned. "I can assure you, I'm dangerous enough on my own."

"Well said! Come, let's go. If they're ever going to approach you, it'll be when you're alone with a poor, defenseless young girl. Farewell, Eresh! So long, Mr. Ranulf! It's a shame we didn't get to explore more of the city together!" Chia said, already waving her goodbyes. As they walked away, she dropped her voice and asked Leandros, quieter, "This is a fun way to end the day, don't you think?"

"I don't know about *fun*," Leandros said. It was more reflex than truth, though. The truth was that he looked forward to working off this restless energy, to learning what these strangers wanted, to being able to sleep again without one hand on his gun.

"There may be more than just the two. I couldn't tell," Chia warned.

"It's a good thing I have an Enforcer at my side, then."

Chia threw back her head and laughed. "So you *do* know! Evelyne warned me you might. Shall I tell her, or keep it between us? It would be very funny to see her face when she learns for herself."

Already, there were less people around them, and the crowds had thinned by the time they ducked around a barrier and turned onto an empty pedestrian street. The cobblestone path was half-torn up, but no construction crew was around today to work on it. Chia and Leandros had to take care picking through the carnage. Curious, Leandros asked, "Is Evelyne not your superior?"

Chia gave a shrug. "She's had the job for far longer than me, but she's not my superior. We don't have superiors. I answer only to the Magistrates."

That explained some of the tension between Evelyne and the others. "I see. I don't suppose you have a gun?"

"No, I don't like guns. They end fights too quickly. Here is perfect, don't you think?"

It truly was an excellent place to orchestrate an ambush. They both slowed their paces to give their pursuers time to catch up, meandering on until, finally, they turned a corner and found two men blocking their way: one with a wide-brimmed hat and one with a brownish beard.

"Prince Nochdvor," said the man with the hat, "You're a hard man to catch."

"I'm being caught, am I?" Leandros asked mildly, making Chia laugh.

The man hesitated, realizing something was off about his prey. They weren't scared. They weren't even surprised. He shared a look with his companion, who whistled, shrill and loud. Chia had been right—it *was* more than just the two. At the sound of the whistle, three others appeared behind Leandros and Chia, at the mouth of the narrow street. Leandros quickly assessed his opponents, then raised his hands in surrender. "You have no idea who you're dealing with," he said. Barely keeping the glee off her face, Chia followed his lead.

"I think we do. We've been after you for a long time, Your Highness," the bearded man said. They had the look of mercenaries, well-dressed but nondescript. Each bore a weapon—short blades, guns, and one with callused fists—with a confidence that only came from experience. There was nothing supernatural about them, at least. Not like that woman from Illyon.

One of the ambushers shoved Leandros from behind. Normally, such a thing wouldn't have budged him, but he stumbled forward, into the man with the hat, his hand flying to the man's chest to catch his balance. They made this too easy. As soon as his fingers made contact with the man's shirt, he twisted his hand in the fabric, slipped his foot between the man's legs, and hooked his knees into buckling. Then, he pivoted, using his grip to lever the man to the ground. It happened so quickly that even Chia took a moment to process it. When she did, she laughed wildly and threw her shoulder into the ambusher closest to her.

None of them had expected Chia to contribute to the fight, their attention fixed wholly on Leandros, and she took advantage of that fact. She caught another with a powerful haymaker while Leandros moved counter-clockwise to her, on to the next mercenary in the circle. He grabbed and twisted the woman's arm before she could aim her gun, then spun and jammed his elbow back into her face, wrenching her arm as he did. While she dropper her gun, he seized it and used it to shoot the man charging Chia. Chia, who'd braced herself for the blow, pouted. "You're ruining my fun, lion cub!"

Leandros grinned, wider and sharper than he normally allowed himself, and dodged a blow from the man with the beard. He felt alive for the first time since the explosion in Illyon. No, since long before that. Flicking the safety on, he made a show of dropping the gun and kicking it away. "My sincere apologies."

When the man with the hat, now back on his feet, came unsteadily at Leandros again, Leandros hit him squarely in the mouth once, twice, thrice, arms moving like the walking beams of a locomotive. Chia, who'd apparently been watching his form, called, "I never would've thought you a pugilist, Captain! Have you done any prize fighting?"

Leandros' opponent spat out a tooth and swung at Leandros; it was obvious and clumsy. "I'm a Prince of Alfheimr, Ms. O'Neill. If I had, I wouldn't tell you," Leandros called back to Chia. It had taken some decades after the rest of the world for bare-knuckle boxing to come to Alfheimr, but as soon as it had, Leandros began regularly sneaking out of the palace to watch—and occasionally participate in— matches. It was one of his greatest pleasures, next to his penny dreadfuls.

"I hope you'll give me a match sometime," Chia said, casually kicking a mercenary that was struggling to their feet.

Leandros plunged his opponent's own knife into the meat of his thigh and watched him fall. With that, only Leandros and Chia were left standing. "I could be convinced," Leandros said.

A shrill cry from behind had them both pausing to look for the source. It came from Eresh, charging down the street with a small pocketknife and Gareth at his heels. The way he held the knife was all wrong; if he tried to stab anyone with it, it would be wrenched from his grip as soon as his opponent pulled away. "Mr. Ochoa, stop *right there*," Leandros snarled, making the dryad stop short. He barely recognized his own voice, vicious and bestial. He hadn't wanted them to see him like this. Chia was allowed, but only because she was like him. "We told you to go home for a reason!"

"They were only trying to help, lion cub," Chia said, though she was clearly delighted by this side of him. She turned to Eresh and Gareth and wagged a finger. "He's right, though. You could've gotten in our way, and *we* would have gotten in big trouble if you'd been hurt."

Eresh stared at the ground, ashamed, but Gareth's eyes were on something behind Leandros. Suddenly, he shouted, "Captain!"

Leandros turned. Behind him, the bearded man was pushing to his feet, already too close for Leandros to be able to move away. He held his knife, pulled from his own thigh, and was already raising it. It was only thanks to engrained instinct that Leandros lifted his arm to protect his torso. The knife bit into his forearm as the bearded man slashed, but he barely felt it: no pain, just a sting and the resistance of blade meeting bone.

The main raised his dagger to attack again, and Leandros didn't think he'd be able to block it, this time. Before he had to, a gunshot echoed through the street.

Then another.

And another.

Just like that, the bearded man dropped again, three bullets in his back. Down the alley, his gun still raised, stood Roman Hallisey.

The world slowed around Leandros. Though he was loath to tear his eyes from this ghostly apparition, he looked down at his arm. There was blood—a sickening, dizzying amount of it. Chia and the others were at his side in an instant, Chia catching and steadying him when he sagged. He could barely feel the wound, which seemed strange; he could see far more of the inner workings of his arm than he was ever meant to.

He couldn't move his fingers, he realized.

"Roman!" Gareth called urgently, but Roman was already approaching.

He looked the same as he always had—no, not *exactly* the same. His hair was shorter, his dark eyes tired. How many times had Leandros imagined those eyes watching him from a crowd, only to look and find them gone? How often had they appeared in his dreams, vanished again with waking? Were they real now, or was this just another ghost? There was only one way to find out. As Roman approached, he drew back and punched him in the face.

His fist met living flesh.

Roman grunted in pain and stumbled back, and Gareth cried out in alarm. Leandros shook out his hand. It wasn't a *great* punch. He'd hoped to break a nose or a tooth, but when Roman touched his fingers to his lips, they only came away with a little blood. Still, Leandros was glad to see him bleed at all. Ghosts couldn't bleed.

Roman glowered at Leandros. "Do you feel better now?"

"Let me try again and I might," Leandros snarled back, his anger catching up with him before the pain did. Sixty years. Roman let Leandros think he was dead for *sixty years.*

"Gareth, remove your waistcoat," Roman ordered, and Gareth obeyed without hesitation. Balling it up, Roman pressed it to the wound on Leandros' arm. "You're losing a lot of blood. You need to keep pressure on the wound," he said slowly, clearly. Begrudgingly,

Leandros replaced Roman's hand on the waistcoat with his own, and then Roman guided Leandros' arm higher with a gentle touch under his elbow. All his touches were gentle. Leandros had almost forgotten. "Keep it held above your heart."

Said heart was beating quickly, unaware and uncaring that Leandros was *angry with* Roman.

"What do we do?" Eresh asked, looking to Roman for answers. As far as Leandros knew, the two had never even met. There was just something about Roman—fully Egil, in this moment—that claimed authority. Leandros wouldn't let him have it.

"Check the bodies," he said before Roman could speak. "I want to know how many are alive, and I want to know who hired them."

"We need to get you medical attention," Roman argued.

"It can wait."

"Only one alive and unconscious, lion cub. I already checked," Chia said. "I have their wallets and identification here—as much as they had on them, anyway. They kept pretty clean."

Roman assessed Chia, his gaze flitting quickly from her ears to her tail to her hand on Leandros' arm, finally ending at the brand on her wrist. His expression twisted with cold distaste.

"Roman is right, Captain. We should get you to a hospital," Gareth said. Hearing that he was on a first-name basis with Roman already, Leandros' expression soured to match Roman's.

"No hospitals. I don't want anyone knowing about this attack," he insisted. That was a weakness he couldn't afford to show. "Ms. O'Neill, do you have any idea who hired them?"

While Chia picked through the wallets she'd collected, Roman sighed. "They're mercenaries from the Broken Pistol. A Council member put a bounty on your head. I've been following you since I found out."

Leandros didn't want to know how long that had been. As for the rest, he didn't have it in him to be surprised. The Alfheimr Council had had it out for him since his father's coup, especially after he started getting closer to Amos and Egil. He felt a headache coming on.

"My hotel is quite close," Gareth suggested. "We could get you settled there and call for a private physician. My family has one in the city we trust."

It was the best offer he'd get, and it was getting harder to think at all, his mind catching up to the shock the rest of his body was already experiencing. He felt numb, tingly. He still couldn't feel his fingers. "Fine," Leandros said. He saw red where his blood had soaked through the waistcoat, but he couldn't feel the damp. "The police will be here soon; they'll have heard the gun shots. Someone needs to stay and explain the situation. Roman, you won't be needed: you stay."

Roman shifted guiltily. "I can't. I need Gareth for something." Gareth gave him a wide-eyed, awestruck look and nodded so vigorously Leandros thought he'd injure himself. Seeing this, Roman sighed and asked Leandros, "You told him?"

"Would you have done it on your own?" Leandros asked. Then, answering his own question: "Of course not. Secrets come as easily to you as breathing."

Roman winced.

"I'll help you to Mr. Ranulf's place, lion cub. I may work for Unity, but I'm still orinian, and that's not a good thing to be when the police come around. Eresh, can you stay?" Chia asked.

"I—what—oh, I suppose," Eresh said.

"Have them take any survivors directly to the island," Chia said with a sweet smile that made Leandros shudder.

"I'm not leaving you alone with someone like her," Roman said at the same time. "You must know what she is, Leandros."

"And who are *you* supposed to be?" Chia asked, resting her hands on her hips.

"Your worst nightmare," Roman said with a smile even sweeter than Chia's had been.

"Mr. Hallisey, that's enough. I trust her," Leandros said. Roman's eyes widened, then narrowed, his expression finally settling into something inscrutable. Leandros couldn't shake the sense of being measured and found wanting, and it made him angry all over again. Who was *Roman* to judge *him*, after all this time? "If that'll be all, Chia and I will go."

Beside him, Chia stuck her tongue out at Roman while Gareth hastily scrawled an address and room number on the back of a visiting card. "My wife is home. Just tell her I invited you and that we'll rejoin you when we can."

"Take your time," Leandros said. He didn't look at Roman. "If I don't have to see *him* again today, all the better."

CHAPTER TWENTY-FIVE

IF YOU HAD ASKED GARETH YESTERDAY, he would have told you he knew Egil well. Not as well as someone like Prince Nochdvor, who'd been close to Egil in life, but better than most. While academic study was no replacement for in-person fellowship, it could still teach you much about a person.

But Gareth did not know this man before him. Roman's—*Egil's* eyes were distant and flat when he finally tore them from Leandros' retreating back. "Let's go, Gareth," was all he said before heading in the opposite direction.

Eager as he was to follow, Gareth paused to ask Eresh, "You're certain you can handle this alone?"

After Leandros and Eftychia had split off from them, it was Eresh who suggested they circle back and help. Faced with bravery like that, Gareth could only agree, but neither had expected to arrive and find bodies strewn, a battle concluded, and their friends speaking casually over the bleeding dead. Gareth avoided looking at the fallen assassins, their eyes unseeing and their limbs splayed over cobblestone. He still hadn't forgotten the thief Egil killed the night they met. He didn't need more empty eyes haunting his dreams.

"Oh, yes. I know how to talk to the police," Eresh assured him.

"Gareth," Egil called, prompting Gareth to scramble after him. Back in crowded streets, Egil raised a hand at the first passing cab, and just like that, it stopped for him. He didn't have to run after it, waving his arms, or wait for another to come by like Gareth often did. This one had stopped simply because Egil ordered it to.

This was the same man who'd spent the previous morning moping on Gareth's sofa. He'd seemed so small, then, but Gareth realized he was more like the shadow he cast along the wall: larger than Gareth could even comprehend. When he held the carriage door for Gareth, Gareth climbed hurriedly inside, unable to resist his friend and hero's cold authority. Egil settled opposite Gareth, rapped his knuckles on the roof, and they were off. "You'll pay the fare, won't you, Gareth?"

Gareth startled at being addressed. "Of course. Where are we going?"

"The courthouse. It's about time I talked to the Magistrates."

A thrill went through Gareth. He was about to see Egil confront Unity. One of his stories was playing out before his eyes. It took a moment for the reality of that to hit him. "Is it safe for you to go there?"

Egil's smile was all arrogance and derision, nothing like the warm smile Gareth was used to. "They can't hurt me. And with the Magistrate's brother at my side, they won't even try. I don't mean to use you, but your status *is* convenient."

"I'm just happy to assist," Gareth said. "But...you won't hurt Moira, will you?"

Egil sighed. "I'll do my best not to," he promised. Shadows from the carriage roof cut across his face, making his eyes look for a moment like they were entirely black. Gareth had always found those eyes too knowing, too stern, too weary for the exuberant young man

Egil pretended to be. Now, finally, he understood why. Egil added, "Speaking of, what did you think of our conversation last night?"

"I hardly know," Gareth admitted. He hadn't understood most of it, but one thing stood out to him as strange: Leandros' reaction when Gareth told him about it. Gareth had been pondering it all morning. "Are you absolutely certain those"—he had trouble even speaking the word—"*Assassins* that attacked the prince weren't sent by Moira?"

A bright curiosity sparked in Egil's eyes. "Do you think your sister is capable of having a man killed?"

"Technically, she has resources. Morally, well…I'm beginning to realize I don't know her as well as I thought. Prince Nochdvor seemed to expect she'd try it, at any rate, and the timing seems strange. Are you going to tell the Magistrates about what happened? Prince Nochdvor said he didn't want anyone knowing—"

"Leandros' pride will be the death of him," Egil interrupted coldly. "I'll keep his secret, but they'll find out, and soon. Did he say *why* he expected this?"

"No, but I suspect I might know anyway. I never told you this, but when the Nochdvors first arrived in Gallonten, I heard some of their conversation with the Magistrates." Gareth proceeded to tell Egil all of it—how the Magistrates pushed for an investigative mission, how Leandros convinced them to let him lead it. He told Egil about the mysterious "orinian woman" the princess mentioned and about Leandros' threats to tell the world—something. Something to do with the kidnapping, something he hadn't voiced out loud. "There are other truths I could tell," he'd warned the Magistrates.

As he explained this last part, Gareth watched Egil for signs of recognition or understanding, but his expressive friend was gone and the stern hero left in his place gave Gareth nothing. "I've never seen the Magistrates so offended," Gareth finished.

Quiet fell in the carriage. Egil's face was serious and thoughtful, hidden almost entirely in shadow now, but he then surprised Gareth by sitting back and laughing. "You do hear a lot, you nosy thing!" he cried. "Well, what do *you* think of this?"

"It just seems strange, doesn't it? Framing Prince Nochdvor, instead of killing him?"

"Very clever."

Gareth flushed at the praise, too ashamed to tell Egil that those were Leandros' words, not his.

"You're right, of course. Unity has ways of keeping people quiet, and they rarely hesitate to use them. If they're so afraid of these secrets, why hesitate with Leandros?"

"Are you asking *me*? Or just hypothetically?" Gareth asked, still a little shaken by Egil's sudden change in demeanor. Without Gareth noticing, Egil had become Roman again. But to sit at such extremes, which version of him was the truth? How could Gareth know Egil so well but not know Roman at all?

Roman sat forward. The boyish grin Gareth knew was back on his face, holding none of the danger of Egil's smirks, and Gareth felt himself relax. This was the smile that made him want to earn Roman's favor, that made him feel like he was part of a secret: him and Roman, against the world. With a smile like that, how had he not realized Roman was the hero Egil sooner? "Hypothetically. Thanks to you, I have a theory; I just need your sister to confirm it."

"Incredible," Gareth breathed. The word and his tone made Roman look away, out the window. Not for the first time, Gareth only realized how disarming Roman's eyes were after they had settled elsewhere. "Quit looking at me like that, Gareth," he sighed.

Gareth stared more. "How would you like me to look at you instead?"

"It's only me. Just treat me the way you always have."

"I…" Gareth began, taken aback by Roman's tone. It was unsettlingly close to desperate. "I'll do my best."

Roman sighed in relief and passed a hand through his dark hair, a nervous gesture that suited Roman Hallisey far more than it did Egil. Outside, gulls shrieked and hooves rattled on hollow stone as they passed over the bridge to Unity Island. "I didn't mean to keep it from you, I just didn't know how to tell you. I'm sorry."

"There's no need to apologize."

Finally, the carriage rolled to a stop before the courthouse. Roman was out first, stretching and yawning while Gareth paid the cab fare. He stood so casually before the solemn stone and sharp spires of Unity's oldest, grandest building that Gareth found it hard to believe he'd attacked this island just two days before. Was he not afraid they'd catch him? "The Magistrates will be in court for another hour yet," he warned Roman.

Roman shrugged. "Then we'll wait. Come with me." He led Gareth around the courthouse to the field behind it, where wild taurel bloomed. Off in the distance, the ground sloped down toward the cliff's face, then nothing but blue horizon stretched beyond.

"Take off your jacket," Roman ordered.

Just as he had back in the alley with Prince Nochdvor, Gareth obeyed without question. He felt exposed, standing out in the open without a jacket *or* a waistcoat, but he busied himself with folding the jacket and draping it neatly over his arm. When he looked up again, Roman had stripped out of his tie, waistcoat, *and* shirt, leaving him in only a scandalous undershirt, his arms bare to the shoulders. Gareth's gaze caught on many scars—Roman had them on his arms, his shoulders, his hands. One knotted, particularly gnarled scar rested above his heart, just visible over the top of his shirt.

"I'm going to teach you how to fight," Roman announced when Gareth still didn't ask.

"What! Mr. Hallisey, I'm in a full suit. I can't—"

"If you learn to fight in a suit, you'll be ready for anything."

"Why don't *you* have to wear your suit, then?"

"Because I already know how to fight," Roman pointed out. Gareth couldn't argue with that. "Earlier, you charged into that alley without a thought. Were you going to fight seasoned mercenaries bare-handed? If so, you're more powerful than I thought. Maybe I needn't go to this effort."

Gareth winced, duly chastised. "I didn't realize you saw that."

"Of course I saw. Like I told Leandros, I was watching. Now, will you learn from me, or not?"

"Yes," Gareth said quickly, then adding, "Please."

"My first lesson is this: pride and a misplaced sense of duty will get you in trouble. It's not your job to defend Leandros, and if you'd joined the fight earlier, you only would have been in his way. Do you understand? Instead of keeping himself alive, he would've had to worry about keeping you alive, too. If you can't win a fight, you need to run. If you can't run, you need to incapacitate your opponent to the best of your ability and *then* run. And you, Gareth, won't be able to win most fights."

Gareth opened his mouth to complain about how blunt Roman was being, but remembering who he was talking to, shut it again and nodded.

"Good. Now, try to hit me."

Gareth hesitated, but Roman only gave an encouraging nod. Hitting *Egil*, his dark hair alight under the midday suns, his expression serious and determined, felt blasphemous. More than that, it felt impossible. But Gareth wanted to be a dutiful student, so Gareth tried. And unsurprisingly, he missed. Roman dodged and swept a leg under Gareth, knocking him to the ground.

"You compromised too much of your balance. Get up. Try again."

This time, Roman guided Gareth: he showed Gareth how to make a fist that wouldn't break his fingers, how to plant his weight and hit opponents where they're weakest. He was a patient teacher, and he had them go again and again and again. By the time Gareth finally did land a hit, he ached everywhere. "You're getting it!" Roman said when he did, laughing. Then, without warning, he feinted a punch toward Gareth's shoulder and *actually* hit him in the stomach, so hard that Gareth grunted in pain and dropped to the ground. Roman frowned down at him, disappointed. "You let your guard down."

"You've been going easy on me!" Gareth accused. That speed—he hadn't even seen the hit coming.

"Of course I have. I'm *Egil*."

It was the first time he'd said it, and it made Gareth shudder. While they fought, he'd almost forgotten. How did Roman do that? How did Roman make him forget? He ducked his head, embarrassed. Floundering and flailing in front of Roman was one thing; doing so in front of *Egil* was another. He wanted to sink into these grasses and disappear into the soil.

He must have made a pathetic sight, because Roman rolled his eyes. "You're just getting started. It took me a lot of time, practice, and training to get as good as I am today."

Gareth found a pebble in the grass and tossed it in Roman's direction. Not close enough to hit him—that would be sacrilege. "I find that hard to believe. I'm sure it was effortless, like everything you do."

Roman dropped into a squat across from Gareth, thoughtfully silent. After a moment, he said, "In my first fight, I was beat nearly to death and left bleeding in the street."

Gareth gasped. "I'm sorr—"

Roman raised a hand to cut him off. "It was a long time ago, but if I'm hard on you, that's why. I had to teach myself to fight; I would have killed for a teacher."

Once again, Gareth ducked his head, his cheeks burning. His

aching muscles, at least, distracted from the shame, so he focused on those. "I appreciate the attempt, Mr. Hallisey, but there comes a point where it's too late to pick this sort of thing up. I'm too old for this."

Almost as soon as the words were out of his mouth, Gareth realized how silly they must sound to someone like Egil: someone timeless. He didn't know how old Egil was; even with all his supposed knowledge, he couldn't begin to guess. The historical records simply cut off after several centuries. Gareth had always assumed Egil must have been maranet, but looking at him now, he didn't possess any of the characteristics of one. Belatedly, all the times Gareth had called Roman *son* or *lad* or *young man* flashed before his eyes in succession. He groaned and hid his face behind his hands.

"You say that too much," Roman said, making Gareth lower his hands again to look at him. He'd sat in the grass across from Gareth and, in a contrarily childlike gesture, was running his fingers through the blades, flattening them just to tousle them up again. "You call yourself old and tired, making yourself the punchline of your own jokes. By repeating the lie, you're not only changing the way others see you, you're changing the way you see yourself. You're not old, not boring, not useless. None of it's true."

"I—thank you," Gareth said, unsure what else he *could* say.

Roman shrugged, then laid back in the grass. They sat in silence for a while, letting the flush from all that activity fade until they'd recovered enough to enjoy the breeze. Eventually, Roman pointed at the two suns occupying the cloudless sky. "Did you know they're getting closer to each other?"

"Who are?"

"The suns. Sol and Del, they're called in Troas. We orbit them, but they also orbit each other. With each cycle, they get closer. We just can't tell because they're so far away."

"Are you an astronomer now, too?" Gareth asked. He couldn't

remember any Egil stories that mentioned it, but it wouldn't have surprised him.

Roman scoffed and shook his head. "I had a friend who was; she explained it to me. Something to do with magnetism. She thinks they're going to coalesce to form one big star, but they're just as likely to collide, explode, and kill everyone. Either way, it won't happen for thousands of years."

Gareth thought, briefly, of Roman and Leandros' volatile reunion. "Atiuh would never let such a thing happen."

"If he exists."

"You think he doesn't? Where do you think all this comes from, then?" Gareth asked, gesturing around them.

Roman shrugged. "Maybe he does. If he does, maybe he's dead, gone, or he no longer gives a damn. Was that too much? What do you say we drop the subject before one of us hurts the other's feelings?"

"Fine," Gareth agreed, a little icily. He mopped the sweat from his brow and glared up at the suns, knowing his skin would be as red as an osun petal later. With his naturally darker skin, Roman probably wouldn't even burn. At the thought, Gareth frowned. It was strange, actually. Troas was the one province on the continent that *didn't* have its own Egil stories.

"You said you're from Troas, didn't you?" Gareth asked.

Roman shot him a sly look. "I was wondering when you'd start asking questions."

"To be honest, I can barely contain them all."

Roman chuckled. Even that sounded boyish, youthful, dangerously close to being a *giggle*. It was no wonder Gareth hadn't guessed his real age. "What do you want to know?"

"Everything."

"*Everything*?" Roman repeated. "A tall order. We'd be here a very long time."

Primly, Gareth said, "Perhaps starting from the beginning would be easiest."

"Ha! Very well. Once, there was a man who loved a woman and a woman who loved the stability the man gave her. And when two people have those kinds of feelings, they—"

Gareth wrinkled his nose. "Mr. Hallisey, please." He hesitated. "Would you still like me to call you that, by the way? Or should I say—"

"If you call me Egil, I'll never speak to you again," Roman said. "I have a dozen names, and while any of them are better than that one, I prefer Roman. How about I start here: I was born in a nameless village in Troas to Christian Hallisey and Catalina Rosario-Reyes. As a traveling merchant, Christian was barely home, so I spent most of my childhood with my mother. I was still young when she died, so I was hauled off to travel with Christian."

"A childhood on the road must have been difficult. "I'm glad your father was there for you, at least."

Roman laughed humorlessly. "I wouldn't say *at least*. Christian was a cruel man, made crueler when he looked at me and saw Catalina. I resembled her too much, he always said. Maybe I still do; it's been so long now that I don't remember what she looked like."

Gareth didn't know what to say to that. He knew little about the field of psychoanalysis, but of course he'd spotted the signs of a troubled childhood in his friend. They were hard *not* to spot. He just had no idea they ran so deep; Roman always seemed so cheerful, so at ease.

Guessing at Gareth's thoughts, Roman gave him a wry smile. "What you think people are—what they seem to be—is rarely the truth. We all pretend, some of us better than others. Everything about me is a construction, Gareth. It has to be, because what's underneath is too damaged to let anyone see," he said. Seeing Gareth open his mouth, he quickly added, "Don't apologize again. I know how dire it sounds, but I don't see it that way. The past is the past, and things are always getting better. There are ups and downs, but I have to believe they always will."

Gareth considered the bags under Roman's eyes, the blood dried on his swollen lip, the bitter twist to his smile. If this was *better*, Gareth was afraid to hear about the *before*.

As if sensing his scrutiny, Roman slung an arm over his face, hiding it in the crook of his elbow. He continued like that, "Anyway, Christian and I settled in Alfheimr, where I started school. But then he died, too, and I couldn't afford the tuition without him. I got kicked out, and Unity found me much later."

"Unity?" Remembering the conversation he'd overheard the night before, Gareth guessed, "You worked for them?"

"Yes, that's why I'm telling you all this now. You know so many stories about me, Gareth, but they mean nothing without context. If you're going to study me, let it be the *real* me. And when you hear what I did for Unity, just know that I was desperate.

"After leaving Alfheimr," he continued, "I was homeless and friendless. Have you ever gone hungry, Gareth? The first week without food is always the worst. After that, the pain dulls and you feel yourself growing weaker every day, inching closer to death. I lived alone in the wilds for a time, but—" Roman cut himself off there, trying to find the right words. "It wasn't sustainable. A hard winter drove me to Gallonten, where I did some odd jobs, but that wasn't enough. I lived on the streets."

That, at least, was part of Egil's history Gareth knew. Some stories said the oracle found him, raised him, and trained him. Others said he distinguished himself in front of some lord or other—stopped a thief, saved a woman's life, performed some small act of heroism. Gareth never would have guessed the truth involved *Unity*, Egil's greatest enemy. He never would have guessed he'd one day have Egil reciting his history *to* him, almost mechanical in delivery.

"Living like that," Roman continued, waving a hand lazily, "You have to beg or steal to survive. My pride, so kindly taught to me by my mother, didn't allow the former, and I wasn't very good at the latter. In the end, some officers picked a fight with me, I defended myself, and I was thrown in jail for it."

"Roman, that's terrible. I'm sorry," Gareth repeated.

"Stop apologizing. Stop saying that like you understand. You *can't* understand," Roman said. The words weren't angry, but that almost made them worse. Roman winced. "Now I'm the one who should apologize. This is hard to talk about, for obvious reasons."

"I—," Gareth began, only to cut himself off. He'd been about to say that he understood, but Roman was right to say that he didn't. He couldn't. Their lives had been about as different as two people's could be. "There's no need to apologize. What happened then?"

"It was in that prison that Unity found me. They offered me a job with security, a salary, and answers to questions I'd long sought. Of course I took it."

"What questions?" Gareth asked.

"That's a different story, I'm afraid," Roman said, wagging a finger. "This, right now, is about Unity. Have you ever thought about where their power comes from?"

Gareth hadn't, but he paused to do so now. "Its laws?"

"Not quite, but good try. Its laws are a *product* of the power, not the source of it. Look at Alfheimr: both the reigning monarch and the province's Council have power in their own ways. The monarch commands the army, issues decrees, and appoints Council members while the Council controls the flow of commerce. You could say those things are the sources of their power, but the answer's even simpler than that: it's their people. Their citizens. If Rhea turns out to be so terrible of a queen that her own people and army stop obeying her, she loses her power. If the Council suddenly starts imposing taxes so steep the people can't pay, in time the Council's funds will run dry and they lose their power. Obviously, these examples are oversimplifications, but they illustrate the point. People lend governments legitimacy; Alfheimr only functions as it does because its people believe in their government. Or if they don't, they at least obey it. They follow laws and pay taxes to avoid punishment, and in so doing, they give their government the very power needed to enforce those punishments. It's an endless cycle, and it's the same for Unity: all of us, you and I, everyone in this world—we give Unity its power," Roman said, gesturing broadly between them.

"Okay," Gareth said, trying to predict where this was leading.

"Now, consider this: unlike Alfheimr, Unity has little financial power of its own and no standing army. When it comes to enforcing punishment, its jurisdiction is limited to interprovince disputes and crimes committed against Unity itself. If an Alfheimr citizen breaks one of their king's rules, the Royal Army can enforce it. So what can Unity do? Why does everyone listen to the distant, faceless strangers trying to dictate their lives? It's not that they believe in Unity, or that they have any amount of faith in it; most of them don't even think about Unity in their day-to-day lives."

"But the Royal Army doesn't just enforce Alfheimr's laws," Gareth argued. "They enforce Unity's, too."

Roman pointed at him, the suns catching on some sharp, excited emotion in his dark eyes. The whites of them seemed to flash in the light, giving him a wild look. "Yes! People follow Unity because their government will punish them if they don't. Their government will punish them because the king demands it. But why does the king demand it?"

"I—I don't know," Gareth admitted.

"It comes back to fear of punishment. It *always* comes back to fear of punishment. But what does a king fear?" Roman shrugged. "Well, it depends on the king. The answer is complicated, but I can sum it up in two words: the Enforcers."

There was that term again: *enforcer*. Roman and Moira mentioned it last night, too, but it still meant nothing to Gareth. Seeing as much on Gareth's face, Roman continued, "Everyone cares about something, and Unity is *very* skilled at identifying and then manipulating those things. That's what the Enforcers were created to do: they exploit weaknesses, uncover secrets, exert pressure on a person's most sensitive spot. They blackmail a judge who gets caught in a scandal. They threaten a man's wife so he votes how they want. They frame a prince who's already distrusted by his people. And then, every so often, when someone steps out of lie, they make quick and tidy examples of them: they crush rebellions, like in Ejera. They assist in coups, like in Alfheim. They destroy industries, like in Adondai. They kill a hero who dared to oppose them."

"Like in Histrios," Gareth breathed. "Then Prince Nochdvor wasn't the one who killed you? Unity was?"

Roman rolled his eyes. "No one killed me, obviously. I'm right here, and I'm trying to go somewhere with this. I need you to understand how dangerous, how monumentally influential the Enforcers are. I need you to understand so you realize how terrifying it is that Unity is sending *four* of them to Orean."

Gareth twisted his hands anxiously in his discarded jacket. "What—what exactly does that mean?"

"That I think we're about to see our Enforcers make an example of Orean—or try, at least."

Gareth blanched. "Four, you said. Who—"

"I'm sure you could name them."

"Evelyne Corscia," Gareth guessed.

Roman sighed. Somewhere behind them, the clock tower chimed a new hour. "Yes."

"Ivor Linde and Aaror Thomason, too," Gareth said. The pattern was obvious: it was the security team. But that meant..."Even Ms. O'Neill?"

"The orinian that was hanging all over Leandros? Yes, definitely her."

Gareth felt ill. "But she's so gentle," he protested. When he closed his eyes, though, he saw that circle of dead assassins again.

"She's trained to come off that way. Gareth, what did you think of *me* when we first met? You trusted me enough to let me drag you, wounded, to a hospital—*after* I openly admitted to following you. You let me near your wife and daughter. You asked me to stay *in your house*, and I could kill you a dozen different ways without even exerting myself."

Gareth swallowed. "What are you—are you saying you were one of them?"

Roman sighed. "Yes. They gave me the name, but they also called me their hound."

"Hound?" Gareth asked. "As in...the Hound of Unity?" The Hound of Unity was a folk figure from the eleventh century; wherever he went, always at Unity's bidding, death followed. Gareth had always dismissed the stories as a shameful fabrication, nothing more than slander; he never would have imagined that the Hound was his hero, all along.

"I'm afraid so," Roman said, not meeting his eyes. "Something else you should know about the Enforcers—to Unity, we're just soldiers, spies, servants, slaves. Unity takes us in when we're young and friendless and pliant and shapes us into weapons. They teach us things that might make us useful: combat, politics, languages. More than anything else, though, they teach us loyalty. They break us down, isolate us from the world, from our families, from any prior loyalties. They strip away our very identities; Troas was my home, but after they took me in, I wasn't allowed to return there." With a sad smile, Roman said, "They even took away my mother's name for me. She called me Amaimon—Amaimon Roman Rosario-Hallisey. Unity wouldn't let me go by it; they insisted *Amaimon* had to die and made me the Hound, instead."

"This sounds like fiction," Gareth said, horrified.

"I wish I had the luxury of agreeing. The Enforcers you've met— they may seem reasonable, but they're not. They may seem sympathetic, but it's only an act. There's nothing left of who they could have been. They are Unity's tools, now."

"If all this is true, how did you get away?"

Roman's answering grin was feral. "A hound that's been beat eventually turns on its owner. I fled Gallonten and hid long enough for them to forget about me, and then I used the name they gave me as a weapon against them."

It was Gareth's turn to look away. This filled the gaps in his research, explained every account that claimed Egil seemed like he was running from something, but he couldn't get past the horror of it. That something was *his* family, *his* ancestors. How could one begin to atone? Well, he'd do what he could. "Anything you need from me, Roman, you have it."

"I'm glad you say that, because it's time to go talk to your sister."

Chapter Twenty-Six

It became quickly clear that Roman knew Unity's courthouse even better than Gareth did. He led them in through a side door, then down narrow hallways to the atrium and on to the Magistrates' Chambers, only slowing when a figure peeled away from the Magistrates' doors to block their way

"Good afternoon, Bellona!" he called in a sing-song. "No, I wouldn't recommend drawing that sword of yours. You wouldn't want to accidentally harm the Magistrate's brother, would you?"

Evelyne Corscia's expression twisted with contempt, but she removed her hand from the sword strapped to her back. "Mr. Ranulf," she said in the soothing tones of one trying not to provoke a predator, "Get away from that man. He's very dangerous."

"I'm afraid I can't do that, Ms. Corscia. We're here to speak with my sister and the others; this will be easier if you let us pass."

"Not a chance."

Roman shrugged, sighed, and rocked back on his heels with all the impish mischief Gareth had come to expect from him. He wondered if any part of it was real. "Then we'll wait until they come out. We can talk right here in the hallway, where anyone might overhear."

"Or I could kill you where you stand," Evelyne replied, her voice deceptively calm. Her hand inched toward her sword again.

Roman tutted. "Then you'd *really* be causing a scene for your employers. Besides, no matter how hard you try, you won't succeed," he said, showing her his palm.

An old scar ran across it, mostly-faded, and Evelyne visibly paled at the sight. In the short time Gareth had known her, she'd always seemed fearless, but faced with a simple scar, he'd never seen anyone so plainly terrified. "How?" she asked.

"I'll tell you if you answer one of *my* questions," Roman said. Evelyne waited, and when she didn't respond either way, Roman continued, "You could have told Moira I was the one who broke into the prison. You could have told any of them."

"That's not a question."

"Why didn't you?"

"Forget it," Evelyne said through gritted teeth. "Wait here. I'll let the Magistrates decide what to do with you."

Gareth watched her go with raised eyebrows. When the doors to the Magistrates' Chambers swung shut behind her, he turned to Roman and asked, "You know her, then?"

"I know lots of people."

Seeing that he wasn't about to elaborate, Gareth then asked, "Couldn't we just follow her in?"

"She'd take any excuse to shoot me. I'll just wait. But don't worry; they'll invite us in."

He was right. Several minutes later, Evelyne returned, holding the door wordlessly open for them with a glare that said enough.

Grinning at Gareth, Roman slipped inside. All three Magistrates of Unity waited for them, arranged much as they had been the last time Gareth visited this room: Moira on one of the plush sofas, Diomis standing behind her, and Malong at her usual place by the windows, the suns on her prismatic scales casting rainbows across the room. There were no Nochdvors here now, though, and Moira and Diomis still wore their formal robes. Also unlike last time, when Gareth had escaped undetected, Moira glared directly at him.

When Roman bowed, dramatic and facetious, none of the Magistrates returned the gesture. He didn't let that deter him and brightly said, "I'll say it if you won't: lovely to see you all. It's been a while, hasn't it? Well, not for you, Magistrate Ranulf. You and I spoke just last night."

Diomis and Malong's heads both whipped toward Moira. "Is this true?" Diomis asked, their round eyes wide. Their hair was done up in a soft pompadour today, their usual kelp diadem resting atop it.

"Don't look at me like that; I had no idea who he was," Moira said, crossing her arms.

"No, but you knew I used to be an Enforcer," Roman pointed out, smiling even brighter as he sowed chaos. He'd barely spoken twenty words. Gareth had never seen the Magistrates so quickly undone. "Remember? You asked to meet in the city specifically so the other Magistrates wouldn't know. But you're right, I suppose it wasn't your fault I turned out to be Egil."

Moira sank lower in her seat and turned her glare back to Gareth. "You know, then. I see you've chosen your side."

"As if I could have chosen any other," Gareth said. "Even if he wasn't who he is, I heard enough from you last night to know where I stand."

"*Enough*," Malong snarled, snapping her wings on the word. Her voice was the rumble of a coming storm. "Explain yourself, Moira. Now."

Moira drew a deep breath, clearly buying herself time to strategize. "Egil manipulated my brother into offering him McDermott's guard position. I was only trying to get to the bottom—"

"Liar. Last night, Magistrate Ranulf told me all about your plans to frame the Alfheimr prince," Roman interrupted before Moira could spin the story any further. "And in return, I told her that I'd tear your island apart and kill every one of you before I allowed it."

Gareth eyed Roman. He hadn't heard *that* part.

"That *does* explain the timing of your miraculous resurrection," Diomis said with a sigh. "I liked you better dead."

"I'm sure you're not the only one," Roman said, smiling. "But here I am, and here's the situation we find ourselves in: the world now knows that you lied about my death. It's not too late to call today's headline a hoax, if you can make sure I won't refute it. Unity can save face and Egil can return to the grave, and all you have to do is leave Leandros alone."

"You're mad. We will not negotiate with you," Malong said.

"You really should. You forget, Magistrate, that I know every secret you and your predecessors ever kept. You thought Leandros' threats were bad? Yes, I know all about those. I know what you did in Histrios, Ejera, Alfheimr, and Adondai, too. I know Leandros threatened to tell everyone about Histrios, and that that scared you. I know *everything* you've been thinking, planning, and doing, and until this morning, you didn't even know I was alive. What do you say to that?"

For a long moment, silence hung between them. It was Malong who finally rose to the obvious bait: "I say that no matter what you try to tell anyone, the world thinks you're dead and mad. You have no proof, so your threats mean nothing."

Roman was no longer smiling. He bore no weapons, but when he took a step forward, all of the Magistrates unconsciously shifted back. Evelyne took a protective step in front of Magistrates Moira and Diomis as Roman said, "I don't have to convince them alone. The new Queen of Alfheimr, the Oracle of Damael, the frìth of Lyryma, even the Magistrate's own brother—do you really think they won't vouch for my sanity?"

Watching Roman boldly threaten the most powerful people on the continent, his eyes bright and feverish, Gareth wasn't sure he'd call Roman *sane*. Still, he nodded.

Roman continued, "Do you think they won't speak up, if I ask? That Leandros won't tell everyone what happened in Histrios the second I say the word?"

Based on the messy reunion they'd just had, Gareth *did* doubt it. The Magistrates didn't know about that, though, and they all exchanged wary looks. "If he wants our help with his uncle, he will not," Diomis said, staring unblinkingly at Roman. "I wonder which of you is more important to him."

"An interesting question, but I propose an alternative," Malong rumbled, her sharp teeth bared. "Ms. Corscia, shoot them both."

"With pleasure," Evelyne said, drawing her pistol.

"You will do *no* such thing!" Moira cried, rising quickly to her feet. She turned on Malong. "How dare you!"

"How dare *I?*" the dragon hissed.

Roman held up a hand, silencing them all. Even Evelyne froze at the wordless command, and Roman took the opportunity to mirror her position, stepping protectively in front of Gareth. "Enough games. As I told Bellona in the hall, she can try to shoot me, but I'll get right back up. And you won't like what I'll do to you then."

"Your folktales have gone to your head. You're a man, not a god," Diomis said evenly.

"Are you certain?" Roman asked, raising an eyebrow. "Certain enough to test it? Then shoot me, Bellona."

Malong's tail thrashed uneasily behind her. Evelyne didn't move.

"Here's what's going to happen: I'm going to accompany your team to Orean," Roman said. When Moira scoffed, he repeated, more emphatically: "I *am* going to accompany the team to Orean. That, or I'll go straight to the papers and tell them everything. From there, I'll go straight to *Orean* and get the magic before any of you can even say the words *international scandal."*

Moira exhaled through her teeth, a sharp *hiss.*

"Magic?" Gareth asked.

"That's all they're really after in Orean," Roman explained, waving a hand. "It was never about Amos Nochdvor. A tower full of nobles blown away in an instant, no way in or out but through a guarded door. No witnesses, no survivors except for a prince and a princess who claim to have seen something impossible. Whether it was magic or science, whoever could pull off a heist like that must be powerful. Whoever controlled magic like that would be *powerful.* And if Unity finds it, they win in more ways than one: they seize it *and* finally get Orean under their heel at the same time. That's why they need Leandros alive—he and Rheamaren are the only ones who saw the orinian woman behind it all. They might still know something useful. Am I on the right track, Magistrates?"

Unsurprisingly, the Magistrates didn't respond, only glared.

"What are you going to do to Orean, Moira?" Gareth asked. Again unsurprisingly, Moira gave him nothing.

Roman scoffed and continued, "I won't let you hurt Leandros, but I won't let you hurt Orean, either."

Watching the Magistrates' expressions harden, Gareth under-stood what all of his Egil stories never said. *This* was Egil's power: not swords and magic, but bold words, a bleeding heart, and firm resolve. He was worth of every bit of faith Gareth had ever placed in him.

"Let me accompany you. You can even keep your Enforcers; it'll be four against one, a race to the magic. It's the fairest way—let the best man win," Egil said.

Moira broke the silence first, her voice bitter. "If you're determined to go to Orean anyway, it seems we can't stop you. Better to have you where we can watch you."

Roman smiled, though his eyes stayed cold. "I feel just the same."

Afterward, as Gareth followed Roman out of the courthouse, giddiness bubbled within him. It was the leftover adrenaline, he was sure, and he'd crash soon enough. For now, though, it was exhilarating. Egil had just walked up to the Magistrates, told them what he wanted, and then gotten it. And the Magistrates had *let him go*. Gareth had never seen anything like it. "I understand what you meant, now, about power," he said.

Roman looked at him. He'd been going back and forth all day, but now he fell somewhere between the strength of Egil and the ease of Roman. Mostly, he just seemed tired. "Do you?"

"You had all of it, back there. If Unity rules by fear of punishment, they have no power if you have no fear. There's nothing they can do to you."

"Can I tell you a secret?" Roman asked, looking up at Unity's clock tower. They hadn't been inside more than half an hour.

Gareth nodded eagerly. "Of course."

"I *am* afraid. And as long as I care about this world and people in it, there's *always* something they can do to me," Roman said. "They just haven't realized that yet."

———

When the orinians left Home, it was without any of the festivities or flair that had characterized their three-day stay in the strange city built into a canyon. They left at dawn, while Home still slept and mist hung low over the city. Only Muir and Senga rose to see them off, happily loading the group—mostly Leileas, who'd been forced to accompany them as punishment for interrupting Galam's song—down with gifts and provisions.

While Leileas bid her parents goodbye, Maebhe stared miserably at the wall of stairs leading up, up, up and out of the city. Her body had recovered somewhat from her dive off a building, but even so, just the thought of climbing those stairs made her legs shake. She couldn't see the top beyond the mist, it stretched so high.

"I could fly you up," Drys whispered, their proximity startling her. She jumped and swatted at them like a pesky fly.

"Quiet, or Senga and Muir will hear you. I don't want them to think I'm ungrateful," Maebhe whispered, glancing back at the frìth. "Was I that obvious?"

"Not at all. I just know you well."

She wanted to point out that they barely knew her at all, but they flared and resettled their wings, the feathers fluffing, and she was promptly distracted. Drys had been meticulous about cleaning them since their escape from Gallonten, and they were already looking much better for it: sleek and magnificent. Maebhe was often tempted to run her hands through the feathers, just to see if they were as soft as they looked, but so far, she hadn't given in.

She wondered at their offer. Her people's stories about the fae said they were never nice just to be nice; they always expected something in return. And Drys had already been *very* nice to her. She was determined to refuse them, but when she looked back up at the stairs, she answered without thinking. "All right, fly me."

Drys grinned and scooped Maebhe into their arms without delay, Maebhe scrabbling to hold on to them and brushing her knuckles along their wings by accident. They *were* soft. Giving her no time to adjust, Drys took off, laughing at the string of curses she let out.

"I don't suppose you'd carry *me* up?" Íde asked Kieran, watching them go.

"I love you, Íde, but I don't think I can even carry *myself* up," Kieran said. He squawked indignantly when Leileas suddenly picked him up and started toward the stairs, carrying both him and Íde in an arm like they were toddlers.

Kieran flailed. "Leileas!"

"I will not drop you," the frìth assured them. She took the steps three at a time, and even put on a burst of speed to try to catch up with Drys. Though she gained on them quickly, her orinians clinging to her fur and armor as if their lives depended on it, the faerie landed on the dewy ground just before she reached the top step.

"Better luck next time, Leileas!" Drys called. From their arms, Maebhe watched Leileas set Kieran and Íde down with wide eyes.

Kieran took one look at her expression and warned, "Don't."

Maebhe threw her head back and laughed.

"Maebhe! It's not funny!"

"It *absolutely* is!"

"Drys, release Maebhe," Leileas said. "Come, little ones. We have a long journey ahead of us."

With Leileas and Drys as their guides, the orinians journeyed into the forest. Lyryma felt different, this deep in—like a held breath, a quiet anticipation. No matter how far they walked, Maebhe felt eyes on her. She normally trusted her instincts, but she couldn't tell if it was real or Senga's warnings and Galam's songs getting to her. But she watched and she listened, so she heard the river long before they came upon it.

Everything in Lyryma seemed to be strange, so Maebhe expected the river to be, as well. Instead, it looked identical to the ones near Orean, only bigger: too wide and deep to cross on foot, unless you fancied a swim. A boathouse sat on its banks, too small to hold any boats that would fit all of them.

"Are we crossing?" Maebhe asked.

"Not yet," Leileas said. Without explanation, she disappeared inside the boathouse and returned a moment later carrying baskets and oars—no, not baskets. *Boats.* They were round, made of willow rods and some sort of hide Maebhe didn't recognize, and each was only large enough to seat a single person. Maebhe had never seen anything like them. She wondered if they could truly support her weight. "We travel down the river. As long as you know how to row, it will not be dangerous. The waters are gentle, this time of year."

Leileas slipped inside the boathouse one more time and emerged with a fifth boat, this one larger than the others but still only large enough to fit the one frith.

"Drys, go first and show the little ones how to use the corougle," Leileas said, propping her boat on the mud and stones and wading into the water. *Wade* wasn't the right word, though—it deepened too fast. Only several feet in, the water nearly reached Leileas's waist. If Maebhe was in her place, she'd be fully submerged. "I will help you all set off."

One by one, Drys, Kieran, Íde, and Maebhe balanced their corougles in the shallow bank and climbed in, Leileas then helping launch them into the water. Maebhe paddled to catch up with Kieran, and as soon as she was close enough, splashed him with her oar. As soon as *he* finished gasping and spluttering, he splashed her back. A war began while Leileas boarded her own corougle behind them.

"Watch the wings!" Drys cried, paddling to get away.

Íde then surprised both twins, splashing them both with a swipe of her oar so powerful it set her spinning. By the time Leileas caught up with them, Maebhe's stomach hurt from laughing.

They spent the rest of the day either paddling or drifting based on the whims of the current, and only pulled to the riverbank to eat or stretch their legs. They started a fire at night, keeping their corougles close by—in case they needed to make a hasty retreat into the water.

Retreat from what, Maebhe didn't ask, but she did watch the forest's shifting shadows more closely. Kieran and Íde fell asleep almost as soon as they were off their feet, but Maebhe stayed awake, listening to the chirps and calls and croaks of creatures that were somehow both familiar and completely alien.

"Would you like me to tell you a story?" Drys whispered, startling her. She didn't know how they knew she was awake, but she turned in her bedroll to look at them. Since they'd volunteered to keep the first watch, they sat cross-legged on a nearby rock, watching the forest.

"Not a scary one, right?" Maebhe whispered.

Drys laughed softly, their face lit by the fading fire, and Maebhe noticed how lovely their smile was. It softened their sharp features, made their eyes twinkle with mirth.

"Not a scary one," they promised.

"Then yes, please."

"Once upon a time," Drys began, their soft voice drowning Lyryma out, "A young dryad bid his parents goodbye and set off to seek his fortune. He took the high road from Home, but he hadn't been walking for long when he heard a voice. 'Is someone there?' it called. Following the voice, the dryad found a faerie caught in a forgotten frìth trap, brambles closed around it to form a cage.

'If you help free me, I will grant you a favor,' the faerie told the dryad.

'Any favor?' asked the dryad.

'Yes, anything you desire, if it's within my power.' Fortunately for the faerie, this dryad was skilled at singing to the trees. He whistled, and the trees released the faerie."

Maebhe tried to keep her eyes open, to listen to the end, but Drys' voice was mesmerizing, almost musical, and it made her mind drift and drift...

The next thing she knew, the forest was bright and Kieran was prodding at her to wake her up. As they went about their morning, Drys didn't bring up the night before, so neither did she.

She followed the others back to the river and, throughout the course of the day, watched the forest around them grow stranger and stranger the further south they drifted. The trees took on towering, gnarled shapes Maebhe had never seen before; the grasses and foliage doubled, then tripled in size. In the afternoon, they passed rows of weeping willows, their great branches reaching over the river in an arc. Small lights like stars dotted the end of each pendulous branch, and Maebhe reached up to feel them trail over her skin. The lights felt warm, like sunslight.

By evening, they reached one of the southern Lyryma frìth villages. The frìth and fae there collected their corougles and greeted them happily, coaxing them again into telling stories and drinking wine until the early morning. With the rising suns, they packed their things half-asleep and said their goodbyes, but before they set off on foot, the residents left them with parting advice: be careful. This forest is dangerous. Darkness lurks amidst the trees.

Despite the warning, Maebhe's fear of Lyryma slowly faded. The forest may be dangerous, but really, *all* forests were dangerous. You just needed to learn how to navigate them. After five days in this one, Maebhe was learning how to navigate it. And if she'd learned anything in that time, it was that Lyryma was *beautiful.*

She'd never seen so much color and life in one place. Red and orange flowers grew on the trees, the occasional petals fluttering past them like leaves in autumn. Those trees—their trunks so thick that if all three orinians joined hands, they wouldn't be able to close their arms around even one—grew as tall as Unity's clock tower.

She'd forgotten the warnings entirely by early evening, when Leileas said, "I think we should hide."

Maebhe looked up from the vividly purple orchid she'd been examining. Before she could ask, Leileas was already scooping her up and carrying her over to a fern twice her height. It had been funny when they'd started their journey, but Maebhe had since grown used to being manhandled by the frìth. Pushing aside the fronds, Leileas deposited Maebhe at the plant's center, then stepped aside to let Kieran, Íde, and Drys climb in on their own. Once they were all hidden, Leileas crouched beside the plant and whispered, "I thought I heard something. Stay there until I know what it is."

Kieran elbowed Maebhe. "Gross! What's that smell?"

Maebhe elbowed him back, harder. "Fuck off. It's not *me*."

"It's the plant," Leileas drifted in. "It will obscure you from whatever's coming, if it has a strong nose."

Whatever's coming. Maebhe bit her lip, straining to hear. It wasn't long before her sharp ears picked it up as well: it started with distant birds screeching as they left their perches, fleeing danger. What followed was a steady *thump, thump, thump* of heavy feet hitting the ground. Branches snapped as a large body moved through the brush.

"It walks on four legs," Leileas murmured, crouching lower, "And has three heartbeats. That leaves two possibilities: one is harmless, the other certainly means our deaths."

Maebhe exchanged a worried look with Kieran. All they could see was the inside of their fern. Outside, silence fell, but after what felt like minutes but could only be moments, Leileas said, "It's all right. Come out if you want to see."

Maebhe crept out of the fern first, Drys following behind, but she froze at the sight that greeted her. It was a great, shaggy creature nearly twice Leileas' height. Nearly *four* times her own. It was shaped like a deer but with different proportions: bigger hooves, a broader breastbone, two sets of antlers. It might've been brown, but it was difficult to tell under the moss growing over its back and sides.

"What *is* that?" Íde asked, still half-hidden in the fern.

"Haven't you seen an elk?" Leileas asked. "This one is young yet. They're usually bigger."

"*Bigger*?" Maebhe repeated, not recognizing the high pitch of her own voice.

The creature lazily swiveled its head toward the group, revealing a third eye on its forehead. It blinked lazily at them. "Is this the darkness everyone's been warning about?" Kieran asked doubtfully.

Suddenly, the creature tensed, its ears flattening as its head swiveled back around, toward some sound.

"Get down!" Leileas yelled just seconds before the elk leaped over their heads, vanishing into the forest with long strides that made the ground shake. Behind Maebhe, Kieran lost his balance and pitched into the fern.

Maebhe whipped back around. Something new moved in the trees, something that had made the elk flee. She searched for it, but it barely made a sound; her own beating heart was louder. The elk's sounds must have covered its presence, but with the elk gone, the soft slither through the underbrush was more pronounced.

"It has no heartbeat," Leileas whispered.

Beneath the stink of the fern, Maebhe smelled rot and death.

There, between two branches, the tip of a wing. Then, low to the ground, a feather-tipped tail. Whatever it was seemed to be circling them. Finally, a long snout peeked out from behind a tree, baring sharp teeth blackened by decay. Next came a rectangular-pupiled pair of crimson eyes, followed by a long neck and scaled body.

It was a dragon, bigger than the ones Maebhe had seen from a distance in Gallonten, bigger than even the tallest frith. Its scales were the color of cinnabar and redcurrant.

Across its breastbone stretched a wide, gaping wound. Where bone and fleshy muscle should have been visible beneath, magma instead swirled across the surface. Trying to look at it for too long gave Maebhe vertigo. She staggered back, having to rely on her tail to help her keep her balance.

"H-hello," she stammered. "How do you do?"

The dragon opened its mouth. At first, it seemed to be smiling, but as its jaw spread wider and wider, Maebhe could see the glow of fire building at the back of its throat. She had forgotten this about the stories of red dragons: they were said to breathe fire.

"Drys!" Leileas yelled.

Before Maebhe realized what was happening, Drys had her in their arms and was taking off. Leileas scooped the others and dove out of the way seconds before a great jet of fire burst from the dragon's maw. Maebhe felt the heat of it as Drys carried her up and away.

When she leaned down to look, a wash of fire covered the forest floor and climbed up the vines of the trees. The dragon was looking right at them; it opened its mouth again.

"Fly south! We'll find you!" Leileas shouted from somewhere behind the flames.

"No!" Maebhe cried, but Drys didn't listen. They changed direction midair and swept south, narrowly avoiding another jet of flame. Maebhe could only hide her face in Drys' shoulder and hold on as the faerie wove through the trees, branches striking and scratching her skin. It seemed like ages before Drys finally slowed, dipped lower and lower, then came to a stumbling stop. Neither fire nor dragon were anywhere to be seen, and they were alone in this dangerous forest.

The second Drys set her down, Maebhe rounded on them. "How could you leave them?!" she demanded. She couldn't breathe; her stomach had tied itself into tighter and tighter and tighter knots during the flight, and now her legs could barely support her. She sank to the ground, frustrated tears springing to her eyes.

She'd only just gotten her family back. Why did this keep happening to them? Why was everything happening to *them*?

Drys blinked, visibly bemused. "Leileas told me to."

"What if they didn't make it out? What if they needed our help?!"

"*I* needed my help, too. You can't fault me for having a sense of self-preservation." They said it like it was the most logical thing in the world.

"Yes, I can! And if they don't make it out because of *your* cowardice, I'll kill you!"

"Oh, don't be dramatic. With its size and damaged wings, that *thing* won't be able to travel quickly in such a dense forest. Leileas can outrun it."

Maebhe covered her face with her hands. "What about the fire?" Her voice came out muffled.

"It's been a damp summer. The fire won't spread far, if at all," Drys assured her. "You have nothing to fear—not for now, at least."

Maebhe breathed. "Okay."

"Better?" Drys asked.

"Better."

"You know, if I was a different faerie, I might be offended. I just saved your life; you should be thanking me, my Mae-*vuh*."

"You—ugh!" Maebhe said. She scooted so her back was to them and took the chance to scrub at her eyes.

"Are you *ignoring* me?" Drys asked.

Maebhe ignored them. That was how the others found them, emerging from the woods just twenty minutes later looking tired and beaten down. Leileas walked with a limp, and the smell of singed fur followed her.

Maebhe jumped up the moment she saw them, throwing her arms around both Kieran and Íde at once. "I'm so glad you're safe. Are you hurt?" she asked.

"Yeah, thanks for just leaving us," Kieran said. Noticing Maebhe's tear-streaked face, though, he frowned and shot Drys a suspicious glare. "Are *you* hurt?"

"No, thanks to Drys. What was that thing? Leileas, Drys, why didn't you tell us there were *red dragons* in Lyryma? They're supposed to be extinct!"

Leileas shook her head. "I didn't know. I wonder if that's what's been scaring animals to the edges of the forest."

The group shared a dark look. Darkness lurks amidst the trees, indeed. When none of them had an answer, Leileas shook her head and said, "Let us continue. I want to get as far from that creature as possible."

Egil V

Gareth and Roman returned to the Ranulfs' rented flat and found Leandros laid out on the couch, the Ranulf family physician kneeling at his side and finishing a long row of stitches. White sheets had been laid out beneath the prince, making the amount of blood he'd lost horribly obvious. He was conscious, at least, and watched them enter with a dark expression.

"I thought you'd be gone longer," he grumbled. At the words, the physician paused his stitching and Isobel appeared in the doorway, the former looking Roman curiously up and down and the latter stomping over to Gareth.

"Where have you been?" Isobel demanded. "You sent a wounded, bleeding man to our home and then just *ran off*? Let me look at you. Were you hurt? Prince Nochdvor said you weren't, but I want to be sure."

"I was in no danger, my dear, I assure you," Gareth said.

"But you could have been." Isobel sighed and shook her head.

"We'll discuss this more later. Mr. Hallisey, don't think I didn't notice your injuries. Let me get you some ice."

Through the exchange, Leandros watched Roman and Roman watched Leandros back. Even at Isobel's offer, Roman touched a finger to his swollen lip and nodded his thanks without ever tearing his eyes from the prince.

"Thank you for coming, Doctor Stewart," Gareth said, settling in the plush armchair by the couch. "How bad is it?"

The physician, a thin man with a bushy handlebar mustache, sat back on his heels and let out a sigh. The sound, defeated and tired, made anxiety spike through Roman. He approached without thinking. He'd known the cut was deep, but he'd forgotten how debilitating injuries could be for people—for *normal* people, anyway. Alfar healed quickly, but that sigh seemed a bad sign.

"He'll live," the physician said, and suddenly Roman could breathe again. "And for now, I gave him a heavy dose of laudanum, so he shouldn't be feeling much."

"I'm right here," Leandros murmured. Now that the physician mentioned it, Roman noticed a slight slur to his normally-precise speech, though it was impossible to tell if that was the blood loss or the laudanum.

The physician ignored him. "He should have gone to a hospital, Gareth. I can't tell the extent of the damage without the proper facilities, so we'll only know how bad it is as it heals. Maybe it's fine, or maybe he'll never use that hand again," he explained in a thick Ejeran accent.

Leandros didn't react to this news except to scowl at Roman. It was such a stark expression for an alfar, even an alfar like Leandros, that Roman took a surprised step back. "Have you finally gotten over your fear of stitches?" Leandros asked. Roman hadn't been looking at the wound, but he did now, glimpsing stark black on pink just before it disappeared beneath a bandage. Feeling immediately queasy, he turned away, and Leandros let out a mean bark of laughter. "It seems not, then."

Gareth raised an eyebrow at Roman. "Stitches? Really?"

"I'm not *afraid* of them. I just don't like them," Roman said.

Fortunately, Isobel's return saved him from further interrogation. She pressed a bag of ice into Roman's hand. "Doctor Stewart said His Highness shouldn't move any time soon, so I invited him to stay with us," she told Gareth. "He shouldn't be living alone with that injury, anyway, even if it's only for a few days. Ms. O'Neill left to fetch his things."

With Leandros' bandage secured, the physician stood. "I'll be back. I need to get a brace from my clinic—something to keep the His Highness from moving his hand too much while it heals. I've already gone over care and maintenance with Isobel, Gareth; she's more than capable of handling any issues that arise, but if I'm needed, don't hesitate to call."

Seeing Roman's curious look her way, Isobel smiled and explained, "My uncle was the old Ranulf family physician. I shadowed with him for years before I married Gareth."

"Thank you again for your help," Gareth told Steward. Then, lowering his voice, he added, "I'm sure I don't have to ask you to be discreet about what you saw here today."

The old physician huffed a laugh. "You don't. His Royal Highness refused to take the laudanum until I made a vow of silence. I don't know what you've gotten yourself into here, Gareth, but I wish you the best with it."

While Gareth escorted the physician out, Roman perched on the arm of the couch at Leandros' feet. He was surprised to find he couldn't read the alfar's expression; there was a time when Roman could read Leandros' every thought.

He tried not to stare, but he couldn't get over how Leandros had grown. He'd always been handsome, disarmingly so, but he'd grown more into his features since the last time they met. As a rule, Roman tried not to think about that meeting, or the look on Leandros' face right before Roman—

Gareth returned and stood in the doorway, his hands on his hips. "Prince Nochdvor, do you still plan on going to Orean? With your injuries, maybe it would be better to—"

"I'm going," Leandros said, leaving no room for discussion.

"Then we need to make sure you're protected," Roman said. "I've disrupted Unity's plans for now, but that doesn't mean the Enforcers won't try anything on the journey."

"I can watch out for myself. I've been doing it for sixty years."

Roman winced.

"Respectfully, Captain, no man can watch out for himself all of the time, especially not one with a serious injury and all the responsibility that you have," Gareth reasoned.

Isobel asked, "What if we find you a personal guard? If Gareth gets to appoint one to the team, you should as well."

"An excellent idea, Bel! I'm sure we could find someone suitable on short notice," Gareth agreed. "Between Roman and this guard, you should be covered."

Leandros narrowed his eyes at Gareth. "What do you mean, between Roman and the guard? We're leaving Gallonten in two days. Roman isn't coming with."

"I am, actually," Roman said in a quiet voice. "The Magistrates agreed to let me just an hour ago."

Leandros sat up. "It's *my* team!" he snarled, his voice louder than most in the room had ever heard it. He tried to stand, lost his balance, and fell back onto the couch, wincing as he jostled his arm. "Do I have a say in this?"

"No," Roman said.

Leandros glared. Roman stared impassively back.

Gareth cleared his throat. "I'm going to check on the spare guest room before Ms. O'Neill returns," he announced, giving Isobel a meaningful look.

Isobel nodded. "And I should tell the cook to make extra for dinner," she said, hastily following her husband out of the room.

It left Roman and Leandros alone. They stared at each other for too long, each second feeling profoundly wrong to Roman. He'd been alone with Leandros more times than he could count, and it had never before been anything but comfortable. From their first meeting, a thread of trust and understanding had unrolled between them. Roman had been the one to cut it, but maybe he hadn't been prepared for the consequences.

"So," Leandros said, finally. "You're alive."

"So," Roman echoed, "You're working with Unity."

"Don't. You let me think you were dead for *sixty years*. Don't act like *you're* morally in the right."

At that, Roman only shrugged. "Me acting poorly doesn't exempt you from doing the same. What were you thinking, Leandros? You know what they are."

"You have no claim to my thoughts," Leandros said coldly, "And no right to my reasons."

"Maybe not," Roman said, "But I have my own reasons for going to Orean. I just hope our goals won't conflict."

That horrible silence fell between them again, even tenser than before. "You would…?" Leandros began, looking uncertain. Looking more like the boy Roman remembered. Then Leandros steeled himself and finished, "If they do, I won't let you stop me."

Roman sighed. He hated this. He suspected Leandros hated it, too. "No, I won't let you stop me, either."

"You should go. I have nothing more to say to you."

Roman nodded, already backing away. "I'll see you around, then."

Roman returned to his room and shut the door. His body was changing before he'd even sunk fully to the floor, the days event's catching up with him. Lifting his tingling hand, he found it faintly aglow. The white light pooled up his arms, high enough that his eyes had probably changed as well.

He squeezed them shut and focused on his breathing, pushing back the magic like he had so many times before.

———

169 YEARS AGO

YEAR OF UNITY 1711

Egil crept through the underbrush as strange sounds echoed through the wood ahead—familiar to Egil, but strange in that they didn't belong in Lyryma Forest.

They were the sounds of people shouting.

No matter how urgent the shouts grew, Egil didn't rush, didn't reveal himself. Though he hadn't encountered them personally, he'd heard of creatures in this old forest that used compassion as bait, mimicking the sounds of people in distress to lure prey deeper. This being some trick of the wood's certainly made more sense than the alternative: that strangers had made it this deep inside. And they could only be strangers; anyone else would know better than to shout here.

He didn't know what he'd expected to see when he finally reached the source of the noise, but three finely-dressed alfar fighting an angry saelcla wasn't it. The bear-like creature towered over them, swiping at the alfar with massive claws. It only took one glance at their stiff sword forms to know who would win this fight.

A fourth boy stood at the back, far from the saelcla. Instead of wielding a sword, he clung to the reigns of their spooked horses, single-handedly keeping all four from running off. Egil crept around the edge of the clearing to him, ripping a large frond from a fern as he went, and whistled to get the boy's attention.

"Give me your matchbox," he whispered.

The boy—*young man*—jumped at Egil's sudden appearance, though his expression remained calm. It impressed Egil; even faced with imminent death, this one kept his composure. In his experience, alfar were good at pretending when it was easy but broke the moment things got difficult. Certainly, this young man's friends and their shrieking were proving that true. "Pardon?" the alfar whispered back.

"A matchbox. You have one, don't you? Give it to me."

"Who are you?"

"It doesn't matter. Trust me."

The alfar stared at Egil a long moment, his ice-blue eyes weighing Egil. Egil felt unbalanced by those eyes, but before he could say anything, the young man nodded, thrust the reins into Egil's hands, and turned to a large dun horse. Egil watched him coo soft consolations to it while he rummaged through its saddlebags, finally retrieving a matchbox and returning to Egil.

Egil used it to set the fern frond ablaze.

Across the clearing, the saelcla stood on its hind legs, towering over the humans at nearly twice their height. It swiped at one with a clawed, eerily human hand and sent him flying into a tree trunk. Before it could strike again, Egil stepped up to it, waving the flaming frond between them. It reeled back, dropping back onto four legs.

"Shoo!" Egil urged, waving the branch again. It wasn't the ideal torch; it burned fast, heat stinging his hand as the flame devoured the leaves. Fortunately, the saelcla retreated before it could burn all the way down, turning and lumbering back into the brush.

Egil dropped the branch and stomped out the fire while the alfar crowded around him.

"That was brilliant!" one said.

"How did you know that would work?" another asked.

Egil stepped away before they could fully encircle him, keeping his back to the forest so he could see them all at once. Too caught up in the excitement and adrenaline, they didn't notice his unease. Guessing an alfar's age was always difficult, but by their manner and dress, Egil knew these four were young. The equivalent of their early twenties, maybe, for other humans.

"What are you doing here?" he asked them. "This forest is dangerous."

"So we were told," one of the boys sighed. He was taller than the others. Older, too, with less baby fat and a trace of blond stubble along his jaw. "I didn't know that meant giant *bears* that attack for no reason!"

"Dangerous means dangerous. Leave before you get hurt."

"We can't," said another, the one who'd been thrown into the tree. He rubbed at his lower back but otherwise appeared unharmed. "Our friends are waiting at the edge of the wood. They dared us to keep going until we found a frìth. We can't turn back now."

"Then you'll die and bring shame on your families," Egil scolded. He met the fourth alfar's gaze, the one who'd given him the matchbox. "Do you really want the blood of royalty on your hands?"

The boys stilled. Surprise flickered across the fourth alfar's face, and he left the horses—much calmer, now that the threat had passed—tethered to a tree in order to join them. "How did you know?"

Egil rolled his eyes. "The crest on your saddlebags gave it away."

The alfar considered this. "How did you know they were *my* saddlebags?" he asked.

"That horse was the first one you turned to—not the closest, not the calmest. And no one coos like that at someone else's horse."

The boy flushed, and the tall alfar said, "Clever. Who are you?"

Egil hesitated. Thanks to his recent partnership with the Oracle of Damael, odds were good that they'd recognize the name Egil. If they didn't from that, they might know him as the Hound of Unity. He didn't much want to be known. Before the alfar could question his hesitation, he picked a name Unity wouldn't be able to trace: "Call me Roman. Roman Hallisey."

"It's truly a pleasure, Mr. Hallisey," the tall alfar said, holding out a hand. Roman didn't shake it, and the boy awkwardly dropped it again. "I'm Helge Evanson. This is Kjell and Oskar, and the one you pointed out earlier is Leandros Nochdvor, grandson to the King."

Roman eyed the Nochdvor prince. He looked like his grandfather—golden hair, pale eyes, and light, unmarred skin. Roman was about to dismiss him, as he already had the others, but then something strange happened: Leandros Nochdvor smiled at him, shy and sweet. It was a strange sight coming from an alfar, especially one from *that* family, and Roman stared a moment longer.

"Join us for a meal," Leandros said. "We owe you for saving our lives."

"I dare say we could have fought it," Kjell sniffed.

"What, like you were fighting it when it sent you flying?" Oskar asked.

"Don't be rude, you two," Helge told them. "I'm with Nochdvor. Please, do sit, Mr. Hallisey. I'd love to hear what *you're* doing in Lyryma, if it's as dangerous as you say. Oskar, get a fire stared."

Roman didn't want to stay, but he couldn't in good conscience leave these boys alone. They'd been lucky to get this far and only encounter a saelcla, but luck ran out quickly in Lyryma and Roman had enough blood staining his soul already. While he was still trying to decide, he found himself being dragged down to sit beside Helge at a small but growing fire.

Kjell broke a loaf of bread and passed it around the circle while Helge offered Roman a basket of fruit. Roman took a small red berry and considered it, then pressed it to his tongue. It was fresh, sweet. These boys traveled lavishly.

"Is a dare really worth your lives?" he asked. He met Leandros' eyes by accident, and the alfar quickly dropped his gaze, a faint blush still dusting the tips of his ears. Roman almost smiled. He'd never met an alfar so easy to discomfit. If he still worked for Unity, he would've found it too easy to pull information from Alfheimr's young prince.

"Yes," Oskar said easily.

"We're students at the Academy, you see, and we're about to enter our final year," Helge explained. "The Academy's the best school in the entire province, and it's tradition that every year, the exiting class gives the rising seniors a dare to complete. Ours is to meet a frith and bring back proof."

Roman raised an eyebrow.

"You don't understand," Kjell said. "You can't know how important these dares are. If we turn back, we'll be the first class in over two hundred and eighty years to fail. Our fathers, our fathers' fathers, they all completed their own dares. We'd be a disgrace."

Roman looked at Leandros. "What about you? You're quiet. Do you disagree?"

Kjell sighed.

"I've disliked this from the start. Our fathers," Leandros began, shooting Kjell a sharp glare, "Were not given dares that are both actively life-threatening *and* disrespectful to an entire nation. In my opinion, being nearly mauled by a bear is excuse enough to return home."

Roman's lips twitched, almost into a smile. "It was a saelcla, technically. Same genus, different species."

The alfar all looked at him with surprise, apparently not expecting a wild-looking stranger they found living in Lyryma Forest to know the difference between a *genus* and a *species*. Roman cleared his throat, suddenly self-conscious. "There are worse creatures here, the deeper you go, which is why I advise you to turn back."

"If you know Lyryma so well, can't you help us? Do you know where we can find the frìth?" Oskar asked. This sparked Kjell and Helge's excitement; soon, Roman had three eager alfar bearing down on him. He rose and stepped swiftly away, closer to the cover of the wood. The alfar all blinked, surprised by his speed.

"If I introduce you to the frìth, do you promise to leave the forest immediately after?"

"Of course," Helge agreed. "We don't *want* to be here. I have a soft bed and warm food waiting for me in Alfheim."

"Then I'll take Leandros Nochdvor, and Leandros Nochdvor only," Roman said. "The rest of you are to stay here."

Leandros' mouth fell open in surprise. The others spoke over each other, each trying to complain the loudest.

Kjell, "Why him?"

Oskar, "Why not take all of us?"

Helge, "Just who do you think you are?"

"Unity and your people have made an enemy of the frìth for centuries; who do *you* think *you* are? Even if you found them, do you really think you'd be welcome? If you even made it to Home, do you think there wouldn't be consequences? Arrogant, *thoughtless* boys. You don't know the harm you could do," Roman spat. "Leandros is the only one who gave a single thought to the frìth. He's the only one I'll take."

Helge spluttered. Soft hands, fine clothes, unearned confidence — Roman guessed he'd never been spoken to like this before.

"We'll be back in a few hours. If the rest of you are going to sleep, keep a watch. Don't leave this clearing and *always* keep that fire lit. Most of the predators who roam the forest at night fear open flames—they should keep you safe until we get back," Roman said before Helge could recover. To Leandros, he added, "We continue on foot. Keep close to me and obey my orders."

Nodding, Leandros shouldered a single bag and followed Roman into the wood. As the glow from the fire behind them dimmed, soon swallowed entirely by foliage, Roman felt the alfar's eyes on him. "Thank you," Leandros said, finally. "For stopping them, and for the compromise."

Roman shrugged.

"How do you know so much about Lyryma?"

Roman looked at him. Though his expression was hard to read in the darkness, it struck Roman as open, innocent. "I live here."

"Your accent's Troasian, isn't it? That's a long way from here."

"It is."

Leandros smiled to himself. He walked beside Roman instead of behind, looking all around him like he couldn't take enough of the forest in. "You're not one for talking, are you? I don't mind it, but tell me if you'd like *me* to stop."

"I wouldn't," Roman admitted.

"Then I'll continue for as long as you like," Leandros said courteously. After a moment, he added, "You know, Lyryma's quite lovely when there are no monsters attacking you. And when you don't have to listen to Helge talk on and on about himself."

Despite himself, Roman laughed. He remembered the first time he'd seen the inside of this forest. He'd been weary and injured, stumbling in after his escape from Gallonten. He'd had Unity guards and other Enforcers on his heels and his heart had been breaking for Bellona, his apprentice, the girl he'd left behind.

For the most part, Leandros respected Roman's silence, though he occasionally asked about strange plants or animals they passed along the way. Roman didn't mind the questions, nor the wonder with which Leandros asked them. With the forest matching their easy silence, they heard the music of Home long before they reached the city. Leandros gasped when he gentle strains first reached them and turned to Roman with eyes blown wide in the dark, but Roman just beckoned him on. Before long, the ground dropped out ahead of them and the city sprawled below. It was lovely at night, like a reflec-tion of the sky; the lanterns lit throughout seemed as distant as stars. But if Roman squinted, he could make out central field and all the small figures that danced and swayed to strange melodies upon it.

"This is Home?" Leandros whispered. He dropped to his knees at the edge of the hill, staring down at the city with evident awe. "From the stories they tell in Alfheim, I was expecting…"

"Not this," Roman guessed.

"Not this," Leandros agreed. "This is beautiful."

"You'd be surprised how many of the stories your people tell about Home are untrue," Roman said, watching Leandros out of the corner of his eye.

Leandros snorted. "I don't think I would."

"Well, there are your frith. Do you need proof for your dare?"

"Just something small, yes," Leandros said. "Can we get closer?"

"I don't know if that's appropriate. It's not for me to invite you into the city. I'm only a guest here, myself."

Before Leandros could reply, a deep voice called, "Egil!" Both Roman and Leandros turned to look, Leandros gasping at the sight of his first frith. Roman could only imagine how she must look to Leandros, with her twisting horns, glowing eyes, and towering height. She approached from the grand staircase, tilting her head quizzically as she took in the person beside Roman. "In all the time you've been with us, you've never brought a friend here."

"He's not really..." Roman began. He paused. He didn't really know how to explain what Leandros was.

"But he's someone you trust?"

Roman considered this. "I suppose."

"Then welcome to Home, little alfar. I'm Senga," Senga said warmly, crouching to be closer to Roman and Leandros' level.

"Leandros," Leandros said in return, dipping into a formal bow.

Senga's ears pricked forward, revealing her pleasure at the respectful gesture. "Welcome to Home, Leandros. You've made it in time for the festivities."

"Festivities?" Leandros asked.

"He's not staying," Roman asked. "Senga, can I ask you for a favor? Can I have one of your whiskers?"

Senga blinked at the unusual request. "A whisker?"

"Yes, a whisker. Leandros needs it," Roman said.

Senga made a considering noise. "I will give your friend a whisker if you both attend our party, first. I've noticed the way you avoid them, Egil. It would make our good neighbors happy if you were to enjoy their wine. Besides, it's Muir's birthday. You must come and wish him well, then tell him a story as a gift."

Roman couldn't argue with that. "We can't stay long."

Together, they followed Senga down the stairs toward the stream of music flowing from Home's heart. The minute they reached the clearing, glasses of shimmering wine were thrust into their hands. A faerie with elegant butterfly wings danced around Roman, playing with his long hair before whisking a bewildered-looking Leandros away for a dance. As a newcomer, someone fresh and exciting, the alfar quickly amassed an entourage of curious fae. Roman watched him for a while—he was all youthful excitement and awkward limbs compared to the ineffable grace of the fae, but he was something solid and true in a sea of the surreal. He was strangely magnetic.

With that thought, Roman drained his glass, then cast one final look at Leandros before setting off in search of a second. If he'd been on his guard, he would have remembered how hard it was to leave a fae party once you'd begun to enjoy it.

Nearly two hours had passed before he found Leandros again. It happened in the middle of a dance, when Roman stumbled after a particularly enthusiastic spin from the faerie he'd been partnered with. He braced himself on whatever was closest, which happened to be Leandros' chest, and laughed as the world tipped dangerously around him. A strong arm caught him by the waist, holding him steady.

Roman blinked, finding Leandros' face very close.

"I barely recognized you with that smile on your face," Leandros said, raising his voice to be heard over the music. "Hello again."

"Hello," Roman echoed breathlessly. He cleared his throat, then pushed on Leandros' chest, putting some space between them. Leandros released him without protest. "We should get back to your friends."

"They're not my friends," Leandros said. He tugged Roman away from the party, deftly avoiding large, dancing hooves. "I think we should sit a while before we try to go anywhere."

Roman shrugged and dropped down into the grass. He knew Leandros was right; it had been a while since he'd had fae wine. He'd forgotten how strong it could be. "Fine. As long as they keep the fire going, they probably won't die."

Leandros laughed, surprising Roman. It was a sound that belonged here, in a forest like this. If magic really existed, Roman had always thought he'd find it in Lyryma. He was right, in a way—he found it in this unusual alfar's laugh. "How much did you drink?" Leandros asked as he settled beside Roman in the grass. "You're like a completely different person."

"I'm not *drunk*," Roman said defensively. "I'm just..." Freed enough to be able to breathe, to emerge from the shell of a man who'd been broken and remade over and over and over. He hoped this would be the last time. *Roman*, he thought, was someone who could smile and feel. Egil was not.

When he didn't finish his sentence, Leandros smiled good-naturedly. "Of course. My apologies."

Roman ignored the teasing and changed the subject. "When does your term start?" he asked.

"Pardon?"

"Kjell—or maybe Helge. *One of them* said you're enrolled at the Academy. A new term starts soon, right?"

"Not until fall," Leandros said.

Roman nodded and twirled a lock of hair around his finger. It was getting long, almost down to his waist if he didn't tie it up. Without seasons, the passage of time was indistinct in Home. Weeks blended into months into years, and through it all, Roman didn't age. He used his hair as a metric of sorts—soon, it would be time to cut it all off and begin the cycle again.

He couldn't guess how many cycles had passed since his days at the Academy. He doubted anyone he knew still taught there, even with alfars' long lives. He thought of the youngest professor on staff back when he'd been enrolled. "Is, ah...Elgar Silge still teaching there?"

Leandros had been watching the party, his foot tapping along to the music, but now he turned the full weight of his attention on Roman. "He's been dead for decades, I'm afraid. But his daughter is the headmaster, now."

Roman sat upright. "Asta?"

"...You know her?"

"We were friends when I—" Roman paused, bit his lip. He'd said too much to stop there. "I used to attend the Academy."

With the expressiveness Roman had come to expect from him, Leandros' eyes widened. "A human from Troas who attended the Academy and lied about his name, now living in Lyryma with the frìth. What a strange creature you are," he said, watching Roman with an intensity that made Roman look away.

"I didn't lie," he said. He suspected he had far more to drink than Leandros had. A mistake. "Roman is my middle name."

"Senga called you Egil."

"That's something else. Don't call me that."

Leandros held his hands up. "If you don't want me to, then I won't. I'm sorry for pushing. I like Roman; it's a good name."

"Thank you," Roman said. Despite the warning bells chiming in the back of his head, telling him he'd revealed too much, he relaxed. Instinct told him Leandros wouldn't abuse this information.

"What did you study?" Leandros asked. "When you were at the Academy?"

"Chemistry. I never graduated, though. I had to drop out before my final year." He almost smiled. "Didn't get to participate in any dares."

"What happened?"

Roman shrugged. "I just couldn't pay the tuition."

Leandros leaned forward, into Roman's space. "You could always return. They have scholarships, now," he said, this sudden excitement the first sign of intoxication he'd shown all night. "You could finish the new term. We could be classmates."

Roman laughed. "I don't know if that's possible."

"At least think about it," Leandros said. He pushed himself to his feet and held a hand out to Roman, who took it with little hesitation. "In the meantime, come and dance with me. Just one song. Then we can find Senga, get her whisker, and you'll be free of me."

SIX MONTHS LATER

The schoolroom was sticky and humid, filled with the chatter of many voices. While not Leandros' favorite place in the world, the Academy gave him what he needed: competent professors and dormitories away from his family.

Helge, Oskar, Kjell, and several classmates who hadn't been included in their fateful summer dare sat around him. Helge was telling some story about a hunting trip he took with his father and Leandros had long since tuned out, his unfocused gaze settled somewhere near the empty blackboard at the front of the room.

When the professor entered, a familiar figure trailing in behind him, Leandros was the first to notice. It was a lean young man with dark skin, a pretty face, and long, long hair pulled up into a ponytail. That face had featured in more than a few of Leandros' dreams since their night in Lyryma.

Roman Hallisey stood out among the broad-shouldered, fair-haired citizens of Alfheimr. More than his dark hair and eyes, he was so exquisitely *sapien,* without an alfar's sharp angles, slitted eyes, or pointed ears. As in Lyryma, his clothes were in a traditional Troasian style—he wore a flowing white tunic partially unbuttoned at the top, a sash around his waist, and a red ascot around his neck. When Roman found Leandros' gaze, Leandros couldn't help but smile broadly.

"Your expression, Prince Nochdvor," the professor warned, and Leandros quickly wiped it from his face. It had drawn the others' attention, and they now noticed Roman as well.

"What is *he* doing here?" Helge asked.

"Mr. Evanson," the professor scolded even more harshly. "This is your new classmate, Roman Hallisey. He is a *personal* friend of the headmaster, so I hope you all welcome him and show him how hospitable we can be at the Academy."

"This is some kind of joke, right?" Helge asked, dropping the Unity-regulated Ellesian language to speak in Eld Alfar, traditionally spoken only among old Alfheimr families. "He's a peasant from the woods. Why would the headmaster have anything to do with him?"

"*Quiet*, Helge," Leandros snapped, also in Eld Alfar. He turned to Roman, who'd settled on a stool at the empty table behind him, and switched back to Ellesian. "I'm glad you could make it."

"Gladr lig at vara hi," Roman replied in crisp, flawless Eld Alfar. *Glad to be here.*

Helge nearly fell off his stool.

As they settled into the term, Leandros made multiple attempts to befriend Roman Hallisey. He tried inviting Roman out with the rest of the students, tried striking up conversations with him between classes, and once, when he was particularly desperate, tried following Roman to the market so he could later "pretend" to run into him. The latter attempt had been the worst failure of them all: somehow, Roman had disappeared from Leandros' sight after just one block.

It frustrated Leandros. He was used to people who hid their emotions, but it sometimes he wondered whether Roman even *had* emotions to hide. Sometimes, when Leandros looked at him, the black eyes looking back were flat, empty. Whenever he was close to giving up, though, he'd catch a flicker of life—the way Roman smiled to himself when the professor got something wrong, the spark of anger that flared when the other students were being foolish, the thoughtful sadness that overtook him on rainy days. These flickers reminded Leandros of Home, when Roman had laughed, danced, and teased Leandros. They reminded him of the loneliness he'd glimpsed in Roman then. After that, he always doubled his efforts, because he knew that loneliness. It was the same as his own.

His chance finally came in the form of a partner project. Leandros visited the classroom early to speak with the professor and ensure that when the assignments were read out, he and Roman would be paired together. Roman said nothing when the groups were named, but he'd shot Leandros a curious, appraising look, like he knew Leandros had rigged it but couldn't prove it. They agreed to meet in Roman's apartment on their next free day to work. Leandros told himself he wasn't nervous about it, but when the day came, he couldn't even pretend to maintain the lie. He was *very* nervous.

He followed the address Roman gave to a corner of Alfheim he'd never been in. It was one of the less-than-glittering neighborhoods of the golden city, where people on dusty, dirty streets gave him curious glances when they brushed shoulders on the sidewalk. The building itself was small, a half-timbered little thing with a butcher's shop on the first floor. Leandros went around the building and climbed the rickety steps to the second floor, planning what he might say to Roman, what they could talk about when not working.

All those ideas fled his mind when Roman answered the door. All he managed was a choked-off, "Good morning."

Roman smiled and stepped aside to let him in.

The apartment was…barren. Nothing more could be said for it. It consisted of only a kitchen, a lavatory, and the main room, and hardly any personal effects could be found in any of those small rooms. Leandros tried not to stare at Roman's bed as they both settled on the ground with their assignment papers spread out in front of them.

They fell into an easy rhythm, focusing on their work. Leandros didn't even need to use one of his planned conversation starters; he'd forgotten how easy it was to be alone with Roman. They worked well together, too, Leandros with an eye for the big picture and Roman for details. They worked *so* well together that they worked through lunch without realizing it.

Leandros was the first to put his journal down.

"I think we've earned ourselves a break," he said, stretching his arms over his head.

"Mm," Roman hummed, still staring down at one of their books with a frown.

"Roman," Leandros pushed. He wasn't sure if they were acquainted enough to use first names. They had in Lyryma, but Alfheim was different and the introduction of the *schoolmates* element complicated things. He was suspected Roman was much, much older than him, too, though he couldn't prove it. "A *break*. This project isn't worth giving yourself a headache over."

"You're right," Roman admitted, finally closing the book. He eyed Leandros—not suspiciously, not warily. Curiously, perhaps. "What kind of break were you thinking?"

Leandros frowned. "I didn't have anything in mind; I'd just hoped we could talk. I'm curious to know how you've been readjusting to Alfheim."

Roman only raised an eyebrow.

Leandros tried again. "Erm. Do you…miss Lyryma?"

"Sometimes," Roman said. Leandros found himself trapped in Roman's gaze. They sat close enough that he could even see himself reflected in Roman's dark eyes. "Leandros, I know you asked the professor to make us partners."

Leandros' mouth fell open. "Oh. I—I only—that is, I thought—"

While he stammered out an excuse, Roman sat up. Next thing Leandros knew, Roman's warm weight was settling on his lap, one leg on either side of Leandros' hips. He leaned in, his breath warm on Leandros' cheek as he whispered, "This is why, right?"

Leandros' mind stuttered to a stop. He turned his head to look at Roman, and before it could start up again, Roman kissed him. His lips were as soft as Leandros had always imagined. Needing to touch, to confirm that this was real, Leandros rested his hands on Roman's waist, making Roman sigh contentedly against him.

It was that sigh that finally broke Leandros' self-control: he kissed back, pulled Roman closer, flush against him. Roman smelled like fire and teakwood, warm and inviting. He was soft beneath Leandros' hands, something Leandros wouldn't have expected just from looking at him. Leandros' hands slid lower, pulling a quiet moan from Roman's lips.

Clarity returned to Leandros, just like that. He pushed Roman off, ignoring the man's surprised grunt, and scooted back until his shoulders hit the edge of the bed. He knew his face must be bright red; he could feel the warmth rushing to his cheeks.

"What are you doing?" he gasped.

Roman looked as surprised as Leandros felt. "That was what you wanted, wasn't it?"

"What I—" Leandros paused, took a moment to process the question. All this time, had Roman thought Leandros was after *this*? "I want to be *friends* with you, Roman."

Roman stared at him, an awkward silence stretching between them. "Friends," Roman repeated, like it was a foreign word. Leandros realized he was embarrassed as well, and they sat there, embarrassed together, until Roman finally asked, "Do you really mean that?"

"Of course," Leandros said. He wondered, not for the first time, what happened to Roman that made him like this, unable to accept kindness without searching for meaning behind it. Leandros knew what Roman looked like when he let that guard down. He knew Roman wasn't naturally cold.

Roman ran a hand through his hair, accidentally pulling some of the shorter locks free of its tie. "I don't...I mean, it's been a while since I—since I've had friends."

"I can tell," Leandros said. He smiled to soften the words. "If it helps, it's the same for me. Helge and the others don't count—they only tolerate me because of my status. And besides, they're awful."

Roman laughed, just as Leandros hoped he would. It felt like a victory. "They are."

Another silence fell between them. Both watched the other warily, as if they might try something else world-altering. Finally, Roman said, "We can try it. Friendship."

A laugh bubbled out of Leandros. He wasn't sure if it was over his own embarrassment or Roman's, but when Roman happily joined in, Leandros felt his loneliness begin to fade. Seeing Roman smile again, Leandros vowed that friendship would be enough.

Before anything else, he would always be Roman's friend.

CHAPTER TWENTY-SEVEN

THE WORDS OF THE MAGISTRATE'S LETTER swam before Leandros' eyes. Over the course of the morning, he'd read it four separate times. Each time had made him progressively angrier.

"We are aware of your past with Mr. Hallisey," the delicate, slanted script read. *"Though he will be accompanying your team to Illyon, he is to be considered an enemy of Unity and treated as such. If you would like our continued support in this matter with your uncle, we advise you to keep your contact with Hallisey limited. Your most humble and obedient servant, Diomis."*

With a heavy sigh, Leandros ran his good hand through his hair. The other was currently set in a brace, an accursed contraption that prevented him from trying to open or close it. Not that he would try, if given the chance. The physician's threat of permanent immobility frightened him more than he let on, and he was already dealing with more world-shattering news than he could handle.

How had his life changed so much in a week? Illyon had been only one week ago. His uncle had been taken from him *one week ago.* When he closed his eyes, he could still vividly picture the woman who took him, from the crimson glow that pulsed beneath her skin to the magic that coiled around her. He couldn't stop her alone. He couldn't stop her without Unity, and now Roman's presence here might ruin everything.

A week and a day ago, Leandros would have said that Roman, alive, was all he wanted and all he would ever wish for. Miraculously, that wish had been granted, but now all he wanted was Roman out of his life again. He stared dully at his manila folder full of Unity protocols and policies, this latest thinly-veiled threat from the Magistrates sitting on top of it. Saving his uncle, the man who'd been there for him when no one else had, took priority over someone who'd faked his own death and let Leandros take the blame.

So why couldn't he get Roman out of his head?

Snarling, he pushed back from his desk and hurled the folder across the room. Papers flew and fluttered everywhere, blanketing the guest room in black and white. Leandros' anger settled with the last of them, leaving him tired. The thought of picking up each page single-handedly was too much, so instead of trying, he grabbed his coat from the bed and hurried out of the room.

He nearly collided with Roman in the hallway.

Their rooms were next to each other in Gareth's modest flat, so it wasn't exactly a surprise to see him. It was, in fact, what Leandros had been trying to avoid by holing himself up in his room to begin with. But while it wasn't a surprise, Leandros wasn't prepared for it, either—let alone for finding Roman so close. In this narrow hallway, Leandros could count every one of Roman's dark eyelashes.

On the surface, Roman hadn't changed in the decades they'd been apart. He'd cut his hair, yes, but he still spoke the same, acted the same, dressed the same. He hadn't even aged, as far as Leandros could tell, but despite all of that, Leandros couldn't shake the feeling that something was monumentally different.

Roman was the first to take a step back, and Leandros wondered what he had done to make Roman stay away in the first place. Roman laughed, a tense, uncomfortable sound, and said, "Sorry."

"No, that was my fault," Leandros said. He cleared his throat. "But as long as we're apologizing, I'd like to apologize for my behavior yesterday."

Roman stared at him, stunned. "Leandros, you…you really don't have to." An awkward silence threatened to settle between them until Roman added, "How's your arm?"

"Fine, thank you," Leandros said, keeping it short. He was in a tremendous amount of pain, actually, but he hadn't wanted his mind addled by more laudanum. "Now, if you'll excuse me."

"Wait." Roman caught Leandros' good arm when the alfar turned to leave, stopping him. Leandros made a half-hearted attempt to tug it free, but unsurprisingly, Roman wouldn't even budge.

Leandros knew this stranger well, though. "What is it? Do you want to check the stitches yourself?" he asked.

Sure enough, Roman wrinkled his nose and dropped Leandros' arm. "Stop that."

"Stop what? What do you *want*, Roman? There's nothing more to be said between us; you made that clear yesterday." And the Magistrates had made it even clearer today.

"I didn't mean—"

They were both so wrapped up in each other that neither noticed Gareth's arrival. When he called to them from down the hall, his voice made them both jump. "There you are! Just the pair I wanted to see!"

Leandros had long since lost control of his expression. He didn't know what it was doing when he turned to his host, but whatever it was made Gareth stop short. "Erm," he said while Leandros struggled to school it into something neutral. "My apologies, am I interrupting something?"

"Did you need something, Gareth?" Roman asked, tactfully deflecting the question. Leandros wasn't tactful; he would have simply lied and told Gareth no.

"Only in that I have good news I needed to share. Isobel found an excellent candidate for Prince Nochdvor's guard. Whenever you're finished here, come downstairs and she'll tell you more about them."

With a shared, lingering look and not another word spoken between them, Roman and Leandros followed Gareth down to the sitting room, where Isobel waited. Since yesterday, the bloody sheets had been cleared off the couch and all evidence of the previous day's events cleaned away. Isobel sat right where Leandros had been stitched up, now stitching her own embroidery.

"Mrs. Ranulf," Leandros said when she looked up. He bowed formally, at the waist, showing deference as he would in Alfheimr to someone of his status or higher. "I would like to apologize for any shameful behavior I exhibited yesterday and thank you and your husband again for your hospitality. I know my intrusion was sudden."

Isobel snorted. "You were ambushed and given nearly enough medication to down a horse, Your Highness. Even if your behavior *was* shameful, I wouldn't hold it against you. There's no need to worry," Isobel assured him.

Leandros nodded and straightened again, though he could feel the tips of his ears heating up from sheer humiliation. Truthfully, he couldn't remember much of what happened after the physician had left. Changing the subject, he said, "Mr. Ranulf mentioned you found a potential guard for me?"

"Yes, a friend of Ofelia's governess," Isobel said, sounding pleased with herself. "I told her she'd be accompanying you to Illyon, but I think the rest should come from you. You should pay her a visit—and take Mr. Hallisey with you. For your safety, of course."

Leandros felt like a child again, his nanny forcing him and Rheamaren to play in the gardens to get them out of the house. This was a "get along and give us some peace" outing, and Isobel barely even attempted to disguise it. "I'm afraid I'm very busy today," he said icily. "I'll have to visit her another time."

Roman shot him a wounded look, but Isobel just smiled. "I thought you might say that, which is why I prepared a bribe."

"I beg your pardon?" Leandros asked, certain he'd misheard. Instead of repeating herself, Isobel retrieved a thick envelope from the table beside her and offered it up to him. Leandros took it reluctantly, but when he peered inside, his breath caught. The envelope contained four booklets, each with dramatic and salacious illustrations on their covers. Penny dreadfuls, and not just any penny dreadfuls: issues of The Carmine Brooch, his current favorite. He recognized the issue on top as the one that had just released yesterday, but the others...He looked up. Beside Isobel, Gareth grinned like a child playing a trick.

"These haven't even been published yet," Leandros said.

"What hasn't?" Roman asked, trying to see over Leandros' shoulder. Leandros elbowed him away.

"Let's say that the publisher owes me a favor," Isobel said with an enigmatic smile. Surprising Leandros, she quickly snatched the envelope back. "You only get this if you go with Roman to meet Wyndie's friend."

Leandros was speechless. Even his nanny had allowed him more dignity. Studying his face, Roman said, "I don't think he's ever been spoken to this way in his life, Isobel."

"I'm sure he'll adjust to it," Isobel said.

"Do I get a bribe, too?" Roman asked.

"Your bribe is that if you go, you may continue to enjoy our generous hospitality."

"But you're letting Leandros do that, too!"

"And Prince Nochdvor offered to contribute to expenses, unlike a certain someone I could name. Not that we'd hear of it, but it's the thought that counts." Isobel added, "I don't care if you are Egil, Roman. You're not Alfheimr royalty."

Leandros allowed himself a small smirk. Seeing Roman receive equal treatment soothed his wounded pride. "We'll make it quick, then," he said. "What's the address?"

Leandros regretted agreeing to this as soon as he stepped outside. Rain beat heavily on the cobblestone streets, washing them clean. While Leandros tested the temperature of it with just his good hand, Roman stepped right out into the street, laughed, and lifted his own so that rain pooled on his palms. When he turned back to Leandros, his smile was wide. "It's not too late to ask the Ranulfs for the use of their carriage, if you don't want to get wet."

It sounded like a challenge, so Leandros joined Roman in the downpour. It was bitingly cold, colder than Leandros' quick test had prepared him for, and he wrinkled his nose at it, making Roman laugh again. "Wait here," he said, disappearing inside and returning a moment later with a black umbrella. After opening it, he passed it off to Leandros. "You really don't want your bandage getting wet."

Gingerly, wordlessly, Leandros accepted it.

The passersby—not that there were many, in this downpour— paid them little mind, and Leandros ached with how much he missed this part of being with Roman. In Roman's presence, he was never *Prince Nochdvor* or *Your Highness*. When it was just the two of them, he could be simply Leandros, and Roman knew everything that meant, all the struggles and baggage it entailed. He was able to exist as just another person in the world, one with a dear friend at his side.

Well. Not so dear anymore.

"Let's go," he said, not giving Roman a chance to reply.

The address Isobel gave them, as it turned out, belonged to one of those ladies' boarding houses that had been making the news lately, known for their strict rules but affordable rents. A pair of young women in university uniforms exited the brick building as Roman and Leandros climbed the front steps, both giggling when Leandros met their eyes. Beside him, Roman grinned and called, "Good morning!"

"Good morning, sirs," one of them called back, her smile shy but *distinctly* interested. Annoyance flickered inside Leandros, but he tamped it down and opened the door for Roman before Roman could flirt more.

Inside, a short foyer led to a tidy lobby decorated with vases of flowers. Leandros wiped his feet on the mat before crossing to the front desk, where an alfar woman with slitted yellow eyes and wrinkles around her mouth sat. Her expression soured when she noticed Roman dripping puddles on her carpet, and Leandros saw where the lines had come from. "Can I help you gentlemen?"

"I apologize for my colleague's state. We're here to speak with a Ms. Theodosia Fairfax."

The woman arched a thick eyebrow. "This is a ladies-only establishment, I'm afraid. There are no men permitted past this point before visiting hours. You'll have to come back this afternoon."

"Ah," Leandros said. Isobel certainly hadn't mentioned this.

"If I don't quite consider myself a man, can *I* go in?" Roman asked. His curls were plastered to his forehead, his white shirt to his chest, and Leandros couldn't bear to look at him for more than a few seconds at a time.

The woman pursed her lips. "Are you a *lady*?"

Roman laughed. "No."

"Then no. I don't know what sort of company Ms. Fairfax is keeping, but if you or she have any problems with our rules—"

"We mean no trouble, I assure you," Leandros said. Like he'd done with Isobel, he dipped into a formal bow. "I'm Prince Leandros Nochdvor of Alfheimr, son of Lorens Nochdvor and nephew to the king. I'm happy to provide identification if you'd like to see it. I'll only be in town two more days and wished to speak with Ms. Fairfax on a matter of business, but if this is inconvenient for you, I'll rearrange my schedule so I can return during your visiting hours."

"Wait," the woman said when Leandros turned to leave. She'd straightened up during his introduction, nervously smoothing her skirt and tucking her hair behind her pointed ears. She glanced at the rain out the window and pursed her lips. "While the rules are quite firm, they only apply to the main house and not the front parlor. It's not our standard practice, but you can wait there while I give Ms. Fairfax a call."

"That would be wonderful, thank you," Leandros said. When the woman smiled, he didn't bother smiling back. He'd learned that outside Alfheimr, people's expectations of him varied drastically before and after finding out who he was. Before, they expected assimilation. They expected him to behave like them. After, they wanted the perfect picture of an Alfheimr alfar: the more aloof and unreadable, the better.

"It's just through those doors," she said, gesturing. As she turned away, she murmured, "Goodness. A prince, in *my* boardinghouse."

The parlor was a wide, comfortable room large enough to seat upwards of a dozen. Today, though, four women played cards and another sat on a sofa and read, but the place was otherwise empty. They had their pick of seating, and Roman chose a private table at the back, away from the women who were now whispering and casting curious glances their way.

A faintly floral smell filled the air. It stuck in Leandros' nostrils and threatened to give him a headache.

"That was clever," Roman said, once they'd settled. "Using your name to get her to help, I mean."

Leandros shrugged. Maybe it *was* clever, but it felt like cheating.

They sat in uncomfortable silence until the alfar woman arrived, giving them—Leandros—a nervous curtsy. "Ms. Fairfax is on her way down. I'm very sorry for my cold reception earlier, Your Highness. I've had some issues recently with the ladies sneaking guests in, and I had no idea Ms. Fairfax had such important friends."

The word *important* made Leandros' mood darken, and Roman quickly jumped in. "This is a lovely room, Ms...?"

"Taylor," the woman supplied.

"Ms. Taylor," Roman repeated, giving her one of his most charming smiles.

"You're very kind, sir, thank you. If this place had not been left to me, I like to think I would have made an excellent interior designer. Oh, but can I get you anything? Tea? Coffee? I think we may have some biscuits from—"

"Why don't you let me take care of my own guests, Ms. Taylor?" a soft voice asked. The woman who stepped up to join their group wasn't what Leandros would've expected of a prospective guard. She was nearly as tall as him, but slender, with a neatly pressed dress and stark white gloves. Her brown hair was perfectly curled, done up in a loose pompadour with artful locks left down to frame her face.

"There you are," Ms. Taylor tutted. "You shouldn't keep a prince waiting, dear."

"I wouldn't have, if I'd known he was coming!" the girl protested. She turned bright green eyes on Leandros as she sized him up—only, she didn't do it in the way Leandros was used to. Instead of looking *at* him, she looked at the space *around* him. Only when she was satisfied with that did she meet his eyes. "Theodosia Fairfax, at your service, but my friends call me Thea. I am sorry about the wait."

Leandros stood. "There was hardly any wait to speak of," he said. He turned to pull a chair out for her but forgot about his injured hand until the last moment. Quickly tucking it behind his back, he pulled the chair out single-handedly, instead. If Thea noticed, she was kind enough not to comment.

"Roman Hallisey," Roman said, holding a hand out.

Thea shook it with a smile. "Pleasure. That'll be all, Ms. Taylor. I believe His Highness would like to speak with me privately." Once the older woman was gone, Thea leaned in and whispered, "And sorry to you, Mr. Hallisey. I know you wanted to take her up on her offer of biscuits, but if I'd followed her out to fetch them I would've been scolded something fierce."

Roman blinked, evidently surprised, then smiled. "I can do without," he whispered back. Back at a normal volume, he said, "She seems strict."

"She means well, and she really does care about her residents. She has a very strong sense of propriety, but she was also the only one who agreed to take me in when I first got here. I'm very grateful."

"Where are you from?"

"Tanisos, a little port not far from Histrios," Thea said, smiling.

"I know it," Roman said. He didn't so much as flinch at the word *Histrios*. Leandros, who'd stiffened, wondered how he could be so nonchalant. Roman being beside him, alive, didn't stop the familiar wave of grief that crashed over Leandros at the name. Suddenly having Roman back didn't save him from drowning.

He cleared his throat. "I have a question as well, Ms. Fairfax, before we get to business. Exactly how old are you?"

"Twenty-five," Thea said, drawing herself up taller.

Leandros looked at Roman. "Is that supposed to be a lot?"

Roman raised an eyebrow. "You're asking *me*?"

"It's enough," Thea said. "At least enough to—well, what would you need me for, exactly? I spoke with Mrs. Ranulf on the phone, but she didn't tell me much. I've been keeping up with the news, of course, so I do know what's been happening with your—well. I'm just not sure where I fit in. My condolences, by the way."

Leandros wasn't sure where this odd girl fit in, either.

"There are people who are unhappy with how Unity and Alfheimr are going about rescuing the king," Roman explained, "And there are people within Unity who are unhappy with how *Leandros* is going about it, specifically. Someone hurt him yesterday, and we're not convinced they won't try again, so we're looking for a guard to stay by his side."

"Oh," Thea breathed.

"Just know going into it that you'll need to be able to act quickly. Leandros loves cuddling up to his enemies, these days, so you might not get much warning."

Leandros scowled at him. "Oh, is that what I'm doing? At least if *they* stab me through the heart, it won't be when my back is turned."

Roman winced.

"Wow. Mrs. Ranulf wasn't joking about you two," Thea said.

"What does *that* mean?" Roman asked.

"Oh," Thea said, eyes wide. "Nothing."

Leandros pinched the bridge of his nose. He took a deep, steadying breath. "Do you have any sort of fighting experience, Ms. Fairfax?"

"Not at all, but I understand why I was recommended to you," Thea said brightly. "I'm rosanin. With my gift, I can read people's intentions. If they're acting out of greed or righteousness, love or hatred, I can tell."

"How?" Roman asked, eyes wide.

"Everyone in the world has an aura—a sort of glow around them that only I can see. Depending on the emotion, the color, texture, and brightness vary. It's hard to interpret, sometimes, but I'm very good."

"That's how you knew I wanted the biscuits," Roman guessed. Cutting to the core of it, he asked, "And you could tell if someone wanted to harm Leandros?"

"Sort of. I can tell if someone *might* harm him. It seems silly, but it's an important distinction. I see the emotion and not the action, but in order for me to see it, it must be *tied* to an action. You opened your mouth to answer Ms. Taylor's offer, and I saw that you wanted something. I also saw a bit of hunger, and guessing your thoughts from there wasn't difficult. Another good example is love. If you loved me but weren't doing anything about it, I wouldn't see anything. But as soon as you held the door for me or gave me a gift or even looked at me out of the corner of your eye, I could see the golden glow" Thea explained. "So if someone approaches Prince Nochdvor with malice, I'll know and be able to warn you."

Leandros and Roman shared a look. Without a word exchanged between them, they were in agreement: she was perfect. The Enforcers were trained to be able to spot dangerous individuals, but Thea *wasn't* dangerous. "What if someone wants to hurt me because they love someone who told them to?" Leandros asked.

"People are made up of more than one feeling at a time. It's what makes us people, messy as it is. I'd see both the love and the ill wishes."

Leandros nodded. Curious, he asked, "What do you see when you look at me?"

"Um. Are you sure you want to know? Some people don't take it well."

"I am, and I can."

"Don't say I didn't warn you," Thea said. She eyed Leandros. "You have a lot of emotions jumbled together, more than I've ever seen from a single person. They're mostly shades of anger—at yourself, more than at anyone else."

"Ah," Leandros said, as calmly as he could manage. Feeling Roman's eyes on him, he gestured vaguely at Roman with his braced hand. "And him? Selfishness? Cowardice? Apathy?"

"Mostly guilt." Thea squinted at Roman, and Roman crossed his arms in front of his chest as if that might stop her from seeing. "Everything is strangely muted with him, so it's hard to tell. I don't know! I thought you wanted a guard, not a couple's counselor." As soon as the words left her mouth, she quickly corrected, "Sorry! I'm sorry. That was rude. Please don't fire me; I really need this job."

Despite himself, Leandros smiled. "We haven't even hired you yet, technically. This will be dangerous. Do you understand that?"

"Before I answer, how much is the pay?"

"I can offer you fifty triems before departure and another fifty upon our return to Gallonten—or Alfheim, as the case may be," Leandros said.

Thea's eyes went comically wide. She nodded so hard a new lock of hair fell to hang in her face. "Yes, yes. Danger understood," she said with a slow-spreading smile. "Did I mention that Danger happens to be my middle name? I can sign waivers to prove it. And a contract, too."

Roman stifled a laugh.

"I'm sure you'll have to, knowing our Unity Coordinator," Leandros said. "But don't accept until I've told you all the details."

"Well, I'm all ears," Thea said, clasping her hands together on the table and looking every part the dutiful student. "Oh! But first, let me get us some of those biscuits."

After briefing Leandros' new guard, Roman and Leandros walked back to the Ranulfs' flat together, sharing Leandros' umbrella. "She'll be fun to have around," Roman said.

"A fine sentiment," Leandros replied, "But I don't have time these days for fun."

Roman stopped. When Leandros kept going, so, too, did the circle of protection his umbrella gave off. It left Roman standing in the pouring rain, frowning after his once-friend. "Leandros," he called, waiting until Leandros had also stopped to say, "You've changed."

Leandros didn't turn to face him right away, watching water run over the cobblestone instead. A bitter smile rose to his lips. With just him and Roman out here, alone, he saw no need to restrain it. "If I have," he said, turning, "It's your fault."

Roman bit his lip. "I never meant for you to think—"

Leandros crossed to him in two long strides. "Oh, you didn't? You know that the rest of the world thinks I *killed you,* Roman, don't you? You understand that my best friend was shot before my eyes and *I* had to take the blame for it?"

Roman fell back a step, eyes wide. "I—"

"Don't. I don't want excuses," Leandros said, cutting him off. He didn't let Roman slip away, closing the distance between them with another step forward. Thea had been right about shades of anger, and this—this simmering in the wake of another abandonment and betrayal—sat closest to his heart. It threatened to boil over, so Leandros lowered the umbrella, plunging himself into the freezing rain. He was *more* than just the anger. He was determined to be more.

"It's been sixty years, Roman," Leandros continued, softly. He searched Roman's face. "Have you been alone all this time?"

Roman was clearly thrown by the sudden change in Leandros, his dark eyes briefly widening. "What?" he asked. That vulnerability was gone in an instant, though, replaced by a coy smile. "Why? Would you be jealous if I said no?"

It was meant to push him away, to stoke the anger, but Leandros only shook his head. "I'd be *worried* if you said yes. You've never done well with loneliness."

Roman's lips parted in surprise. Raindrops dripped off his curls and ran down his cheeks, and Leandros raised the umbrella again, ensuring they were both under it. He'd figured out what had been bothering him about Roman, the monumental change that he hadn't been able to see: this person before him was a ghost, after all. This was never his Roman. Leandros could only assume *his* Roman really had died in Histrios.

When this Roman smiled, it was a pained imitation of the smile Leandros knew, an act put on for the benefit of everyone around him. When this Roman laughed, it was only an echo of the real Roman's, of Leandros' favorite sound in the world. When this Roman thought no one was looking, his eyes were dim. He reminded Leandros of the Roman he'd seem during their first meeting: distant, defeated, empty.

Roman was right here, but it didn't ease the grief that had long settled in Leandros' heart. Roman was *right here*, but Leandros still mourned him.

Roman looked left and right, as if he was planning an escape. "After everything I—You—" His expression crumpled. "Can't you go back to hating me?"

"Is that really what you want?" Leandros asked.

"It would be easier," Roman replied. While Leandros agreed, that wasn't an answer. Roman also hadn't answered Leandros' earlier question about being alone, and with Roman, that avoidance was an answer in and of itself.

"What about that girl—the actress?" Leandros asked.

Roman's eyes widened again. "How did you—ugh, *Gareth*." He flushed and ran a hand through his hair, mussing up his curls and shaking water everywhere. "My time with her was short, even for a normal human's standards. She was great, but I think we both just wanted to stave off the loneliness. It was never…more than that. At least, not for me."

Leandros looked away. If he continued to look at Roman while standing so close, he might do something foolish. "Well," he sniffed. "She was too young for you, anyway."

Caught by surprise, Roman laughed. It still wasn't quite the laugh Leandros remembered, but it was closer. "You know that you'd be too young for me too, then, right?"

The moment Roman uttered the words, they both knew they had been a mistake. It had been sixty years since Histrios, but the last words Leandros had said to Roman were still branded in both of their minds. This came uncomfortably close to addressing them, and Leandros stiffened. Roman flushed further. "I didn't mean—"

But Leandros held a hand to stop him. His pride stung, his anger burned, and he couldn't stop the words that came out of his mouth next: "I can assure you, Roman, that I haven't the slightest interest in being your *friend,* let alone anything more."

Roman recoiled like he'd been struck, his expression twisting with pain before settling into hurt. "Leandros—"

"Don't," Leandros said, already backing away, banishing Roman back to the rain. He turned to leave. "Don't try to be my friend again, not now. If you ever cared about me, just let me mourn in peace."

Chapter Twenty-Eight

Maebhe stepped out of Lyryma Forest and sank to her knees. The open air, the familiar slopes of her home valley, and the silhouette of Orean glittering in the distance overwhelmed her. She ran her fingers through the grass, dewy and damp, and felt the cold soak through the cloak she'd borrowed from Roman.

Íde crouched beside her and laid a gentle hand on her shoulder. Her smile was amused, but Maebhe could see the relief in it. "Are you all right?"

Maebhe grunted and flopped the rest of the way onto the ground. Kieran sat on her other side, Íde joining after a moment's hesitation. Finally, they'd made it home.

The group sat at the top of a large hill, the strange, magical realm of Lyryma simply a wall of trees behind them, now. Out here, there was no dangerous foliage, no strange songs or red dragons. Ahead of them stretched Creae Valley, the air open and the grassy fields spotted with patches of golden flowers. Maebhe could just make out the tree-covered hills of Rossmor Forest in the distance. She loved Rossmor. The trees were such a respectable size.

To their left sat Orean, built between two mountains and walled in with the valley's famous silver brick. From this distance, they made

Orean shine. Illyon sat at the other end of the valley, smaller than Orean and not nearly as sparkling.

"Why are we stopping?" Leileas asked. She lurked in the forest's shadows and wrinkled her nose at the thought of leaving it. "We're so close."

"Leileas, just enjoy having a break from that damned forest," Drys said.

"I *like* this damned forest. We don't have to see any of that." Leileas waved distastefully at the smoke rising from Illyon's chimneys.

"And we don't have to deal with dragons that are supposed to be extinct," Maebhe countered.

"Neither do we, normally. There is something wrong, and the problem is not only with Lyryma."

Maebhe couldn't disagree.

"Enough of this gloomy talk," Kieran said, standing. "Let's keep moving. The sooner we warn Orean, the more time King Riordan will have to prepare for Unity's arrival."

Pushing to her feet as well, Maebhe ran to Leileas and jumped, clambering up the frìth's side to perch herself on Leileas' shoulder. Leileas let out an amused snort and, together, the group started down the hill.

Soon, even Leileas had to crane her neck to look up at Orean's walls. A line of officers waited for them at the edge of the city, having seen the massive frìth coming down the hill. Their uniforms and caps were all identical, only one of them set apart by a gold cape. Kieran had the same cape sitting in his closet.

"Kieran, is that you?" the gold-caped individual called when they were close enough. He raised a hand to shield his eyes from the suns and squinted at the group, his round face almost entirely covered in dark, swirling birthmarks. "And Íde, too! We weren't expecting you back until winter! Where's Maebhe?"

Maebhe waved from her perch on Leileas' shoulder. "Hello, Captain Song!"

The orinian captain looked up, his eyes widening. "Maebhe! Who…who do you have with you?"

"This is Leileas, and that's Drys. They're friends of ours," Kieran said. "Song, we need to see King Riordan immediately. It's important."

"You know these people?" Leileas asked Kieran, bending and examining Captain Song with open curiosity, her large, shaggy flat face only a few feet from his. Maebhe took the chance to jump down.

"We work together," Kieran explained.

"Your name is Song?" Leileas asked approvingly. "Kieran is correct, Song. We need to see your king."

Captain Song nodded weakly, trying not to lean away from Leileas' scrutiny. He beckoned one of his officers over. "Tell his Majesty to expect us."

The officer nodded and, with a fearful look at Leileas, dashed off, then Song and his procession led them through the city gates. Once inside, Maebhe finally shook the weight from everything she'd seen and done on this journey off her shoulders. Back in these familiar streets, Unity could not hurt her. Gallonten was so very far away.

In terms of design, Orean was an unusual city in that it was more like a city built *around* another city. There was the old city and the new: the old city was walled off, separated by deep canals. It had stood since the Great War, probably longer, and was where the king and his court conducted their business. Only authorized personnel were allowed to enter, and that was partially for the public's own good—it was full of crumbling old buildings that had survived millennia only to be eroded by them—and partially to protect the king's privacy. It also kept people away from the dark castle at the city's center.

The new city was the Orean that had grown around the old. It was the city that made up Maebhe's whole world. Because of the hilly landscape, its streets were convoluted. To reach the palace, they'd have to walk up and down hills, around bends and through neighborhoods. It was a shame Leileas couldn't fit in a carriage, because Maebhe's feet were killing her.

They were paraded through the new city's streets, orinians everywhere stopping what they were doing to point and stare at the frìth and the faerie. When they passed a group of children playing in the street, the children peered up at Leileas with wide eyes and open mouths, and Leileas paused to peer back. "They're so small," she said to Maebhe, in the same voice Maebhe used when she held a kitten.

The other unusual thing about Orean was the way it had expanded. Rather than build further and further down the mountain, Orean had built upward. Modern buildings stacked on top of old ones until Orean became a hodge-podge of architectural styles and towering structures. It was colorful, too, so much more than Gallonten. It was colorful not just in the red and blue rooftops of the new city, but in flags, signs, lanterns. Even the clothes lines stretching from house to house were vibrant, with banners and silk ribbons hanging off them. Leileas had to duck whenever they encountered the latter.

When they reached the old city's walls, they encountered more guards. Maebhe thought their parade would stop there, but instead, Captain Song led them through the gates and over the canals, then down the quiet, paved paths to King Riordan's palace. Maebhe peered excitedly around as they walked, looking at everything she could find *except* for the castle that loomed behind the squat palace. All of Orean liked to pretend *that* place didn't exist. It was a sinister old thing, char-blackened and ancient. Its eastern wing had been torn away, leaving its innards exposed. Maebhe guessed it had been centuries, at least, since any glass sat in the windows, and now ivy climbed freely up and through them into the shadow and darkness.

Captain Song didn't so much as glance at it, leading the group inside the palace and down long, echoing hallways lined with statues. Surprisingly, the ceilings were high enough for Leileas, who only had to duck in the twisting stairways. When they reached the king's chambers, the captain had them wait outside while he went in.

Maebhe surreptitiously wiped her palms on her trousers. She'd never met King Riordan before; he mostly kept to his palace and the old city, to his wives and his parties and his wine. She'd never done anything this important before. It all hit her all at once, here in the grand halls of the king's palace. Their whole trip back was for *this*. It was to get *here*.

When Captain Song returned, she wordlessly followed her companions up to the king's chambers. They were given a double-door entrance, palace guards on either side watching them pass before shutting the doors solidly behind them. Maebhe's ears flattened to her head. They found themselves in a round room, with tall windows circling them all around. Some of them were propped open, making soft blue curtains billow in from the east. From here, Maebhe could see Tellaos' castle even better. She was so distracted by it that she almost missed the king himself.

King Riordan was settled in an armchair far from those eastern windows, far from that blackened castle. The modern furniture seemed out of place in the otherwise ancient palace, but the man him-self did not. He was an older man with silver-streaked hair and weath-ered skin that was highlighted by light birthmarks. He stood when they entered, folding his delicate hands in front of him and inclining his head in greeting.

Kieran bowed and Maebhe and Íde quickly followed. Maebhe's heartbeat pounded in her ears.

"Rise," King Riordan said in a voice younger than his appearance suggested. It didn't match the lines around his eyes or the tired slump of his shoulders. "It's been many years since one of the frìth has visited us here," he said to Leileas, who had managed to worm her way through the door. "You are welcome, of course, but what brings you out of your forest? I hope nothing is wrong."

Leileas pressed a fist to her chest and bowed. "Your subjects' story brings me here, Your Majesty."

King Riordan looked at Kieran, Íde, and Maebhe with a raised eyebrow, his stare making Maebhe want to inch behind her brother. He beckoned Kieran forward. "I know you. You're a captain of my guard, are you not?"

"Yes, Your Majesty."

"What is this story, then?"

Kieran cleared his throat. "Are you aware that the alfar King Nochdvor is missing, sire?"

Riordan's thin lips pressed together. "I am."

"You know?" Maebhe asked before she could stop herself, tone accusatory. Kieran shot her a horrified look, but Riordan only glanced between the twins with mild curiosity. "Your sister?" he guessed.

Before Kieran could answer, Maebhe dropped into another hasty bow. "Maebhe Cairn, Your Highness. Kieran, Íde, and I just returned from a holiday in Gallonten, where your people are being rounded up and thrown in prisons."

Riordan stared at her, looked her slowly up and down. Also at odds with his appearance, his eyes were bright. "Explain yourself, Ms. Cairn."

It was Kieran who answered, taking a step back in front of his sister. "Shortly after the Nochdvors arrived in Gallonten, we were ambushed in our hotel by Gallontean Police. Maebhe escaped, but Íde and I were taken to Unity Island, where we were questioned by Unity officials. They thought we were spies."

From there, Kieran went on to explain their questioning, escape, and the journey through Lyryma. When he reached the end of the story, Íde fumbled in her bag for the newspaper they'd brought with them from Gallonten, one of many that blamed Orean for Nochdvor's disappearance. She offered it up to the king alongside Roman's letter. King Riordan took the papers with him to one of the windows, his back to the group while he read. Over his shoulder, the whole valley was visible. Maebhe wondered if Riordan had been here, looking out at Illyon, the day the alfar king had been kidnapped.

"It was Egil who rescued us. The frìth confirmed it. He's alive, and that letter is from him," Kieran said. "It explains everything he knows about Unity's plan."

Riordan scoffed and tossed the newspaper aside, onto a side table. "They can turn our city upside down, if they like, but they won't find their blasted king," he spat. He turned to them, inclined his head in a deeper bow than before. "It was good of you to bring me this information. I'll see that you're all duly compensated."

Relief flooded through Maebhe even as a part of her insisted it couldn't possibly be so simple. Was she really free of this burden? Was it done? "What will you do about this?" she asked.

"Maebhe," Kieran hissed, but the king held up a hand to silence him. He approached, slowly, and took Maebhe's hand. He smoothed it over reassuringly and said, "Ms. Cairn, I can't imagine how stressful this last week has been for you. You may rest easy, now, knowing that I will handle it. Do not concern yourself with the details."

Reluctantly dropping her hand, he turned to Drys and Leileas next. "Will you be staying in Orean?"

"Yes," Drys said immediately, practically *scowling* at the king. Bemused, Maebhe wondered what Riordan had done to offend them.

Leileas shook her head. "My message has been delivered and I must return to Home." Her expression darkened, then, her thick brows furrowing. "There are matters I must report to my people."

Riordan nodded. "I thank you for coming. You are welcome again in Orean anytime."

Leileas repeated her salute from earlier. "And know that if you need Home's assistance at any time, you need only ask."

Outside the palace, Leileas said her goodbyes. She crouched so that she was eye level with the orinians and said in her low, gentle voice, "It was an honor to meet you all. I'll miss you, little ones. Please come visit us in Home whenever you like."

Maebhe threw her arms around the frith's neck. "We'll miss you too, Leileas. Be careful going back through that forest alone, please."

Leileas pulled back and did her strange, grimacing smile, and that was the end of it. She was led back to the city gates by Captain Song, and Drys didn't join her.

"Drys, that's your debt repaid, isn't it?" Maebhe said to them. "Why aren't you going back to Home?"

"Are you trying to get rid of me, Mae-*vuh*? My debt to Egil is repaid, but I think you owe me a debt of your own," Drys said, throwing an arm around her shoulders and starting back toward the new city. Maebhe laughed, leaned into their side, and then pushed them gently away—it wasn't a rejection, not outright. Drys brightened, seeming to realize as much. "Really, I'd just like to explore Orean," they said. They looked around, their eyes catching on the old black castle.

"You're not exploring *there*. In fact, none of you are coming to the old city again," Kieran said sternly, following their gaze.

"What! Why am I being included in this?" Maebhe exclaimed while, at the same time, Drys asked, "Why not?"

"Because it's not allowed. And because *you* get in trouble wherever you go," Kieran said, giving Maebhe a pointed look. "Drys, you're welcome to stay with us, but don't expect us to be gracious hosts. I think I'm going to sleep for the next week."

Kieran, Íde, and Drys began walking away, following the path Leileas had departed in, but Maebhe hesitated and looked back at the darkened castle.

"Maebhe?" Kieran called. "Are you coming or not?"

Maebhe tore her eyes away. They dropped to the palace, and out of curiosity, Maebhe looked for King Riordan's tower. Just as she found it, blue curtains were drawn hastily shut. "I'm coming."

———

"Come along, Ofelia," Isobel said, holding the sleepy five-year-old's hand as they walked along. The rain had stopped, but a terrible fog had replaced it. The air was damp, heavy, and Gallonten was quiet. They passed only a few others on the streets.

"You really don't have to come all this way, Boop," Gareth said.

"We're seeing you out of the city," Isobel said. "It's the least we can do. Who knows when we'll see you next."

Roman and Leandros, walking ahead of them, kept quiet. When they finally stopped so Gareth could say his goodbyes to Isobel and Ofelia, they kept their distance. Things were awkward and uncomfortable between them, still; they'd spoken as little as possible since they'd gone to meet Theodosia Fairfax two days before, and since the bitter confrontation that had followed.

Roman watched Gareth. He and Isobel were always so gentle with each other, so tender. Watching them made him hurt in a way that felt both confusing and warm. He stiffened in surprise when Isobel came over and hugged him goodbye, whispering in his ear, "Promise you'll keep him safe."

"I promise," Roman whispered back before they broke apart. When they did, he noticed tears gathering in Isobel's eyes. She wiped them quickly, turning to Ofelia and holding out her hand.

"Come along, Fe. It's time for us to go home; we'll see your father again soon."

Roman, Gareth, and Leandros watched them disappear into the city smog. When they were fully out of sight, Leandros sighed and smoothed out his coat. He really did wear mourning blacks, like Gareth had said. Roman was just having trouble believing it was really for him. "Are you all right, Mr. Ranulf?" Leandros asked.

"Hm?" Gareth said, finally tearing his eyes from the place his wife and daughter had vanished. "Oh, yes. Quite. As right as I can be."

Leandros nodded, then gave Gareth's arm an awkward pat. "The others are waiting. We should be off."

"Wait!" a distant voice called. "Wait for me!"

A young woman in a crisp dress emerged from the fog, running toward them and waving her straw hat excitedly. She wasn't exactly dressed for the journey, but Thea Fairfax struck Roman as someone who would dress however she wanted, regardless of the occasion. She was out of breath by the time she caught up to them, but that didn't dim her bright grin. "I passed Mrs. Ranulf and Ofelia on my way, and Isobel said that if I hurried, I might catch up with you. I'm glad I did; I hate showing up to things alone."

Leandros offered her a small smile. "So do I. Now please, let's go before anyone else delays us."

Far outside the city, Unity's security team, half a dozen horses, and three loaded wagons waited. There were no Unity or Alfheimr symbols on any of their belongings, nothing to give away the official nature of their mission. They looked like any other group of merchants or travelers preparing for a journey, even the Unity workers helping them load their supplies dressed in plain, unassuming clothes.

Eresh saw them first, waving with his clipboard and jogging over, looking tired but as excited as Thea. "Good morning! Ms. Corscia and I have been here for hours already. It didn't quite feel real even as of yesterday, but it certainly does now, don't you think? You've packed everything you need, all of you? You haven't forgotten anything?" He looked over the group, counting heads. "All of your bags arrived ahead of you, so you needn't worry about that."

"Is this everyone?" Thea asked Roman in a loud whisper.

"Oh! I forgot you haven't met anyone yet." Eresh spun to try to locate the rest of the team. He and Thea had met the day before, when Leandros brought her and Roman to the island for paperwork. Eresh had been cold and jealous of Thea for about an hour, and then he'd gotten over it, finally finding in her someone who matched his energy. He pointed. "There's Ivor Linde, Aaror Thomason, and Eftychia O'Neill, of the security team. Trinity Smith, our negotiator, and Cathwright, a skilled barrister. Ms. Corscia is also around here somewhere. It's a lot of names, I'm sure, but we'll all grow much closer on the journey."

"Gods, I hope not," Roman murmured. When Eresh and Leandros turned away to discuss business, he asked Thea, "What do you see when you look at them all?"

"Nothing suspicious yet," Thea said. "Ms. Smith and Cathwright are reserved, but it's just nerves."

"And Mr. Ochoa?"

"Him, I'm not sure about. There's something flickering under the surface. His motives aren't what they seem; he's driven by some sort of duty. He means no harm, at least."

"A duty to Unity?" Gareth asked.

"Maybe," Thea said, though she didn't sound sure. "Oh!"

A slouched, languid alfar stopped in front of Roman. "So *you're* Hallisey," he said. He wore heavy leather, two pistols at his hips, and an eye patch over one eye. The two other members of the security team flanked him: Eftychia O'Neill on his right, draped in bright fabrics, and a broad, scowling man with a bow and quiver on his left. "You might not remember, but we met at the Ranulfs' place, the other day."

"I remember," Roman said. He smiled at Ivor, then at Eftychia and Aaror in turn. Thea tugged urgently on his sleeve, her eyes wide in warning. "That was right before you let me in to see your Magistrate without even checking if I carried a weapon. I'm sure that went well for you, after the fact."

Ivor's expression darkened. He sneered not just at Roman, but at Thea beside him. "You don't seem so scary, old man. Let's go toe-to-toe, you and I, and maybe I'll teach you a thing or two about picking fights you can't win. You can even bring your little dormouse—she looks like she could throw a better punch than y—"

"Ivor," said a cold voice. Thea jumped in surprise, finding a woman beside her where there had been none moments before. Evelyne Corscia didn't look her way, her eyes locked on Roman like he'd attack if she even dared to blink. "What did I say about talking to him?"

"You're not in charge of me, Evelyne," Ivor replied.

"I am, at least for this journey," she said, her voice as gentle as a whisper. Eresh and Leandros had paused their conversation, as had Trin and Cathwright. The whole team watched this exchange. As soon as Evelyne realized this, she finally tore her eyes from Roman and turned Leandros. "We're ready for final inventory checks, Captain. Eresh."

"Yes, of course," Eresh said quickly. "The captain and I were just wrapping up."

Evelyne nodded. "Eftychia, Aaror, go secure the last of the luggage," she said crossing her arms. As she did, the movement highlighted old battle scars that criss-crossed her bare arms. When

Ivor tried to pass her, she held one of them out to bar his way. "You—apologize to the girl."

Ivor looked like he'd been slapped. "Excuse me?"

"She's the captain's assistant. She's not a part of this, and you will not involve her in it."

"Evie," Eftychia said with a pout, "I'm sure Ivor didn't mean anything by it. Dormouse is actually a very cute—"

Evelyne raised an eyebrow, the simple expression making Chia bite her lip mid-sentence.

"My apologies, Ms. Fairfax," Ivor said, sweeping into an exaggerated bow. "Big day, you know. Lots to worry about. I didn't mean to take that out on you."

"You're forgiven," Thea said, half-hidden behind Roman. With that, and with another glare at both Roman and Evelyne, Ivor swept away, Aaror at his side and Eftychia skipping after him.

"Tell me if he bothers you again," Evelyne told Thea. "Or give him a fright yourself. It's not difficult. I'm sure you've got it in you."

"Oh! Yes. Wow. Thank you. That was…" Thea stammered, then trailed off with a cough. Behind her freckles, her cheeks were bright red. Finally, she managed, "Inspirational. You're very kind."

Evelyne blinked, surprised, then smiled. It softened the harsh planes of her face, almost overshadowing the hawklike set of her gaze. Beside Thea, Roman raised an eyebrow.

"Thank you for intervening, Ms. Corscia," Leandros said.

"It wasn't for you," Evelyne said, cold once more. She looked from Roman to Leandros. "I hope you're ready for what's ahead, Captain. Eresh, inventory. Come."

Eresh and Gareth left with her, leaving Leandros, Roman, and Thea alone. "You should have told me you had a history with Ms. Corscia," Leandros hissed.

"You don't—," Roman started, his eyes wide. He schooled his

expression quickly and shrugged. "It's nothing of note. Not more than I have with any other Enforcer."

Leandros narrowed his eyes at Roman, then turned to Thea. "Ms. Fairfax, can you tell when people are lying?"

"I'm not lying!" Roman said.

"I sometimes can, I sometimes can't. It depends on *why* they're lying. But if Roman's lying, I can't tell," Thea said, staring over at where Eresh and the security team were working.

Leandros sighed. "Fine. And the security team?"

"They do want to hurt someone," Thea said, turning her attention back to Leandros. Her gaze slid, then, over to Roman. "For now, Your Highness, it's not you."

Leandros drew in a sharp breath. To Roman, fervent and emphatic, he said, "Be *careful*." And with that, he was also gone, rejoining Eresh and Evelyne. As soon as he was out of earshot, Thea asked, "So what's the story?"

"Story?" Roman asked.

"You were *definitely* lying."

Roman winced. "Thank you for not telling him."

"I can see that you're trying to protect Ms. Corscia," Thea said. "I don't know form what or why, but that's the only reason I didn't tell."

Roman nodded, avoiding Thea eyes. "I'll tell you the story later."

"Liar," Thea said, smiling.

At that, Roman smiled back. "Only sometimes."

Within the hour, Unity's team finally left Gallonten behind, the road unwinding from Unity's capital leading them on toward Lyryma Forest and, beyond that, Illyon.

———

A whistle blew, followed by the crashing of metal and a release of steam as Dinara strolled down the train platform, suitcase in hand. She was always loathe to leave Gallonten, and no amount of heartbreak felt here could change that.

"Hurry up, Di, or we'll leave you behind!" Gemma called out an open window, the whistle blowing again and cutting off anything more she had to say.

Dinara scanned the train for an open car. As she hurried toward it, though, she nearly collided with someone, catching their shoulder with her own.

"Oh, I'm so sorry!" Dinara said hurriedly. At the sight of the woman's face, she gasped. The upper half of it was hidden beneath a veiled hat, but Dinara saw enough of her to know she was orinian. She had the birthmarks, though there was something *wrong* with them — they were like open wounds, an almost-liquid orange glow swirling in the gaps. Horror froze her in place, and she could only stare.

The woman turning to leave, though, spurred her into action. "Wait!" she called. She caught the woman by the wrist; even through her gloves, she could feel how *cold* the woman was. It seeped through the thin leather and crept up her arm. "Are you coming or going, ma'am?"

The woman only tipped her head down to hide more of her face.

"It's okay, I won't tell anyone," Dinara whispered. She understood why the woman wouldn't want anyone seeing her; people would already view her as suspect just for who she was. Such sinister-looking scars would make it worse. But she seemed to have been heading toward the station exit, and if she made it into the city proper, Dinara wouldn't be able to help her. "You shouldn't go to Gallonten. It's not safe for orinians right now."

"Why not?" the woman asked, tasting the word as it rolled off her tongue. Her accent was unusual; it certainly wasn't like Maebhe, Kieran, and Íde's had been. It sounded stiffer, older.

"Haven't you heard? The King of Alfheimr is missing. Unity is launching an investigation into Orean. There might be a war."

The woman took an alarmed step back, raising her head enough for Dinara to see wide, glowing eyes. "Why warn me?"

"You mean because I'm sapien?" Dinara asked. "That shouldn't matter. I don't want you to get hurt if I can help it."

The woman frowned at Dinara, a delicate furrow appearing between her brows. She looked like she had another question, but the screech of the train whistle and the low creak of wheels grinding into motion made Dinara jump. "I'm sorry; I have to go!" she called. Pressing her hat to her head so it wouldn't fly off, she ran and jumped onto the nearest train car even as the massive locomotive began to roll out of the station. She landed on the narrow stairs, her heavy skirts whipping around her, and turned just in time to see the strange woman—still watching her—disappear from view as they left the station behind.

Dinara shook herself and continued into the cabin, smiling when she saw she'd chosen the car the costume crates had all been stuffed into. She recognized the markings on one as containing the Players' masks and tried not to think of the last time she'd rummaged through that crate.

"So much for a quiet trip," a voice said, making Dinara jump.

"Tabia! You startled me," Dinara said. The older actress was nestled between two crates, a book in her hands. "I promise not to bother you too much."

As they left Gallonten behind, Dinara returned to the narrow stairs between cars. Months earlier, when the Webhon Players had wound their way south, the world had been green. Now, while the long grasses still swayed, the trees recognized the approach of autumn. The leaves had changed in preparation, like wildfire in color and scope.

It reflected how Dinara felt inside: changing, readying herself for something new. Holding onto the door's handle, Dinara leaned out of the car as far as she dared. She laughed when the wind hit her, blowing her curls all around and tugging at her skirts. It was cold, but far colder where she was going—north to Adondai, the capital of the Sheman province.

There, the whole world awaited Dinara, if she could only gather the courage to chase it.

CHAPTER TWENTY-NINE

ROMAN SHIVERED AND RUBBED HIS HANDS TOGETHER to generate friction. The first real chill of autumn had struck, made more bitingly cold by the suddenness of it. The cold stung his fingers and cheeks, and when he breathed, it clawed into his lungs, painful and purifying. Summer had lost its footing, and because the universe was cruel, it had done so on the very day they'd left Gallonten. Perhaps Atiuh saw what they were doing and disapproved of their mission.

Roman snorted at the thought.

No one else seemed bothered by the cold, but they sat nearer the fire than Roman. He alone kept his distance, watching and thinking. They'd set up a small camp, their modest tents surrounding them and the captain's trailer parked nearby. The trees of Lyryma towered over the team on one side, but despite their looming presence, spirits around the fire ran high. They always did, at the start of journeys like this. Even the coldest among them, Evelyne and Aaror, smiled as they listened to Eresh tell a story about Representative Biro tripping at Unity's spring ball.

As Eresh's story reached its end, Trin said, "Mr. Ranulf, aren't you a writer? Will you give us a story as well?"

Gareth jumped at suddenly being addressed, and Roman almost laughed at the nervous, panicked look the man shot him. If he had to guess, most of Gareth's stories involved a certain hero. "My writing is mostly nonfiction," Gareth said. "Not very suited to this sort of setting, I'm sure you can imagine."

"You study Egil, don't you?" Thea asked. She had a wool blanket wrapped around her like a cocoon. "An Egil story sounds perfect."

Roman stood and approached the fire, Gareth wincing with every step. "Go on, Gareth. I bet you know an Egil story we don't."

Ivor, prodding at the fire with a stick, rolled his good eye. Leandros, sitting between Gareth and Thea on a toppled log, coughed to hide a laugh. Though Gareth shot Roman an exasperated look, his cheeks turned even more flushed and blotchy.

After more prodding from the others—particularly Trin and Thea—he finally conceded. It wasn't without another nervous glance toward Roman, though. "Oh, very well. I suppose I do know an Egil story or two. In honor of our destination, I'll tell a story about Illyon. Or Ehloran, as it was called in those days."

It began as most Egil stories do, in the halls of Devikra Stormsong, the Great Oracle of Damael. Egil was her most trusted agent, her dearest friend. Whenever her visions posed problems only he could fix, she summoned him to her gilded halls. On this day, Egil entered and bowed low before the oracle, the air between them heavy with incense and cleansing herbs.

"My lady," he said, kissing the hand she offered to him, "How may I assist you?"

With an imperious wave, the oracle's servants left them alone. Devikra reclined on a bed of lavish pillows and regarded Egil carefully. "Heed my words well and do as I ask," she said. "Many lives depend on it."

"Of course, my lady," Egil said, for disobeying the oracle always came with consequences.

"Go to the city of Ehloran. When you reach the white tree at the center of the city, travel north. Continue north and do not stop."

"Why?" Egil asked, unable to stop the question.

Rather than answer, Devikra said, "You will know when you have reached your destination."

Egil held his tongue, though more questions burned on its tip. This was the way of the oracle's prophecies—they were mere glimpses into the future. They created more questions than they answered. Egil had seen them fulfilled enough times to know that much. He also knew that the oracle was never wrong, so he bowed again and left to prepare for the journey, making all haste to Ehloran and finding the white tree, whose petals had just begun to fall.

He turned north and, on foot (as he knew not how far he had to journey), he began to walk. He walked up and down the hilly streets of Ehloran, always pointing due north and not letting distractions break his stride. He passed through a market, the smells of the foods there taunting him. A beautiful woman in a glittering dress danced in the street to swift music, and he longed to stay and watch. When he reached a tall fence, he paused, but he could not disobey the oracle, so he climbed. Finally, at the city gates, he was forced to stop when an alfar man dressed in rich robes fell at his feet.

"Please, Egil!" the man cried. "I am Trym Bech, leader of this city. I ran as soon as I heard you were here. My daughter Rylia has gone missing. Please, I need your help finding her. I fear something terrible has happened."

Egil thought about the oracle's words. *You will know when you have reached your destination.* Egil did not yet know, so he said, "I am sorry, I cannot. If your daughter is still missing when I return, I will help you find her."

Egil did not know that, the day before her disappearance, Lady Rylia's father announced she would be married. The intended prince, who'd come from Alfheim for the lady's hand, was a kind man, but Rylia loved another, a young woman of humble birth. Confronted with the choice to marry someone she did not love or break her father's heart, Rylia chose to flee into Lyryma. But distraught and alone, confused by the darkness, she lost her way.

A witch who lived in the forest, a daughter of Tellaos, found her and spirited her to Tellaos' realm, intending to feed the pretty young noble to the soulless beasts who roamed the dead forest there.

Egil stepped around Rylia's father and left Ehloran, continuing down into the grassy fields of the Valley of Creae. He walked until he reached the borders of Lyryma Forest, and then he walked further yet. He walked until his feet ached and his eyes drooped, and finally, he reached his destination.

As the oracle had said, he knew it immediately. On the strange, winding path before him, Egil saw the swirling of dark magics. Shadows swelled and sharp branches hung low, and Egil knew—for Egil knew many things about magic—that if he continued down this path, it would lead him to the place between worlds. Egil thought quickly. He pulled down winding vines from the tall Lyryma trees, tied a thousand together to make a rope. He tied one end of the rope to a tree root and the other around his waist so that he would be able to find his way back.

Thus secured, Egil started down the path. Slowly and somehow all at once, the trees changed. He found himself in Tellaos' dead forest, which was silent except for the sounds he himself made. No birds sang up high, no creeks bubbled in the distance, and no wind rustled the decaying leaves under his feet. Egil continued through the forest until he heard a woman's cries for help. Following the sound, he found Lady Rylia weeping at the base of a twisted tree.

"Who are you?" she asked when she saw him.

"I am Egil. Your father sent me to find you," answered Egil, and Rylia knew she was safe, for Egil was well known, by this time. Egil helped her to stand and, with his rope made of vines, began leading her back to their world. A voice stopped them, then, crying out, "Stop! You will not take her! Stop!"

It was the witch who'd brought Rylia to this realm.

Egil instructed Rylia to follow the rope back. Then he turned to face the witch, who shot lightning from her palms, meaning to kill him with her magic. The lightning struck Egil in the chest and the witch cackled, sure she had won, but when the lightning died Egil had not fallen. He had not even been harmed.

"Are you a child of Tellaos, too?" the witch asked him. For if he had magic, he must have been born of one of the Guardians.

"I am Egil. My magic is my own," Egil said. He drew his sword and pointed it at the witch. "I am taking the lady back to her home."

"You cannot!" the witch wailed. "The beasts of the forest were promised a meal! They will become violent if they do not have it!"

"Then *you* shall be their meal," Egil said. Leaving the witch among the shadows, he followed the reeds back to Lyryma, where he found Lady Rylia waiting. Together, they returned to Ehloran, and the Lord of the city thanked Egil with a grand celebration.

Roman stared into the fire while Gareth told his story, his mind far away. He closed his eyes and saw the shapes of the flames burned against his eyelids, Devikra's face among them, disappointed and pitying. Gareth was getting it all wrong.

Roman hadn't been working for Devikra long when this happened. It came after they'd met in Damael but before he met Leandros in Lyryma. He hadn't been any sort of functional person, then. He'd been damaged and angry, but Devikra had given him the chance to turn that into something good—to reclaim Egil, the title Unity had given him.

She'd had a vision of Lady Rylia being kidnapped, that part was true, but she'd ordered Roman not to go. Conscience heavy with the weight of his past sins, desperate to do anything he could to offset it, he'd gone anyway and he'd found Rylia safe at home. It was his arrival and the chaos that followed—Egil was becoming a household name, by then—that created an opening for Rylia to be kidnapped. Finding her hadn't been as easy as Gareth made it out to be. It had taken weeks and a heavy ransom, but Roman finally managed to track them. And to get Rylia back, he had to kill them.

He'd returned to Devikra with even more guilt added to the weight on his shoulders and the blood of petty extortionists on his clothing. Devikra had given him that look, then, half-disappointed and half-pitying.

"If I hadn't gone, she might have died," he'd told her.

She'd replied, "If you hadn't gone, she wouldn't have gone missing." Roman had learned then not to play with fate, and he'd learned that the oracle's visions always came with tricks.

"Roman?"

Roman startled, snapping back to the present to find Leandros and the team staring at him. Leandros' brow was creased with concern. How many times had he called Roman's name?

"Hmm?"

"I asked if *you'd* tell a story," Leandros explained. "As I recall, you used to be quite good at it."

Beside him, Gareth nodded. His cheeks were still blotchy, but no longer tomato-red. "Please, Roman. Put your stage voice to use."

"Well," Roman hedged, looking around at the expectant group. He didn't feel like storytelling, especially in front of Enforcers, but of course Leandros knew that. A story would draw Roman out of his ruminating, at least. Of course, Leandros knew that, too. "All right, fine. But nothing about Egil."

Thea whooped and the diplomats cheered politely, but before Roman could say a word, Evelyne stood. She shot him a glare and stormed off.

"Don't mind her," Ivor drawled, sitting back on his hands. He looked like he might fall asleep at any moment, but his gaze was sharp and locked on Roman. "She's just grumpy."

Roman didn't let himself watch her leave, claiming her newly-vacated seat, instead. "I'll stick with Gareth's theme and tell a story about Creae Valley. How many of you have heard of Runderath?"

Today, Calaidia knows peace—or something like it. It hasn't always been this way. For the years of the Great War, violence and tragedy were all anyone knew. Bloodshed was a way of life, death a price to be paid. During that war, we fought, we died, and we fought on still.

Unity didn't exist, then. No government could stay in power long enough to soar to its heights. As soon as the conquering class showed weakness, someone else rose up to overthrow them, and behind it all was Tellaos, one of the Guardians Atiuh made to protect Calaidia. Tellaos believed the world would do better without its greedy, selfish mortals, so he pitted everyone against each other and stoked the flames of war.

And where were the other Guardians? Why weren't they stopping him? No one had seen them since the war began, but one day, someone did.

Runderath was a young alfar Captain, a fierce fighter and a small-name hero. It happened during a rare stalemate. The suns hung crimson in the sky and Runderath picked his way through a bloody battlefield, searching faces of the fallen for the men he'd lost. No other commanders bothered; there were too many dead, and the nameless faces were just that—memories that would fade. Runderath thought differently. Memories they may be, but they were memories he would honor.

Aside from a lone dragon flying off in the distance, its mournful keen echoing through the valley, Runderath believed himself the only one on the field, so he was surprised when he came upon two figures with their backs to him.

"Ho there!" Runderath called, approaching them. "The alfar army will be coming through soon! They won't be happy to see outsiders here, so you'd best go, for your own sakes."

The figures turned toward Runderath, and Runderath stopped short, the hairs on the back of his neck standing on end. The figure on the right, a human clad in black armor with silver-streaked hair, kept his eyes on the horizon. He wiped them like he'd been crying.

When the other turned, Runderath saw that the ground beneath her feet was charred. Her eyes, flat black with specks that glowed like smoldering sparks of a dying flame, bored into him. Her skin, golden-red like a sunset, was covered in swirling patterns that flickered, twisted and glowed like tongues of fire. Long wings, shimmering and incandescent like a dragonfly's, stretched behind her.

"Why would you warn us?" she asked. "*You* are alfar."

The man beside her met Runderath's gaze. Though he looked not nearly as alien as his companion, he unsettled Runderath more. He was solid, weighty, eternal. His eyes had seen many things and the weight of them all shrouded him like a cloak.

"I am not cruel. I would not see two nonviolent creatures harmed for being in the wrong place at the wrong time," said Runderath.

"And how do you know we are nonviolent?" the woman asked with a dangerous smile.

"I am unarmed; you are not. You could have killed me on sight."

The man inclined his head in acknowledgment. "And what are you doing here alone, unarmed?"

"Searching for my fallen men, that I may administer last rites," Runderath answered. He had been through so much, felt so much pain and seen so much death, that he no longer feared either. So he asked, "And you?"

The man and the woman looked at each other and, at once, began to pace around Runderath in slow, concentric circles.

"We are trying to decide how to stop our brother," said the woman.

"We cannot oppose him directly—both out of love for him and because of the laws our god laid upon us," the man continued.

"But we cannot stand by while he destroys the world our father made for you," the woman said, passing in front of Runderath.

"Tellaos must die," the man said.

"If he does, the war will end," the woman added.

The man stopped in front of Runderath. "We need a champion who will fight him in our name. I look into your soul and I see light, Runderath id Kamar. Will you be our champion?"

Runderath opened his mouth and found he could speak no words, for he finally knew whose presence he stood in. Atuos and Ellaes, Atiuh's Guardians. He bowed by way of answer, and when he straightened, Atuos smiled.

Ellaes pressed a kiss that burned like fire to Runderath's forehead and said, "With this I give you a taste of our magic, that you may meet Tellaos as an equal."

Atuos drew his sword, made of the same fathomless black as his armor, and offered it up to Runderath. "With this, I give you our blessing. Face Tellaos with courage and heart, and you will not fail."

Runderath took the sword and felt some light emotion rise in his chest. He realized it was hope. "Thank you. I will not fail."

"Be brave, Runderath. We will be with you in spirit," said Ellaes. With that, they were gone, vanishing in the time it took Runderath to blink. Without the weight of Atuos' sword in his hand, or the fire of Ellaes' magic in his heart, Runderath would have feared he'd imagined them.

Runderath did not return to his army's camp. Instead, he turned east and began the journey to Tellaos' mountain. On this mountain was a castle the Guardian loved more than any others, which sat overlooking a bloody battlefield. Its walls were darker than the nights in Rhycr and stronger than the scales of the dragon who lived inside. Anyone who entered—aside from the great serpent himself—never left. This castle stands today, in the heart of Orean. This is the bloody history of Creae Valley.

Runderath fought his way through the valley to the base of the mountain. He climbed it, Atuos' sword strapped to his back, and burst into Tellaos' castle. From there, he climbed the winding stairs to Tellaos' watchtower, confident in himself and his mission. Finally, Runderath faced the black serpent.

"Tellaos!" he called, "I have come to end your reign! No longer will the people of Calaidia fall prey to your games!"

The dragon laughed, loud and terrible. "Is that so, little hero? What's to stop me from killing you where you stand?"

"I have magic, that I may meet you as an equal, and I have this sword, a blessing from those who would see you defeated."

Tellaos stopped laughing. He knew those words, and suddenly he recognized Ellaes' magic in Runderath. In his rage, he blew a jet of flame at hero. But when the flames cleared, Runderath stood in the same spot, unharmed. He raised Atuos' sword and charged.

On the battlefield below, soldiers of every species paused their fighting to gaze in wonder at Tellaos' castle, which rumbled and shook in great waves. Then, the dragon's watchtower began to crumble, and all anyone could do was watch as it collapsed, leaving the southwest corner of the castle open and exposed. As if a spell was lifted, all dropped their weapons and began to cheer. They knew, in their hearts, that Tellaos was dead.

Later that day, a party went up the mountain to search the rubble. Stories were already circulating about the hero who'd been seen fighting his way to the mountain, and they hoped to find him alive so they may thank him. But neither Runderath nor Tellaos were seen again.

From that day on, the Story of Runderath the Mighty, the hero who stripped Tellaos of his power but perished in the process, was told across the content.

At that, the diplomats around the fire began to clap, expecting Roman had reached the end of his story, but Roman held a hand up. "I'm not finished."

The night following Tellaos' defeat, the great dragon clawed his way out of the rubble while the mortals celebrated in the valley below, unaware. Tellaos found two figures waiting.

"Your plan failed," he snarled at them, "I'm not dead."

"We did not mean to kill you," Ellaes said. Soft flames flickered across her skin, their glow the only light on the dark mountainside. "Only to punish and humiliate you."

Atuos took Ellaes' hand and said, in a voice harder than diamonds, "And now, to bind you."

Together, Atuos and Ellaes bound Tellaos' magic within him. Using their magic, they trapped him in a weak mortal form so he would no longer have power over the people of Calaidia. Then, with heavy hearts, they denounced him as a Guardian and left him to live the rest of his mortal life alone.

When Roman fell silent, Eresh blurted, "That's not how the story goes! Tellaos can't *live*!"

Roman stood and stretched. "It's the story I've always been told," he said. The popular version ended with Runderath slaying Tellaos, but this was the version his mother had told. It was one of the few things he remembered about her. "Do you really think it's so easy to kill a Guardian?"

"Well—"

"Either way, it's just a story," Roman continued with a shrug. "I'm tired; I think I'm going to retire for the evening. I'll see you all bright and early again tomorrow."

———

An orinian woman with glowing scars carved into her skin stood on the bridge to Unity Island. She pressed herself against the stone wall, looking down at the water swirling below. For longer than she could remember, she'd been chased by something, a feeling she couldn't name. A creeping feeling, like the brush of fingers on the back of her neck, or shadows shifting at the corner of her vision. The black waves reminded her of that feeling—angry, insistent, inviting. They called to her, just like the grasping darkness.

But she couldn't give in to it. There was a closer call, even more insistent. It was near, now. She pushed herself away from the rail and turned to face it.

A man walked down the bridge toward her, the hard soles of his snakeskin boots clicking on the cobblestones with each deliberate step. He looked human—handsome in a broad, hard-edged way. His eyes, the pupils rectangular like a goat's, rested on the clock tower above and behind Mercy.

"Beautiful, isn't it?" he asked as he neared. There was no one around but them. Finally, he looked at Mercy and smiled, his teeth too many and too sharp. If Mercy's heart still beat, the sight would have stopped it. The man's smile dimmed as he took in the fading glow behind her skin, and he cupped her cheeks between his hands. "Oh, I've left you alone for too long. You've almost run out. Mercy, are you still with me?"

Mercy shivered and covered his hands with her own. His hands, the only things keeping her tethered to this world. Instead of answering, she asked, "Why are we here, love? Why did we come to this awful place?"

"Mercy," he warned, voice low. He leaned down to kiss her forehead. "I know it's awful, but I needed to see it, just once. I needed to see it before I destroy it." He looked up at the clock tower again. "The Guardians' pride and joy, their solution to everything. It meant so much to them. To *him*."

He took her hand and pulled her toward the Island. "Let's get a closer look."

They hadn't moved more than twenty feet before Mercy yanked her hand back, saying, "I can't." When he kept walking, she called, "Tellaos! We can see it from here. I don't want to go further."

"Yes," Tellaos said, his voice like the slither of a snake through tall grass. "Yes, you're right. Mercy, come to me, and then we can return home. I swear it."

It was then that the two of them noticed a procession approaching from the island. Horsemen rode at the front and at the back, a sleek black carriage between them. The carriage slowed as it came upon the god and his late wife. Then, it stopped, and a woman peered out the window.

She was on the older end of middle-aged and she carried herself rigidly. Her eyes were wide and fixed on Mercy; she paid Tellaos no mind.

Tellaos began to scratch the scales that peeked over the top of his shirt collar. Looking between his lover and this woman, he asked impatiently, "Who are you, then?"

The woman finally looked at him, taken aback. "Moira Ranulf, a Magistrate of Unity. I could have you thrown in prison for speaking to me that way."

Tellaos sneered. "You're no Magistrate of mine. Mercy?"

Mercy took a step towards the carriage, but Moira Ranulf called, "Guards!" The two horsemen were there in an instant, one barring Mercy's way with his sword and the other training a gun on her. A breeze swept past them, blowing Mercy's veil away from her face, and Moira sank even deeper into her carriage. "You're the one the Nochdvors saw," she breathed.

Before Mercy could advance, Tellaos held a hand up to stop her. "Pardon?" he asked. "What was that?"

Moira was pounding on the roof of her carriage, no longer listening. "Go! Drive! Get me away from here!"

Tellaos sighed, then signaled Mercy on. He looked away as his wife killed the horsemen, wincing when he heard bones snap and Moira scream. He scratched his arms, the mortal body Atuos and Ellaes trapped him in not enough to contain the multitudes swirling inside of him.

Moira's screaming stopped.

"I hate having to do that," Tellaos said, turning back around. "Mercy, is there any chance someone in that throne room survived when you grabbed the king?"

Mercy frowned, her delicate features twisting in thought. "I don't know. The magic was overwhelming."

"We're going to have to find out." Tellaos continued to scratch, then stamped his foot. "Damn Atuos! Damn Ellaes! Damn this body! Mercy, come here."

Mercy approached, but when Tellaos held a hand out to her, she skittered back. "No, wait. I don't want to feel it again so soon."

Tellaos kept his hand out. "I won't force you, Mercy, but if you do this one last thing for me, everything will get better. I need your help. I need my body back, love."

Mercy reluctantly approached. "What do you want me to do?"

Tellaos whispered the answer in her ear. When she nodded, eyes wide, he said, "Now, open up."

Tellaos put something in Mercy's mouth. It was insubstantial like smoke, yet solid enough that he could hold it between his fingers. It was alive—alive, but not living. It writhed and squirmed in his fingers like an angry black centipede.

The warped, twisted power of the thing hit Mercy immediately, spreading warmth all the way down to her toes. The glowing in her veins flared bright, so bright that she watched Tellaos' pupils shrink. She'd been cold earlier, but now she was too hot. This was too much, not enough. Burning, freezing. She couldn't contain it. She must.

Tellaos watched her through it all. Finally, she breathed in, and her heart quietly, faintly began to beat again. That other call, the one that echoed the crashing black waves, felt much further away.

"There you go," Tellaos murmured. "It's almost over now."

He wrapped an arm around her waist and pulled her to him. She raised her hand into the air and used the magic Tellaos had given her, just as she had when she'd stolen Amos Nochdvor away.

Around them, Unity's bridge began to collapse. It started at the ends, heavy rocks falling to the water. The bridge tore itself apart stone by stone, taking the bloodied carriage with it, but the patch Tellaos and Mercy stood on remained intact, hovering above the water.

Tellaos laughed, pulled Mercy tighter, and kissed her. Mercy snapped her fingers and, like that, they disappeared as the last of the bridge fell.

———

Aleksir Bardon sat stiller than he had in his life, eyes wide and fixed on the white dragon in the center of the room. The dragon was bowed low, unable or unwilling to look at the recipient of his message, but Aleksir looked at her. She sat upright and rigid, her face an impassive mask. Aleksir had worked with her long enough to recognize things others would not—the subtle pursing of her lips, the flare of her nostrils. The Oracle of Damael was *angry*.

"What did you just say?" she asked.

The dragon bowed, if possible, lower. His long snout nearly touched the ground. "Unity Bridge has collapsed, my lady. No one was harmed, but Magistrate Ranulf seems to be missing. I flew here as soon as I heard the news."

"Thank you for bringing this to my attention," she said. All around her, her courtiers whispered and shifted. The looks they shared with each other all asked the same question: Why hadn't the oracle foreseen this?

Devikra Stormsong stood, and the whispers fell silent. "Unfortunately, there's nothing even I can do to prevent natural disasters such as this. Please, see our messenger to a spare room and get him whatever comforts he requires. Send a missive to Unity offering our aid. Another vision may be coming on, so I'm afraid I must return to my chambers. Aleksir?"

Aleksir followed Devikra out of the hall. Once it was just the two of them, Devikra began to pace, rubbing her temples as she passed back and forth in front of Aleksir, who watched her warily. "The *entire bridge*?" she hissed. "Bridges don't just collapse!"

"What do you think happened?" Aleksir asked.

"I'm more concerned about why we didn't see it coming. Aleksir, dear, will you go ask Wil about it? I have something I need to do first, but I'll meet you upstairs."

"Yeah, sure. You all right, Devikra? You seem sort of…worried," Aleksir said. It was out of character for her.

Devikra took one of Aleksir's hands and patted it fondly. "I'm fine. Don't you worry about me—I'll be with you shortly."

"Sure."

Aleksir left Devikra standing in the hallway, weaving through the temple and down long, winding stairways until he finally found himself in a cool basement. He knocked on a heavy door before entering a large room, everything about it orchestrated to make the space comfortable for the oracle.

The oracle herself sat in the room's small kitchen space, and Aleksir dove to catch the door before it slammed, instead guiding it shut with just a soft *click*.

Aleksir slipped his shoes off, let the room's calming atmosphere do what it was designed to do. It was filled with soft, heavy fabrics—sofas that looked like they'd swallow you whole, pillows on the sofas and grounds and anywhere they could feasibly fit, paisley patterned curtains that diffused the suns' rays and set the room alight with a cool glow. Aleksir padded over to the small kitchen.

"Wilhara," he called gently. The oracle ignored him, tapping her charcoal against the counter and squinting at the sketchbook in front of her. "Wilhara?"

When she still didn't respond, Aleksir said more firmly, "*Wil*."

Wilhara looked up, apparently surprised to find Aleksir standing there. An alfar with orinian blood, Wilhara's ears were sharp but expressive, flattening against her head in surprise. Paired with her doe-like eyes, she looked perpetually frightened. The set of her mouth, in contrast, made her look vaguely annoyed. Aleksir knew she was rarely the former, but frequently the latter. He was very fond of her.

Wilhara was the true visionary behind the oracle's persona. Devikra taking public credit was a front that worked well for both of them—they knew their strengths and their weaknesses. For Wilhara, dealing with people was one of the latter.

"Oh, Aleksir. When did you get back?" She spared him an effusive smile in the time it took to locate and sip her tea, then went back to studying her drawing book. Aleksir recognized the bitter smell of that brew. It never meant good things for Wilhara's headspace.

"Just this morning," Aleksir said. He'd been annoyed when Devikra had suddenly pulled him from Gallonten, and now he was even more so. He wondered what must be happening in the city today—what Egil must think of this bridge business. Aleksir wished he'd gotten to say goodbye. "Did you have a vision?" he asked.

After a minute of consternated silence, Wilhara asked, "Hmm?"

Aleksir glanced at the drawing book, where Wilhara recorded her visions. They contained an array of people and places she'd neither met nor visited, and she'd found it was easier to draw than describe. Then Devikra, who'd seen more of the world, could interpret them for her. Aleksir liked to think he provided the moral support. Really, he just ran errands.

"Are you having a bad day?" Aleksir asked, rephrasing the question.

"Oh, very. The visions won't stop."

"What do you mean?" Aleksir asked.

"I've had a dozen today, at least."

"A *dozen*?" Aleksir asked. It was usually considered huge if Wilhara had more than five visions in a week. Aleksir pointed to her book. "May I?"

Wilhara pushed the book at Aleksir. "I suppose you might as well. I don't know what any of it means."

Aleksir flipped through the newest pages with a frown. There were a lot, and they all seemed to be related. There was Orean, wonderfully sketched, with a dragon flying above it. The next page was almost the same—same city, same view—but without the dragon. Following that, everything was on fire and a giant smudge blocked out a third of a page. Aleksir peered closer—not a smudge, but frantic scribbles. That explained the charcoal all over Wil's dress, then.

"It was like living shadow," Wilhara said quietly. "I didn't know how to draw it."

The next page made Aleksir gasp. It was Unity Bridge, falling into the water. "When did you do this one?" he asked Wilhara.

Not picking up on his urgency, Wilhara regarded it and tugged at her skirts, smoothing them out only to tug them into wrinkles again. She deposited more charcoal on them as she did. "This morning, I think. No—wait, yes. Yes, right after breakfast."

Aleksir stared at her. According to the dragon's report, that would've been around the time that it happened. He turned the page again and blinked in surprise. It was Egil—a dozen sketches of Egil smiling, frowning, crying. His eyes, his mouth, his hands. There were other faces he recognized, too—Leandros Nochdvor, Maebhe Cairn. There was a dancer on a stage, a woman with cold eyes and a sword strapped to her back. There was even a drawing of himself in here. He looked up at Wil. "What is this?"

Wilhara rubbed her eyes. "I don't know. I just kept seeing your faces, one after the other, and the visions are so blurry. They change so fast. That's not the last of them."

Aleksir turned the page again, then quickly shut the book. He felt ill. "There's no way. How did he...?"

"I don't know. I just see him like *that* over and over again like that. I don't know!"

Aleksir grabbed Wil's hands and rubbed soothing circles into the backs of them. "Hey, hey, it's all right. We'll talk to Devikra about it. I'm sure she'll have answers."

Wilhara nodded. "Yes. Okay. Where is she?"

"She went to—Shit. I meant to tell you. Unity's bridge is gone."

"The bridge is gone," she repeated slowly. "Like my vision."

"Yeah."

"When?"

"This morning."

"But I *saw* it this morning!" She shook her head and clenched her hands in her skirts. "I usually get more warning than that! First, I missed King Nochdvor's kidnapping, and now this. What's happening to me?"

Aleksir was saved from having to answer when the door flew open. It struck the wall, and Wilhara flinched at the sound. Devikra stormed in, all righteous fury and terrible beauty, looking significantly more tired than she had downstairs. When she noticed Aleksir and Wilhara staring, she tucked it all neatly away behind a smile. "Wilhara, dearest, I wasn't sure if you'd be up. I'm sorry about the noise."

"I understand. Aleksir told me what happened."

Devikra joined them at the table and dropped into the seat across from Wilhara. "How strange this all is. Wil, you didn't see anything about this, did you? Something we might have missed?"

Without prompting, Aleksir opened the drawing book up to the page with the falling bridge and showed Devikra.

"When did you…?"

"This morning," Wilhara said.

Without looking up, sensing more than seeing Wilhara's distressed look, Devikra said, "Don't fret, Wil. There's nothing wrong on your end. I know what's causing this."

"You do?" Aleksir asked.

"Wilhara is rosanin." Devikra looked up. "Rosanin abilities don't work on the Guardians."

"The Guardians?" Aleksir waved a hand. "Ellaes and them?"

"Ellaes, Tellaos, and Atuos, yes."

"But they're not real."

"They're very real. They're as real as you or I."

"It's true," Wilhara said. "I forgot about—I mean, it's happened before. Tellaos has changed my visions." She met Devikra's eye, then quickly looked away. "It was a long time ago."

Devikra nodded. "And I suspect it's Tellaos again. Your visions have been acting up since Nochdvor's kidnapping, right? I fear he had a hand in that, too."

"What does he want?" Aleksir asked.

"That's a good question. I could only theorize."

"So if Wil's visions can change now," Aleksir said, a concept that defied everything he'd ever learned about the oracle's visions, "What about all the other ones she drew today?"

Devikra looked sharply at Wil, who passed the book back to her. Devikra spent more time on each drawing than Aleksir had, her eyebrows drawing closer together with each page she turned. Normally, Wilhara's drawings were clear and logical, not frantic and chaotic like these. Aleksir watched Devikra run her fingers over two almost identical drawings of him—identical except for his expressions, one happy, one anguished.

She said, "Your visions are inconsistent because you're seeing the different possibilities. Every time Tellaos changes course, he changes the futures you see. He must have been doing a lot of thinking this morning."

Wilhara flipped to the page of Egil drawings and tapped at it insistently. Devikra eyed the pages, then Wilhara. "You want me to help him?"

Wilhara sighed, relieved, and nodded. She turned the page. "This was the only one that was clear."

Devikra studied this last image for a long time. Wilhara fidgeted;

Aleksir looked away. He couldn't bear to look at his hero, not like that.

"I'm sorry," Wilhara said. Again, she said, "That was the only one that was clear."

"I have to warn him," Devikra said.

She stood, and Aleksir and Wilhara shared a look. "Will that help?" Aleksir asked. "I thought there was no changing Wil's visions."

"It will help," she said. She said it so certainly, too, that Aleksir believed her. "Aleskir, are you coming?"

"To see Egil?" Aleksir asked, perking up. "Can I?"

"You *are* the closest of friends now, from what I read," Devikra said dryly. "Make up your mind quickly. This threat is one he won't be able to stop alone."

"I'm coming," Aleksir said. He considered this news about the Guardians, and he considered Egil. He asked, "Does he really have magic? The first time we met, I thought I saw something weird."

Devikra stilled. "What did you just say? Weird how?" she asked.

"I dunno, just…odd. I swear, for just a second, his eyes turned all black like some sort of monster's. Devikra? What is it?"

"He's in more trouble than I thought. We have to go *now*," she announced. "We'll be back soon, Wil."

Before they left, Aleksir glanced one more time at Wilhara's final drawing, a drawing of Egil laying dead among the ruins of Orean. He wasn't a religious man, but he said a quick prayer to Atiuh.

He hoped, desperately, that Devikra could prevent this, but he also remembered the hatred on Egil's face whenever Aleksir had mentioned her.

He prayed that Egil would let them save him.

THE STORY CONTINUES AT

WWW.QUEERENIGMA.COM

Acknowledgements

There's a story about Hans Christian Andersen I like to tell where the man, while visiting Charles Dickens, received a bad review and was found sobbing face-first in Dickens' front yard. I tell it because it's relatable, and I'm sure many writers would agree. In the years I've been working on Fractured Magic, I've experienced moments of uncertainty and insecurity, and those have often come with lots of dramatic bemoaning and lamenting. To that end, I'd like to thank my fiancé for always putting up with my "Hans Christian Andersen-ing," as we call it. And for always being much more patient than Dickens was.

I'd also like to thank my friends in the Worms Pit, for always hyping me up when I need it and giving me a reality check when I ask for it. And on that note, I'd like to particularly thank Jasmine — your beta reading has been phenomenally helpful, but on top of that, you're the best cheerleader an author could ask for, and I appreciate it so much.

Finally, I'd like to thank all of the readers who have been here since Fractured Magic 1.0. I am truly not exaggerating when I say you're the only reason the story has become what it is today, as well as the only reason I've been able to keep writing it.

ABOUT THE AUTHOR

Emeric Rowene is a storyteller and an artist based in the Twin Cities. They are the author of FRACTURED MAGIC and THE CASE FILES OF SHERIDAN BELL, a fantasy homage to the golden era of detective fiction. While most of their work sits squarely at the crossroads between old school fantasy and creeping gothic horror, they can also be found picking up a magnifying glass or exploring new planets. In their works, they carry on the storied queer tradition of exploring the haunting and the monstrous.

Beyond their books, Em is an attorney with extensive knowledge of fanworks and copyright. They have a B.A. in English Composition and have several years' experience as an SFF developmental editor. When not writing, they can be found reading or gaming, likely trapped under one of their five cats.

Content Warnings

- Graphic Depictions of Violence
- Body Horror
- Depictions of Mental Illness, Panic Attacks
- Kidnapping
- Police Violence (Mentioned)
- Suicidal Ideation (Mentioned)

A full character guide is also available at
https://www.queerenigma.com/fm-character-guide/

FOLLOW QUEER ENIGMA BOOKS

FOR UPDATES:

Join the mailing list for updates on Fractured Magic Vol II and Em Rowene's other works:

www.queerenigma.com

Follow Em Rowene:

 @emrowene

 @queerenigma.com

 @emrowene

www.ingramcontent.com/pod-product-compliance
Lightning Source LLC
Chambersburg PA
CBHW052347110726